THE WITCH OF BALINTORE

A Medieval Mystery

'What happened after the seven years? You felt homesick suddenly?'

'Disease came among us, some kind of grippe, but fatal in most cases.'

'And she died of it?'

'No, strangely, I did.'

I thought she must mean something else. She didn't.

Lady Marian MacElpin (known in Spain as Doña Mariana de la Manga), now twenty-four, and still fighting the label "witch" that has haunted her since childhood, travels for the first time to the land of her ancestors.

There, in the far north of Scotland, called upon by chance to act as interpreter for two Arabic-speaking slaves whose master has been murdered, she meets her Scottish grandmother (a witch, of course) whom she had long believed dead; she becomes embroiled in ancient myths and legends (sheltimen, mermaids, elps, the Queen of Elphame) - no less fantastic now, in the flesh, than they had seemed in the tales her father told her when she was a child; and she falls (yet again) into the unsympathetic hands of authority, this time in the form of the local Master Executioner and his obnoxious son, and the skeletal black-robed Dominican Friar, Brother Arsenius, Inquisitor.

I listened to the wulcats. They seemed to be all around us. Was it something natural? Or was it Mouraig ...? How could it be?

Long minutes went by. The yowling grew louder and louder, closer and closer. It sounded like hundreds of cats.

Suddenly they all stopped.

The door opened. Brother Arsenius came swiftly down the stone steps.

Anyone else wearing flip-flop sandals like he was wearing would make a flip-flop sound on those stone steps. Not him. He entered like a draught, silently.

Other Books by James Munro

Poetry
Reluctant Rebel
The Wizard's Sister
Sweeney Jim & Other Poems
Better Than Sleep
Fin de Millennium & The Jesus Bhakti Poems
Fin de Millennium: Selected Poems 1964-2000
Drinking-Up Time

Novellas in Verse
The High Place
The City

Novels

Medieval Mysteries
Thirteen-Card Spread

Tales of the Dark Ages
Children of AN
Colum's Day

James Munro

THE WITCH OF BALINTORE

Published by James Munro through Lulu.com.

For more information, visit

www.BetterThanSleep.com
or
www.Lulu.com/JamesMunro

To
My Mother

Special thanks to Marilena,
who first read Witch and pronounced it good,
and gave me constructive advice which I took.
To Jenny Hewitt, who edited the first version;
her enthusiasm and encouragement
meant much to me.
And of course, as always, to Anna, without whom …

Timeless our meeting,
Of past and future all the now and here
Of many lives, the ever-blossoming tree.
I am old and alone, but boundless
All is everywhere,
Once is forever.
(Kathleen Raine, The Oracle In The Heart)

ONE

The Rose In May

In London, May can be like June or it can be like March. Yesterday, which was May Eve, was worse than March - worse even than Andalucía when the weather breaks and the autumn rains come. At least that rain is warm. This rain was cold, and it beat down on the open river and on the roofs and in the narrow streets all day long, then after a short pause at dusk, all night long too.

At dawn, the sky was clear, a pale, washed-out blue. I know, I was watching. The patter ("pitter-patter" - some of these English words are so expressive!) of the rain on the shutters had kept me awake. Then the sun rose and everything was washed again, this time in pale gold.

I didn't go back to bed. I threw a cloak over my night gown, pulled on an old pair of boots, stepped over Yahia, who sleeps across the doorway of my chamber (some guard) and went out and walked by the river. Dawn is the one time a woman can stroll there alone, or sit unmolested and gaze at the water swirling under the bridge. Only how can you sit when everything is sopping wet? And how can you find the May Dew when everything is dripping with rain?

But it was May Day and it promised to be fine. We ought to do something special. All right, in Spain *el primero de mayo* is nothing special, but I had grown up listening to Papa's tales of his home in Scotland, and one of his favourites was how on the first of May - Beltane, they call it still in the north - the lasses celebrate by bathing their faces in the May Dew and the menfolk light the needfires using the nine sacred woods.

Last year, I went with Tom to his village in Essex. It was fun, especially in the forest after the feasting and dancing were over. Tom (who is my man - in the sense of man-servant, the man who does for me the many things that Yahia cannot) went off with the May Queen - a childhood sweetheart of his, apparently - and I ended up with the blacksmith. It is one day in the year when social rank counts for nothing, and all the better for that.

I should have gone with Tom again this year.

When I got back to the house, it was no longer dawn. It was morning, everyone was up and about, and a messenger from Kennington Palace was waiting.

Kennington Palace meant Princess Joan, an ageing siren in a pink room. I have a lot of sympathy for her, but none with her growing interest in the forbidden arts. It is motivated entirely by her obsession with her own beauty: *Mirror, mirror, on the wall ...* Fortunately, I don't have such a mirror for her. Also, she has a deep-down superstitious fear of magic which can only, in the long run, spell danger for me.

I ate breakfast as slowly as I dared (the messenger would report back) then took Yahia upstairs to help me dress in an appropriate manner: in this case, a simple outfit which would not attract attention. Princess Joan views the women around her as background: anything perceived as an attempt at competition can prove fatal. We decided on a plain red velvet kirtle with no surcoat, elegant boots, and a light cloak I had had since Avignon. A cap and veil. No jewellery.

Outside, the sun was hot now, for the first time in the year.

The messenger led me through the Priory grounds to where a Royal Boat was waiting at the Prior's private jetty. The oarsmen kept their eyes averted as he handed me down into it. Then, when I was safely seated, he nodded to them and they began to row.

The river was crowded, but we bore the royal insignia. We sped along, and everything from the stateliest barge to the flimsiest wherry made way for us.

I sat back like royalty and gazed around, breathed in and out deeply. I caught the tang of the sea drifting up river with us on the breeze, the smell of drying kelp and sun-drenched saltmarshes.

Does summer always come here on the first of May? At Beltane?

But whatever the weather, you need to be in the country to celebrate Beltane. You need a village green with a Maypole all decked out in flowers and trailing ribbons. You need the forest close by, or at least a wood large enough to get lost in. Tom's village, St Osyth, set between the forest and the marsh, has everything. And his father's house faces the open sea, is almost on the beach, like my own old home beside the Mar Menor in Spain.

I miss the sea. Any sea. The North Sea is not the Mediterranean, it is cold and grey, but it is beautiful, and the great sandy beaches, though windswept and empty, are beautiful, too. Last time I was in St Osyth, I swam for hours, every day, remembering when I was a child in Spain. I used to spend all day in the water then, very often, summer and winter.

Princess Joan is a talker (talker-talker-talker), filling the pink room with words. Everything blurs. My eyes do not see her, they see only pinkness, nor do my ears hear the words.

It is always the same.

But today, there is something new. I hear sounds of laughter coming up from the courtyard, catch glimpses of sunlight between the pink curtains.

Real laughter. Real sunshine - while I, for my sins, which are many, sit here dreaming in this stuffy, smoky, over-heated pink-on-pink room with Princess Joan, who is in fact Joan of Kent, mother of the King and widow of the Black Prince. The Black Prince and the Pink Princess. Even the voluminous silks and satins and ribbons and bows which festoon her are pink. There is no light, no air, which is not pink. Even I must look pink, and be growing pinker by the minute from the heat, and from sheer exasperation.

She looks up.

'*N'est-ce pas, Marianne*?' Well, isn't it?

Isn't what what? I have no idea what she has been talking about. I gaze back, smile fixed on my face, trying to feel again the awe I felt when first I met her two years ago. She has aged since then. Once lauded as "the fairest lady in the land" and "the most amorous", and famous for her shocking attire - gowns full of "windows", and even on occasion men's garments, doublet and hose (though who am I to judge her for that?) - she was still, a year ago (is even now in the view of many), among the most beautiful women in the kingdom; but "among" isn't good enough for her.

'It was of me, they say, that Master Chaucer was thinking when he wrote "and she was fair as is the rose in May". *Qu'est-ce que tu penses, Marianne*?'

She always speaks French since discovering that my French is at least as good as my English. She is, of course, fluent in both.

'I have not heard that, madame. But yes, why not? You are the Rose of England. And pink.'

She gives me a suspicious look. Then smiles. The Rose of England.

I'm sure it was *not* of her that Geoffrey was thinking. His muse, his goddess, was by all acounts Duchess Blanche of Lancaster. Though I have heard it said that Geoffrey's own sister-in-law, the dusky Katherine Swynford, John o' Gaunt's mistress, has been the inspiration for many of his more recent poems, replacing pale Blanche as goddess and muse even as she replaced poor, dead Blanche in Duke John's bed.

Gossip. But in this case I should love to know …

I did my best. I cast her horoscope, and sweetened it, as she likes it. I read her palm - again! - and flattered her all I could. I gave her more of the unguent I had learnt to prepare while I was still in Spain, in Cuenca. It would smooth out the wrinkles on her face, but nothing I could do would refloat her sinking breasts, firm her thighs, tighten her buttocks. Nothing I was prepared to do, anyway. The risks were too great.

'But *you* are not ageing at all, Marianne!' An accusation.

Even that was dangerous.

'You look *exactly* as you did when I first met you, yet you must be nearly thirty now, and I am only forty-something.'

I was twenty-four. She was fifty-something.

'Do you know how to read these new cards? They're the latest thing from Italy. Tarocchi, they're called, I believe.'

I shook my head. I had no intention of being the bearer of the bad news I was sure the cards would hold for her.

I hadn't pleased her. They brought me back to Southwark in a common wherry and dropped me off at Fish Wharf. I had to make my own way home from there, alone and on foot. I don't mind the stink - it is no worse than the stink of other, far worse things that you breathe in with every breath here in London - but I hate the way my feet slip and slide in the slime as I try to walk.

There's another problem, worse than dead fish. Live men.

One of the guards at the bridge gate knew me, so I got a polite 'Good day, my lady,' from him, but as I rounded the priory, it began.

'Look at *that*!'

'You touting, Poppet?'

Soliciting is forbidden within the City of London. Southwark, though, where I have made my home, lies south of the river. Here it is not only permitted, it is actively encouraged; after all, the Bishop of Winchester owns all the stews and half the brothels, and those he doesn't own his retainers "protect" - for a price. I had my cap on and my veil down over my face, but still everyone assumed I was a whore, and every man had something to say:

'The wanton. Look at the way she walks.'

'Touting? That one? She'll have a waiting list!'

'Aye, look at her, fair dancing along.'

'Mustn't keep their lordships in suspense.'

Even right outside the church. Especially right outside the church.

'Hussy. Thinks she's too good for the likes of us.'

The church, ironically, is called St Mary Overie.

'Aye, but she'll pleasure the Prior.'

'Or bed the Bishop.'

'Or fuck a friar.'

Some village Wycliff off a cabbage barge, catching that last oh-so poetic line (almost worthy of Master Geoffrey), bellowed 'Fuck the Friars! All of them!' which was greeted by a chorus of jeers and laughter.

I ignore it usually, unless I find myself completely surrounded. But today, when two men, father and son, stood right in my path as I turned into Clink Street, I was in no mood to step aside.

'What about *this* one, son, eh? Eh? The *way* she moves! Exquisite ...'

'Expensive, too, Papa. Look at her clothes.'

Though hardly more than a boy, he was taller than his father.

Papa had to show off. 'She'd halve the price if a man knew how to satisfy her - wouldn't you, love-lips?'

I looked him up and down. He was powerful, red-faced, choleric, flabby, what had once been firm flesh and muscle turning to fat. And wealthy. I should have said nothing: but "love-lips"?

'For you,' I said, 'I'd double it.'

The boy sniggered.

'Watch your tongue, slut,' the man snarled. 'Impertinence is a punishable offence.'

I could have answered him - the language of the whore-house in Cuenca still came easily - but I wanted to avoid trouble, not stir it up. So now - a little late - I bit my lip (My "love-lip"? No, I think he had somewhere else in mind.) cast down my eyes and kept them down in a display of humility, as I had been trained to do in the harem in Granada.

The man took it for fear. A woman - some filth off the street - to snub *him*, turn *him* down? At his age, and in front of his son? Whore.

'Who gave you the right to wear velvet, eh? Eh, whore? And tan boots like a lady?'

He stepped forward, raising his hand -

'*Strike first, lass*,' my father used to say, '*and strike fast*.' But I no longer carried the hidden stiletto. I no longer needed it. I was quick on my feet and I knew a dozen ways to tumble a fat, angry man like him. Ferchard, old soldier and master of unarmed combat, my father's friend, had made sure of that.

Or else, I could ...

I raised my eyes. His hand, I noticed, despite the soft expensive clothes, was encased in a studded leather glove. Like an executioner's glove. That would hurt

The son was staring at me. He said, suddenly, 'She's *not* a whore, Papa. She's *a witch*!'

'She's a whore! You heard her!'

Something snapped inside. But it wasn't rage that swept over me. It was a kind of torpor. I had had enough. Whore - slut - hussy ... witch. The son was wiser than the father, too. Witch. Without doubt the opinion of the princess, if truth be told. Suddenly, I no longer cared. All these years spent trying to avoid just such a public denunciation, and now, in a moment, all would be lost.

I let him hit me - watched his eyes (they were bloodshot) as his hand came down on the side of my head. It was slow, but hard and heavy when it landed, knocking me sideways, sending me sprawling in the mud.

Then his boot hit my ribs, and as I cried out I heard the boy say, 'That's enough, Papa. Papa! She'll put the Eye on you! Papa!'

I arrived home with not just my feet but most of my body covered in the usual London mix of mud and shit and blood.

Yahia, my eunuch, was waiting. He always is. And he is always pleased. If he had a tail, it would wag.

He pulled off my boots, then he and Khadija - my maid, also from Spain - removed my disgusting clothes and wrapped me in a red and black silk kaftan - this from Fès, it had been a present from Ibn Khaldoun, though I never agreed with him that red suited me.

I refused to discuss my swollen face, I did not mention my aching ribs, I stormed up to my chamber in the blackest humour I had known for months.

"Flounced", Papa would have called it, a favourite word of his: "flounced out of the room" and up to my chamber.

I missed Papa, too. I missed Spain. I had had enough of London, of Joan of Kent and her like - even of Anna, the new

Queen, who had been my friend as I thought since we met in Paris five years earlier, when she was still a child.

Should I go back to Paris?

But I had been back, several times. The filth was worse than in London. They didn't have the ravens that scavenged everywhere here. All they had were rats and pigs, and the wolves that howled outside the walls in winter and when the river froze padded silently into the city on the ice - and that one unforgettable dawn so nearly ate what little the Church had left of me.

Not Paris. It was too dangerous. The Church hunted all year round. And not Spain, not yet anyway.

There was a timid knock on the door.

It was poor Khadija, whom I bullied so much. She sat with me on the bed and waited till I calmed down, as she had when I was a child.

Then she called Yahia, and told him to fetch his drums.

She gave me a sash and said, 'Dance for us, child.'

I tied it round my hips.

I sank first into the floor dance, for when one is down one must *be* down; only so can one rise. I knelt. I sat back on my heels, and folded myself forward over my knees, forehead to the floor. After a moment, I raised myself and sat back on my heels; I leant over backwards, my bottom pressing down between my feet, my back arched, the back of my head on the floor, my arms stretched out beyond my head in the posture of submission to God, the sky, the lightning, the thunder; I, the queen, the earth, having bowed, now submitted.

Then, slowly, I rose until I was kneeling upright once more. Now my arms were snakes that wove their own dance, pulling me upwards till I rose tall upon my knees. The drums began to beat. I breathed right out then sucked right in and did the belly ripple, the wave, the roll ... I breathed in again, gently, letting no one see (though both these knew), and fluttered my belly, faster and faster, following Yahia's lead, till in one swift move I was on my feet. My pelvis kept the beat now for a little while, then I did a shoulder shimmy and suddenly I was well again, I was me again, alive and young and full of strength. I clapped my hands and the music stopped.

I had danced out my sorrow, come to terms with my life and the world.

I was ready.

They bathed me and dressed me, and left.

It was too late to do anything for May Day. But thinking of Paris had reminded me of the Albanian scrying cards.

Princess Joan had mentioned them that morning. Tarocchi, she had called them - apparently that's what they were called now in Italy - but from what she said they were the same cards. I had claimed I knew nothing about it. It was true I was no expert, not like I was at palmistry and astrology, and various other arts best left unmentioned, but I had been taught to scry with the cards by experts, and I had not forgotten.

I opened my Moorish chest, which had belonged to my grandmother, Sebah of Córdoba, and felt around in the bottom of it for the pack of scrying cards.

They were carefully wrapped in a black silk cloth. I unfolded the cloth and spread it out on the table, then held the cards for a moment clasped in my two hands. When I was ready, without shuffling them, I laid them down on the table and cut them.

No big spreads. I simply wanted to know my situation now, and be given some indication of the future, some idea what to do.

Two cards.

The Present and the Future.

I turned over the first card. It was number IX, the Hermit.

Think of the numbers as Arabic numerals, they had said: they are important. Number IX - 9 - was the last of the single numbers. After that, we begin again, set out again on a new road, or on an entirely new phase of our life. It symbolises growing up. It symbolises getting married.

The card itself, the Hermit, the old man with his staff and his lamp, implies a need for retirement, for solitude, for time to relax and reflect, far away from the rush and the noise.

Well, yes.

It can also signify a refusal to change - the besetting sin of age - was I getting old? - the old man peering into the gloom, sure that he is right, that what always has been is what should be.

I turned the second card. Number XVIII. The Moon. The card Lorina had turned up for me in Paris.

In Arabic numerals it is 18, 1 and 8, which is to say 9 again. Here, there is no old man. There is nobody. It is the only card with nobody on it at all.

There are two dogs - two wolves? - one dog and one wolf, Lorina had told me - looking up at - howling at? - the moon. And behind them, crawling out of the water, a crayfish, clambering up into the light of the moon. In the distance are two towers: between and beyond them lies another world.

It made me think of the shelti-world.

And the shelti-world made me think of Scotland.

TWO

Dyngvale, in Scotland

'And why not?' Ferchard's eyes are pale, like the sky up here in Scotland on a summer evening, and when he is angry they grow even paler. 'Why shouldn't she be? As the executioner's wife, she'll hold a respected position in the community.'

We are having a meal in a tavern in Dyngvale, a grey town on the shore of a grey rain-swept sea-loch, while Ferchard, who is Dyngvale born and bred but has not been back for half a century, makes enquiries.

It appears that his only surviving relative is a niece named Effie, who is married to the Master Executioner of Ross.

'All right,' I give in. 'I'll come, I'll meet this *executioner*, but -'

'Will you stop saying *executioner* like that?' The white beard he wears unfashionably small on his jutting chin stands still for a moment like a nervous chicken, then starts wagging again. 'How was I to know my sister, poor Euphemia, had died? And her husband and their two sons, and her two other daughters - and my cousin Patrick and his son, and grandson - all wealthy merchants.'

'Wealthy or not, some must survive the rigours of the climate or they wouldn't need an executioner. I notice *he* survives.'

'It wasn't the climate, Marian, it was the plague, the Great Mortality. Effie survived. I survived.'

'You survived by living anywhere but here. And now you are here, let's hope this *hangman* - '

'They don't hang men of nearly a hundred.'

'You're not nearly a hundred. You're seventy-five.'

'Seventy-five is nearly a hundred.'

'In that case I'm still nearly a new-born babe.'

'You *are* still nearly a new-born babe. People flatter you, make you believe you're something special. Aye, you have something of the spaewife in you from your Scots grandmother, Marian Vass - I knew her - which makes you feel important, and I don't mean just the look, either, though you have that in plenty, too, but ...'

He likes to think he is in charge. He is, of course, in a sense. In this world every woman, queen or kitchen-maid, abbess or courtesan, has to come clearly under the aegis of some man, and I have no one else.

Ferchard - Sir Farquhar - was an old comrade of my father's, and accompanied him into exile when the Bruces finally defeated the Balliols. They travelled as far as Rome together, then went their separate ways. Ferchard wished to journey on east to Jerusalem, while my father preferred to head back into France, then south to Spain, where he finally settled, and married, in Andalucía. Years later, Ferchard, an old man now, came looking for his old friend, and found - not his friend, for my father had died - but me, Mariana, the half-Scottish, half-Spanish, eighteen-year-old daughter who was all that was left and whom, needless to say, he took instantly under his wing, i.e. under his aegis.

At least he fits in up here, in his old-fashioned breeches and little white beard. Nearly everyone in London - and Paris - is clean-shaven. Or wears a full beard. My father had a trimmed beard, though ... and my Spanish grandfather, Don Joaquín ... and my Scottish grandfather, Sir Magnus. And they all wore breeches.

'She was a good woman, your grandmother, a beautiful woman, fifty years ago - aye, more than a little like you - and she really did have the Sight. That's no uncommon thing up here, of course, but she was special. Some even held she was a witch.'

The less said about that, the better. Ferchard knows almost nothing of my life in Spain before his sudden appearance.

My teacher when I was a child, the Kabbalist Rabbi Yacoub ben Amar of Murcia, though a true mystic, abhorred all forms of magic, and did his best to cultivate in me a horror of witchcraft. At the same time, an almost equal fascination *for* magic was planted and nurtured in my heart by my grandmother, Sebah of

Córdoba, though what *she* meant by "magic" - thc magic of women, so closely related to the mystique of belly-dancing (which she also taught me), and to birth and growth and love and loss and death - was something quite different from what Uncle Yacoub meant by "magic" (*black* magic, which had its origin with the Devil).

After my father died, I lived for a year and a half with a practising witch in a bordel in Cuenca, when I was fifteen, sixteen. A time I have tried hard to forget.

Then, later, when the Wheel of Fortune had turned and I had become Lady Marian MacElpin once more, I went to the north of Spain with Ferchard, and to Provence, and Avignon, with its permanent row of stakes in the great square directly below the *Palais des Papes*, and saw everywhere witches being burnt, and I realised that in the eyes of the Church at least, all magics were one, that to be a wise woman was in itself a sin, and to claim that women *could* be wise was heresy.

'Anyway, I didn't *bring* you,' Ferchard announces suddenly, 'I *accompanied* you. It was your idea to come to Scotland.'

'How was I to know it was so far? To *here*, I mean, not to Scotland. It's nearly three weeks since we crossed the border.'

Our host comes over with news. 'My boy's returned, master. It seems the Executioner, Master Robert, is at home, and is expecting you. And so is Mistress Effie. It's the large house down at the end of the street - the lad will show you.'

We follow the pot-boy out of the Ross Arms and up the road past the Whore & Hounds. It looks much better than the inn we chose, but I hadn't liked the name much, and I certainly hadn't liked the painted sign that hung outside.

The executioner's house is large, and the buxom woman with the big gold earrings standing in the doorway waiting for us can only be Ferchard's niece, Euphemia's daughter. For a moment, Ferchard hesitates, then surges forward. 'I'm your Uncle Farquhar, Euphemia's brother, Mistress Effie, and - '

'Don't you "Mistress" me! Oh, I've heard so much about you! Big Ferchard, she always called you.'

'And this is Lady Marian MacElpin - '

'Oh, my lady - '

'Don't *you* "my lady" me!'

We both laugh, and she ushers us over the threshold into the dark house.

'Your father must have been Sir Andrew. My mother told me all about when he and Uncle Ferchard went off into exile - '

'On pilgrimage,' Farquhar corrects her, quickly.

'Yes, pilgrimage,' she goes on, oblivious, 'with Sir Andrew. But she didn't really know Sir Andrew well. She knew your grandfather better, my lady - Sir Magnus MacElpin. She was always saying what a fine gentleman he was.'

'My father grew up mostly in Dun Edin, that's why. But he was a fine gentleman too.'

'Oh, I'm sure he was. Robert, come here.'

A large man who has been hovering shyly in the background now comes forward.

'This is my husband, Master Robert Ross. Robert, this is Lady Marian, Sir Andrew MacElpin's daughter. And Sir Farquhar, my Uncle - Big Ferchard! And big he is still! As big as you, Robert, and there's not many men that are, even in these parts. You'd have made a good executioner, Uncle Ferchard.'

'Me?' He is delighted.

'Ferchard couldn't be an executioner,' I say, spoiling it. 'He's a Taurus, a Bull.'

They don't understand.

'The Bull is a fighter, it is brave, it is beautiful, but it cannot win. It is the sacrificial offering. No Bull, no Taurus, could ever be a torturer or executioner. Now you, Master Robert: I suspect that you were born under one of the other Earth signs, when the sun was in Virgo or Capricorn, and that you have a lot in common with Ferchard. Torturer and victim do have, but your sign - '

'What's this about me as a victim?' Ferchard interrupts (having been surprisingly patient). '*I*'ve never been the victim. *You* are the one who - '

'Shh. Your sign, Master Robert, will be Virgo, probably, if you're as good at your job as I suspect.'

'Oh, he's good at his job,' Effie says, proudly.

The executioner scratches his ear. 'Well, I - ah - '

'When were you born? When was he born, Mistress Effie?'

'The last day of August his birthday is, every year.'

'Then I was right. You were born under the sign of the Virgin, Master Robert.'

'The Virgin?'

I can see that the executioner is beginning to wonder whether maybe this strange young foreign woman who claims to be of ancient Scottish stock is mocking him. No one is allowed to mock a Master Executioner.

'Virgin?' Effie crows. 'He's no virgin, nor was he when I first knew him - or should I say he knew me!'

'That's not what I mean. Virgo is the constellation where the sun was - '

'It's astrology.' Ferchard helps me out, which I don't deserve after teasing him about being a victim. In his view, it's unmanly to be a victim. I flash him a smile as he explains: 'It tells you about yourself, depending on the date you were born.'

'Ah, astrology. Aye, but - '

'Marian's very good at it.' Then, no doubt thinking we would all benefit from a change to a less mysterious - and less dangerous - subject, he adds: 'She does palm-reading, too. She's done it for people in London, and before that in Paris. Very important people, some of them.'

'Palm-reading? Oh, read mine!'

'All right, but not now, Mistress Effie, later, when - '

'Not Mistress Effie, just Effie. I'm sorry, yes, you must be exhausted. Do you remember that awful old woman you hanged a couple of years ago, Robert? She did palm-reading, didn't she?'

'Aye, but she was old and ugly, and a witch.'

Sweet Jesu, I hope they're not talking about my grandmother!

'She had the Eye, too, you remember?' She grimaces.

They can't be talking about her. They would know her name, know it was the same as mine. I look at Master Robert.

He scratches his great bristly chin. 'I never believed that story of her riding around on a wulboar, though.'

'Naked through the forest, aye.'

'No, no. Her daughter, maybe.'

'Her daughter, too. And where did *she* suddenly get that famous beauty of hers from if not from her mother? An ugly little brat as a child, she was, then suddenly she looks like the Queen of Elphame.'

'Hush, woman. She's gone now.'

'Aye, she's gone all right. Fled, before Master Robert could get the truth out of her.' Effie sighs dramatically at the injustice of the world. Her lips part, her eyes widen, her bosom heaves

I notice Ferchard gazing at her.

She is like a statue of Juno I once saw in Avignon. Same breasts, exactly. Same lips, same arms.

Where did *she* get *her* beauty from?

Another great sigh. Then: 'You're quite right, Uncle Ferchard, it's not a job that anyone can do. Kenneth, though, our son, he's quite different from Master Robert in most ways, more like me, and yet he's good, Master Robert always says so.'

I look back at Master Robert, realise *he* has been gazing at *me*.

'Young Kenneth? Aye. Best apprentice I ever had, and I'm not saying that because he's my own. On the contrary. Now, come on in through here and - Ferchard - may I call you Ferchard? - you'll have a dram, won't you?'

Ferchard would and did, and another two or three, while I took a much-needed bath with the assistance of Effie, her two little daughters and a giggling maid-servant. Afterwards, I introduced the girls and Effie to some tints and hues I use as eye-shadow that they had not come across. And to anklets, which I wear as a souvenir of Ibn Khaldoun, who used to love me in them. And they introduce me to the great golden armlets which are still fashionable up in the north. Effie sees how much I like them and makes me a present of a pair of coiled snakes to wear on my upper arms. When I protest, she insists, saying they had belonged to Ferchard's mother and were by rights his. I give in. I love them.

Then we go out for a stroll. It is one of those Highland evenings that go on and on, so unlike the sudden, dark, hot Andalusían night.

The one main street we have seen already: a few two-storey houses and many single-ends, a square down by the firth, another square at the other end of the street. That was where the Court House stood, with - as Master Robert points out proudly - the torture chamber down below and the public pillory and stocks up outside in the square alongside the whipping-post.

The gallows were down at the other end, on a promontory overlooking the firth, and there behind the scaffolds grew a single elder tree. It was hardly more than a bush. I gazed at it, then went over and cupped a cluster of flowers in each hand and held them to my face. The bourtree, tree of the Goddess. How many others know that now? I wonder. Has this bare promontory always had a special use? It has a special atmosphere. The gallows, though, are empty, and so too is the firth. The tide is out and only flat mud can be seen, stretching away bleak and cold and lonely into the distance. A few gulls wheel and call.

Master Robert stands beside me. 'Sometimes you see millions of birds on the mud-flats, but not tonight. It's too late; those that spend summer here are already roosting up on the moors. And many of the ducks and geese have flown north. They'll all be back though, in the autumn, and what a clamour there'll be!' He smiles. 'Will you be here still, then, Lady Marian?'

'We may be. You never know.'

'It's not written on your hand?'

He is smiling, but he is wondering about me.

I smile back, disarmingly I hope. 'It is written on the hand and written in the stars for those who can to read, but I still never *know*.'

He thinks about that a little, and seems satisfied with it. Then he changes tack. 'Where is your home now?'

'In London.'

'Ah, London. A great city, they say, but the Inglis … God be thankit for the French, we do say up here!'

'Amen,' I murmur, diplomatically.

'You're not Inglis at all in any way, are you, my lady? Only with you living down there …'

'No, I am half Scots - you knew, or knew of, my father - and the other half of me is Spanish. My mother was Doña Maria de la Manga. Does that sound Inglis?'

'That dark hair must be part of the Spanish half.'

'So the Spanish half is the top half, you imagine?'

'Well, no, it doesn't seem that simple. Those sea-green eyes are not the eyes of a Spanish woman. And there are strange red tints in that nigh-black hair'

I laugh. Let's get straight to the point. 'In Spain, eyes like mine can get a lass called *bruja* - witch - if she's not careful.'

He regarded me, sombrely. 'Here in Scotland, some of the things you say - and say you know - could get a lass in trouble, too. So be careful, my lady. Very careful. Especially if you travel out of Ross and into Sutherland, where I should not be able to protect you.'

Effie, who has been walking ahead arm-in-arm with Ferchard, laughing and chattering, now calls: 'Come on, you two, it's getting cold. And what can you be talking about at all that's making you look so grave?'

Back in the house, we eat and drink, and talk, and the talk now seems to be all reminiscences of the Great Mortality, or Black Death, in which so many of Ferchard's family perished, and indeed so many of mine. Was it God's punishment on a sinful world? Sinful in what way? In that we tolerate the presence of the Muslim infidel in the Holy Land, and in Catholic Spain, as some would say, and send no more crusades to root them out? In that we tolerate the presence of Jews, the "Christ-killers", in our cities?

'I have known many Muslims - Moors - in Spain,' I say, not mentioning, of course, in the present company, my own very mixed descent on the Spanish side, 'and they have been good people mostly, just as Christians are good people mostly. And as for the Jews - '

'And as for the Jews, yes, as you say,' Effie interrupts me, 'they are the devils, the demons, the workers of evil in our society.'

It turns out that, like so many people all over Europe, they believe Jews to have been responsible for the plague; that they poisoned the wells or cast spells as they feasted on the roasted corpses of Christian infants, butchered as Herod, King of the Jews, had butchered those other infants long ago. I remind them that the Jews too had been decimated by the plague.

'Aye,' says Effie, 'and the survivors didn't last long either, I can tell you, not up here. There are no Jews left in Ross now, are there, Robert?'

'No, nor anywhere north of Inverness. Some still skulk there, I believe, protected by the Bishop.'

'Why? Does he owe them money?'

Ferchard laughs. 'More likely because he *wants* to owe them money. When he does owe them money - especially if it's a lot - he won't - '

Big Robbie joins in the laughter. 'Aye, there's something in that. They say that Earl Robert was deeply in debt to some Jew whose house burnt down one night with him and all his family trapped inside.'

'How "trapped"?'

'It was surrounded by irate citizens armed with knives and spears and cudgels.'

Irate thugs.

'But the Bishop is not like that,' Robbie continues. 'He protects them because, he says, they are people, like other people - '

Effie snorts.

'And - ' Big Robbie clearly does not like being interrupted, even by her - 'And he says Jesus Christ and his Holy Mother were Jews too, so - '

'That's ridiculous!' squawks Effie.

Robbie gives up, holds out his pot for the maid to refill it with ale.

'Well, isn't it?' Effie appeals to me and Ferchard.

He shrugs, and I say: 'I thought everyone knew they were Jews - and St Peter, too, and St Paul - all of them.'

She looks at me reproachfully. '*God* is Jesus' Father. You'll be telling me God is a Jew next.'

Ferchard does not look at me at all. Which is a very good thing.

THREE

On With The Old Love?

In the morning, it rained.

Ferchard and I stayed in the house with Effie and the girls. I read all their palms and told them about London and Paris. Effie said they weren't interested in Spain, at any rate not the south of Spain: wasn't it still infested with Saracens and Jews?

I admitted it was.

Nor would she let the girls come with us when the sun broke through and we decided to go for a walk. She said it would rain again, more heavily.

She was right. We'd got as far as the Court House when suddenly it was like standing in a waterfall.

Ferchard pointed at the nearest inn, the one with the awful name, but I was bored with taverns after nearly six weeks on the road. Then we realised we were right outside the torture chamber where Master Robbie and his son had been working all morning.

I think Farquhar would have preferred to stay out in the rain.

I didn't ask him. I ran down the steps and he followed.

They had a tinkler there, accused of stealing eggs from the poultry yard of a local house - one of the large ones, neighbours, it turns out, of Master Robert and Mistress Effie. The woman of the house had not actually witnessed the theft but there seemed to be fewer eggs than usual and who else would have stolen them? Oh yes, she'd noticed him hanging about nearby ...

'We found a shilling on him, but no eggs. So Kenneth scourged him. He still won't confess. Now he's going to put the pilliwinks on him.'

'Pilliwinks?'

'These. They're finger-screws.'

Horrible things. 'Is that the law?'

'No. He's a tinkler. Laws don't apply to him any more than

they do to serfs and bondservants. Less, in fact. Bondservants do have some rights under the law.' He smiles. 'But as they're not allowed to testify, no one knows when those rights are violated.'

'And tinklers?'

'The courts don't recognise the existence of tinklers.'

'So they don't have to be tortured?'

'They don't have to be put to the question, true, my lady, because we don't need a confession. They're not supposed to be here. They have no rights here, inside the town limits, no business here.'

'And he'll hang?' asks Ferchard, gazing at the tinkler, a strange little man with long fair hair and cropped ears.

'Maybe.'

'For a first offence?'

'Begging your pardon, my lady, but it's not a first offence. He's been a tinkler, which means he's been a thief, all his life. We hang any tinkler that's been charged with theft, as a matter of course. If they've just been picked up and brought in for no reason, we simply scourge them and release them outside the town with a warning not to return. Executions though, within the town boundaries, even the hanging of a tinkler, must be authorised by the Sheriff. And that's good, that's the rule of Law, which holds sway in the town. Outside,' he shrugs his great shoulders, 'beyond the town boundaries, tinklers and other outlaws - all those outside the Law - may be killed with impunity.'

'Then he will be hanged?' Ferchard is, predictably, on the little tinkler's side, despite all the big-man affectation.

'We await the Sheriff's decision. You never know. He may decide on a simple amputation.'

'One of the hands? And the pilliwinks?'

Kenneth has been locking the man's wrists and neck into a kind of pillory, one of a row of three which stand beside a rack and directly beneath a large crucifix. Now he applies the pilliwinks to the fifth finger, the pinkie, of first one trapped and helpless hand and then the other. The man watches, as they always do, in disbelief, eyes wide still with the pain and shock of the whipping and with the terror of what is to come.

'The pilliwinks? Oh, Kenneth is doing that for practice, only -

while we wait on the Sheriff.'

Blood oozes around the tinkler's nails, then he screams as the finger-tips burst but even his screams do not prevent me from hearing the bones fracturing, splintering.

Still he does not admit to stealing the eggs. But then why should he?

I glance at Ferchard, who looks sick. He catches my eye: Shall we go? I nod. But then the man's wife and two children are brought down. Like her husband, the woman is small. Her yellow-gold hair, though, is tied back with a leather thong, and she has blue-green eyes that I find quite beautiful.

'Whin? Is that you, Whin?' he sobs, when he sees her. 'Will I tell them I did it? Will I?'

'That way you'll hang, man!'

'What good will I be to you with my hands all destroyed?'

'What good will you be to me hanged?'

The boy, the younger of the two, begins to giggle. Or sob. His sister, prevented by Master Robert from running to her father, turns to her brother and tries to shush him, talking to him urgently.

'Use the Gaelic or the Norn, lass, so we can all understand, or hold your tongue.'

'What language is that they're speaking?'

'It's not a language, my lady, not a real one, just Shelta, or the Elphin tongue.'

'I'm sorry, sir,' the girl says, in the Gaelic we have all been using. 'I was just telling Otter - he's my little brother - not to get upset, our da'll come with us after … when … and we'll be …'

The man screams as another of his fingers splits and then the bone inside it cracks.

I nod to Ferchard and we go up and out. The woman, Whin, tells the children to go with us.

The rain is easing off. We stand in the doorway, gazing out at it. There is silence, the children awkward with us: we are strangers - more than strangers - and the situation too is strange and shocking for them.

I smile at the girl. 'What were you saying, sweet?'

'Just that it's nicer when we're all together. We had been. All together, I mean. We had been since Beltain came, and the yellow was on the broom, and we set out on the roam - but then my da went off on his own gathering flysvamp for a shelti-trip and Ma said "Let him" and told him when to meet us on a day in a place we know out along the Tarbat coast.'

I let her chatter; it was good for her, and for the lad to listen to her.

'When the day came, the day we were to meet, we sent Otter over on the Mickle Ferry with our things and Ma and me took to the sea, which is what we love to do, swimming all day far away from the shore. We swam off the great beach at Dornoch, yesterday, early, while the sun was still down from the night before, and we came back to land at Whiteness on the other side of the firth as the sun was setting behind the hills for another night. Otter was waiting for us, weren't you, Otter? He gave us our things and we dressed and Ma lit a fire behind the dunes and we cooked the fish we'd brought out with us. Then Otter took me to see a funny old woman who was on the beach. But Ma came and said "That's not a woman ..." and I wanted to know what she meant, but I must have fallen asleep ...'

She was small for her age compared with one of us but she was beautiful, like a doll, and charming too.

I realised that Big Robbie was standing behind us. He too seemed charmed. He sighed and said, 'The Thane's policy in these cases is to find a place for the children in the hope that they'll learn to fit in. The lass - what's your name, child?'

'Kari, sir.'

'Kari'll go to one of the big houses, perhaps to the woman whose eggs were stolen.'

I stared at him. What was he talking about? 'But we don't know that the eggs were stolen.'

'Exactly. I'll let her have the lass cheap, that'll be fair. And Fergus at the Whore & Hounds will take the boy. He's skinny but he's strong-looking.'

'I want us to be together,' protested Kari. 'I want - '

'You haven't been listening, catkin.' The woman - Whin - was standing behind Master Robert. 'You're to go to a new home and live with a grand lady - well, not such a grand lady, not like my lady here, but you'll be living in one of the grand houses and -'

'Ma, I don't - '

'Kari,' I interrupted her, 'I don't think it's going to be possible for you to stay with your ma and be all together any longer - I'll check with Master Robert, but - '

'It's not,' he grunted.

'So how would you like to live with me?'

Kari looked doubtful. Then she smiled. Better the bogle you know.

Master Robert said, 'We'll talk of that later. For the moment, you'd better come back down, Whin. And you, lad.' He pushed the boy ahead of him back down the steps, and I heard him tell Kenneth to 'strip those filthy rags off him, shave his head and welt his buttocks a bit - make him look like just the lad for Master Fergus ...'

Whin did not follow him down.

There were two benches facing the square.

The rain had stopped. Some children were playing now, and a couple of dogs.

The sun came out.

The benches were dryish because they were under the eaves, so Kari and I sat on the one farthest from the door, in the sunshine. Whin sat with us.

'That poor boy,' I said to Ferchard, 'he hadn't done anything, just come looking for his father ... Ferchard, I miss the sun!'

He gazed at me. 'Let's go back to Spain.'

'Oh, yes! When?'

Though Whin knew nothing of Spain, the look on her upturned face showed how much she loved sunshine. Now, she reluctantly opened her eyes and joined in the conversation. 'It's his own fault. Their own fault. I told them to wait in the wood, but no, they had to follow me into the town and get caught too.'

'It was my fault, Ma, not Otter's. He would have waited. I said we - '

'I know. I know you. But he must learn he doesn't have to do every stupid thing any scaldie lass tells him to.'

'I'm not *any* scaldie lass, I'm his big sister! I'm like his ma when you're not there!'

'Well, now he's learning the hard way that you're not so like his ma - a very hard way if he ends up at the Queen.'

'The Queen?' Ferchard looked at her. 'Aye, I remember. You mean the Whore & Hounds.'

Whin preferred to explain to me. 'Have you seen the sign, my lady? At the inn? The picture shows the Queen of Elphame. Only *they* say it doesn't, that she's a whore.'

'Mariana?'

I looked up, into the sunshine. A man on a horse was speaking to me but I was dazzled. He must *know* me. Who ...?

He got down off his horse, came towards me.

It was Raoul.

'Raoul?'

Then he was in front of me and I was standing up and we were in each other's arms and - oh, I was at home there, at home in someone's arms as I had not been since Paris.

'Mariana, I thought I would never find you.'

He had been looking for me? All these years in London I had been so easy to find, and now in the north of Scotland …?

'Where were you looking?'

'Why - here. I started here and - I found you. But I *thought* I would never find you.'

'But why would you look for me here?'

'Where else should I look?'

He nodded to Ferchard, and I remembered that the last time I'd seen him, in Paris, I'd said I was coming up here to my father's country. I had got no further than London; but how was he to know that?

'Mariana, there has been a murder.'

A murder? 'Who?'

'Not here. In Tain, where I am staying.'

'Tain? But why are you staying in Tain?'

'I - oh, it's a long story. Let me go and get settled in at that *auberge* with the bizarre name - *'Comment s'appelle l'auberge?'* he called to his companion.

I knew.

'Don't worry, I know,' I said. 'Go on then, and I will see you later - in an hour? Come to the executioner's house -'

'The *executioner's* house?'

I nodded, smiling.

'Mariana, you have not changed. And that is a good thing. We shall need you as you were. *Salud.*' He saluted Ferchard, mounted again, and rode off with his companion.

Need me? And *as I was*?

'What was that all about?' Ferchard did not like Raoul. But Ferchard did not like any young man who showed more than a passing interest in me.

'A murder,' I said. 'In Tain.'

'A *murder*? They must have known you were coming.'

I smiled. 'They thought I was already here.'

'Now, my lady.' Master Robert emerged into the sunlight, blinking, again. 'What do you want the lass for? And what do you want her as?'

'I want her to wait on me, be my maid. She will come to me as a bondservant, all the papers duly made out.'

'Then you will take her south with you.' He gazed at me. 'Best thing. At least she will never be hunted, as her mother will again in the very near future, unless I miss the mark, and her brother too, no doubt, one fine day. With the Thane not resident, and the Sheriff we have here now, and the lairds to the north - Baron Hugh up at Foulis Castle, for one - so keen on the hunt … '

He sat down beside Ferchard on the bench.

'We had a tinkler boy in here a while back, not much older than her. He should have been hanged but they ordered his thumbs chopped off instead. As a warning, they said. A lenient sentence.' He turned and shouted down the steps, 'Kenneth, send the lad up out of it, too! Give him some kind of breech-clout to wear!' Then turned back to us: 'The Bailie relieved me of those thumbs. And I happen to know that they came into the hands of Baron Hugh, who promptly invited all his grand friends to the hunt. With the boy's thumbs to work the dogs into a frenzy, they couldn't go wrong. But they did go wrong. They lost the boy out around Balintore. Some mist came up out of the ground - summoned up by witchcraft was their story - and the boy was last seen swimming out to sea off Balone Castle there, heading north. No one knows if he reached the Sutherland coast - or indeed if what they had spotted out on the sea really was him at all.'

'What do you think?'

The boy Otter came up into the sunshine, sobbing. All his lovely hair had gone.

Master Robert motioned him to stand a little away from us. 'Wait there, lad. And don't run off.'

He turned back to me. 'Some say it wasn't the boy, it was a seal, yet the seal had been the boy - they had seen him, had seen him there, and then there was only the seal.'

Ferchard was interested. 'You mean he was a shape-shifter.'

'You've heard of that?'

'Aye. But I've never seen it.'

'And you're not sure you believe it.' He shook his great head. 'Well, no more do I, but ... Some of them are like seals - are seals, if you believe all the local stories. Or mermaids. Who knows if he ... I hope he got away. I hope so, yes. But he was in a bad way even before the hunt.'

Ferchard says: 'If he drowned, how much better that is than being torn down by hounds or caught alive and carried back to the castle trussed up and slung from a stake.'

Robbie stares at him. 'You've been on such a hunt?'

'I became involved in one once, yes. To my eternal shame. One of the reasons I left here and went on pilgrimage.'

'And another was love, or so my wife tells me.'

'Aye, another was love.'

'Love?' This is new. I always understood that it was politics. 'I might have guessed.'

Ferchard looks at me.

He blushes.

Another characteristic of the Taurean. The male Taurean. Not blushing. Love.

'I'll be going for a wee walk,' he says.

We watch him go, stepping round the puddles, at home here in the rain and the mud even after all these years.

Then I turn back to Whin. 'Whin, do you know when you were born? The date? Or when your children were?'

'The boy, no, save it was in winter. The lass was born on St Colum's Day. Someone said so, said it was a good omen.'

Gemini. 'Do you remember the time of day?'

'It was very early, when the summer sky was brightening again. We were in the north, on the coast, near Thurso. I could see Hoy pink against the summer night.'

The more I see and hear of this woman, the more I like her. I take her hands, study them one by one, then both together. The finger tips are square. A mark of practicality, of having one's feet on the ground. Of being conventional. And I suppose she is, by her own standards. And she is a Mercurian, the Mount of Mercury very prominent on both hands, which certainly matches her physical features - the smallness, the beauty, the strength - and means that she will be at her best faced with a challenge, but could also be dangerous. There is something strange, a combination of physical suffering and superiority, majesty even, that I have not come across before in anyone.

'That is my - Line of Life, you call it?' She nods towards it.

I let go of her left hand, but keep hold of her right still, palm up. I trace the Life Line all the way round the Mount of Venus with the nail of my right index finger.

'And the Line of Death?'

'Line of Death? Some call the Line of Mercury the Line of Death, but -'

'Where?'

I show her on my hand, where it is clearly marked, running up towards the Mount of Mercury and the little finger. She looks at her own hand. There is no such line there.

I smile. 'Don't worry, Whin. You will live for a long time to come, have two more men, another son, other daughters.'

She gazes up at me like a child, believing. Then glances at her son.

I take the hint. 'Otter?'

He gives me his hands. He raises his head and looks at me. I look back into his eyes. He is crying still. The whites of his eyes are bloodshot, his face swollen, his whole hairless little head it seems, bruised, but his eyes are clear, mostly green and hazel, but giving a blue impression too. Then I look down at his palms. No woman, no children, at least not clearly and not yet. Something strange there too, with a very clearly defined Line of Intuition, but for the most part it seems a short and bitter life and a violent death in circumstances over which he has no control. Probably a Capricorn, like poor Richard, in London. Poor? Well, but which of them is better off? Which will live longer? Which has more enemies? More "friends" who would benefit from his death? King Richard will one day be my concern, of that I am certain - through Anna, his queen, I have been moving closer to him - but he is not my concern yet. And nor is this poor sobbing bairn.

An elderly man greets Master Robert. I overhear him say only that there has been a murder. Then, mumbling, they go down into the chamber.

Whin is waiting for me to say something, but Kari elbows her brother aside and holds her hands out. She meets my gaze with a nervous smile.

I take her hands, look deep into her eyes. 'So you are a Gemini, born on the ninth of June … I'll look that up in the Almagest when we get home, but Gemini suits …' And Mercury rules in the Night House of Gemini, which seems right for her - she is rather a detached little thing - so it must have been night still when she was born. It is more likely that her mother noticed Hoy turning pink shortly after Kari was born.

Her palms, too, are clear and easy. Not a long life, but long enough. A lot of luck, some happiness, some children, travelling, meeting strange people, learning new ways, new languages, new customs. I tell her some of this, that she will travel, meet new people, have a lucky life. She glances back at the whimpering boy. I follow her glance. He will do all right as a pot-boy and sweeper, at least for a while. He is cut out for it as Robbie observed, and good for nothing else. It is cruel, but if he doesn't do it some other boy will; it is a job that has to be done, just as Big Robbie's is a job that has to be done by someone.

The elderly man comes back out with Master Robert and Kenneth.

I introduce myself and ask for news of the murder.

'What murder?'

'The murder in Tain.'

The man looks at Master Robert.

Master Robert looks at me. So does Kenneth.

'What do you know of the murder, Lady Marian?'

'Only that it occurred in Tain. And that one or more French - officials? - are somehow involved.'

There is a moment of silence while all three of them stare at me.

Then Master Robert asks: 'Will you be taking both of the children? Only -'

'No, the girl alone. Sell the boy as you intended.'

They turn away from us, talking together.

Whin nudges me. 'My lady, I remember now. He was born before mid-winter, same as me.'

'Let me see your hand again ... Ah.' So mother and son are both Sagittarians. Psychics. And with their wild, animal, side at the service of the spirit, the freest, the least predestined. The best. But ...

The messenger leaves. Big Robbie turns back to us.

I ignore him, carry on talking to Whin. 'Whatever, Whin. The pattern of his life and of his future - like yours, like mine, like that of his sister - is written, written already: written in the stars and written on the palms of his hands. As above, so below.'

'Aye, he has the gallows in his face, that one.' Robbie seems to think he is agreeing with me. 'I examined the faces - and eyes and brains and teeth - of many a hanged man while I was serving out my apprenticeship in Edinburgh. He'll come to no good.'

He and Kenneth go back down the steps.

I follow them. I want to learn more of this murder. I want to know what is happening, what the messenger said about the tinkler.

I notice once more the crucifix on the wall. It is a large, realistic one, even by Spanish standards, with an appropriately agonised and writhing Christ upon it. Christ the Son of Man. The son of men. 'There is another' - I point - 'whose sufferings and death were written in the stars. And no doubt on his palms.' Another Capricorn. Why had I not thought of that before? Or had he too been really Sagittarius? They hadn't used the same calendar, so when a couple of days would make all the difference, how could one be sure?

'Will you deliver the boy to his new master this evening?'

'No, we'll keep him here a couple of days; make sure he's tame and biddable all through, not just on the surface.'

'Like beauty, good behaviour can be just skin deep, you mean.'

He smiles at me.

That's better.

'Exactly, my lady. Whin here is a good example of that.'

'Are we speaking of her behaviour?' *Or her beauty?*

He studies Whin.

She raises an eyebrow at him, which he ignores.

'Beneath that charm, she's as kittle and as deadly as a wulcat. And I do *not* say that simply because she's a tinkler. There are good people and bad of every kind. Look at this heretic they've caught up with in Tain - a monk, a theologian, I don't know - all white and holy on the outside, like a sepulchre, all filth and corruption within. And look at the gallows meat I am presented with every week of my life.'

Heretic? And what about the murder? Are they connected?

'But in Alba now,' he continues, 'there is no place for such as Whin. Save as game for the lairds till none are left.'

In Alba now there is no place for me, either, if the truth be told: look what happened to us. But will we meet again, Whin and I, some other time, some other happier place, where we can talk?

Then Whin says, 'Alba was our land.'

We all look at her.

'Alba is our word, and - '

Kenneth peers into her open mouth. 'You talk too much.'

Her mouth snaps shut.

He laughs. If he had his way, her tongue would need somewhere safer than her mouth to hide.

'What about them?' I am becoming more and more involved. 'What was the Bailie's decision?'

'Tinkman is to be released as he stands.'

'As he stands? You mean no - ?'

'No amputation. The application of the pilliwinks has been deemed sufficient punishment.'

'But that's wonderful!' Then I realise. 'They want to hunt them.'

'Aye, they do, for sure.'

'What happens exactly?'

'Tell her, Whin.'

Whin glances at Kenneth; then, keeping her eyes on me, she begins: 'They hunt us like animals. But we are not animals. The law should protect us.' Kenneth sniggers again but she goes on doggedly: 'The law is quick to arrest us, to hang us like real people, but when - '

'My lady,' Master Robert interrupts her, 'as I told you, the law affords no protection to any of them - there are others, the Urisgaig, the Glaistig, the - well, there were others. You don't see many now. And better not, for them and for us.'

'How do they hunt you, Whin? With hounds? On horseback? Do they use bows? Spears?'

'I've been chased by hounds. I've been shot with an arrow - through my leg, here.' She pulls up her skirt, shows us a scar on her thigh. 'And will be again. Arrows always strike the same place twice, we say.'

'No more than you deserve,' says Master Robert, very pompous, 'you with your skirts up like that.'

'Up?' She laughs. 'I'd thrown my clothes *off*, all of them, left them for the dogs to worry while I went up a stream a while - and then, like a sharger bairn, came out in front of another hunter, a stalker with a bow and arrow this time. It was his lucky day - well, almost. I could have ended up with my head stuffed and mounted on the wall among the stags and bears and wulboar in one of those castles.'

'You were running naked?' I feel some of their excitement merely imagining her.

'That's why I'm here now, my lady. If I'd been dressed, I'd be dead.'

'It's no wonder they hunt you. They see you running naked through the forest …'

'They hunt me first.'

'But the dogs won't kill you and nor will the men, not if they catch you dressed like a Christian woman.'

'They know I'm not a Christian woman. Some even say not a woman at all. In a castle up on Sandwood Bay in the far north west, they have the head - and torso, with the breasts - of what the laird claims was a mermaid once. He says the men who caught her had to cut the tail off her - here, round here, just below the navel - when the fishy part of her began to stink. But he was tricked. And the serving-maids know he was tricked, that's why they took me in and showed me her. They know she was my cousin.'

'Your cousin?' I gasp.

'Tricked?' chuckles Robbie. 'That's as may be. Though I doubt very much if the serving-maids think he was tricked.' He looks at his smirking son. 'Ah, even I have never had the chance to cut off a mermaid's tail.'

Kenneth licks his thin lips with a darting, excited, tongue. 'Not yet,' he hisses, and stares at Whin, then at Kari.

I glare across at him. 'The girl is mine.'

'Kari's not a mermaid!' Whin protests. 'And nor was my cousin, of course she wasn't. We swim very well, that's all, we of the Elpin, especially the women among us. We know our way through water in the dark as we do through woods, and we can stay under for a very long time. Then when we do come up, sometimes there is somebody there - somebody who has not been expecting us ...'

I smile and nod. 'And people are deceived, not seeing your legs.' Do I believe her? Or is it simply that I'm on her side?

'People are gullible,' says Robbie, with a sudden about-face. But his mind is on something else. 'Look how they were deceived by this monk. He calls the Church "a whore" and criticises society for "punishing the poor".' The huge man crosses himself nervously. 'He's a Cathar, or something. Didn't they all run around naked?'

'A Cathar, and a Lollard, and an Albigensian.' Kenneth seems to be the family expert on heresies.

'Which means?' I demand, eyebrows raised.

'Which means the stake, my lady.'

Why is he leering at me like that? 'Seriously. Do you know?'

Master Robert is about to say something but is interrupted by the return of the same messenger, and turns away with the man.

'Oh, I know. I've been studying the subject. A Master Executioner these days needs to know all about heresy. *And witchcraft*. It means he preaches that absolution should be free. It means he preaches that the Church should hold no property of its own: it should identify with "the poorest of the poor" - with such as Tinkman there, and Whin, living from day to day like animals, content to be poor. Is the Church responsible for *them*?'

'Are you content to be poor, Whin?'

'And if I were not content?'

'Whin, if you were not content I'd have hanged you long ago,' says Big Robbie, overhearing. 'My lady, you are needed in Tain. Do you know Tain? On the Dornoch Firth?'

'I know of it, yes. My father spoke of it. It was one of his favourite places.'

He nods to the messenger, a thin, elderly man who sniffs. 'My lady, the message states simply that there has been a murder (sniff) in Tain, that both the victim and the principle suspect are strangers, Moors, (sniff) and that this suspect speaks only Arabic. It requests an interpreter (sniff) from here, or failing that, from Inverness (sniff). The messenger from Tain was, it seems, accompanied by a Maître Raoul de Cocherel (sniff) acting on behalf of Captain Jaufre le Fou of the French Expeditionary Force in Scotland. Maître de Cocherel is apparently in search of a certain Lady Marian MacElpin ...'

We all wait for the sniff. It doesn't come.

He clears his throat impressively. '... to whom, should she be found in Dyngvale, or in the vicinity of Dyngvale, we are requested kindly to deliver this message and desire her to meet the said Maître de Cocherel (sniff), with a view to accompanying him on his return to Tain, there to act as interpreter and liaison between the Moors (sniff) - the suspect and his sister - the Scottish Authorities, and the French officers who find themselves embroiled in the affair. (sniff)'

'What shall I tell him, my lady? That you will meet him?'

'Yes. Yes, of course. I have already arranged with Maître de Cocherel to meet at your house in one hour's time.'

Another silence.

'And how did you manage that?'

I explain.

He nods and ushers the messenger over to the steps, his arm

round him, telling him to bring the *maître* to his house, where Lady Marian is at present residing. He watches as the man goes up the steps and out through the open door.

Then he turns to me.

'How did you think I knew, Master Robert?'

'Don't ask.'

I laugh.

'You had better take the lass and go on home, my lady. The gentleman will be waiting.'

'What will you do with her parents? Will you release them now, before you come?'

'Aye. I'll take my cart and drop them off beyond the town limits, somewhere out on the road to Muir of Ord. They'll do better there than over towards Foulis.'

He comes up to see me and Kari off. 'Don't worry. My good wife is sympathetic to tinklers - more so than we are, anyway. Kenneth's on the other side altogether.' He glances back at his son fondly as we emerge into the daylight, then suddenly shouts: 'The boy! He's gone!'

The other children are still there, playing, but they tell us they didn't see which way he went. If they had, they would have given chase.

Kenneth comes running up, with Whin following him. 'He won't have got far. I'll gather some of the lads, and their dogs. The Bailie's son has an elphound.'

He seems pleased.

A crowd is gathering. I put my arm round Kari, who has started sobbing, and lead her away up the street to the executioner's house.

FOUR

Once Is Forever

Unsure what to do with him, for they'd never had a *Frangach* - a Frenchman - in the house before, they put Raoul in a room on his own and left him with a glass of wine to await me.

Effie showed me in and there he was, sitting on a stool before an unlit fire.

For a moment again we gazed at each other, remembering, readjusting: then we were in each other's arms. I clung to him, crying - why was I crying? - and wondering why I had ever left France.

I heard a cough, and a squawk. I looked round. The cough had been a discreet one from Effie; the squawk had come from Kari, whom Effie wanted to remove from the scene, by the elbow, or by the ear if necessary.

I said, 'Leave her, leave her here, Effie. She'll be all right. She's frightened, I think, in this big, strange house.'

'She'd be frightened in any house. She's probably never been in a house before.'

'That's true, so - '

'Aye, but you can't bring a tinkler bairn in just like that. There are things to be done. She has to be fed, she has to be cleaned. She'll have to be clothed: those things she is wearing, those - what are they? cat-skins? - they must be alive with fleas and lice and - '

'Yes.' It was making me itch simply listening. 'I'll bring her through in a moment.'

'No, no, I'll do it. Just tell the lass to come with me. Now.'

'Kari, go along with Mistress Effie. She wants to feed you, that's all, and give you some nice clothes to wear.'

'But you'll be here?' She was crying, all the events of that long day piling up on her. I held her to me, promising, comforting, irritated more by Effie's shocked face over the child's shoulder than by the thought of catching fleas or lice. I'd caught so many fleas, anyway, from the beds we'd slept in the last few weeks, that there was probably more risk of Effie, or her upholstery or her bedding, catching them from me than from poor Kari. Still, I wouldn't mention that or I might find myself being taken by the ear and stripped and disinfested alongside Kari. Which, now I came to think of it, I had been, all but, the previous evening. 'I'll be here, sweet, waiting for you.' I pushed her gently towards Effie and watched them go, then turned back to Raoul.

'Give me some of that wine - no, no, don't worry, I've drunk from your glass before. *A toî*, Raoul.'

'I've missed you.'

'It's been four years.'

'Four long, lonely years ... I'd rather walk than sit here. Shall we walk? The sun is shining now.'

'I know,' I smiled. 'I've just come in.'

'Oh. Yes. And you must be hungry. Would it - ' *déranger* was the word he used, disarrange, discommode, *inconvenience*, yes, that was it - 'Would it inconvenience your hosts, do you think, if you were to dine with me? At my *auberge*? I saw what looked like a very tasty lamb turning on the spit.'

It sounded extremely tempting. It had been years since Raoul and I ... 'I'd adore to. But there is that child - '

'She's in good hands now.'

'Still I must tell her - and them.' And Ferchard.

A few minutes later, Raoul and I were strolling arm in arm up the muddy main street and it was as though we had never been apart.

Did he have more than dinner in mind? I hoped so.

When we reached the inn, I paused to look up at the painted sign. 'Raoul, is that a whore?' I asked him, remembering the conversation outside the courthouse. 'Or a queen?'

He gazed up. 'Better ask is she the huntress - I mean is she leading the hunt - or is she the quarry? I cannot tell; but I suspect the latter.'

Whore, then.

Or cast-out queen.

As no private dining room was available, we sat in a corner of the crowded tap-room and roast lamb was set before us on trenchers of warm fresh bread. Raoul put a piece of meat to my lips. I took it in my teeth, chewed and swallowed it, and licked my lips. It was delicious.

He smiled. I was his again.

We ate, Raoul feeding me all the choicest bits from his cut so that he finished first. I passed him the rest of mine and we ate that together.

All this in silence.

Then he took a swallow of wine, sat back, and gazed at me. 'I've missed you, Mariana. I miss you all the time. I miss you in the summer, in the evenings, sitting in the shade, with a glass of wine. And in the winter when I'm cold and I remember how we used to make each other warm.'

'On summer evenings and winter nights?'

'I miss you in the spring when I remember how you came into my life like a sunlit morning, like the first warm evening. And I miss you in the autumn when I remember how you left me.'

My poet.

'I didn't leave you in the autumn.'

'No, I know, but ...'

'Give me your hand.' I remembered it. The same long, strong Line of Life; the deep, clear Line of Head; the Line of Fate terminating at the Line of Heart - this last not so good, and still very clear. I had often wondered if the cause of this broken heart - wrecked life even, it may be - was to be me? I prayed not.

I'd heard, when I returned to Paris on a visit, that he had moved on to Avignon to continue his studies. Now he told me that there he had become involved in politics. He had obtained a post under Enguerrand VII de Coucy (the great French general and statesman) while Coucy was in Avignon, and remained in Coucy's service. We talked a little of the changes that had taken place in Avignon since I had been there, then I said, 'But what are you doing here in the north of Scotland?'

'I'm with the force sent by King Charles to help the Scots prepare - to encourage them to prepare - for the invasion of England.'

'An army?'

'Not exactly. Only some one thousand five hundred men. The army will follow later, when the Scots army is ready.'

'And you? You're not a soldier.'

'Coucy asked me to accompany the expeditionary force and report direct to him on the situation in Scotland. I spent some time in Edinburgh then, when I heard that Jaufre le Fou was being sent north, I got myself attached to him. You remember Jaufre? Capitaine le Fou?'

'Vaguely.'

'We started in Inverness, moved north here to Dyngvale, then, after a few days, when we had spoken to everyone that mattered, went on up to Tain - again for a few days. The "few days" have now extended to nearly three weeks, but that's all right because from Tain, Jaufre and I can get to other small towns and local leaders and back again either the same day or the following day.' He smiled. 'To be honest, we are not achieving much. Myself, I am not achieving anything. But it is very pleasant - or was until this happened.'

'Until what happened? Tell me about it. Tell me about this Moor who was murdered.'

He looked round, raised his eyebrows.

'No one here understands French,' I said.

'How do you know that?' He stood, took my hand, helped me up. We made our way between the tables to the stairs. I had been the object of attention, most of it admiring, some curious, but none particularly hostile, ever since we arrived; now I caught one or two openly appraising glances. What were they thinking?

When we were safely in Raoul's room and I was undressed and he was stroking, caressing, remembering me, he said: 'After all, who can tell when they gaze upon a naked woman, whether she be queen or whore?'

I smiled up at him. That was very true. The important thing was not what she was but how she was treated. What was done to her.

What *was* being done, in that painted sign?

He ran his hand over my smooth mons veneris, my hairlessness - it was complete - a legacy of my days among the Moors in Granada, and murmured, 'I'll never forget the surprise I had the first time I saw *this* - this *nakedness*. I simply could not believe it ...'

I smiled, remembering. Unlike among the Moors, in Paris it is a mark of the prostitute, especially of those employed in *les étuves*, the bath-houses, what in London we call the stews. And of the queen? His eyes left mine, moved down, his face brushed between my breasts and over my stomach, then he began to kiss me there, his lips running over the cleft, and his tongue found better things to do than talk. Words gave way to actions, time to timelessness, to the eternity we find only in the arms of someone we love ...

But eternity came - it always does - to an end.

A church bell rang.

Time restarted.

I found myself lying beside Raoul.

And soon I was calm enough to start talking again. What strange creatures we are. 'So,' I repeated. 'Who was this Moor, this man who was murdered? And what was he doing in Tain?'

He sighed. A deep, contented sigh. 'Abdelwahed ben Youssef. A man everyone loved. No, not everyone. Jaufre didn't love him. Do you remember the murdered miser, the alchemist? When you were in Paris? And you saved our friend Jaquet from the scaffold?'

'I remember that I could not have saved him without you, Raoul. But tell me about Jaufre le Fou and this Moor, ben Youssef.'

'Jaufre? That is nothing, simple bigotry. Abdelwahed ben Youssef of Fès is - was - a Moor (I can't get used to the fact that he is dead; he was so alive) and Jaufre is from Arles, in the south of France, which makes him almost as fanatical as a Spaniard. You should know.'

Yes, I should know. I grew up in Spain. Be half-this, half-that, though, and you won't be a bigot. Jaufre le Fou was pure *provençal*.

'How is it?' le Fou had asked Raoul once, 'that this Moor has adapted so well to life in the north of Scotland? Is his homeland so barren and so totally unamusing that even Scotland seems *habitable* by contrast?'

To Raoul it had seemed that ben Youssef was simply interested - genuinely interested and genuinely friendly. And adaptable. Nothing upset him, not even the weather. He rode around the countryside, with the French-speaking Finlay MacKay to translate for him, talking to everyone, enjoying their joys, sharing their sorrows, and they, who were normally so taciturn, talked back to him: 'He was so foreign, so strange, so full of laughter and warmth that it was as if the sun, unable to come itself, had sent its ambassador, and the poor, pale people, who had forgotten what it was to smile, bared their hearts and basked in the brightness of him.'

He enquired about their myths and legends. That of the Queen of Elphame, especially, had caught his interest. She seemed so real to the people, riding by in her white cloak and golden sandals with her great hound loping along behind her; not like a tale out of the distant past at all. Though she hadn't been wearing golden sandals when he had seen her ...

'*He had seen her*?'

'So he told me.'

'And you believed him?'

'He was not the sort of man one did not believe.'

Apparently, Raoul and ben Youssef used to sit in the tap-room of the inn and have long conversations while they waited for the rain outside to stop. Sometimes, as we had done, they talked of Paris, where ben Youssef too had stayed. 'It is the heart of Europe,' the Moor would pontificate. 'It is to Paris that I return, always. It is, to Europe, what Fès is to the Maghreb.'

And they would reminisce about their lives in Paris, where Raoul had been a student of theology, though he had spent more time in the bars and taverns than in the lecture halls.

'Perhaps that is why Allah, the All-seeing, decreed that you should transfer your patronage from the taverns of Paris to those of Tain.'

'A little harsh.'

Ben Youssef laughed. 'The ways of Allah are inscrutable. Ah, if you could go to the Koranic University of Fès, my home, to study real theology! But they would not accept you. They could not: you are not a true believer. They might, however, in Granada. A school exists at the Great Mosque there that is run on liberal - that is to say, unorthodox - principles, though the theology itself, I believe, is sound.'

All this talk of Paris, Raoul confided to me now, and especially the mention of Granada, had brought back to his mind a girl - *a lady* - he had known in Paris. His lady, to whom he wrote sonnets and for whom he would willingly have laid down his life at any time. Or so he liked to believe. She had been from the south of Spain, Al Andalús, Andalucía - her mother had been Spanish - but her father was a Scot, from right up here in the far, far north, if he remembered rightly. Doña Mariana de la Manga. Lady Marian MacElpin.

Me.

He asked me once in Paris what "la manga" meant. 'It's the name of an arm of land, hardly more than a sandbank, that sticks out and surrounds a little sea, the Mar Menor, near Cartagena in the south-east corner of Spain. That's where I am from.'

'The cities of Al Andalús -' ben Youssef was still in the alehouse with Raoul - 'Granada, Córdoba, Sevilla, Murcia, Cartagena, and the rest - they are beautiful, but they are not like Fès, Fès el-Bali. Very soon now I shall return. I shall teach at one of the schools, one of the *medersas* for which Fès is famous -'

'What will you teach, Abdelwahed, my friend? Are you a theologian?'

'No more than you are, Raoul, my friend. I shall teach what I know, what I have learnt on my travels, and I shall never travel again.'

'Never?'

'Not even so far as Fès el-Jdid. That is the new city nearby where the Sultan has his palace and his bodyguard: *Nasranis* - Christian mercenaries - most of them.' He spat. Then laughed. 'That's theology! Go on, let's see you do it!'

Raoul spat across the crowded room, over a shoulder, between two heads - if this was theology, this he *could* do - out through a window and - oops! - splat onto the cheek of some poor woman who chose that moment to pass by.

'You should never, ever, spit on a woman. But it was written.

Thus the All-knowing decrees that even the best of theologians - and you I see now are indeed among the best - sin inadvertently.'

Raoul, shocked by what he had done, sat watching the doorway, but the woman did not come. She must have thought it was a present from a passing bird. Or perhaps she hadn't noticed it in all the rain.

Ben Youssef was homesick today, despite his love of this strange land. 'The government ministries are in the new city, of course. And that is better. The old city is golden and peaceful, and redolent of Allah in every brick and tile, every courtyard, every palm.'

Raoul yawned.

Abdelwahed ben Youssef had two slaves, Rachid and Souad, brother and sister, both young, who, between them, did for him all that a man might reasonably want done. He did not take them with him when he went out with MacKay each day, for they had no French and would not have enjoyed it; neither did they appreciate the local scenery and weather as their master did. So they stayed home. "Home" was wherever they happened to be - in this case, their lodgings in Tain - for their master was a great traveller, and they, who were now seventeen, eighteen, had been mere children when he bought them at the great slave-market in Tangiers prior to crossing over to Europe, prior to starting this long journey of exploration that had become almost, to him, a pilgrimage: for though of course it was in no way comparable to the *hadj*, the great pilgrimage to Mecca, it was quite like the wanderings of the Christian pilgrims whose path he so often crossed and whom he sometimes even joined for a while.

'Next, I will leave you all and make my own way on west to see the famous brightness in the sky, the halo, that surrounds the holy island of Iona, and after that ...' - "you all" being Raoul and the rest of the French with whom he had come this time from France to Scotland.

But Raoul, the theologian, was asleep. And at his feet, in the warmth and fug of the bar-room, La Pauvre, a poor, cowed, skinny stray that had attached herself to him on sight, now too slept, and snored and twitched and dreamed that she was human, as perhaps she had been once - who knows? - in another life.

Perhaps she had once looked like Souad.

Souad was beautiful, and Abdelwahed ben Youssef kept her almost entirely secluded. Raoul and le Fou, *le capitaine*, saw her eyes from time to time - they could hardly help it, travelling together - and as le Fou said, one could infer almost everything about a woman from her eyes. They had even caught the occasional glimpse of her *en déshabille*, less than fully clothed and veiled, when they had called at ben Youssef's lodgings on some trumped-up errand. But this only served to confirm their extrapolations and to further inflame both Raoul's fantasies and le Fou's lust or, as he preferred to put it, ardour. Le Fou, despite his name, was no fool, at least in the opinion of his superior officers; however, he was, like Raoul, cold and bored, and French, and a long, long way from home ...

He has changed, Raoul, my old admirer, my poet, my Parisian. Grown up.

In truth, he is not a Parisian at all. Despite his name - Raoul de Cocherel - he comes from Normandy. He is quite tall, though not particularly well-built; not particularly anything. His skin is pale, but not as pale as it was in Paris - he must get more fresh air, more sunlight, here - and his hair is a rather boring brown, but clean, glossy even, not lank and greasy like most men's. And most women's when their caps come off. How does he do that?

'How do you do that?'

'Do what?'

But I am looking into his eyes now, and he is gazing back into mine. He has lovely light-brown eyes, hazel-coloured. 'Do what, my lady?'

'Keep your hair so clean, so glossy?'

'My hair? Oh, I see. I use a special soap we make in my village. It contains cider - at least I think it does. It certainly smells as if it does!'

'You must let me have some.'

'You? But your hair is perfect. I have been trying to think of words to describe it. You see dark swans sometimes on the rivers and lakes of Normandy, which at sunset ...'

I leave him talking while I think about ben Youssef, about the situation in Tain. If we disregard, for the moment, the so-called suspect, then the murder could have been local, some local jealousy or antagonism. In two or three weeks a talkative foreigner can upset a lot of people. Or it could have been orchestrated from abroad, be something out of the itinerant Moor's no-doubt-colourful past catching up with him. Or it could have been political: was his being with the French expeditionary force merely a happy chance seized on by the experienced traveller or was it more than that?

'Tell me about the suspect, Raoul.'

He was coming to that.

Souad was beautiful, he told me; but Rachid, her twin brother, was not. He was big. He was simple. And he was a eunuch. He had just been castrated when ben Youssef bought them as a brother-and-sister pair. It had been clumsily done and it had been done too late; the boy had never really recovered. But ben Youssef had not been looking at the boy. No one had. All the bidding had been for the girl, and by the time he got her - caught up in the excitement of the chase - he had paid much more than even she was worth. The boy, of course, was worth nothing. He had kept him, though - the girl had wanted him - and since then, it was true, the boy had made himself useful guarding and waiting on her, and doing housework, and heaving their luggage about when they were on the move.

One morning, Jaufre, ever watchful, saw ben Youssef ride out from Tain with MacKay to the Mickel Ferry and cross over to Sutherland, where he disappeared into the mist on the road to Dornoch. He posted one of his men on the look-out for the return of the ferry with ben Youssef aboard, and prepared to move in.

'The girl has bright eyes,' he assured Raoul, 'and is therefore bright, unlike her dull-eyed brother. She must know at least a few words of either French or Spanish. She must: they have been travelling around Europe for years.'

He called at ben Youssef's lodging and talked to Rachid so seriously and at such length that the poor boy, understanding nothing and worried lest it might be urgent, let him in and took him through to where Souad, in a sort of muslin kaftan, was busy doing something to her nails.

When their eyes met, he thought she was going to scream, to

put her hands to her face - to her breasts, which the kaftan covered but did not conceal - and, yes, scream. But instead, she watched him with a half smile as her brother poured out the story, while he gazed back at her, noting the skin, dark as honey and no doubt as sweet to the tongue, and the black eyes he had admired for so long and that he saw now were not merely bright and cold like precious stones but glowing, smoking, with passion. She listened to her brother, calmed the poor creature down, and sent him out of the room - insisting - then said, '*Capetán. Qué quiere Vd aquí*?' What do you want here?

'You speak Spanish?' he answered in the same tongue.

'*Castellano? Sí.* A little. From when I was a child, before Sidi ben Youssef bought me. So. What do you want?'

What did he want?

'Don't worry, Raoul,' I laughed. 'I'll get that story from Jaufre himself when I speak to him.'

They talked a little, then Souad sent him away and told him not to return. She thought that was the end of it.

As did the *capitaine*.

So the following day, still with no clue as to how to instil enthusiasm for war against England into the local barons and lairds and leaders of men, he cast his eye in another direction: that of *Sasunn* Bella, wife - or at any rate, woman - of the late Harald Skinner.

As a widow, Bella now came under the aegis of her father-in-law, one Thorfinn Skinner, a man feared and avoided even by the fighting men among his neighbours. He beat and abused her, and - so rumour had it - he was assisted in this by a slave, a strange silver-eyed creature named "*glaistig*" Coll, who was deputed to watch poor Bella's every move.

They lived on the Tarbat coast to the east of Tain, on their own land, with their own boat, and they never let Bella out alone. Raoul though, and Jaufre le Fou, had seen her in the town with her father-in-law, seen all eyes turn. The wind played with her long blonde hair and, no matter what they did to her, the sun caressed her cheeks and tried to catch her bright blue eyes, and it was as though the old days of the Vikings and their women had returned, for Thorfinn himself was a great sea-going man with a full beard and a heavy leather belt and he matched this fine, tall, Saxon girl as Odin, king of the Norse gods, would match Freya, goddess of love, were they to come back and walk down the High Street of Tain once more together.

'So what happened, Raoul?'

Again Raoul had warned Captain le Fou - this time with feeling, for it was Raoul himself, I suddenly realised, who found Bella, *la belle anglaise*, like Freya, divine, whereas Souad, equally *belle*, and dark, and from the jasmine-scented south, was much more to his captain's taste. But Jaufre had eyes and ears now only for what he laughingly referred to as *le plat du jour*, the dish of the day.

And Jaufre le Fou was not one to stand back and wait for his slower, shyer, friend.

This time Jaufre was lucky, for Thorfinn went out in his fishing-boat and a storm blew up and Thorfinn did not return at the appointed time.

Jaufre rode out to Bella at the Skinner steading.

And that night, Abdelwahed ben Youssef of Fès was murdered somewhere out there between Tain and the steading. His body was discovered by the slave, Rachid, who had gone out at dawn in search of his missing master. He found him lying by the cart track with a hole in his chest and his back. His horse was grazing quietly nearby.

They arrested Rachid, supposing that he, as a Moor, must have murdered his master, another Moor.

Mulling it over, I realise that the tinkler family I have befriended may well have been on that same beach out to the east of Tain at the time of the murder. I would have to find out exactly what they saw and heard. And who was the old woman "who was not a woman" that Kari mentioned? What was she doing there? And what did she see?

Raoul walks me back to the executioner's house. He is to sleep at the Whore & Hounds and leave for Inverness at dawn. We arrange to meet in Tain, in two days' time, on the Sunday.

FIVE

In Which I Join The Tinklers

Big Robbie, the Master Executioner, was a good man: a good husband to his wife, Effie, a good father to Kenneth and his two little daughters, and - there could be no doubt of it, one had only to look at him - a good executioner.

I liked him. He liked me, too, I could tell. As he entered the room that evening, his eyes swept round and having rested upon me he had to find something to say.

'The Frenchman's away, is he?'

'To the Queen for the night, and then to Inverness,' his wife replied.

'Aye, well, he'll have to report to his superiors.'

I notice that at home they - or at least Effie - use the old name for the inn.

He is, I know, curious about Raoul and what I might have learned from him, but I am still thinking. I feel no desire to speak of it yet.

Big Robbie sighs. 'Young Kenneth will be late home, no doubt.'

'Why?'

'He's with the Bailie's son and some other lads, hunting the tinkler brat that got away.'

'Poor mite.'

I look at her. Where is the logic?

'Will they catch him?' she asks.

'Oh aye.'

'And when they have caught him, what will they do with him?' She looks at him, but he is drinking his ale. 'And the mother was there, you say? As well as the father? Who scourged her? She wasn't? Better. Though I mustn't be sentimental. After all, they're not like us, tinklers. I mean, they don't feel pain the same. They're more like witches. You don't think this one was a witch, do you? Only Mistress Iseabal says she was sort of - well, she said "beautiful", in a wild, ugly, kind of way. Of course, a good whipping would put her off coming back to Dyngvale again, causing a nuisance. If we didn't do something, we'd be overrun.'

I choose between a dozen possible responses: 'She'd come back anyway, to find out about her children.'

'No.'

Just like that.

'No. As I say, they're not like real people, like you or me. She'll forget them, have some more, same as a cat or dog.'

Robbie chuckles. 'But she'll remember Kenneth. She'll remember, even though she didn't get her whipping. She'll remember and guard her tongue.'

Effie flushes with pleasure. 'Master Robert's getting soft; everyone says so, but what a boy he's got, they say. And he's studying the hearsays now.'

Her husband interrupts: 'Heresies, aye. He'll be off to Tain tomorrow to assist Brother Arsenius. Wonderful opportunity for the lad. You must meet the good Brother, have a chat with him. And the heretic, as well. Perhaps you can make him see reason.'

'He is already condemned, this heretic?'

'Was long ago, I understand. In Toledo or Avignon or - I don't know. By the Pope himself, they do say. Then he escaped. Arsenius, a Black Friar, and Inquisitor in his own right, was assistant to the Chief Inquisitor at the trial. He has spent years hunting him down, and found him at, of all places, our local monastery, the Abbey of Fearn. He is, of course, well out of patience, and more than ready to burn the blaggard and be done with it, but, naturally, being a religious man, he longs to see the sinner repent.'

'Naturally. Yes, I'd like to talk to him. Not Brother Arsenius, the other man.'

'I may see you in Tain, later. There'll be this young Moor of theirs to execute.'

'Will he hang? Master Skinner can hang him without you.' Effie didn't want him away.

'He may. But he's a slave, remember, and he murdered his own master in cold blood. There'll be many who say that hanging's too good for him. They may want him boiled, or burnt.'

'Tell me about these Moors.'

'All I know - Lady Marian will know more - is that the victim was wealthy and is believed to have been stabbed by his slave, who is a eunuch, and hardly more than a lad. His sister was their master's concubine, and said to be exotically beautiful. Or so the messenger from Tain informed me when I caught up with him at the Bailie's house. Apparently, she was always veiled from head to foot when she appeared in public, with only her eyes and her toes on show, so the women of Tain took leave to doubt this tale of her beauty, but their husbands and their sons, and of course their fathers, believed it to a man.'

I believed it too. I knew Moorish girls. What I could not credit was that either she or her brother would under any circumstances murder their master. Especially while they were far from home, strangers in a very strange land.

I told them so.

'But why not?' demanded Effie. 'Now they're free. And perhaps she always hated him. I know I would have. And her brother, of course, would have hated him too.'

'No, they're not free. They weren't his children, they were his property. Like all the rest of his goods and chattels, they become the property of his heirs and successors. His son, if he has one.'

Big Robbie nodded. 'Like any bondsman, aye. They'll have to be held in custody till ...'

It struck me then that ben Youssef might have prepared certificates of manumission, freeing them in the event of his death. Interesting.

I would set out that night, after all, I decided. Tain was anyway close to some of our family lands, those lands of my grandfather's, which had been confiscated from us and given to others: our punishment for having supported the Balliols, and not the Bruce and his cronies.

I told Effie I would be leaving, and taking Kari with me.

'She'll run away.'

'No - '

'You don't understand. How will you ever be able to stop her, or catch her? Either leave her here or keep her chained to your horse.'

Then Kenneth returned, flushed and happy, to tell us that "the tinkler brat" had been caught.

'Was he killed?' asked Robbie.

'No, though he was mauled by the dogs a bit,' Kenneth grinned.

'Where is he now?'

'I left him all trussed up and hanging from a cleek down in the chamber.'

'He'll be all right till morning?'

'Aye, but Baron Hugh got wind of the hunt and was very put out, so the Bailie told him about the two older ones. Said we'd kept them specially for him. So then I told him where you'd dropped them off.'

'And he was happy with that?'

'Oh, aye. He's going to set gillies to watch them tomorrow, and arrange a Great Hunt for Sunday.'

I made a second decision. Or rather, choice.

I took Ferchard on one side and sent him off to the apothecary to get me two unguents: one of adder's tongue, vervain, thyme and touch-and-heal for Tinkman's back, and another garlic-based with boneset and comfrey, and also parsley as it was for his hands and the hands are ruled by Mercury. When he had gone, I went through to the kitchen where Kari had been making herself useful, sampling the various dishes on the table.

'Listen, Kari. I'm going north to Tain tomorrow, and you're coming with me. Just you and me.'

'And Sir Farquhar?'

'He's staying here for the moment. Now, if you want to run away any time while we're on the road, go right ahead and do so. I shan't try to stop you. I'm on your side. None of this was my idea. I just want you to remember, though, that the next time you're picked up by the Bailie or his men, the least that will happen to you is having the letter F for Fugitive branded on you - here - for all to see. And Master Robert will say he warned you, and he'll have Master Kenneth scourge you. And ... so please, don't run away, for your own sake.'

'But I wasn't going to. I wouldn't. I - I love you, my lady. I don't want to be out there hungry in the rain and cold with the hounds coming closer and closer like poor Otter. And like my ma. They'll catch my da and then they'll hunt her too, I know they will.'

'But they won't catch her, will they?'

'My ma? No! She's too sleekit and too swift for them. But if she had to wait for me ... I'm not like her. I never will be.'

'I think you're very like her. You just don't realise it yet.'

'Oh no, you haven't seen her. She's a wonder.'

'I have seen her. And I can imagine her out on the hill - and in the sea - '

'Oh yes, in the sea, she's like a mermaid - but so am I; I can do that. My da used to say I'll be a mermaid when I grow up, all the time I mean, fishtail and all, and never be able to come up out of the sea. Do you think I will?'

'You never know. But in the meantime, we'll find a lonely beach somewhere on our travels and you can show me how you swim. And if it turns out that you do have a tail, why, then I'll leave you there. What good would a maid with a tail be to a grand lady in London?'

Kari laughed, and watching her I thought again of my father's lands which, it seemed, had all been lost. Not such a grand lady. Probably not a "Lady" at all, if the truth were told.

'Kari, when we leave here, just you and me, we'll go out first along the road that leads to Muir of Ord. You know it?'

'Yes, my lady.'

'Master Robert left your ma and da out along that way, somewhere beyond the town limits. Do you think you can find them?'

She was looking at me, as if not sure she could trust me.

'I've sent Sir Farquhar out to fetch unguents from the apothecary for your da's back and hands. And we'll take them some food, too, to help them survive.'

'Will you? Will you really do that? Oh yes, I know where they'll be.'

'And can you find it, in the dark?'

'I'm an Elp.'

I looked at her.

She was right. That's exactly what she was. They were Elps. As some of my own ancestors must have been, or where did my name, MacElpin, come from?

'Talking about seeing in the dark, Kari, I shall want to know what your ma saw last night on the beach outside Tain - you know, after you fell asleep? Something happened there during the night that I need to know about, because it involves a friend of mine. Did you see - or hear - any riders go by on horseback?'

She was staring at me still, but she said nothing.

'We'll ask your ma when we see her, yes?'

She nodded then, big eyes still gazing up at me in puzzlement, but not distrust, not really, not any longer. She wanted to be on my side.

'There was a horse went by on the cart-track before we met Otter, I remember that. Then later they came back from Tain, I think. You'll have to ask Ma.'

When Ferchard returned, I told him that I was setting out at once and preferred to leave him behind so that he could spend time with his family.

'You mean with Effie? Marian, you are my family now, you know that.'

I was moved. 'I do know that.' I hugged him. 'I thought you were bored with the journey. That your only purpose in coming here was to visit your family, see your old home again.'

'My only purpose in coming here was to protect you. As for the journey, I've enjoyed it. Mostly. It reminds me of when we were on the road before, when we came up through Spain and France four years ago, heading north. Those four years - where have they gone? It's as though we merely broke our journey in London - '

'That was more than four years ago, Ferchard. I was only eighteen when we left Spain. And we spent a winter in Avignon -

and Italy - or I did. And the next winter in Paris.'

'And then London. But travelling ever further north, together - till now.'

'We could always go on. Where does one go on to from here? Ultima Thule?'

'I don't know where Ultima Thule is, but we could certainly go on to Orkney and Sheltland.'

'And then? Beyond Sheltland?' I wondered.

'Norroway? Lappland? Finnland? We would take ship from Sheltland and head north once more, and this time go on right to "the land of the midnight sun".'

'It's light at midnight here - '

'Lightish, sometimes, yes, but the sun does set. Up there, I've heard, it never sets at all from May to July. Which must affect the horoscope quite dramatically.'

'It will simply mean that there is no House of the Night,' I said. 'Everyone will be born in the House of the Day.'

He was not really interested, he'd only been teasing. And he wasn't happy. What was wrong?

'Why do I talk about the four years - six - whatever it is? What happened to the fifty years? It seems like yesterday I went away for what should have been one year, two, no more.'

'There must be old men here, Ferchard, who were boys when you were a boy.'

'And remembering them as they were, not having seen them age and change from day to day and from year to year as they have seen each other, will I want to see them now? Will they want to see me, the me I am, as opposed to the me that they remember?'

'If you came back to life, back to Earth, for a visit in, say, another fifty years, would you want to see me?'

'Of course I would. And that's my answer. But still, in the here and now … it's that Raoul. You want to be free to be with him.'

Ah. So that was it. 'I *am* free, Ferchard, whether or not you are nearby.'

'Perhaps Khadija is right. Perhaps it is time to marry you off to some fine gentleman with a strong right arm.'

Khadija was my nurse, had been my mother's nurse, was still with me now, waiting for me at our home in London.

'You know you wouldn't,' I said.

'What marry you off, or marry you off to someone with a strong right arm?'

'Either, I hope. And he'd need a very strong right arm.'

'She's thinking of you. Khadija wouldn't - '

'Khadija! Khadija's the least submissive of women, despite being a lifelong slave - yet she's a great believer in submissive women.'

'Lass, she bends with the storm, that's all. Something I should have thought *you* might have learnt during your time in Granada. Well, all right then, off you go on your own. But not dressed up as a lad. Promise me. That Jack Cutting you pretend to be nearly got me killed. And nearly got you killed twice. Not to mention getting you that dreadful beating. You remember? In Paris, when the Abbé Soxxal had you brought in and questioned?'

Could I ever forget? I laughed. 'Don't worry. I'm getting much too buxom now to pass as a boy.'

He gazed down at me. 'Ay, well, you keep them covered, or you'll be getting into other kinds of trouble.'

'Ferchard, whenever you wish to, whenever you are ready, come and find us in Tain.'

'Us?' The glint was back in his eye.

'Kari, the tinkler girl - '

'Ah, yes.'

'I want to spend some time alone with her, get to know her better - give her a chance to get to know me better - in familiar surroundings.'

Before I left, I took Big Robbie on one side too. I thanked him for his hospitality and for all his kindness. 'But, Master Robert, there is one thing: I feel I must ask you to warn your son that my family have many old friends here in the County of Ross. Countess Euphemia, for example, an old friend of my father's and grandfather's, also dabbles in astrology; and if she was to learn that your Kenneth had looked at me - *me* - in an insolent - knowing - manner when the subject under discussion was heresy and witchcraft, he would be lucky if it was only his tongue he lost. The Countess of Ross is not known for her clemency.'

He was shocked. 'Ah, my lady. Aye, he did, I remember. But he's only young - '

'The "tinkler brat" is only young, yet he hangs trussed in the torture chamber for the night. And what harm did he ever do anyone?'

'Oh, you're right, yes. I'll go and let the tinkler br- lad down now, at once, and make him more comfortable.'

'Your son said he'd been mauled by the dogs, so dress his wounds before they fester.'

'You're right, you're right. I will. And tomorrow morning, first thing, I'll have a word with the boy - Kenneth, I mean.'

'You'll have more than "a word" with him.'

'Aye, my lady. You'll get no more insolence from him, I promise you.'

'Then good night, and once again, my thanks, Master Robert. I was sure that you would understand.'

We leave by the South Gate as evening falls, and in a few moments are clear of the outlying hovels with their barking dogs and crying babies and children playing in the mud.

Now the quiet waters of the firth in the dusk lie to our left, and on our right dark forest and hills.

Kari, up behind me on the grey mare Ferchard found and hired for us, is uncertain where to stop. It all seems unfamiliar to her, no doubt, for she is seeing it all from a quite different viewpoint. Normally, she confides, her lips to the back of my ear, they would not even walk along the track, they would make their way through the woods to the west and avoid the track altogether.

We ride on in silence a while, then: 'There. They might be over there, if he dropped them off on this stretch of the road.'

We slip down off the mare. As I fasten the rein to a tree, I hear right behind me the call of what sounds like some large bird. I peer round but can see nothing. Nervously - I am on completely unfamiliar ground - I follow Kari into the wood.

After a moment, we hear the sound of water running between the trees. Kari touches my arm and points. 'Down there.'

They have a little fire going, but are well hidden among the dark alders that line the burn. Whin has cooked a fish and is feeding Tinkman, pushing bits into his mouth. They show no concern at our approach.

'How is it they don't hear us coming and hide?' I ask Kari.

She smiles up at me: a smile of approval, but also of superior knowledge. 'Did you hear the capercaillie cry out then chatter right behind us just now?'

'Was that what it was?'

She grins. 'No, but that's what it sounded like. What it was was me letting my ma and da know that we were coming and not to be frightened. Ma?'

'Kari? And my lady?'

'Hello, Whin. No, don't get up, finish your food.'

'I have finished, I'm just feeding Tinkman. Would you like some?'

'No, no -'

'We ate a lot, Ma, before we left.'

'*You* did,' I laugh. 'If I ate as much as that - '

Tinkman has been looking at me, as though unsure who I am. Now he says, suddenly, 'You'd be real b-bonny, my lady, were you a pound or two plumper.'

Ah! He's coming round. 'Well, thank you, sir. Then I'll keep young Kari company at the table from now on.'

'Take no notice, my lady. He finds me too thin, as well. He finds everyone too thin except his golden girl - fat little Kari here.'

'Ma! I'm not - '

Tinkman is still naked from the waist up, and his back looks bad.

'If you could stay like that - yes - so I can get at your back. I have some unguent here I brought with me from Tain.'

'I couldn't do anything much for him except get him into the water to wash it and cool it. He wouldn't put his hands in.'

'How are his hands? A little better?'

I look at his hands. They never will be better, not completely. And he won't let me touch them, so I return my attention to his back. Gently, I sooth some of the ointment onto the bruised and swollen flesh, the ploughed up skin, dabbing it on then smoothing it over. He sighs.

'Ma, while I was asleep the other night - Ma?'

'Yes, I'm listening, blossom. What other night?'

'Last night, I mean, near Tain, along the sands out Tarbat way there - '

'When we met Otter, and were waiting for your da. How is my poor Otter? Was he badly hurt when they caught him? He wasn't killed, was he? I'd have known if he'd been killed.'

'No, Ma, but he was mauled a bit - '

'Mauled *a bit*? Hounds don't maul "a bit" ... Well, they'll come after me next, the hounds that mauled my little Otter, and when they do, they'll *die a bit*.'

She is so poor, so powerless, this outlaw, this non-woman, so helpless in this modern world of towns and houses and laws and money and law-courts and judges and torturers and shops, as helpless as any poor animal - there are no elk or reindeer left in Scotland, or so I have heard, and not that many wolves or bears or wulboar either - and yet how full of power, too, how certain of herself, at a time when even kings, even the two popes, doubt themselves and all they stand for ... And how remorseless, once aroused, like the vengeance of Wul of the forest, or the anger of AN of the sea.

I smile to myself. Old names are coming back to me out of the tales I heard as a child when my father came and tucked me in and kissed me good night.

And yet I am glad I am not Baron Hugh of Foulis Castle or Master Kenneth Ross or one of their dogs.

Where had *she* been on the night of the murder? Where? There.

'And where is he now, my otter kit? Back in the torture chamber with that Hel's-son Master Kenneth?' She spits and makes a strange sign with both hands. 'Hel is a Viking goddess,' she informs us all, but with a glance at me to make sure I am listening, 'a Viking goddess, huge and blue-eyed and cold. She has yellow hair so pale it is almost white, not white like snow, but yellow-white, like death; and if she mated with some carrion-eater come out of Orkney, some twisted troll with the stench of decay in its mouth and the aura of fear before and behind, she'd give birth to one such as him.'

I look at her. 'I don't like him either,' I say, still soothing the salve into her man's back: more of Kenneth's work. 'But your boy is not with him, he's with Master Robert. I warned him to keep young Kenneth right away from Otter.'

Now she smiles - and turns back to Kari, and I see from Kari's eyes that Whin is smiling at her, too.

I say, 'You're right, though, they will be coming after you next, Whin. They say that when Baron Foulis - Sir Hugh, you know him? - heard that he had missed the hunt for the tinkler boy, he said they should have waited, should have told him, there was time - and they should have told him "the brat" was for sale in the first place.'

'And if he had been there the brat would not have escaped with his life,' Whin says. 'Aye, I know him.' She spits and makes that sign again. 'The one who hunted young Badger, Yorlin's boy, to his death. Drove him into the sea, where he died, somewhere off Tarbat Ness. He was no swimmer. Better than Tinkman, though. He'd rather die on the beach, wouldn't you, Tink ... When's it to be? Tomorrow? '

'No, Sunday.'

'Sunday?'

'The day after tomorrow. Tomorrow, he says, he'll set gillies to watch you ... It will be a Great Hunt, apparently,'

'You hear that, Tinkman? Tonight, now, as soon as you're ready, you must go down the firth and onto Black Isle and hide up somewhere there. And I'll go west towards the Falls of Rogie and Loch Garve. Then at dawn, I'll let myself be seen somewhere near Strathpeffer. It will draw him away from you and I'll be better off too on my own. I can go where I will and do as I will. Oh, Yewel, my man ... Yewel, yes ... and why not? The yew will do - the yew will do very well - for dogs and, too, it may be, one day, for men.'

I understand. I know some of the properties of the yew, and have the feeling that very soon I will learn to what use she plans to put them. The dogs? The men? I say only, "We must leave you now. We too travel through Black Isle tonight. We go to Tain and I prefer not to approach along the main route from the south. Also Kari has promised to show me where you waited for Tinkman last night. Would he like to come with us?'

'He is safest on his own. Unless the dogs pick up his scent, he'll never be noticed. Will this salve be good for his fingers too?'

'What's in it?' asks Tinkman.

'St John's wort - that's devil's scourge - '

'I know St John's wort. We call it touch-and-heal.'

'It's also known as balm-of-the-warrior's-wound. I brought another one for your fingers, one that may speed the healing. Where is it, Kari? Ah, here. Yes. This contains boneset and garlic. Soothe it in gently, as much and as often as possible, if you can bear it.'

'Oh aye, I'll bear it.'

'I'll do it for you the once, anyway, now,' Whin says.

'Why don't you come with us, Da? The lady says you can.'

'No, lass, I'm better on my own now till my fingers heal. Like any other wounded thing.'

'And where he'll be going, he has a store of flysvamp. He'll hide himself up and go on a shelti-trip.'

'Aye, I have a little store on Black Isle, by the cairns up Culbo way. It's in the forest,' he explains to me. 'You don't want to go into the forest. You stay on the track along the side of the firth.'

A shelti-trip - the soul's journey to the shelti-world: but Flysvamp? I ask Whin.

'It's just a kind of mushroom he likes to pick and dry and store, and then enjoys chewing later, when he passes that way again.'

Just a kind of mushroom? I see. But now I am thinking of Culbo on Black Isle and my father's tales of home.

'Ma, when I was asleep last night, did you see that horseman again? The one we saw riding into Tain with the woman with long blonde hair up behind him. You remember?'

'Yes, I remember. Why?'

'My lady wants to know. Something happened out there last night. A man was killed. She must help them find out who did it.'

'Why you, my lady?'

'Because the man who was killed was a foreigner, a Moor, and the man they suspect of killing him is also a Moor and no one there speaks his language. I do.'

'He has brown skin and brown eyes, this Moor, and a grey

beard, and wears strange clothes? And has a long, curved dagger hanging at his side?'

I nod. 'That sounds like the one who was killed.'

'Aye, I've seen him. I saw him talking to the folk in Golspie, in the market place. He seemed a good, a kind, man. What is it you want to know? Who we saw? A man rode by on a horse with a woman up behind, heading for Tain, as Kari says. Later, he and she rode back out towards the steading. It was darker by then, but I could see her hair. She was a young woman, tall, as tall as the man, and with beautiful Viking hair. Later, the man passed again, on his way back to Tain once more, but this time more slowly, on his own, and that was when I fell asleep.'

I smile. Big, with beautiful Viking hair? She must have looked like Hel to Whin.

'Are you sure that was the same man?'

'No, I just assumed it was, and we made up a story about them, Otter and me, what they were doing. I said he picked her up and took her into Tain, to the Spider & King, for a drink and a chat and maybe something else, then took her home again. The otter kit, who is the dreamer of the family, said she was a princess out of Norroway and was being held in thrall. The man - the first man - was rescuing her. Then the second time we saw her, this he thought was with another man, maybe the man whose thrall she now was; she was being brought back, and now, of course, she was in trouble. Well, that was for sure and didn't need any great imagination, not if you know that man - Thorfinn the skinner. Then the third rider, the one on his own, was that same man again and, according to Otter, his slowness and heaviness now were because he'd already exhausted himself punishing the poor princess and he still had to go after and kill the other man, the man who'd tried to rescue her. But that first man had probably left with the man in black, the man Otter said had come all the way from Norroway to rescue her too. As I say, he's a grand story-teller, and I shall miss him on long winter nights.'

Man in black?

I should have saved the boy as well, not only Kari. Perhaps there is still something … But not tonight.

'And the woman he saw on the beach? Who was that? And

what was she doing exactly? Kari says you told her it wasn't a woman, wasn't a person at all.'

'She was neither young nor old,' Whin chanted. 'but by turns the one and then the other, and by turns hideous as a bogle and fair as the girl on the back of the horse.'

'But what was she doing?'

'She was working a spell. It was a spell for a storm, or so Otter told me - he heard the words.'

'What kind of spell?'

'A spell against a man on a boat. A spell with a wee doll. How did it go? He remembered it, but I don't. It began something like :

I mak the heid, I mak the han,
I mak the feet, I hae the man.
I pit the man into the wave …

then something about his grave. We saw the storm come up, go down.'

'A worker of witchcraft, then?'

'Aye, but like the weather itself, she was neither good nor evil, foul nor fair, but both, as it were, coming and going.'

'You cannot put a name to her? Not even the name of her kind?'

'I can, but I would rather not. When you leave Black Isle and cross over to Nigg, ask for the Witch of Balintore. She will tell you what you need to know.'

'This was not her?'

'Oh no, nothing like her. The Witch is - like you, my lady, but old now, very old.'

SIX

On The Black Isle

We rode north through the half dark of the summer night. Following Kari's advice - and her father's, I remembered - we kept to the coastal path. We saw no one, and we heard nothing except the occasional nightjar churring and burbling for minutes on end and a fox calling in the distance. If we stopped and listened, we could hear more sound coming from the water that lay to our left than from the forest on our right.

I asked Kari about this and she told me the firth was noisy because the tide was high and turning and, as for the forest, very soon it would come wide awake quite suddenly. Realising I was not at home in these surroundings, she appointed herself my guide. I could see she was going to be useful. It was Kari who told me that the bird we kept hearing and that seemed to be following us was a nightjar - and of course that the tree we were sitting under with Whin and Tinkman was an alder. I know the properties of the alder but I wouldn't have recognised one in a wood in daylight, let alone at night.

The conversation with Ferchard was worrying me.

I had often been asked, of course, whose authority I came under. My father was dead and my two elder brothers had died in the Great Mortality when they were children, so I kept up the fiction of my twin brother, Magnus. Where is he now? they asked. He's on his travels. And who did he confide you to? To Sir Farquhar here.

It is not true. Or perhaps I thought it might be true, at least in part. Perhaps Magnus had been on his travels all these years. For though the symbol of Scorpio - our sign, one of the four fixed signs - can be a scorpion, it can also be an eagle, as it is in the signs of the four Evangelists: the eagle that soars up and away, following the setting sun.

We were in fact born on the 28th of October, 1357, the day of St Jude, Patron Saint of the hopeless, in Cartagena (New Carthage) in the south east of Spain. My father, Sir Andrew MacElpin, had been living there in exile for years. He had married my mother, Doña María de la Manga, and had two sons: my elder brothers, Edward (Eduardo) and James (Iago), who died, as I say, in 1349 during the Great Mortality. Eight years later, Magnus and I were born. During the next visitation of the Black Death, in 1361, María, our mother, died, and Magnus, then aged three, disappeared in all the panic. Everyone assumed that he had run off and died too, somewhere, unnoticed and alone. No, not those who knew him. Not my father; not my grandmother, Sebah, nor Khadija, the slave who had looked after my mother and now looked after me; and not me either, as I grew older and thought about it. To me, it always seemed he had simply gone away.

We were supported in this by Uncle Yacoub ben Amar.

My father, in his "spare time" as he put it - his time was all spare - studied languages and philosophy under Uncle Yacoub, and I sat with them; sat literally at their feet. Then, as my father grew discouraged and gave up and spent more and more of his time away from us on his own under the trellised vine with his flagon and cup, saying nothing at all, I went on learning, gradually learning all that Yacoub knew, or at least all that he considered suitable for the ears of a Hebrew maiden. I should explain here that my mother's mother, Sebah of Cordoba, was the daughter of a Muslim father and a Jewish mother, and it was this Jewish strand in the family to which Yacoub ben Amar belonged. Though in the eyes of the world I might be of noble Scottish blood, and of almost equally noble Spanish birth, and a Christian through and through, in the eyes of Yacoub, I was the daughter of the daughter of the daughter of Rebecca of Salé in Morocco; and descent among Jews being through the mother, as Jewish as Rachel or Judith or Esther or indeed the Holy Mother Mary - Maria, Mariam - herself.

I learnt Hebrew and Arabic. I read through the Koran and picked up something of Islam. I read the Hebrew Bible and learnt much of Judaism and of the history of "my" people, and too of mysticism and gnosticism, for Yacoub's mind - and heart and soul - were always on the Kabbalah. I learnt astronomy and astrology, and the basics of medicine. And I learnt palmistry. I took to such subjects. I have a feeling for the future that my father said I inherited from the Scottish side of the family, from his mother, a spaewife, one who knows, one who has The Sight. Which is interesting, when you think that a student of Kabbalah, such as my master Yacoub, is referred to reverently as one who knows, one who understands.

I still remember my father repeating over and over, when I sat with him as I sometimes did at his table under the vine trellis: 'Yacoub says wee Magnus will return. There was no early death written in his hand. And what will he do if he returns and finds us gone?'

What indeed? For my grandparents died and my father died, and for four years I too was separated from Khadija and my home. And when, after many adventures, I found my way back, I was "grown up", and old enough to take charge of my own affairs.

It was then, as I say, that my life line fell in with that of Sir Farquhar de Dyngvale, my father's old friend, Ferchard. And now we were family, along with Khadija, who looked after us, and Yahia, my eunuch. But did he have authority over me? That kind of authority? Could he really marry me off to whoever he chose? Not that he would, but - I couldn't help wondering - did he have the right, the power? Ferchard would never do anything, never allow anything to happen, that might hurt me, of course, but I could imagine someone *like* me, with an uncle *like* Ferchard, only not quite like Ferchard. After all, it was I who had the money, the property, and would have for as long as I remained unmarried: the money we lived on was mine, Khadija was mine, Yahia was mine. The house we lived in was mine. I could throw him out. Ferchard, I mean. Or could I? Could he just marry me off whenever he chose, having previously made some arrangement to the effect that when all my worldly goods passed into my husband's hands, a generous share passed straight back into his own? Two rich men; one penniless woman, with no redress whatsoever, living the rest of her life at the beck and call of her new husband and his family.

It happened all the time.

I looked up, looked round. I had been nodding off to sleep.

We were coming to the north coast of Black Isle. Soon the path swung right, towards the east. The sky was already pink though it was still the middle of the night by normal standards. We stopped in the dunes fronting a little bay - Udale Bay, Kari informed me - and we slept for a while.

I woke suddenly. Kari was shaking me and pointing. I sat up and looked. The tide had gone out. Beyond the flat mud that now filled the bay, the sea was sparkling. And beyond that lay what must be the Bay of Nigg in the distance and over to the right the Hill of Nigg, the Nigg peninsula, home of the heroes in many of my father's tales.

And then I saw what Kari had woken me to see. An enormous blue-grey thing that couldn't be a fish, yet was too big to be a dolphin. Dolphins we had off La Manga, and sometimes they even found their way into the Mar Menor, but I had never seen anything like this. Except once in a dream world. 'It's a whale,' I breathed.

She nodded, amused.

'But how did it get there?'

'It came up the firth too far, and into this bay, then couldn't turn round and get out again.'

'Why? I mean, why couldn't it?'

'They can't go backwards. It was trying to turn round, I expect, but to do that it would have had to move partly forward as well, and into even shallower water.'

'Are whales not as clever as dolphins then? The dolphins where I come from are far too clever to get themselves stranded like this - unless they are very old or very ill, that is, or badly injured.'.

'It's a young one, I think. It may have got separated from its family. Whales are clever: the cleverest of all animals my ma says, cleverer even than us -'

'We're not particularly clever, I think, sometimes.'

She laughed. 'Ma says people who live in towns and cities are stupider than any animal that has the sense to prefer the forest or the sea.'

'You'll be able to find out for yourself very soon.'

'Oh yes! I'll be living in a town, won't I?'

'In a big city - London!'

Her eyes were shining. 'I will?' She didn't seem to share her mother's prejudice against the urban way of life.

'You will. But you were telling me about the whales. If they're so clever …'

'They're also the biggest and they find it difficult to manoeuvre. How would you cope in a body that size?'

'Unless I was in deep water with no obstacles at all around me, I wouldn't cope at all. It's alive still, isn't it? Look at its eye. It's watching us.'

'It wants us to help it.'

What did it see as it saw us sitting there? What did it think?

'Will we? Help it, I mean?'

'We can't.'

'Perhaps we can get the men from the town to help us lift it back into the sea.'

'The men from the town will cut it up and take it home in pieces. I've seen it happen before, when I was with my da.'

'And he said they were right to do that?'

'No, he thought it was a shame. He's a good man. You didn't see him when he was well and happy. And he always had everything we needed with him. Like he would have had a pot with him and the makings of a fire, and we'd be able to have a hot drink. But not now, even if he was here. They took everything away again. They always do, even from him, who has nothing.'

'And unto those that have, more shall be given.'

'What?'

'Nothing, sweet. Your da is the blessed one, no matter what the world and the Church may say and think - and do.'

We sit and gaze back at the whale. 'Your da is right about the hot drink too. A hot drink does make all the difference on mornings like this. But without fire -'

'My ma can make fire, anywhere, any time. It's the pot you can't do without.'

'Always? Even when it's wet and rainy?' As it so often is up here.

She nods. 'And she's shown me how, many times, but I just don't have the knack.'

'Or the magic.'

'No! It's not - it's not - really, my lady! My ma doesn't know any of - of that stuff.'

She is terrified of being accused. They must all be. 'I didn't mean real magic; I just meant it seems like magic when someone does something so quickly and easily that we can't do at all. You wait till I show you some of the things I can do!'

She considers me, doubtfully. 'Like?' Then suddenly smiles that wonderful smile of hers again. 'Oh, I know! Like reading people's palms and knowing what will happen to them.'

'Exactly, yes. And now, can we go out to see that poor whale? Talk to it, touch it a bit, comfort it. I mean, it's going to die, isn't it. It's drying out.'

'Aye, and when it's in water the water supports it, but when it's on land it can't breathe because of the weight pressing down on its chest.'

'I see. I hadn't thought of that. That's awful! But will we be able to walk on this - what is it? Is it just mud? It looks rather soft.'

'I shouldn't if I were you, my lady. You'll get filthy - '

'Only my boots -'

'You'll sink into it. You'll probably fall over. You might sink right in - and then what would I do?'

She is right, of course.

We eat some bread Effie gave us for the way, then, in silence, ride on along the coastal path towards Cromarty and the ferry.

After a mile or so, we come to a small steading with a couple of cottages and some goats that Kari tells me are sheep despite the long, straight hair and four - yes, four - horns.

A man comes out of the door of one of the cottages to look at us, followed by a woman holding a baby. And they do just that: look at us.

I say, 'What a beautiful day! What a beautiful child!'

They gaze at me glumly.

Kari says, 'There's a whale stranded back there a mile.'

Their eyes brighten - even the baby's - until she adds, 'It's my lady's'. Then their looks become guarded again. 'But she doesn't want it. What can she do with it?' She waits.

Not being sure yet what is going on, I wait too.

The man says, 'You're just a tinkler girl.'

The woman spits and crosses herself.

Kari says, 'This is the Lady Marian MacElpin. Deal with her or we will go on into Cromarty and report our find there - and then if you so much as touch the whale you will lose an arm and a leg.'

The man studies the far horizon for a while. The woman brings the baby closer to see the horse.

'What is its name?' I ask.

'Magnus, my lady. It's a boy.'

Magnus. Like my long-lost brother. 'My grandfather was Sir Magnus MacElpin. God's blessing on the child, for his sake.'

She holds the baby up to me. She's not giving it to me, is she?

Kari, who seems already to read my mind sometimes, laughs and says, 'She just wants you to hold it for a moment, for luck.'

The man comes forward, a silver shilling between finger and thumb. 'Is the whale fresh?'

'It's still alive,' Kari answers.

'Let my lady tell me that.'

'It was still alive half an hour ago.'

'And how big is it, my lady? How long, from snout to tail? Longer than me?'

'Oh yes. More than twice as long, I would say.'

'Aye, well, with the tide going out, she'll still be there. Will you take a silver shilling for her, my lady?'

'But she's not - ' I begin to say, then feel Kari dig me in the ribs. This girl is getting cheeky - but the whale is really hers, I suppose, not mine, so … 'Yes. All right, then. And your name is?' I pass the baby back down and accept the coin.

'Callum, my lady. Callum Vass.'

Vass was my grandmother's maiden name, that and Gudmundsdottir, which I think was her mother's family name. I feel surrounded by my own past, my own ancestry.

'Then, Callum Vass, the whale is yours. Good luck to you, and God bless the child, wee Magnus' - and I remembered my father calling my brother "Wee Magnus". I open my purse, put the shilling in and take a gold mark out. 'Here, this is for him.'

The woman suddenly smiles, knowing at last what she should be doing in this totally unfamiliar situation. 'I have a fire going, my lady, and a hot drink ready. Will you get down off your horse? Can I help you? My name is Shusie, by the way.'

The house is dark, of course, for the windows are tiny, but it is fresh-smelling and seems clean. It has sleeping benches against the south and west walls and Shusie sits us on one of these. 'Will you have the hot drink? It's made with broom and elderflowers, and there's honey in it, and it's ready, as I say. Or I can give you good fresh milk.'

Kari drinks milk and eats an oatcake - but with honey, she doesn't want to miss out on the honey - while I just have a cup of the herb tea. It is delicious.

To make conversation (and because I like fishing, casting my net wide, when involved in any kind of mystery) I say, 'We're bound for Tain. Have you heard any news from there at all?'

'Aye, I was in Cromarty yesterday, and I heard of a killing there - some foreign traveller like yourself, my lady.'

Foreign? Me?

'Not being from these parts, my lady, perhaps you should take care - if there is someone out there who doesn't take kindly to strangers.'

I smile. 'I will take care, Callum Vass.'

'And too I heard tell that Thorfinn Skinner had been lost at sea, and I thought: disappeared he may be, but not at sea, or at least not on Sunday night.'

'How do you know?'

'Because I saw him myself, on the beach over the other side between Blue Head and Red Nose.'

'Were you in your boat?'

'Aye, and I sailed on by. I was on my way down to the cave where my old master, Fursey McFarquhar, lives now. A holy man, he is, a hermit, and a healer too, if you can get to him. I take him supplies once a month by boat - it's easier that way - and see he's all right.'

'You spoke to this Thorfinn Skinner?'

'Not I. When first I passed him, he was pulled up on the beach, as I say, and when an hour or two later he passed us by, sailing on west into the firth, the Moray that is, I waved, but he did not respond.'

Strange. 'Did that surprise you?'

'No, my lady. It would have surprised me if he had responded.'

Shusie, who had been gazing proudly at him as he spoke to me, now giggled and said, 'Thorfinn Skinner is awful - awful quiet, anyway, I'll say no more. And perhaps it's just his job - his jobs: hangman, he is, you see, when they need one, and that's not very nice, and cattle-slaughterer too, as well as having his own boat and steading like my Callum.'

My fishing had born fruit, so to speak. I had learnt a little from Whin, and from Callum here, of one at least of those involved in this Case of the Murdered Moor. But only indirectly involved. He was, after all, a hangman, a man of the law, and also he didn't claim to have disappeared: that could be simply a mistaken assumption on the part of people expecting him back.

By now, Callum was impatient to see to his whale as the tide would soon be flowing again. We too had to be on our way. But as he was putting his bow and his quiver of arrows on his back, getting ready to go, he remembered one last item of news. The dead Moor had been mutilated: his scrotum slit open and one ballock removed.

'Sounds like witchcraft to me,' he muttered, and told Shusie to keep the door closed and not talk to anyone while he was away.

Kari, I noticed, for the first time since I had met her the previous morning, and despite all she had been through in that time, looked frightened.

SEVEN

The Witch of Balintore

At Cromarty, Kari wanted to swim across the firth, to show me she could do it; and she would get there before me, she boasted.

I didn't like the idea. 'You're coming with me on the boat to help look after the mare. Later, we'll stop somewhere - '

'I know somewhere.'

'All right.'

'And I'll swim?'

'You shall swim.'

When we got off the ferry, we rode north to Nigg village through dazzling sunshine - my face was getting sunburnt and though I did not want to put on my cap and veil, I was glad to be facing away from the sun. I never got sunburnt in Spain.

As we rode, Kari told me more about Tinkman, her father, how much she loved him and how she thought sometimes that he loved her; but mostly he seemed not really to care.

'He cares,' I said. 'But what can he do? Life is hard, and sometimes nasty, and even a father with money and property can do very little. After all, it is your life you are living. My father said to me once, "I wish I could protect you from all that." But he couldn't. He died. And I have been bought and sold, and been beaten till I thought I would die. I never gave in and wanted to die though. I wanted only to escape.'

North of the village, we followed the track east round the base of the great Hill of Nigg and so made our way back to the sea. The open sea, this time. Kari brought us down past a little settlement that she said was called Sand-vik, and then out along a grassy path to an endless beach of fine windblown sand, with turnstones and oystercatchers in the distance along the water's edge. Hurrying here and there, too, on the dry sand and among the dead seaweed and sea thistles, were some old friends from Spain - and from London and Essex - wagtails, lots of them, including several greenish-yellow ones I had never seen before. They were like strange wild sisters of the tame canaries that we have in Spain.

We sat there to rest and talk. Kari told me that the houses, the fishing village we could see in the distance to the north, was Port-an-Ab, Abbotshaven, though some of the people who lived there called it Balintore - they were good people, too, not like in Dyngvale. Then further up, beyond Balintore, where the cliffs began again, was Kattar-bol: all around there, wulcats roamed.

Balintore? Wasn't that where the old woman lived, the one Whin had advised me to talk to? The witch.

Suddenly, Kari stripped off and with a laugh ran down the beach into the sea, where she disappeared and stayed under so long I thought she had drowned. But then I saw her head pop up, far out to sea, and I understood what Big Robbie meant when he said you could never be quite sure what you were looking at: an Elp - one of these little people I was, so unexpectedly, getting to know and love - or a selchie - one of the strange mythical creatures, half-human and half-seal, of whom - of which? - my father used to talk and dream over his wine when he became nostalgic and began to miss the cold winds and great grey heaving oceans of the north. In fact, I think he always missed them, that the hills and the sea-lochs and the endless beaches were always in his mind, always there in his heart, but it was only at night, after a second or third carafe of wine, that he would speak of it.

Hours went by.

One pale star was shining - pale *planet*, Saturn, *that* I do know. The sea was almost silent. The breaking of the waves seemed slow. Could that be so? Slower than the Mediterranean? Slower than the waves that broke, on a quiet evening, on the outside of La Manga, the arm of land that encloses the Mar Menor? Perhaps it is the size of the sea? This North Sea goes on for ever, they say; it is not enclosed like my sea - and I don't mean the Mar Menor, I mean the great Mediterranean itself, which is just a lake, a Mar Menor, compared to this.

I looked round. There was no one in sight. In the half dark, I stood up, pulled off all my clothes, and ran (I am not one for testing the water) straight into the sea.

It was cold. I dived down beneath the waves as Kari had done, and followed her into the gloom. Cold, yes, but not much colder than the Mediterranean in the spring before the sun begins to heat it up again.

I swam out and out and out till I was forced to come up for air. No sign of Kari, but just to be in the sea once more was wonderful.

Down again, to the bottom. I have always preferred being underwater. After a while, my eyes adjusted. I swam north now over the flat expanse of rippled sand that formed the sea bed until I saw some rocks, then headed towards them. I could make out seaweeds and anemones and corals - no bright colours, of course - and various small fish. Some of the fish whisked away at my approach but others came to inspect me. One or two little mouths nibbled at me, experimentally. They felt like kisses - and reminded me of other times in the sea. Then a huge eel stuck its head out from between two rocks. That mouth would do more than nibble. I too whisked away.

Up on the surface again, I found I had come a long way from where we had left our clothes. Slowly, enjoying every minute, I swam back. And when I got nearer, saw Kari, sitting there waiting for me.

I swam up onto the sand, till I was resting on my elbows then stood up.

I was naked, but it didn't matter.

Yes, it did. That wasn't Kari.

It was an old woman.

She gazed at me as I walked towards her.

'Marian?' she asked. It wasn't really a question.

'Yes?' I was shocked, but I tried not to show it.

'Marian Gudmundsdottir?'

Gudmundsdottir is, as I have said, though not my name, a family name, my great-grandmother's name.

'Who are you?'

'Gudmundsdottir is one of my names, too, my dear. But you may call me Mouraig.'

'Mouraig.'

I needed to dry myself.

'Excuse me a moment, Mouraig.'

'Of course, my child.'

I went up to where my horse was waiting on the path, and took a towel from the saddle bag.

When I returned, the old woman smiled and said, 'You are with Whin's girl?' Again, it was not really a question.

I wanted to say 'You know Whin?' but I stopped myself. I was looking foolish enough already. Of course she knew Whin. Instead, I said: "Whin suggested that I look you up while I was in Balintore.' And this time I caught her out.

'She did?'

I nodded, and carried on rubbing myself with the towel. I was cold. 'I need to find out about the old woman - who was not a woman? - and who was not old, but neither was she young? - who cast a spell for a storm over on the Whiteness coast on Sunday night. And cast it too over the image of a man.'

'Ah, the little poppets. She's using them again, is she? I should have realised when that druid storm blew up on Sunday night, then blew over so fast. That's Coll. Old Coll, they call her, though it's true that she can appear to be young at times: which is more than I can do. How I would love to know that trick!'

Her eyelids looked a little sore, her cheeks were slightly sunken, and her skin was wrinkled, but her green eyes were bright still and her hair, though mostly white, still bore traces of the hawthorn red it must once have been.

'Coll's not one of us. She's not even one of them. She's a glaistig.'

'A glaistig?'

'Thorfinn Skinner caught her one night years ago when he was fishing in Loch Eye. As a glaistig, she prefers fresh water to sea water, of course. He bound her and, when he got home, branded her, and she has been his thrall ever since.'

'Thrall?' I began pulling on my clothes.

'It's the old Viking version of slavery.'

'She cannot leave him?'

'No. If they run away they become out-law. An outlaw is as if he were dead, a wolf's-head. Anyone can kill him - or her - without risk of penalty.'

'Probably as a glaistig she is out-law anyway. Whin and Kari and the others - Tinkman and Otter - seem to be.'

'Oh yes, certainly.'

I sat down beside her. I didn't want to put on my hose and boots, I preferred to be barefoot.

'Can you tell me any more about this spell of Coll's?'

'Oh, she will have made a wee boat from bits of his boat, and a wee poppet - a mannikin - from bits of Thorfinn himself - hair, fingernail trimmings, spit, semen, blood - all kneaded together with a lump of bread he had fingered and toyed with and discarded. And then ... then she will have sung ... Who heard her?'

'Whin's boy. Otter.'

'Aye, he would. He doesn't miss much, that one.'

'Whin remembered some of the words: "I mak the heid, I mak the han - "'

'Aye ... She will have sung first, sung her song to the rising moon and the wind and the sea, and the wind will have carried the song across the beach and back to the boy, and a strange wild voice he will have heard, a voice like the voice of a whaup on a bare white coast or a dark lonely loch. Then clouds will have covered the moon; and her voice, so clear and bright in the moonlight, will have grown suddenly harsh and ugly.'

She had forgotten me. She patted the pouch which hung at her belt and began to chant, exactly, I was sure, as Coll had chanted:

'I mak the heid, I mak the han,
I mak the feet, I hae the man.

I pit the man into the wave,
for he sall have nae ither grave.

Wave, brak the heid! Wave, brak the han!
Wave, brak the feet! Deil tak the man!

I pit the man into the sea:

Deil tak Thorfinn and set me free!'

We sat in silence for a few minutes after that.

Thorfinn Skinner …

'Do you suspect *him* of the murder?' she asked.

I hadn't spoken. Not aloud … 'You know about the murder?'

'Everybody knows about the murder. Not everybody knows that Lady Marian MacElpin is on her way to Tain to interpret for the two Moorish slaves. And very few know her well enough to predict that she will attempt to solve the crime and save the boy Rachid from the gallows or worse.'

'And why should she do that?'

'Because she does not believe that he killed his master any more than I do. And also, of course, because she thinks she is clever - far cleverer than the Bailie and his men. Or Capitaine le Fou.'

She smiled.

And so did I. And as I did so, I saw myself in her smile.

'You are my - clever - grandmother, aren't you,' I said.

Next moment we were in each other's arms, laughing and crying, and I remember thinking that although she seemed so fit and supple and wide-awake, when I held her she felt thin and light and - fragile - and I mustn't hug her too hard. But it was wonderful! I had lost *everyone*, and now, after years without any real family, had found my Scottish grandmother. And what a woman she was! What a woman she had been, yes, by all means, but what a woman she still was now too.

'You'll spend the night with me,' she announced.

'Yes. Of course I will. But what about Kari?'

'She'll follow us. Leave her clothes up there where you left your horse.'

'How will she know where -'

'She could find you anywhere. Anywhere out in the country.' She pointed to her tracks across the sand.

'Ah. Yes. She'll know that someone came and sat beside me, and that later we went off together. Which way? Back the way you came?'

'Yes. And she'll know who - she knows my footprints - and

she'll know roughly when by their condition, considering the dampness of the sand, the force of the wind, and so on.'

I was convinced. I also realised suddenly how useful Kari might turn out to be.

'But, Mouraig - oh, what shall I call you? Shall I - ?'

'*Not* Grandmother. Everyone calls me Mouraig.'

I looked at her. 'Some call you the Witch of Balintore,' I said, smiling.

'Aye, they do. Well, they would, wouldn't they. I'm old, I'm -'

'You're not ugly!'

'I had no intention of saying I was. I'm old, I'm a woman, and I know certain things they don't know - like how to cure the hasty - the murrain, a cattle disease - and so, despite the appelation "witch", they look after me. They need me.'

'Big Robbie - Master Robert Ross, the Executioner down in Dyngvale - was telling me they hanged a witch a year or two ago. She was "old and ugly", they said - that's where I got the phrase from.'

'That was poor Agnes. Agnes of Strathpeffer. Aye, they did.'

'But you must be careful!'

'As I say, they need me. And Agnes was, really, quite dreadfully ugly, it is true.'

I laughed. What else could I do? Then I thought: well, but it wasn't only that she was ugly. 'She practised astrology, I heard. Forecast the future, and so on. Surely Countess Euphemia does that too? She's famous for it.'

'Yes, but Euphemia gets it wrong, always. Poor Agnes got it right. Euphemia, by the way, is a friend of mine, one of the very few who know my true identity. She would be a valuable ally in time of need. Don't worry about me, I'm careful enough. And I don't practise astrology. Though I heard that you do - and palmistry.'

'How? Who told you?'

'Ah. Who told the Witch of Balintore? She knows, she is one who knows …'

That phrase, my father's phrase.

There was so much I wanted to know!

We left Kari's things and made our way slowly along the

grassy path above the beach, not riding but leading the mare, and while we walked I plied her with questions which she did her best to answer.

'Wc are of the Dispossessed, my dear. They talk a lot about the Dispossessed, the noble families of Scotland that lost their lands in England - lands *in England*, mark you - as a result of supporting the Bruce and his gang against the English crown. They do not speak much, if at all, of those who lost their lands *in Scotland* for supporting the Balliols, who were the kings by right, against the Bruce. With my husband - your grandfather, Sir Magnus - dead, and myself left landless and under continual threat of being pronounced a witch (though I wasn't, not really, not then, just a simple spaewife), I decided to change my identity: change everything. And the best way to do this was to go right away for a while - for a long time - and then come back as that other person. So I went north to Orkney and stayed there a few months, using my new name, Mouraig Gudmundsdottir - '

'Your real name, originally, was Marian, wasn't it? The same as mine.'

'Yes. I am really, somewhere deep down inside, Lady Marian MacElpin. But - now, that is you, my dear, and I am Mouraig the Witch, to you, to everyone. Nobody on Orkney knew except one old serving man I had brought with me to see me on my way, get me started - he insisted, and I knew he could not last long. Indeed, he died on Orkney, in Stromness, and when he'd been buried and the masses sung, I took ship for Norroway, via the Sheltlands. And there, at Lervik, the Shelti capital, I fell in with a pilgrim woman. She had travelled in the east, had been beyond Jerusalem, beyond far Samarkand, beyond even Pamir of the Mongols, and there, among the great mountains that they call the roof of the world, she had taken shelter with a hermit in a cave among the snowy peaks and he had counselled her to turn back now, go home, and try to settle there, either with a husband and a family, or, failing that, to set up on her own as a holy woman, a hermit, like him. If though, he had said with a smile, she could not settle down, if the call of the road, the call of the open sea - which she had described to him, for had never seen the sea nor ever would - was too strong in her, then she should travel on, but west this time, into the setting sun, forever west; and there, both on her way and at her journey's end, God would show her great wonders. In Holland, by the Zuider Zee, where she had grown up, she found no man with whom to set up home - the ones she liked were either married or too old - '

'Isn't that always the way! What was her name?'

'Margrethe. And she was an Aquarian, before you ask, born in the night house where Saturn rules.'

'Ah.'

'And nor did she feel any desire to stay there on the beach or in the nearby wood as a hermit, so she went down to the port of Haarlem, and there, in an ale-house, she spoke to an old, retired ship's captain and asked his advice. He suggested she head first for Kirkwall on Orkney, and the tomb of St Magnus; and that was where our paths first crossed. I hadn't noticed her but she had noticed me. When she saw me again in Lervik, she was moved to speak. The old captain had advised her to go on from Lervik to Rejkjavik in Iceland, where - and he used the same phrase as the hermit in the mountains - she would see great wonders, and then - and this was the greatest wonder to me - she was not to stop there but to go on west from Iceland to Greenland - I had never heard of it - and then on to Vinland. And there, he said, she should settle and stay, for that, in the opinion of one who was too old now to do aught else but sit in an ale-house and listen to the promptings of his heart, was God's will for her.'

'And that is what you did? The two of you? You went with her?'

'Aye. And I stayed with her in Vinland seven years.'

'One day I will travel more. I know France and England, and Italy, and Spain, of course, and Andalucía and the Maghreb, the lands of the Moors, but that is all. Talking to Ferchard, I wanted to go east, but now after listening to you I want to go west to Greenland and Vinland.'

'And one day you will, I am sure. I'll draw you a map before you leave Scotland, and tell you all I remember of the lands in the west.'

'What happened after the seven years? You felt homesick suddenly?'

'Disease came among us, some kind of grippe, but fatal in most cases.'

'And she died of it?'

'No, strangely, I did.'

I thought she must mean something else. She didn't. I looked at her in horror.

Then she was smiling, laughing at me.

'Many of us died, it seems. Too many for coffins. When I awoke - or came to, I should say - it was dark. I couldn't move, I couldn't breathe, I thought I was in a nightmare. I tried to scream but I had no breath. I was suffocating. I had been buried! I was wrapped in a white sheet intended to serve as a shroud, and it held my arms. I suppose my whole body convulsed, I don't know, but somehow, suddenly, I found myself sitting up out of the shallow sandy grave where they had laid me so hurriedly. I was screaming, but I calmed down when I realised I was out and safe, I called for someone, anyone, to come and help me. No one came. They had all gone, fled from the illness. I was quite alone. Margrethe had gone on without me.'

'And you didn't go after her - after them? You must have felt so alone, so frightened.'

'Aye, but I had no idea which way they'd gone. I walked west on the main trail for a few hours but found no trace of them, so I came back to the settlement. We had no ships there, we had only canoes and curraghs made with animal skins over wooden frames, nothing that could carry all our goods and equipment - it was more likely that *they* were carrying the boats. So I waited at the settlement by myself. I waited all through the winter - the local people helped me survive - and in the spring I began to think about making a curragh and trying to get back to Greenland.'

'Local people? I thought you were all alone.'

'There were small groups - family groups - of a people who called themselves Algonquin coming and going in the forests nearby. They had never bothered us nor we them, but when they realised I was on my own, they came sometimes to see if I was all right and brought me presents of meat and other foods.'

'And you didn't want to go with them? I mean live with them?'

'Not *live* with them, no, but ... Listen, Marian. Like you, I grew up as a witch by inheritance and by training. And like you - no, don't say anything, I know, I can tell - though I served out my time as a novice on the Black Isle and in Caithness, I never underwent the trial, the fasting, the solitude and trance, which throw open the shutters of the mind and prepare one for the rite of initiation. In my case, it was because I married young and left home. With your grandfather, in Edinburgh, I moved in a different world altogether. Oh, there are witches in Edinburgh, but they live and work among the poor. The only time one such as I would ever meet a witch face to face was if we were in need of a love potion or a charm or a spell to protect us from harm or to make us more beautiful or to counter a curse or to control the weather, and then we would have to take our skirts - and our lives - in our hands and go searching the filthy wynds that ran along behind the tenements or, more easily, but perhaps more dangerously, find a witch down at the port of Leith among the whore-houses.'

It sounded very like life in London and Paris - and the witches sounded exactly like the witch I had lived with and worked for in the bordel in Cuenca, in Spain. She was right, her background was not so different from mine - except that she had only visited, while I had lived it.

'Then an Algonquin shaman - like our sheltiman - took me under his wing. I spent the summer with him in the forest. He taught me to fast, he taught me to dream. He taught me to heal, with herbs. He taught me about travelling into the shelti-world in search of a shelti creature for one who is ill, or in search of his soul if his soul has gone missing or he is under a curse. In Scotland, I'd only heard of this, never experienced it. In the fall, he left me. I had to stay alone out there in the wilderness from *Pidgi'pibun* - the beginning of winter, roughly our Samhaïn - to *Wa'bigun* - the time of the flowers, our Beltain. I did it - I mean I didn't die again! - ' she laughed, 'but the strange thing is that now I remember very little of it. The cold, the dark, the wolves ...'

'The wolves didn't hunt you?'

'They didn't need to. I was there, among them.'

'You mean they accepted you? As one of them?'

'As happens with the wulcats here? No, that's something different. The wolves seemed oblivious of me. I used a cream the shaman gave me, rubbed it in all over my body. At first I thought it made me invisible, but it didn't, not to animals, only to people. He told me later that to animals it made me seem like a plant ...'

I shivered thinking about it. 'You stripped out there in the snow and rubbed this cream, this unguent, in all over you?'

She smiled. 'Yes, but I didn't feel the cold. Especially not with the cream on. It had something in it that heated me ... Then, when the sun came back and the snow melted and the rivers ran and the birds sang and the fish jumped and the flowers came out I was declared a shaman in my own right and invited to stay with them as a wise woman, a medicine woman; but now suddenly all I wanted was get back to my own people, my own land.'

'But how could you? How *did* you? What happened?'

'I was lucky. A ship came - Harald Sixfingers' ship, which I'd seen before, years earlier, in Reykjavik. It got blown off course in a storm while making for Greenland. I'd returned to my hut in the deserted village and made my home there again. Well, I woke up one fine morning and listened and realised that the storm which had been crashing off the ocean for days had finally blown itself out. I opened the door and looked and there she was, the Ran, standing to in our bay. And that was that. Harald brought me as far as Thurso before turning south for Dublin. He wanted me to go with him - go on with him, stay with him - but I was having none of it. I gave him a kiss for his pains - it was all the gold I had - and set off for Golspie, where there was an old Wise Woman I'd known when I was a lass. I thought she might be able to help me again, and she did. Then I came here. No one knew me on this stretch of the coast. I've been here ever since.'

I looked at her, this old, old lady who had seen so much, done so much, and I was proud. 'And you set up home here then as Mouraig Gudmundsdottir.'

'By that time I *was* Mouraig Gudmundsdottir, I'd been her so long. For nine years by the time I came back. And I've been living in Kattar-bol by Balintore, Kattar-bol of the wulcats, nearly forty years.'

We had passed through Balintore, named Port-an-Ab, for the Abbot of Fearn - the monks owned most of the land around Balintore now - and were following the path along the top of the small rocky beach that led to Kattar-bol.

'These cliffs are a haunt of wulcats?'

'That's right. They prey on the seabirds that foolishly go on nesting here. As do I.'

I laughed. 'Which? Nest here, or prey on the seabirds?'

'Both.'

'I've never seen a wulcat, though I've seen a lynx on the high sierras in Spain.'

'I'll introduce you to one or two of them, tomorrow perhaps. I'm tired now. Let's go on in.'

I realised then that the wooden hut in front of us was in fact her house. It stood at the bottom of the cliff, sheltered certainly from behind, but not protected at all from the sea.

'Come in, my dear, and welcome. Make yourself at home. You are at home.'

'Thank you,' I said, moved. 'Mouraig - grandmother - thank you very much for that.'

It was small, but not as small inside as it had seemed from the outside, and it was warm and comfortable. A fire glowed in the fireplace and over it something tasty simmered in a large pot hanging from a swee - a long swivelling arm with a cleek - a hook - on the end. I took my cloak off, and my boots, and when I saw her going to the pot, filling a dish from it, I said, 'Let me do that. You're tired.'

'No, no, I'll do it. It's just my legs that are tired. You wash. There's water there.'

When I'd finished, she gave me the dish of stew and some bread, and we sat down together on the sleeping bench.

'What's this in the stew?'

'It's hare. You like it?'

'It's perfect. I hadn't realised how hungry I was.'

'Whin's girl will come ashore carrying fish to cook on the beach. No idea of time, but wonderful swimmers.'

'Oh, yes. I saw how she went into the sea. You'd think she was a mermaid.'

'Think? She *is* a mermaid. They're what mermaids are. Let's hope she brings the fish here with her, and doesn't throw them back. We'll have them tomorrow.' She looked at me? 'You look a little like a mermaid, too. No doubt the Elpin blood coming out.'

I found myself laughing and blushing, ridiculously flattered by the comparison with Whin and Kari. 'I don't know about being a mermaid, but I used to swim a lot when I was a child in Spain. I still do sometimes when we go from London to the Essex coast. And you?'

'I swim still, yes. But only at night.'

I looked at her. How old was she exactly? 'Am I right? Were you born in 1300?'

'I was. On the twenty-third of March. Soon after sunset.' She was gazing straight back into my eyes. 'Well, you're the astrologer. What would you say about a woman who was born under the sign of Aries, died and was buried in her fortieth year, and still goes swimming in the moonlight at the age of eighty?'

'I would say, Who needs astrology? This woman has it all. But show me your hand: I like to combine the two skills.' I put my empty bowl down.

'Would you like some more?'

'Oh - no, thank you.'

She held out both her hands and I took them in mine and held them there, not bothering to do more than glance at them, then letting my mind run free. 'You are proud and passionate, impatient, brave, still full of fire -' I could feel it '- and yes, still potentially destructive, still in love with the world, but not, or no longer, with people.'

'That sounds like my *fylgia* - my shelti creature - the brown bear.'

'You still do that? Have shelti creatures?'

'No. Only the Elps, and not all of them, these days. *Fulga* is their word for it, almost the same - they use it for the skin as a totem as well as for the totem animal itself … I found my brown bear while I was in Vinland. A shaman must have a totem.'

I looked again at her hands. They were old hands, the skin loose and mottled, but the lines were clear and she wore a ruby set in gold on the middle finger of her left hand.

'Your colour is red, of course, Mars being your ruling planet. You still see very well, don't you - at least in the distance.'

She nodded.

'But you don't hear too well, I think.' *Much of your hearing seems to be done by telepathy, in fact,* I thought, but did not say.

'Yes, it is,' she said. 'You are quite right. Not many people have noticed that. Euphemia did - she doesn't miss anything. And Coll, of course.'

'Ah, yes, you were telling me about Coll. She really is something strange, something different?'

'She really is. And he has her in thrall by virtue, as I say, of having caught her and branded her. If you ever get a chance to examine her, you will find that her whole body is covered in fine silver down. Totally unlike even the hairiest human - and I should know, your grandfather was one of the hairiest humans I ever met!'

'Was he? My father was much less hairy than most of the men where I grew up.'

'Your father took after me. Anyway, Thorfinn branded her on her flank, just here.' She showed me, touching herself just below the right hip. 'Burning the hair away, of course. Now the hair has grown back and the seven years have gone by and she wants - and should get - her freedom. She told me this last time I saw her but I haven't heard yet what happened. Knowing Thorfinn, though, I imagine he refused and renewed the brand, thereby binding her to him all over again.'

They certainly maintained the old traditions here. It was worse than Spain. 'But can he be a suspect for the murder?'

'Not if he was out in the boat and it seems he was. In fact, he seems to have been lost at sea. Which is no great loss, but makes you wonder: did poor Coll's storm actually work?'

'He wasn't lost at sea, Mouraig, not on Thursday night.' I told her what Callum Vass had told me.

'Now that is interesting. Still, if he had already put to sea when the murder was committed ...?'

'Could he have turned back, briefly?'

'He could have. He might have run for port during Coll's brief storm. But no one says so. No one saw him. And anyway, he could hardly be accused of returning in order to commit a murder under those circumstances, could he?'

'No. And there's another point in his favour, too, quite apart from the question of what possible motive he could have had for killing the Moor: and that is, what possible motive could a man like this skinner have had for mutilating the Moor?'

'No. That smacks - though I say it myself - of witchcraft.'

'Yes, but if we keep it simple, what connection could there be between a man like him and some foreigner just passing through?'

'Who knows? You must talk to Bella, as well, when you go to the Skinner steading.'

'Ah. Bella, yes.'

'His daughter-in-law. A tall, blonde, Saxon girl from down London way. And a widow, if she was a wife. Thorfinn's son died soon after - '

'She may be the girl Whin and her children saw that night on the back of a horse.' I told her their story.

'It certainly sounds like her. But how strange. We'll talk some more tomorrow, perhaps - and after you have visited the Skinner steading and been to Tain. I must sleep now.'

'And Kari?'

'Don't worry about her. You can sleep here.' She pointed. 'And there are furs in that chest.'

EIGHT

Sasunn Bella and Glaistig Coll

'Get up, lass! The sea is calm, the sun is shining!'

I tried to open my eyes.

She had porridge ready.

She had been up for hours, obviously.

I am not a little girl any more.

'Mouraig, I have things to do before I eat. I wash, I do my exercises, I meditate.'

'You do?'

'I do. Has Kari turned up?'

'She's outside.'

I peered out through the door, both ways.

'Not there. At the back. She tends to sleep out there among the herbs in summer. They all do. No, let her sleep. There's a jug of water and a basin on the table.'

I washed - all over, to Mouraig's amazement - then looked round for somewhere to do my exercises. There was no room indoors, so still dressed only in my chemise, I went outside onto the beach that lay immediately below the little house.

'Are you going out in just your cutty semmit? And with your hair all out and hanging loose?'

'Is that not all right?'

'Well, let me come with you to lend you the weight of my respectability. Though there's many would say I just add to your disrespectability.'

'You? I'm sure you are the height of respectability,' I laughed. I was sure she was not, and loved her for it.

I started as I always did with my own exercises, the ones I had practised since I was a child: the head slides that loosen the neck and the shoulders while swirling the hair and throwing it backwards and forwards; the rib cage slides, which move the rib cage independently of the hips and the shoulders; the moon circle, the small circle of the hips, and the sun circle, which is the great circle; and finally the double circle. Then stretched right up and with snake arms sank to the sand.

'What was *that*?'

'That was belly-dancing. I learnt it from my grandmother - my *other* grandmother - Sebah of Cordoba.'

'Sebah? That's not a Christian name.'

'No, she was a Moor. And half Jewish. ' I rose to my feet. 'And then, of course, when I was in Granada, I learnt more of this - it's not just dancing, it's a whole way of - of being a woman. I was *trained* in it.'

She gazed at me.

But I didn't want to talk, I wanted to do the other half of my exercises, the quite different ones I had learnt from Ferchard. I raced up and down, my short shift hardly hindering me at all. I leapt and whirled, I practised my kicks with enthusiasm, sending sand flying everywhere. I was, I knew, like a child let off the leash, and when finally I came to a stop in front of her, I was laughing, as well as panting (the result of too much time spent sitting in taverns, no doubt).

'And *that*?' She looked even more astonished than she had at the belly dancing.

'*That* is system of fighting that Farquhar - Big Ferchard - picked up somewhere on his travels. From a fighter in Alexandria, I believe he said. He taught me so that I would be able to defend myself ... He cares very much about me.'

'I'm sure he does. And you fight with your feet.'

'Basically. They're much stronger and have a far longer reach than the arms. But you have to practise every day.'

'And who knows that you know this?'

'No one, except Ferchard. You. Khadija, my old nanny: she was a family slave and I brought her with me to London. Yahia, my eunuch, and Tom, my - my manservant.'

'So, it's a secret.'

'Oh yes. And now - '

'What's next? Meditation? Meditation, I know.'

We sat down together and, my mind being on Granada, I went into a deep memory meditation, focusing on that day when I saved the life of Ibn Khaldoun - and became *his* slave, and was later given the eunuch Yahia, and my freedom, as a reward. Yahia was another who was unconditionally on my side and he, too, was waiting at home for me in London with Khadija and Tom.

When we came up from the beach, I went round to the little herb garden behind the house. It was protected by the house itself and by walls to the north and west. Kari was curled up in the corner out of the wind. At my approach her eyes opened; and her ears, the one I could see anyway, definitely moved.

'Hello. Did you sleep all right there?'

She nodded and yawned, then got to her feet and walked past me round to the front of the hut where the sun was shining. 'I'll sleep a bit more ...'

I gave up on her. Back inside, Mouraig had put some porridge in a bowl for me and, while I ate, we talked again. I told her something of my past, up to the point where my father died of drink and discouragement.

'Aye, and homesickness, I'll be bound,' was her comment.

The smell of the peat fire, and through the open door the sight of the sea and the open sky, the cry of the gulls: I knew what she meant.

'He should have come home, lands or no lands, and brought you with him. Wasn't it enough for him that his three sons - my grandsons - had died there already?'

'They died in the Great Mortality, Mouraig. There was nothing that could be done. And from what I hear, plenty died in these parts too.'

'Aye, they did. And you say young Magnus might be alive still? Well, let us pray that he is, and that he be restored to us one day as you have been, God be thanked.'

'But how can he be, when he doesn't know who he is or where he's from? He was only four - not even four. When I was freed after my years in captivity, I knew where to go, I knew where home was. I knew who I was.'

'You? You were a captive?'

'Oh yes. That's another story, though, and for another day. I still have one or two questions you can help me with, then I'll be on my way. I must speak to Raoul and Captain le Fou, and I must listen to the stories of the two Moorish slaves.'

'Raoul?'

'I knew him in Paris.'

'Ah ha. You must bring him to see me.'

I laughed. 'You mean, for you to see him.'

She nodded and gazed at me. Then picked up the thread of the conversation: 'So. What are your questions?'

'I need to know all there is to know about Master Thorfinn Skinner. His *ménage à trois* with Coll and Bella could have something to do with the murder. After all, it's quite a coincidence that, on the night in question, Coll and Bella were both seen in the area where the murder occurred and nobody else was, while the skinner himself disappeared.'

'Mm. He works in Tain as cattle-slaughterer and skinner, one or two days a month, I think, except in those days before Samhaïn when the winter killing is done. He has a share in the local tanning and leather business. He is also the town hangman. He's not a master torturer or executioner like your friend Robert Ross, but he's all we need up here and he does the job very effectively when it's required of him - or so I hear.'

'He slaughters and skins only cattle? Not pigs or sheep or -'

'The shepherds deal with the sheep themselves, usually, and there is a pig-sticker who goes around the country seeing to the pigs. Or the butcher, Master Ronald Brodie, sees to it. He's the brother of Master Brodie the Bailie. You'll be meeting him, of course.'

'And Master Thorfinn does the questioning? What happens if he is not available?'

'For that he is, always. Oh, I see what you mean. Yes. And they're going to want to put the boy's sister to the question, as well. As a slave, and a witness who may well be partial, she has no defence against it, has she? Except you. And possibly one or two of the men - Captain le Fou perhaps. Or your Raoul - I hear she is very beautiful.'

I ignored that. 'And Thorfinn goes out in his boat - how

often?'

'I don't know. Overnight, I imagine, once or twice a week. He'll be after fish, but also seals, and anything else that moves. He may stay out longer if he's hunting something.'

'And who works the steading?'

'Harald used to help, and Thorfinn had a man bonded to him by the court who worked in the fields, till one night he ran away and was never seen again. At least, that was Thorfinn's story. Myself, I think he probably killed the poor loon, which, as he wasn't in fact his property, he shouldn't have done. Then Coll came on the scene. Now I think of it, she arrived before the bondsman "ran away", so there may be another mystery there.'

I groaned. 'I don't want more mysteries, I want light on the existing one. Do you think it does throw light on it?'

She shrugged, and held the shrug, then relaxed and went on, 'He works Coll like a slave - which she is, of course, by her own terms, the traditional terms governing relations between her kind and ours. Then young Harald returned one day after a lengthy absence (he was also thought to have been lost at sea in a storm when in fact he had simply been blown away to the south) and he had a young Saxon woman aboard: *Sasunn* Bella. She too has been worked like a slave, especially since Harald died - also somewhat mysteriously - about a year ago. Some say she *is* a slave, never was Harald's wife at all. That he won her or something. He would never have bought her, the Skinners are too mean for that. Anyway, Thorfinn was mean with Harald, so Harald would never have had the money to buy her.'

'She would have cost a lot?'

'A fortune. She's a goddess - Freya incarnate. Or perhaps our own native Mour, the goddess after whom I am named.'

'Could there have been some kind of liaison between her and the murder victim?'

'That you will have to discover for yourself, but from all I have heard he was an elderly man and respectable. Friendly and open, yes, but very correct.'

'Did you ever meet him?'

'No, but I've spoken to those that did.'

'He was here with the French deputation, I understand.'

'Yes. Talk to them about him, they knew him best. Is Thorfinn Skinner your main suspect? Everyone around here, of course, suspects the murdered man's two slaves, and if not them, then one of the French soldiers. An outsider, anyway. Not one of us.'

'Who do you suspect, Mouraig? Just on instinct.'

'Baron Hugh, the Master of Foulis.'

'Ah ha! Why?'

'I though at first it couldn't be Sir Hugh because of the mutilation. Then I realised that could have been done to mislead us, and therefore the murder itself could have been committed by anybody, not just someone who might practise witchcraft. The Baron, Sir Hugh, is a great hunter - especially of women. And I have heard that he caught a glimpse of the Moorish girl somewhere and began pestering her owner to invite him up to his lodgings, let him have more than a glimpse. He was rebuffed.'

'Of course. How old is he?'

'Oh, thirtyish. Thirty something. Then he offered to buy the girl and was told she was not for sale - at any price.'

'And that was the end of the story?'

'Yes. Or was it?'

'I see. Has he tried to get hold of the girl?'

'I don't know.'

'I'll soon find out. When I've spoken to - '

But just then Kari came running in. 'There's a man here. One of them!'

'One of whom?' asked Mouraig.

I followed her to the doorway, with Kari hiding behind me. It was a young monk, tall and skeletally thin.

'M-Mistress Mouraig?'

'Aye, you know me, Brother Martin. What can I do for you?'

'M-Mistress, the Ab-b-b-Abbot himself sent me. It's his p-p-p-piles, and the p-p-p-pilewort and the feverfew that the Father Ap-po-po-pothecary gives him to drink don't seem to help him at all. B-But I'm not to tell anyone else, and esp-p-pecially not Father B-B-B-Basil, the Ap-po-po-'

'Yes, yes, the apothecary, that you have been here to me - that you've been sent here by Father Cyril - that's the abbot,' she explained to me. Then added with a smile, 'The good abbot does not believe in giving credit where credit is due. Brother Martin, tell Father Cyril to get up off his doup and walk, then walk some more, and do some work, then walk again, and not to ride, never to ride, to walk, as I say, and to eat less meat and cream, and fewer sweets. And tell him if he does all this, and only if he does all this, then drinking an infusion of the leaves of the blackberry bramble three times a day may help, as may using a decoction of yarrow as a compress -'

'A compress?'

'Yes, applied there, between his legs, where it hurts.'

'Ah. Yes.'

'Have you got all that?'

While the monk was repeating it as best he could, I went into the house and fetched him and Kari each a bowl of the porridge, which Kari ate greedily but the monk hesitated at first to accept and then prayed over at some length in surprisingly fluent Latin before finally wolfing it down at least as fast as Kari had done.

When he had finished and was about to take his leave, Mouraig suddenly asked after Master MacDalorg.

'D-Drostan? They're going to b-b-b-b-b-b-burn him.'

'So I hear. Well, tell Father Cyril also, from me, that a guilty conscience can cause constant constipation - remember that: c-c-c-c-c - and constant constipation can cause piles. All right, you can go.'

The poor man bowed and ran off up the hill to Fearn and his abbot, leaving Kari laughing and me trying not to.

'Not that I imagine for one moment that our good, fat, little abbot is suffering with his conscience,' said Mouraig. And spat, like Whin.

And Kari, still giggling, said, 'Do you think he'll remember the b-b-b-blackberry b-b-b-b-b-b-bramble? And the c-c-c-c-c bit? What was that?'

'If you don't know,' I said, 'you shouldn't laugh at others who do. I've no doubt Brother Martin understood very well.'

'Kari, eat some more brose, child, quick, before you leave. And hurry! You're keeping your lady waiting.' Mouraig winked at me as Kari hurried indoors with a nervous glance in my direction. At least the child didn't pout.

'Drostan?' I asked. 'Master MacDalorg? Is that the theologian who was condemned for heresy in Toledo - or Avignon - and escaped but was pursued up here by some Black Friar called Brother Arsenius?'

She raised her eyebrows. 'Was that a question?'

I laughed. 'Master Robert told me about him. What he didn't mention was his name. Oh, and he also said that his son, an obnoxious youth named Kenneth - do you know him? - would be coming up to Tain to assist the oh-so-conscientious Brother Arsenius in his attempts to persuade the poor old man to repent.'

'I see. Well, now we know what's in store for those two slaves, don't we. So let's hope you get there before this - um - obnoxious youth. Whom, incidentally, I do not know, and I pray I never come to know.'

'Amen to that.'

I took the saddle round to the back where the mare had spent the night by the wall outside the herb garden, and put it on her. Mouraig had followed me, and we stood and gazed up at the cliffs where the gulls nested. Of the wulcats there was no sign.

'It's the time of day,' she explained. 'When will you be back? Tomorrow evening?'

'I hope so.'

'Then tomorrow evening I will show you to them.'

Kari appeared, wiping her mouth with the back of her hand. I was going to have to teach this child some manners. 'Have they got kits, any of them?' she asked. 'They're dangerous when they've got kits. The other day I disturbed one who must have had kits because she came out at me spitting and snarling, with one of her front paws raking the air at me like this -' she showed us - 'all the claws out ready. And I remembered seeing my ma do that back at a wulcat, like this -' she spat and snarled and tore the air with imaginary claws - 'and the wulcat turned and fled. So I did the same - but the wulcat kept coming!'

'What did you do?'

'I turned and fled.'

I laughed, and Mouraig said, 'Yes, well, your ma is something special.'

They both sighed.

'And I'm not a cat girl, she says. In fact I'm not a forest girl at all, though I have something of the rowan in me, and of the birch, she says: I should stick to the seals and the beaches and the sea, and being a mermaid. But it's not fair, 'cause she's both.'

'You're going to become a city girl, Kari,' said Mouraig, 'which is one thing your ma will never be, not in this life.'

'Is it nice, the city?'

'In its way, it's wonderful. I lived in Dun Edin for many years when I was young -'

'And would you go there again?'

'I would if I were young again, at least for a while.' She kissed Kari and said, 'Anyway, I'll see you before you leave. We'll talk some more about it then.' She kissed me next, and with a murmured 'God bless you,' went back into the house.

Kari and I watched her go, then mounted the mare and set off once more on our journey.

We rode first to Loch Eye, which is an inland loch, not large, but surrounded by bushes and trees. That morning in the sunshine with the birds singing, it was beautiful.

So this was where Master Thorfinn the skinner had captured the glaistig Coll. At night, of course, the loch would have a very different atmosphere.

We stopped to sit and relax for a while by the water - Kari was not in a talkative mood and nor was I - then rode on north to the bare grey, blue-green coast. No trees here. Once more we sat and gazed, this time without even getting down off the mare.

The tide was coming in and the bay was almost full.

'Was the tide in that night you were here? When you saw Coll?'

'Coll? Oh. Yes. Coming in. Much the same as it is now.'

'Are we near where you were then?'

'Me and Ma were along here, waiting for Da and Otter. Otter was over there - ' she pointed - 'waiting for us, and that's where he saw her.'

We dismounted and she showed me everything on foot. I insisted. It was easier, and much better, that way, despite Kari's protestations. Being on horseback was a novelty for her.

'We were sitting here, among these grassy dunes, sheltered from the sea wind. This is where I fell asleep. My ma was sitting over there.' She pointed.

'And your brother?'

'He'd gone back to watch the - Coll.'

'And what was she doing, your ma?'

'Nothing. Waiting for my da. We were tired. We'd been in the sea all day, and we hadn't slept.'

We went to look at where Otter had hidden to watch the glaistig, and then down onto the beach. I wanted to know what she had been able to see.

'That's the Skinner steading there, in the distance?'

'I don't know.'

'Let's go and find out, shall we?'

As we rode along the beach path, I wondered about the riders they had seen. How much time had passed between the first and second time they rode by, and then again between that and the third time? I would have to ask Whin. But when would I see her? What if she was caught and killed in this terrible hunt which was - *today*. Would she survive? How had she survived that time she had been shot through the thigh with an arrow as she came up out of the water? Had she killed the man?

The path led to the steading, then along the outside of a stone wall till we came to the gate. It was closed. Not locked, but I was hesitant to go in uninvited and it had no bell or other means to attract attention. Master Thorfinn did not expect visitors - nor get many, I imagined.

Then the problem was resolved as a large hunting dog - 'A wolfhound!' Kari hissed - came running to the gate, barking and growling. She was terrified of it. With reason, from the stories I had heard in Dyngvale.

'The dog's inside, we're outside. Don't worry,' I said.

'And when someone comes and opens the gate? Oh, let's go!'

Someone was coming, a tall young woman with long, blonde hair held back now in a pony-tail: it could only be Sasunn Bella. She had a sweet, lazy smile, and suddenly I felt welcome and the dog, sensing this, fell silent.

'Good day,' I said, in English. 'I am Lady MacElpin.'

'Good day, my lady.' She was clearly puzzled, by me, by my title, by my addressing her in English.

'Is your master at home?' I wanted to clear up the question of her status.

'No, my lady, he's - everyone knows he's been missing at sea since Wednesday night.'

'I thought he might have returned. May we come in for a while? Quench our thirst, perhaps?'

'"We"?'

I looked round. I was alone. I smiled. 'The child must be on the beach. No matter. Just don't let the mastiff go after her, will you. She was frightened of it.'

'No, of course not. Hey! Beetle-bane! Come here! Stay with me.'

The great hairy creature did so - seemed happy to do so.

'Come in, my lady.'

'"Beetle-bane"?' I laughed.

'I tease him. He's a wolfhound, and Master Thorfinn calls him Wolf-bane. I call him things like Beetle and Butterfly-bane. Butterfly-brain.'

'In front of Thorfinn?'

'No!'

'We were approaching the door of the house. It wasn't the tumble-down hovel I had expected from all I had heard of Thorfinn Skinner. It was a substantial wooden house well able to withstand the weather it must get here on the north coast of the peninsula, but it had something forbidding about it, something silent, even though the girl Bella seemed relaxed and happy. But was that because she thought Skinner was gone for good?

She sat me down and asked if I would like ale; they had a barrel on tap. Master Thorfinn didn't normally permit, but seeing I was a Lady …

'Water will be fine, Bella, thank you.'

I looked round the kitchen-cum-living room where we were sitting. It contained no luxury, no decoration, but everything seemed strong and well made, just as it had outside. Big wooden storage chests. A beautifully constructed hearth, with only a small fire burning on this warm day.

The table we were sitting at, and the stools, were excellent, quite exceptional.

'Is all this Thorfinn's work, Bella? The furniture - the house itself? It is beautifully done.'

'No, my lady, it was Master Harald's work, most of it. This table and these stools he made not so long ago, shortly before he died.'

'Where did he learn to do such work?'

'He was apprenticed to the carpenter in Tain when he was a boy, so he told me. One of Master Thorfinn's notions.'

'I see.'

I decided not to push her for her story, but to come back again. She wasn't the sort who would clam up overnight; on the contrary. And I would have more time to sit with her. Now I wanted to know about Thorfinn and Coll.

'Has your master ever stayed away before for so long? For three days or more? I mean, do you expect him home any moment, or do you really believe he has been lost at sea?'

'He's never been away so long, my lady. But that doesn't mean he won't walk in tomorrow or the next day. Master Harald was away for more than a month once and everyone apparently thought that he was dead and gone. Then he came sailing back one day with a big smile on his face and me on his arm.'

I could understand the smile on his face; but had there been one on hers?

'My master is a very good sailor, they say - well able to weather a storm like that one.'

I noticed the "is". I also noticed that she stressed the word "that". 'Like what one, Bella?'

'Like the one on Wednesday night, my lady.'

'Was there anything special about that one?'

She looked at me. She had perfect blue eyes. 'You know there was, my lady, or you wouldn't ask. Coll is always doing things like that. Witch things.'

'She doesn't want him to come back?'

'She never has, but especially not now. He's going to brand her again, and she'll fight and he'll beat her and ...'

'And you?'

'Me?'

I let the question hang in the air a moment, then changed the thrust of it. 'You. Where were you on Wednesday evening, Wednesday night? Were you here, at home? Did you go out at all? How did you know what Coll was up to? Did you see her on the beach?'

'I saw her set out, and she had her puppet and bowl and things.'

'And you knew what they were?'

'Only because she talks to me sometimes, tells me her plans and her dreams; like when it's cold and dark outside in the winter and we are all alone here, just her and me. Then other times she behaves as if she distrusts me.'

Why? It was obvious why.

'Not that she does distrust me. She -'

I should have listened. Instead, I interrupted: 'So what are you telling me? That you stayed here in the house all evening?'

'Yes, my lady.'

'What time did Thorfinn leave?'

'I'm not sure of times ever, my lady, but it was early. The chickens and geese were still out. And the goats. I hadn't milked the goats yet when he went.'

'And what time did Coll go - and come back?'

'I'm not sure when she went. It was later. I was in here, doing something. And when she came back it was dark. As dark as it gets at this time of year.'

I smiled. 'I know what you mean, yes. I'm a stranger up here too.'

'Oh, I know, my lady. I mean, I knew. Where are you from? You speak English like - like me. I'm sorry, it's just that -'

'I understand. I live in London now.'

'London!'

'Mm.'

'Oh … And do you know Colchester? The Hythe?'

'I do, yes. Is that where you're from?'

She nodded, her eyes brimming with memories, the tip of her tongue pressing into her lower lip with sudden homesickness. And I felt for her, oh I felt for her.

'I'll come back another time - tomorrow perhaps, or the next day - and we'll have a chat if you'd like to.'

'Oh, I'd like to, my lady!'

'I want a word with Coll now, though, before I leave. Is she here?'

'No, she's out with the pigs. The master told her to take them out along the road to Tain these next few days and let them forage at the edge of the wood. She'll be about a mile from here, no more. Are you going that way?'

'Yes, I'll keep an eye open. And I'll be back to see you again soon, I promise. Oh yes - one other thing: do you know your birthday, Bella?'

'My birthday?'

'Yes, the day you were born. And the time, if you know it.'

'Why? Oh - I'm sorry, it's just ... I was born on the tenth of May, in 1361. But I don't know what time.'

'So you're a Taurus.' Another victim then, like Farquhar, only more so - a real victim. And yet she had been lying. Why? And twenty-four years old; the same as me and I had taken her for eighteen or nineteen.

As I rode away from the steading and it grew suddenly colder and began to spit with rain, I wondered what else I had taken her for. For sweet and innocent? What about that beautiful anklet? How did she come to have that? It not only looked like solid gold, it looked as though it had been wrought in Fès or Byzantium or Hindustan, and by a goldsmith who never worked for anyone below the rank of emperor or sultan.

Perhaps she was telling the truth, though, and it had been another woman on the horse that night. But then again, Mouraig had never doubted that it was Bella, which implied that there was no one else like Bella in the area. And also that it was, at least potentially, in character. I would have to check up on what other tall blonde beauties there might be within range. Raoul would certainly know. And the Bailie, too, this Master Brodie, the brother of the town butcher.

We saw Coll sitting on a fallen tree-trunk where the track began to flank the wood that covered all the country to the south - the edge of the great Morangie Forest, Kari told me, which here stretched out a long green arm between Loch Eye and the sea.

'Is that her?' I murmured. I knew from the sudden tensing of the hands at my waist that it was. Kari was frightened.

Coll, though, showed no sign of fear as we came up to her. She was youngish - or was she? - and everything about her was pale: the pale complexion, the great shock of silver hair. Not beautiful, like Whin, but she had the same aura of wildness. That she was sitting there at all, looking after pigs for a man who would, if he returned, abuse and beat and brand her again, was strange and unfitting; it meant that she had been bent to his will, bent, but not broken: you could tell at a glance that she would never be tamed, would never tamely accept the abuse as her lot.

'Coll?'

She nodded slightly, warily.

'Would you mind if I sat with you a while?'

Again she made that slight, cautious, movement of the head that implied assent.

Kari slid down first, on the side away from Coll. She kept the mare between them the whole time we were there.

I dismounted next and sat down beside Coll with a murmured 'May I?' Then I said, 'Coll, I am Lady Marian MacElpin.'

That didn't impress her much.

'Coll, last Wednesday evening - when Master Thorfinn disappeared ...?' I made this sound like a question. All I got back was the same barely-perceptible nod. 'Who did you see? Who came? Who went? Bella? Anyone else ...? Master Thorfinn? What time did he go? Were you at home all the evening? All night?'

After a long pause - for reflection? for memories to resurface? - she said, softly, 'Coll saw.'

I waited. Nothing more was forthcoming. 'Coll saw?'

'Aye. Coll saw.'

I looked up to the heavens. The rain clouds were not passing over, though the wind was getting colder. 'Did Coll see Bella?'

'Aye.'

'With *him*?' It was a flash of inspiration.

'No, the other one.'

Ah. Ah ha! 'The … tall one?'

'Tall?'

'Foreign? Not from around here?'

'Oh. Aye, speaking foreign. Coll heard them.' Then: 'The other one, it was. Not the one she wants. Who wants her.' Coll grinned suddenly.

'And he came to the house?'

'Coll heard. Master didn't hear. Master never hears, but Coll hears.'

She touched her ears.

The rain was starting again, this time in earnest. Coll got up and with a wave to Kari disappeared into a grove of aspen, the leaves shimmering in the grey wind and sky as the storm came on.

Kari took my hand and quickly led the mare and me between the trees into the wood, then, as the rain suddenly pelted down, pulled me under a holly tree, itself beneath a sheltering oak. It was there that I became one of them. Family. And that sitting there with me, so happy and relaxed, Kari became family to me.

NINE

At the Spider & King

Pale sunshine followed the rain. I could hear a thrush singing now, outside the tavern, and a colony of jackdaws squabbling in the trees.

Raoul looked at me. He smiled. 'Jaufre will be coming and going, but he says I should stay here in Tain with you.'

We were at the Spider & King, where he had found a room for me and Kari, and where he and Jaufre le Fou also had their lodgings. We'd left Kari in the room, asleep, and walked a bit, followed closely by La Pauvre, a drag-tail bitch that had attached itself to him - or to which he had attached himself? - while he showed me something of the town. Then we had come back to the inn for a drink and a chunk of venison pie.

'He asked you, or you decided? Are you your own master here?'

'Oh yes, completely, except in so far as I have committed myself to him. He is a great organiser, as you know. But yes, I decided. I have always to weigh Coucy's long-term interests against the situation we find ourselves in at any given moment.'

He looked at me. Smiled again, this time uncertainly, as though not sure how far he could trust me.

'*Entre nous*, I am never quite sure what his long-term interests may be at any given moment. I haven't seen him for months. The last time I saw him, he was still flat on his back after a fall from his horse in Avignon. But he is a fascinating man. An extremely powerful one, too, since he gave up his English allegiance and committed himself, finally, to the French King Charles. He is thinking of marrying again and …'

That soft voice of his! It had always put me to sleep. He

talked about the political situation in France and in Europe as a whole and what Coucy was really up to, but I couldn't keep my mind on it. I kept remembering Coll and thinking about her and Bella, and this Master Thorfinn Skinner. Out on the road, at the edge of the forest, talking to Coll, I had been wondering just how good her hearing was, but got no chance to find out. And of course, as I suddenly realised now, sitting talking to Raoul, in French - and remembering Kari's puzzled face - Coll could not have understood what she heard: so how could she have known that one foreigner loved Bella and was loved by her, and that the other did not and was not? And were they Raoul and le Fou? (Which one was Raoul?) Or had one of them been Abdelwahed ben Youssef? Understanding everyone, I sometimes forgot to wonder to what extent they understood each other. How, for instance, did Coll communicate with Bella? And yet Bella had said they talked together while they were sitting out the long dark winter evenings.

Raoul must spend a lot of time down here in the tap-room. Must have spent a lot of time sitting here with ben Youssef.

I want to *see* this ben Youssef. I try to imagine him sitting here in the long brown burnous and white turban that Raoul says he still always wore, even after so many years in Europe.

'What did ben Youssef drink?' I ask.

'Ale, wine, whisky - whatever was going. He wasn't fanatical. But never enough to loosen his tongue or render him careless in any way.'

I have had the story, but all in one lump, and all from Raoul. Now I need to chew it over for myself, get the taste of it. Digest it, as my old mentor, Yacoub ben Amar, would say. It is ages now since I spoke to him, even in my dreams, but I always think of him at times like this; try to imagine what he would have said, what he would have asked. He would have wanted other viewpoints, other perspectives; and he would have wanted detail.

'Raoul, I agree with you about Rachid. But who do you suspect?'

'Me? You are the solver of riddles and mysteries, my Mariana, not me. And this is quite a mystery, isn't it, this Case of the Mutilated Moor.'

The name has changed - and with it the emphasis.

'I still haven't met most of these people. And I haven't spoken to Jaufre le Fou. What about him? Could *he* be the murderer? *Could* he be?'

Raoul shakes his head. 'Of course not.' In his eyes I think I see some doubt. But then he smiles past me, over my shoulder. '*Mais le voilà*!'

I am about to start meeting "these people", and in particular Jaufre le Fou, who claims to remember me from the Paris days but whom I hardly remember at all.

Oh. Him.

Raoul stands up and performs the introductions. *Le capitaine* is still tall, dark and handsome. And still from the South. He bows over my ungloved hand. Then kisses it with wet, hungry, lips, and murmurs while doing so, 'We are neighbours, demoiselle. Two of a kind.'

'Oh, yes. I understand that you also have a room - '

'I mean, demoiselle, that I, like you, am from the South, that we meet once again as exiles, this time in a land without sun, without warmth -'

'Ah. I see. And this is …?' I have turned back to Raoul, and to le Fou's companions, one of whom, a small bearded man, is obviously local.

'Finlay MacKay. Finlay was ben Youssef's almost constant companion,' Raoul explains, as he seats the three men and pours them drinks. 'At least he was when he was out and around and not sitting in here with me. Ben Youssef liked to meet people, talk to them, but of course he had no Gaelic so Finlay used to interpret for him. As Roger here does for Jaufre.'

'You speak Arabic, Master MacKay?' I ask, in Gaelic.

'No, my lady. Only the Gaelic, and French.'

We return to French for the sake of the others as I ask him to tell me about ben Youssef.

'He was a good man, my lady. Not a Christian, but good.'

Le Fou poufs. I remember that "pouf".

MacKay ignores him. 'He had a kind heart. He liked Scotland - but he liked France, too. He liked all the many lands he had travelled through. And this was because he liked people. He was interested in them, in their lives, even in their children and the games they played. He actually learnt one game and the song the lassies sing when they play it.'

He sang softly:

'Here we gae roon the jing-a-ring
The jing-a-ring, the jing-a-ring,
Here we gae roon the jing-a-ring,
Aboot the merry-matanzie.

Twice aboot and then we fa,
Then we fa, then we fa,
Twice aboot and then we fa,
Aboot the merry-matanzie.'

'So you don't believe his servants - his slaves - would hate him enough to want to kill him?'

'No, my lady. No, I don't. I am quite sure that they loved him.'

'Both of them? The woman and the man?'

'Yes, my lady. Rachid is not very bright. His attitude towards their master would simply reflect his sister's feelings, and her feelings were quite clear. You had only to see them together, her and ben Youssef.'

'And you did?'

'Several times.'

Le Fou has been out of the conversation too long. 'She says he is innocent, and she should know.'

'You've spoken to her? You can speak to her?'

'Oh yes. She speaks Spanish.'

'And Rachid?'

'No, I don't think so. Anyway, if it does turn out that he is not the one, that someone else - one of us - is the murderer - '

'What do you mean, "one of us"?' demands MacKay.

'I mean a Christian ... one of us. Then in that case, killing a Moor is hardly a crime.'

'It is around here.'

'It is in France, too,' says Raoul. 'Even killing a Jew is a crime, though people tend to look the other way.'

'Where I come from, in Provence, and in the civilised parts of Spain, if you kill a Moor you're a hero.'

Raoul - like me - is unimpressed. 'That may be true, *mon capitaine*, when there is a war going on, but - '

'*May* be?'

'*D'accord*, it is, it would be. But when there is no war going on - like now - then what is it? *Le sport*? *La chasse*?'

'Sport? Don't talk to me. I fence for sport, I joust sometimes, I kill, if needs be. You? You are no soldier. What do you know of sword-play?'

Years ago in Paris they had been just like this, the two extremes of France and of French culture, the one like a peacock, the other in grey, provoking each other. Jaufre has already referred to his *pays*, Provence. In a moment, one of them will mention Normandy.

I notice a man in black watching us, listening to us.

'And don't talk to me of the hunt, either,' Jaufre continues, implacably. 'Me, I hunt like a man, with my spear, face to face with the boar, or I chase the deer on a horse through the woods with my dogs. But you? You are from Normandy. What do you know of the hunt?'

'*Nous avons aussi la chasse dans mon pays*.' We too hunt in Normandy.

'With a crossbow?' derisively. 'That is not sport.'

The man in black looks foreign to me - Italian. Or Spanish? Should I introduce myself?

'Killing an old man is? Yes, he was old, his beard almost completely white. Killing a defenceless old man by stealth, in the middle of the night -'

'How do you know all that? The time, the manner - '

'Oh, come on. You'll be telling me next that - '

'People are remarking on the amount of time you used to spend in his company.'

MacKay yawns, equally unimpressed. 'That applies to me, too.'

'Yes, but you have an alibi … I suppose.'

'I was at home with my wife.'

'That's something, at least. Raoul has no alibi at all.'

'I understood that you were - '

'He refuses to swear that I was here with him. How - and why - should I swear that he was here with me?'

'But you weren't!' Raoul protests.

'So much for comrades in arms, for Frenchmen together in a foreign land.'

'Tell them you were with Bella. She will be your alibi.'

'And you?'

'I didn't ask you to give *me* a false alibi.'

In the silence that follows this interchange, the two Frenchmen both end up looking ruefully at me.

'Whatever will milady think of us?' asks le Fou.

I smile. I am thinking, of course, that if le Fou was with Bella, then he is not the foreigner whom Bella loves; so is it Raoul, my Raoul? Or was it ben Youssef? But I say, 'Milady supposes that neither of you really needs an alibi if you can argue so openly about giving each other a false one. Or that you do not realise yet how much you are going to need one.' I let that sink in. 'And milady wonders who and what this Bella may be?'

Le Fou takes up the challenge. '*La belle anglaise*. If her master ever learns that she and I were - '

But MacKay interrupts him. 'Thorfinn Skinner? I heard that he was lost at sea.'

'Bella says he probably took shelter somewhere down the coast. He's done it before. It seems they all do it.'

'Aye, that's right enough.'

'He'll be back. You'd have been doing everyone a favour if you'd given me an alibi and let me give you one, Raoul.'

I doubt if that would help Bella if he does come back. Or, in the long run, le Fou himself.

'How do you communicate with *la belle anglaise*, *Capitaine*?'

'Jaufre.'

'Jaufre.'

'I know some words of the English,' he says, in English, 'and she speaks French - the French *normande* that some still speak in her *Coulcestre*, her *Aissexe*.'

I smile. Raoul speaks no English so far as I am aware, but he would be more than happy to speak to her in that "French *normande* they speak in her *Aissexe*". It suddenly occurs to me that she could also have communicated in the same way with ben Youssef.

I ask Raoul and Finlay MacKay.

Raoul doesn't seem to know, but MacKay says that now he comes to think of it, ben Youssef did have a few words with the lass in French one evening as they were riding by the steading.

'What about?'

'Oh, nothing - I wasn't paying any attention. He just introduced himself, asked her who she was, how she came to speak French, and she told him a little of her background, I think. Then we went on towards Tain - I was in a hurry, I remember, and we soon went our own ways.'

'Could you tell me what day that was?'

'Last Sunday. No, the Monday.'

'What exactly is - was - ben Youssef doing here?' I ask. 'Was he officially attached to you?' I look at Jaufre le Fou, let him hold my gaze. 'And what exactly are you doing here?'

'Paving the way for the army of Coucy and Clisson that is to follow from France, and subsequently -' he goes into English, showing off now, '- subsequently, join the massed Scots in an invasion of England. The problem is that the Scots will not mass. And who can blame them? Better the inside of a cold, bare "castle" or some draughty windowless hostelry than outside, travelling through the rain and mist that pass here for summer.'

'*Ah oui, mon capitaine, mais les soirs*! The evenings here! The sunsets go on and on!' It is the impressionable Raoul. So he does know some English.

'And if they go on for ever, who cares, when the evenings, like the dawn and the day, are a mass of lowering grey cloud? Give me five minutes - give me one - of - nothing special - just an ordinary, warm, scented evening in Provence! Five minutes of jasmine blossom and one bright star in a sky turning from blue through pink and yellow and green, and silver, and so back to blue, the darker, warmer blue of the summer night, a night of wine and music; a night of love.'

'Some years though, they say, the sun does shine,' says our poet, not to be outdone.

'For an hour or two - a day or two, *peut-être* - at some point, some time between *Pâques* - *Pâques*?'

'Easter. But it will still be winter here then.'

'*Ah oui*, between Easter and *le Jour des Morts* - '

'All Souls' Day.'

His English is *better* than le Fou's.

'Though presumably the poor dead souls would rather remain in their graves than face another night of this.'

MacKay, who doesn't have English but is aware that this *petit salaud* is criticising some aspect of his Scotland, announces that his wife will be waiting for him.

Raoul hints that he and I would rather be alone, so Le Fou and Roger, too, take their leave along with MacKay.

The man in black has gone, must have gone unnoticed while we were talking.

'Is Jauffre right, do you think, about Bella and the alibi?'

Raoul looks thoughtful. 'He is more likely than I am to need an alibi.'

'Perhaps he thinks he can have this Souad all to himself ... as *his* slave.'

'Not likely. He would think of the harem, of slaves like Souad, as a Moorish custom. Jaufre is a very intolerant type, Mariana. He can't cope - couldn't cope - with ben Youssef at all.'

'Because he wasn't a Christian.'

'Because he wore strange clothes and prayed strange prayers to a strange god and kept Souad in seclusion.'

'Then it is at least possible that our brave *capitaine* murdered Abdelwahed ben Youssef in order to liberate Souad, is it not?'

'It is, yes. It is possible as a motive, but it is not in character.'

'Are you sure?'

'Yes. No. Aren't you supposed to ask me at this point for his date of birth?'

'Do you happen to know it?'

'No. Can't you guess? You guessed in Paris once or twice, I remember, and were always right.'

How can once or twice lead on to always? That is how legends start. 'Once or twice in - how long did I know you in Paris? On and off, nearly two years. You see? It's most unusual to be able to tell, just like that - '

'Yes, but - '

'And how well did I know Jaufre? We met occasionally in a bar, in your company. And usually he had his own girl with him and hardly glanced at me. What I'd like to be able to do is hold his hand, read his palm, look into his eyes. Read him.'

'He'd enjoy that. Just from what you've seen of him, though, can't you make a guess?'

'I can. But don't you quote me on it later. It must be one of the fixed signs. He will never change, I think, not in this incarnation. And a Fire sign, for he seems headstrong and well-named to me. So, Leo … And Leos tend to quarrel with their friends,' I finished.

'Un Lion? Could he then be the murderer?'

'*A* murderer, oh yes. For like all those born under one of the Fire signs, he may, like fire, become dangerously destructive when things go wrong. But *the* murderer? No, I doubt it. For this murder was planned.'

'C'est merveilleux, ça.'

'Yes, but it is not evidence. Much more to the point is whether he has an alibi. A real alibi.'

'The murder could have occurred quite late in the night,' Raoul observed. 'At dawn, even, or just before dawn.'

'True. And do you not find it a little strange, a little too much of a coincidence, that Master Skinner should choose that same night to disappear? Do people believe in this disappearance? Was Master Skinner a good hand with boats? What have you heard?'

'That such a storm - for though it seemed a veritable tempest to me, it was by their standards hardly a storm at all - such a storm would have meant nothing to him. He had weathered out such storms hundreds of times.'

'So is it possible that he is still alive, in fact, and in hiding somewhere?'

'You mean Master Skinner could be the murderer? He could have put in to shore again for a while when everyone thought he was out at sea. And of course there was that storm. He might have had to turn back. But why would he want to kill ben Youssef?'

I smile. I can come up with no motive as yet, but the timing is suspicious. 'Raoul, Master Thorfinn is alive and well.' I tell him what I heard from Callum Vass, that the skinner was seen heading south off Black Isle on the Monday morning.

Now I want to talk to Rachid.

I would also like to meet Master Drostan MacDalorg, the "heretic".

TEN

Another Hunter, Other Prey

Master Robert, the executioner, was big and warm: you forgave him anything - everything - on account of his smile and his voice and his strength, and that warmth, and the fact that not forgiving him was a bit like not forgiving God; but Brother Arsenius was thin and cold and unforgivable. Oh, he was strong, too, but strong like rock, his grey eyes and white teeth (whiter than any teeth I had ever seen) hard and cold as stone in mid-winter; and he smiled too, but his smile was not like Master Robert's smile, it was a grin, and it was skeletal.

To Kenneth, he seemed perfect. All that his father was not.

Kenneth had been welcome both in the chamber and at the scaffold since he was a toddler, on the principle that the things he became familiar with as he grew up would never later worry or upset him. And the result was that he seemed more at home in the torture chamber than at home.

I looked round this other, smaller, chamber - hardly more than a holding-room, which it was, officially - trying to see it from his point of view. It was dark, but warm, with a fire and two torches burning. He loved all the implements: you could tell that from the way he handled them, the shiny steel, the leather and the wood, all polished and oily and smelling of oil and sweat; but overlaid by the smell of fear, and of blood, and ordure, like in the killing yard at a butcher's, of singeing hair and burning flesh, like in the back yard of a tavern where the spit was kept turning all day long. But this wasn't food, wasn't animals, this was real. This was people. Ah yes, I could understand his fascination.

Rachid had been put to the question already by Kenneth, under the supervision of Brother Arsenius. They had been asked by the Bailie, Master Brodie, to take over when Kenneth arrived from Dyngvale and there was still no sign of Master Thorfinn.

He was on their rack, a rickety old contraption they referred to as the "ladder", and he was unconscious. It obviously worked.

Brother Arsenius inspected him. 'Release him a little and bring him round, will you, Kenneth.' He turned back to me. 'When you arrived, my lady, we were working on the other one while we let the Moor have a rest and come round in his own good time. Kinder, really, but if you insist on speaking to him ...'

'I do insist, Brother.' How could he call it kind to leave the poor boy stretched out on the rack unconscious and with his joints all at breaking point?

'Perhaps while you are waiting you would like to come through here and meet our heretic. He is conscious.'

I glanced over at the figure on the rack and realised this was going to take some time unless - oh, no! '*Don't* drip ammonia into his nostrils, Kenneth. I'm in no hurry. Just ease the strain on his joints, as Brother Arsenius says, and give him a little cold water perhaps; ease him and give him time to recover.'

I turned back to Brother Arsenius. 'Yes, I would like that.'

Master MacDalorg was an old secular theologian. He was a Master of Divinity of the University of Oxford and had, I learnt later, spent many years teaching in Milan; been one year in Rome under Pope Urban in 1377-8; then gone to Toledo and taught there for four years before deciding at last to return to his native Scotland for a breath of fresh air and sanity. However, he had been invited to visit France before he retired.

'And there, at Carcasonne,' Brother Arsenius informed me, 'he was charged with heresy. He was found guilty, but misguided friends and students managed to get him removed to Toulouse - where he was condemned again. He was then taken to Avignon, to appear before the Pope himself, but never arrived. His escort was ambushed and he was taken north.'

By "the Pope himself" he meant Clement VII, of Avignon, whom he represented, and who was recognised in Scotland as in France. England, of course - England and France seem never to agree about anything - recognised Urban VI of Rome as the true

Pope.

'I pursued them to Norroway,' he went on, 'then I lost them. They tricked me. His companions turned south again, south and east, into Saxony, and thence to Bohemia, and Prague, and the university there, while he, alone, crossed over to Sheltland, and made his way down into Scotland. I should have guessed. I knew that - like me - he hailed from Scotland.'

In Scotland, he had gone to the Abbey of Fearn, on the road to Balintore, intending simply to live there in retirement. They had been proud to have him ...

It was a dark, airless, little cell, and he was sitting on a narrow bench, which, with a brim-full bucket, was all there was.

I noticed his hands first, lying limp on his lap. They looked like Tinkman's hands. All the nails seemed to have been torn out. But what else? It wasn't the pilliwinks. Was it needles? Up under the nails till the nails came loose and fell off? Then I looked at his face, glanced into his eyes, trying to assess the extent of his injuries - they have to be careful with an old man like this if they don't want him to die. The short white beard was bloody, but I couldn't tell what they had been doing to his mouth or if it was only his nose that had been bleeding.

He had brown eyes, the gentle eyes of the woodland, bloodshot now of course, but soft and deep. Eyes that reminded me of someone. Who? Then I remembered: my own master when I had been a slave, the young - relatively young - and handsome Ibn Khaldoun.

Brother Arsenius spoke. 'Now, why don't you tell Lady MacElpin some of the nonsense you have come to believe? Make her laugh. Tell her what you were telling me earlier - from Meister Eckhart, wasn't it?'

'Meister Eckhart was a Christian man, a good man, a philsopher and mystic who - '

'Tell her what he said, Drostan. The Church will decide whether he was a good man and a Christian, or a heretic like yourself. Has decided.'

The old man ignored him. 'Eckhart said, He who witholds but a pennyworth of worldly goods from his neighbour, knowing him to be in need of it, is a robber in the sight of God. And whoever spares a penny for himself to put it by against a rainy day, thinking, I may need that tomorrow, is a murderer before God.'

'And do you believe that, Master MacDalorg?' I ask.

'Not literally, perhaps, but - '

'You see, my lady? He doesn't even believe it himself, and yet he is dying for it. Shall we go and see whether - '

'I'd like to listen to Master MacDalorg for a while, Brother, if that would be all right? Alone.'

'Why?'

'I am interested. In Paris I saw heretics burnt, and too in Avignon. In London, they don't, but it will come, I'm afraid. Wyclif was lucky to die in his bed.'

'John Wyclif? He would never have died in his bed in the County of Ross, or in Caithness or Sutherland. He would have been put to the question and burnt - as indeed he would have anywhere in Scotland. We know how to treat heretics and traitors here. And witches, who are both. Not like in England.'

'No, indeed,' I retorted. 'More like in Provence, or Christian Spain, where a burning is an everyday occurrence and arouses little interest unless a famous heresiarch is being burnt - burnt alive - or a beautiful woman. Or what had been, before she was tortured, a beautiful woman. In Valencia, I once witnessed the death of a woman the mob considered a saint. The Church did not agree. For her, the whole city turned out. To their disappointment, she had confessed under torture; but now at the stake she recanted. It had only been to ease her pain, she said: she had had no idea that pain could make her tell such lies. Pain can make you say anything, I know, I know, but she hadn't known. Now she spoke once more of her visions and said they could never take that away: soon she would be with God, would be in the arms of Jesus, be comforted by the Virgin Mary herself. They lit the fire and burnt her alive as a relapsed heretic while the crowd fought to get at her, fought the executioners to get bits of her before she was reduced to ashes and dust and swept up and dumped in the river. Her name was Juliana. Santa Juliana they were calling her already, within minutes of her passing.'

'That in itself is heresy.'

'It is, isn't it.'

His grey eyes studied my face. Then he gave us one of his death's-head grins. 'Drostan was cast out of the Church - which means out of Heaven - three years ago. And was handed over to the secular arm for execution. He is not about to become a saint by public acclaim, I assure you. I'll leave the door open.'

Silence.

The old man and I studied each other.

'My lady, I am in no condition to preach sermons,' he lisped.

'Please, don't cause yourself any further distress for me, Master MacDalorg.'

'Drostan will do very well. It is the name the good Brother uses. It is the name my mother gave me ... What is it you want, my lady? Is this just a - a curiosity visit? I'm sorry; you don't seem like one of them.'

'One of them? Ah, you've had silly women pestering you.'

'Yes, in Carcasonne. And in Toulouse, surprisingly. Ones with influence enough to get past the guards. Forgive me.'

'No, you forgive me. There may have been something of that in my desire to talk to you, but all this is no novelty to me. What I am interested in is religion. Religions. Other opinions, other beliefs.'

'You are?'

'Yes. Seriously interested. I know all the tenets of Islam, and all the prayers - '

'In Arabic?'

'Yes, of course.'

'Aah ...' He is impressed. He has a worry though. 'But you *are* a Christian?'

'Both my parents were Christian, and so am I, but ... not unreservedly so. I have studied the Kabbalah with a Hebrew scholar - a Jew, Yacoub ben Amar, of Murcia. I also studied astrology with him. And I continued my studies in astrology and theology at the Sorbonne in Paris.'

'In my time, they did not accept women students.'

I smile. 'I was an unofficial student.' Am I tiring the poor man unbearably, or am I helping him by taking his mind off it a little? 'I enrolled as my twin brother.'

His eyes twinkle at that. 'Ah, yes. The masquerade. I

remember a certain Henri who turned out to be *une certaine* Henriette. Such a clever girl. I wonder where she is now …' But he is serious when he asks: 'What do you mean when you say, "not unreservedly so"?'

'I mean that I can see some good in different points of view. And I can see some bad points, not in Christianity itself, perhaps, but in Christianity as it is mediated to us by the Church.'

'Are you sure, my dear, that we are alone?'

I tiptoe to the door and peep out. 'We seem to be. Most of all, I am suspicious of the Church's claim to be the only means of salvation and its condemnation of all who differ. In Spain, for instance, they are determined to drive out to Morocco all the Muslims, all the Jews, all those who do not embrace the Catholic Faith. But why? Why should they do that? This idea that the people who live in a country are all one big family, that they must all hold the same beliefs and practise the same religion, and that if they do not, this justifies their compatriots in torturing and killing them … this can only lead to untold suffering and bloodshed. And I don't need the Kabbalah or astrology to tell me that.'

A long pause. A small smile. 'I thought you said you wanted to listen, my lady.'

'Ah. Yes. I'm sorry. You asked me what I meant by - '

'I know I did. And "When you state your beliefs, don't try to be brief" is wise advice … Perhaps that was my error. Not enough detail. Not enough argument. Not enough confusion. Anyway, you don't need to listen to me. You are heretic enough without that.'

I realised suddenly that I had placed myself in this man's hands. Would he try to save himself by informing against me?

He must have seen the sudden uncertainty in my eyes. 'I am just Drostan, remember. No longer part of the university. No longer part of the Universal Church. At least, according to Clement.'

'And you no longer believe that salvation is only through the Universal Church?'

'No. Which is fortunate in the circumstances. But then the Church can hardly seem other than partial - and fallible - to one in my position.'

'They would say it is the man who is fallible.'

'They would, yes.'

'How did you first come to question the Church?'

'One of the turning points came when I was studying Pope Innocent III's crusades against the Cathars and the Waldenses. Did you know that these "heretics" were against the taking of human life, even in war? *Even in judicial execution?* Which was reminiscent of the teaching of Someone Else who ended up being executed by the priesthood of the established religion of his time. But it is as you say: be they Jews or Moors, or Cathars, a whole group may be massacred simply because they are different, because they are who they are; prejudice in the strictest sense of the term.'

'What star sign were you born under?'

'I went on to question the current view of the Incarnation - as did Master Abelard before me. Have you read his *Dialogue Between a Philosopher, a Jew and a Christian*, by the way? No? You should. Of course, they are not enamoured of *his* views either, so his writings are hard to come by, even in Paris. Be that as it may, it seemed to me, seems still, despite the attentions of Brother Arsenius and his ilk, that our modern reading of the Incarnation borders on Monophysitism.'

'That Jesus was God, not man, and occupied a human body in appearance only.'

'Something like that, yes. I wished to re-establish that the Lord had a soul, had a mind, of his own.'

This man played with fire and enjoyed it: a latter-day Peter Abelard, indeed.

'When were you in Paris, Master?'

'Oh, twenty-five years ago. No, thirty-five - for six years.'

If I had been there then, would I have been his Heloïse?

Wake up, Mariana.

'That Jesus was not simply God in a human body,' he continued, 'but was himself and could fight back and disagree. I cited the raising of Lazarus, where Jesus, upset at the death of his friend, changes everything; rewrites what was written: rewrites history. I cited the healing of the man born blind - also in the Fourth Gospel, the gospel where Jesus is depicted most clearly as "one with the Father" and yet this latter miracle is staged, at least in the mind of the Evangelist, to show that Jesus could and would find wrong, and change, what had been ordained. Preordained.'

'Dangerous, in this day and age.'

'Dangerous in any day and age. At least in any day and age when people care. But I would rather live in an age when people care than in one where they do not.'

'Drostan, tell me: what star were you born under?'

'Under Pisces, on St David's Day. Ah yes, you are an astrologer.'

'That's the same sign as my father. I would like to hold your hands, but - '

'No.'

'What did they do to your mouth? Shall I fetch a cloth and some water? Clean you up a bit?'

'It is nothing. The apprentice slapped me. He wants to learn about all the major heresies - and grows impatient with his teacher when he fails to understand. But that other poor boy, the Moor. Will you interpret for him? He is innocent, by the way.'

'The problem will be proving it.'

'The victim was another Moor, I understand, so take your own advice: look for signs of xenophobia.'

'Mm. Yes. Though it could just as well be personal. Most murders seem to be.'

'Of course.' He sighs. Relaxes a little. 'So tell me about Pisces. Just don't tell me I may wed a dark-haired, green-eyed stranger, though, and live another thirty years in marital bliss: I'm afraid I shan't believe you.'

The only possible response to this in the circumstances is my most beautiful smile … Then, my eyes still shining, I am sure, I say: 'It is a Water Sign - '

He interrupts me: 'Your eyes are elpin eyes -'

'You're saying that because of my name.'

'Oh no, no, I'm not. There were many of them around the Shin, by the river and in the forest, when I was a boy, but now there are very few anywhere. They hunt them, you know.'

'I know.'

After a moment, he says, 'It is a Water Sign, yes. Which

means?'

'Which means that you are likely to be emotional and sensitive. It is also one of the mutable signs, so during this lifetime you will change and develop, make spiritual progress. That sounds right, doesn't it?'

He smiles. 'And the Pisces image? The Fish?'

'Two fish, usually, connected by a silver cord.'

'Ah. The body and the soul, separated yet still attached. As in astral travel? And if it is one fish only?'

'Then it is the symbol of Christ.'

He crosses himself with his poor bleeding hands and Brother Arsenius, outside, calls, 'Lady MacElpin, leave Drostan to his foolish thoughts and dreams. The slave-boy Rachid is recovered.'

He was being held up in a sitting position by a man who turned out to be some kind of officer of the law, representing Master Brodie the Bailie. They must have sent for him while I was with Drostan.

They introduced him as Niáll of Lairg.

I didn't care. The boy Rachid was dying, I realised. He could hardly breathe. His heart was failing. He had, literally, been broken on the rack.

I had seen such things before, but never in one so obviously simple-minded, so obviously innocent.

When I protested, Brother Arsenius shrugged - why all the fuss? He's only a Moor - and looked at Kenneth.

Kenneth, for his part, had not believed, he said, that the prisoner could be unable to understand the simplest question. 'How was I to know? Master Brodie told me to get a confession out of him as fast as possible. And that's what I was doing. I mean, I just had to make him agree that he'd killed his master. What was difficult about that? He understood, of course he did, and yet he kept pretending he didn't. I lost my temper.'

'Don't blame the lad,' said Brother Arsenius, kindly. 'He did his best. What do you expect? Even his famous father could not, I am sure, extract a formal confession from a Mohammedan slave who speaks no known language - and leave the slave in one piece.'

I gave up on them, and with a glance at Niáll, who nodded to me, turned my attention to Rachid.

'Salaam wa laikum.'

His eyes opened.

'Rachid? I am a friend. What have they done to you? No, don't answer that. Tell me simply: are you dying?'

'Salaam wa laikum, lalla,' he whispered. 'Yes, by God's mercy, I - I think I am dying.'

'He thinks he is dying,' I told Niall.

Niáll nodded. A man of few words.

'Let's hear his story and then try to move him out to - I don't know, to somewhere else.' I said. 'Will you put the questions, while I translate them?'

'No, no, my lady. You - '

'All right, I'll question him, and then translate his answers.'

'Fair enough.'

It was a painful process, not just for Rachid but for me too. It took a very long time for him to understand the point of the questions and to whisper and gasp out the answers, much longer than it seems, here, now, when I retell the story.

'I'll try to get you out of here, Rachid, but first you must tell me what happened that night.'

'The night Sidi ben Youssef was killed?'

'Yes, Rachid, that night.'

'He went out on his horse, lalla, and he didn't come back.'

'Was he alone?'

'Yes.'

'Did he say where he was going?'

'Not to me, Lalla - Lalla - ?'

'Mariana. That's Maryam.'

'Lalla Maryam. Souad said later that he had told her.'

'Told her what, Rachid?'

'That he was going for a ride out to - I don't remember the name, lalla.'

'Tarbat? Whiteness? The Skinner Steading? Balintore?'

He didn't know. I would ask Souad about it, later. I would need to confirm the whole story with her, in fact.

'So at what time did you start to worry about him?'

'I waited for him, lalla. Souad went to bed, and I waited, as I always wait. But he didn't come. Then very early in the morning - it was still night, but it was light, you know - I went out looking for him.'

'How did you know where to look?'

'Lalla Maryam, I didn't. I woke Souad and she told me what road to look along.'

'How long were you walking before you found him?'

'I don't know, lalla. A long time.'

'Tell me what you saw when you found him.'

'He was lying in the grass beside the road. I saw his horse first, then I ran, and I saw him.'

'Was he lying on his front or on his back?'

'On his back.'

'And did you know at once that he was dead?'

'Yes, lalla. He was still and - cold. He was dead.'

'Could you see a wound?'

'Yes, there was a hole in his chest. In his shirt, and in his chest.'

'You looked?'

'Yes, lalla. I opened his shirt where it was torn, and - '

'Was there a lot of blood?'

'No. No blood. Just a dirty stain on his shirt. And on his back, too, when I turned him over. When I put him on the horse.'

'And a wound in his back? A hole? Yes? Which hole was bigger, was worse? The one in his chest or the one in his back?'

'They were about the same, I think, lalla.'

'And his *burnous*?' His cloak.

'It was lying on the grass nearby.'

'As though it had fallen off him? Or as though it had been put there?'

'Put there, lalla. It was all - all together.'

'Bundled up, you mean?' He nodded. 'And the weapon? Was there any sign of whatever was used to kill him? An arrow? Something like that?'

He had seen nothing. Not even ben Youssef's own knife. That had not been there.

'And how big was that knife, ben Youssef's own knife? Could that have inflicted such a wound?'

'It was quite big, yes, but -'

'How big?'

He tried to show me but couldn't use his arms, so I showed him. 'This size? This? This the handle, this the blade? Yes?'

The blade had been about a foot long, the handle smaller, hand-sized. It all depended on how fat he was, really. I could find that out later. The boy had had enough.

I translated this last part for Niáll, stressing the missing weapon and the burnous, the long cloak, its being put there, its being bundled up.

But Niáll was not ready to let me go. 'Ask him why he mutilated his master's body.'

'But - '

'Ask him, my lady.'

I asked him.

'He says he didn't. He doesn't know what you are talking about. He knows nothing of any mutilation.'

'Ask him if it wasn't because he himself has no ballocks. A kind of jealous obsession.'

'But why of his master?'

'His master had been fucking his baby sister for years.'

This was my "man of few words". I must avoid these quick character judgments - at least if I don't have the date of birth and a good long look at the palms and into the eyes.

I asked Rachid. He didn't see the point of the question, and still protested total ignorance of any mutilation.

'But were you not jealous of Sidi ben Youssef?'

'Jealous?'

'He used to lie with your sister.'

'She was his. Who else should he lie with? Should she lie with?'

I translated, and shrugged.

'And you believe all this, my lady? We have no evidence for any of it.'

'But surely ... Who else saw it? Who came along then?'

'No one, my lady. It was - if it happened at all as he says - not long after matins. He was back in Tain before Prime, and he walked. Ask him what he did next.'

My mind raced. What would he do next? Of course. He would put the body on the horse and take it home.

I asked him. Yes, that was what he had done. Fortunately, though, he had been seen entering the town, so there was one piece of corroboratory evidence.

Who had seen him? The Bailie's brother, Niáll told me. The butcher. Master Ronald Brodie. He had stopped him, spoken to him, asked him about the body on the horse, but, on seeing that it was the body of ben Youssef, and finding himself unable to communicate with Rachid, he had called at his brother's house and alerted him to the situation before going about his own business.

'The Bailie went straight round to ben Youssef's lodgings. He found things as they have been described: Rachid here trying to get the body up the narrow staircase, the girl - Souad? - having hysterics, the landlady and her other guests having the time of their lives, especially the men.'

'Why "especially the men"? Oh, I see. Souad ... '

'Yes, my lady.'

'Were you there?'

'Yes, my lady.' He grinned.

'Well, I can confirm all that later, when I see Souad. And of course talk to your master, the Bailie.'

Niáll stood up, letting Rachid down flat on his back again, but it became obvious at once that he could no longer breathe in that position. He was completely helpless.

Niáll and Kenneth lifted him over to a bench by a wall and propped him up so that he could breathe.

'He needs attention,' I said. 'At once. A physician, and when he's been treated and can breathe a bit more easily we must find him some kind of home where he can rest and recover.'

Kenneth was still ignoring me, as pointedly as he dared. Niáll, though, I noticed, was looking at me as if I was from another world. Not so much incredulously as tolerantly. Amused. Well, I was from another world. So?

'Where is his sister? I heard she was at the Bailie's house.'

'Aye, Mistress Brodie's taking care of her.'

'Then he should be taken there, to Mistress Brodie's. The best person to care for him now is his sister.'

Niáll laughed. 'Let's go and talk to Master Brodie. And you can talk to Souad as well, while we're there, my lady.'

Master Brodie, the Bailie of Tain, was a peaceful man and he liked a peaceful life; now he was upset. Not only did he have the prospect of a burning on his hands, but he also had a murder, foreigners whose language he could not speak, witchcraft and interfering aristocrats.

Actually, I think he rather admired Master MacDalorg; but then he also seemed to admire Thorfinn Skinner, for quite different qualities. He could not abide Brother Arsenius.

Mona, his wife, was sweet: small, red-haired and rosy-cheeked. Quite different from the slender, golden-skinned Souad. Yet she had clearly taken to her, and now seemed to want to protect her as much as I did.

The introductions were made, and I spoke to Souad for a moment in Arabic, explaining who I was and that I was there to help her and Rachid tell their story and answer questions, and to help them in any other way I could. I also told her, when she insisted on knowing how her brother was, that he had been tortured and was in great pain still and very weak.

'Is he dying, Lalla?' The tears were in her eyes.

'I hope not. The first thing we must do, though, is get him out of there.'

'He should never have been put in there! He was just trying to help. If he had killed his master, would he have brought him back like that?'

'It seems unlikely, doesn't it? Anyway, let me tell these people your brother's story first, then I'll translate for you.'

When I had finished, Master Brodie himself seemed to agree that Rachid had been telling the truth.

Niáll, though, was still sceptical. 'Now question the girl. Without telling her first what her brother's story was. My lady.'

I ignored the way he said that. My lady.

She had, she said, been woken by Rachid, early - very early. He had told her that the master was still out. What should he do? Should he go and look?

'And what did you say? Exactly.'

'I cursed him, may Allah forgive me. I was sleepy. Then I said something like, "Yes, of course, but stop disturbing me!"'

'And he said?'

'He said sorry, then stammered out his problem: he didn't know which way Sidi Abdelwahed had gone. Did I? I did. He had told me before he left that he was going east along the Tarbat road. And he had said something strange, as well, that's right. I've only just remembered it, lalla. I didn't tell Rachid. Sidi Abdelwahed said, "What would you do, Souad, my joy, if you were owned by a cruel and violent master who used you ill? Think ... Would you - take a lover? Someone who would use you kindly?" "Sidi! No, I - I -" My mind had flown to Captain le Fou, who had approached me with just such a suggestion on his lips. "Or would you kill the cruel master? Poison him perhaps?" "Sidi Abdelwahed, how can you say such things - ?" "I am merely enquiring, merely wondering, what you can conceive of yourself as doing were your master to make life intolerable for you." "Yes. Yes, I see, but - but to kill someone ..." "Or would you pray to Allah that you might somehow fall into the hands of another, gentler and more civilised master?" "Yes - yes, that is what I would do, Sidi Abdelwahed." "Perhaps you would pray that you might be free?" "Oh, no. No, I would never - I told you, I don't want to be free." "Hmmm," he said, and he smiled and kissed me, and he went. And I never spoke to him again.' She started crying. '"I don't want to be free!" - those were the last words I spoke to him.'

'Ask her what happened next.'

She had gone back to sleep, only to be woken again by Rachid. Now he was shouting from the stairs, waking everybody, and this time she had been furious - till she saw ben Youssef's body and remembered their earlier conversation.

'What did you do, Souad?'

'Nothing, lalla. What could I do? I just started screaming - wailing - like this.' She suddenly ululated, loudly, making everyone jump. No one in the room apart from me, or so I thought, had ever heard such a sound before. I was wrong, of course. Master Brodie and Niáll had both heard it when they arrived that morning to see what was going on - and had promptly arrested Rachid, put ben Youssef's body in the church - he was not a Christian, but where else could they put him? - and brought Souad, who was hysterical, round to Mistress Brodie to look after her. And she had been here ever since.

'Ask her about the mutilation.' Niáll seemed almost to be giving me orders.

'Does she know about it?' I asked Master Brodie.

'No, my lady, not so far as I know. How could she?'

'Did she have any chance to examine the body?'

He shook his head.

'Souad. Did you know that apart from the wound made by the sword or arrow or whatever it was that killed him - '

'The wound in his chest - yes.'

'That your master's body was also cut in another place?'

She looked completely mystified. 'But what - where - ?'

I told her. Now she looked sick.

'Do you think your brother could have done that?'

'No!' she said, in horror. Then she screamed, 'No! Of course not! Never!'

'But he himself had been castrated and - '

'You mean for revenge - or - or - or jealousy? It wasn't Sidi Abdelwahed who did that to him, it was - well, that doesn't matter. Lalla Mariana, Rachid loved our master. He would have died for him. Why do you think he went rushing off out in the middle of the night? Because he was worried, upset. And where was I? I loved him too, I loved him very much, he was father to me, and husband, and lover, he was everything. But I didn't love him like - like a dog. Rachid worshipped him!' She gazed at me. 'You who speak our language but are not one of us, can you understand that? *I* was asleep. *Rachid* was out in the night, scouring the country for him.'

Now I gazed at her for a moment, at the tears welling up one by one in those lovely Spanish eyes and trickling slowly down those perfect Spanish cheeks. Hadn't le Fou said she spoke Spanish?

'*Sí, señorita*,' I said, '*entiendo muy bien*. I understand very well. But are you so sure,' I went on in the same language, 'that I am not one of you?'

Now she stared at me.

'We will speak of that later,' I said softly, going back into Arabic, 'when we are alone. There are one or two more questions that I have to ask you still, and then we will try to get something done about Rachid.'

She nodded submissively, but her eyes were shining with sudden happiness, sudden hope. She had found a friend.

'We are interested in the weapon that was used to kill your master. Did you see that there was a hole also in his back? Where the weapon came out - or went in.' She shook her head and I went on: 'Could someone have done that with Sidi Abdelwahed's own knife, the knife he was carrying? Only the knife has disappeared, so we have no idea how big it was. Also, I have never seen your master, so I have no idea how big he was. Could his knife have gone right through his body and come out the other side?'

'No, Lalla Mariana. It might just have reached the other side, I suppose, but …'

I translated, and waited for them to speak, but when they did not, I said, 'So. That is all right then. Now what are we going to do about the boy?'

'The boy?' They all looked at me.

'He is innocent, we have seen that. He has been tortured - quite wrongfully, in my view - and not by a Master Torturer but by a mere boy, an apprentice. And now he is dying - will die, unless he can be moved at once to safe and friendly surroundings and nursed back to health.'

'We can't do that.'

'There is no evidence - '

'There is,' I protested. 'There is the sister's evidence. It corroborates his story in every detail.'

'How do we know she is telling the truth?'

'Of course she is telling the truth. Look at her. And if we don't act soon - now, at once - that boy will die.'

'He is a slave,' said Niáll. 'He must stay where he is. Isn't that so, Master Brodie?'

'Yes, yes, I'm afraid it is. And she too is a slave, so - '

'Oh, no. No, no, no, no, no.' This was the first time Mistress Mona had spoken, but now she was quite firm. 'She stays here with me.'

'I didn't say - '

'I know what you're thinking, both of you.'

I knew what they were thinking, too. Suddenly, the question was no longer whether we could rescue Rachid. It was whether we could save Souad. And argue as we might, Mona and I could do little more that afternoon than delay the making of a decision and prevent Niáll from marching Souad straight down to the holding-room there and then, just as she was, and getting started on her.

I left her in Mona's hands, finally - what choice did I have? - and made my way back to my room at the inn, and poor little lonely Kari. I had been expecting to spend the evening with Raoul, but realised now, belatedly, that Kari presented something of a problem. I could of course treat her as a bondmaid - a slave, in effect - leave her shut in the room, tie her to something if she seemed likely to flee, beat her if she protested. This was, after all, how most people would treat her: it was not wrong. Or I could treat her as I did in fact treat her when not Raoul but Jaufre le Fou knocked on my door. I dressed her up and took her down to the tap-room with us.

She ate a slice of the venison pie, then sat with a cup of wine in her hand, sipping it uncertainly, and looking around with wide eyes, fascinated by the people and the place, but most of all by the presence of herself there with them, almost like one of them.

And meanwhile, Jaufre and I talked of this and that. He was not my kind of man, he was a peacock, but he was charming, too, as only a Frenchman - and in particular one from the Midi - can be, and for that evening at least I fell under his spell. As had Bella: she had been with him, not Raoul, who had been at best her second choice, as it seemed to me then. And Souad, too, had succumbed, if one believed Jaufre's account of his visit to her.

'What do you know of this Moorish girl, Souad?' I had asked him, probing.

'Souad? I've seen her, but …'

'You mean in the veil she wears whenever she is to be seen? Which is not often, from what I hear. And how do you come to know that she speaks Spanish?'

He laughed and winked at Kari - who of course understood

nothing of all this but was enchanted by him - and proceeded to tell me the story of ben Youssef's departure on the Mickle Ferry for Dornoch, and his own visit to Ben Youssef's rooms - Souad's rooms - and how they had spoken together in Spanish.

He had asked her about her knowledge of Spanish.

'I speak it from when I was a child, before Sidi ben Youssef bought me.'

'And he never lets you go out, never lets you use it?'

'No.' Demurely. 'I am his. And he prefers me in. Anyway, he doesn't know I still speak Castellano. Or that I ever spoke it.'

'Doesn't know?'

'Why should he? My mother's last words to me, shortly before they took me away from her, were that I should please my masters - yes, of course - but keep some things back from them. Have my little secrets.'

'How old were you when - ?'

'When he bought me? Eleven. And yes, before you ask, I was still a virgin.'

'And don't you ever get lonely?'

'Lonely?'

'I mean … Have you ever had a friend?'

'A friend?'

'Someone who - who was your friend and came to visit you. When ben Youssef, when your master, was not at home.'

She was laughing at him, he knew. But then she said, 'Oh yes. Yes. And Rachid is very good. He understands. But that was in Toulouse, and in Milano, great cities, not in a tiny little ten-house town like this, where everyone knows what everyone else is doing every hour of the day and night. It is too dangerous.'

She held out her hand to him. He took it, wondering, studied the perfect nails, and touched the fingers to his lips.

'They are plain and bare.' She was referring to her hands. 'Ben Youssef does not like henna - except a little on my feet.' She showed him, watched him admire them. 'Come and see me in Edimburgo - or - or in Paris, in any city where you and my master happen to be at the same time. But be very, very careful. He carries a garrotte and, unlike his big dagger, it is not for decoration.'

He still had her hand in his, he told me, and now he turned it over and kissed the palm. He studied it, and kissed it again, so soft, so sweet-smelling, and so pale compared to the glossy golden skin on the back of her hand and on her arm. And all so bare - she was right - compared to her feet.

London, he decided; yes, London would probably be the best place if - if - they ever got there.

'I will visit you in London,' he told her.

'Londino? *I* go to Londino. But you? I do not think so. The Scots have no interest in your war. Not even their king. Have you met their king?'

'How do you know all this?'

'My master has. He says he is an old man, and no warrior.'

Was ben Youssef a spy? he wondered. And if so, for whom?

'He talks to me, tells me everything when we are alone together.'

For Coucy? He knew Raoul was Coucy's man: and it was Coucy, he remembered, who had imposed the Moor upon them. 'Take him anywhere. Let him see everything, talk to everyone.' For the English? It was possible. For the Pope in Avignon? A Moor? Hardly.

'Did they get anything out of Souad's brother?' he asked, suddenly.

'Not really. A false confession. And they broke him on the rack to get that.'

'But a confession?'

'A nod to leading questions he could not understand.'

'I see.'

'I had the true story out of him afterwards, and that was confirmed by Souad when I spoke to her, but he is the murderer as far as they are concerned. Now they intend to put poor Souad to the question to corroborate his testimony, which was that Rachid murdered his master with her connivance.'

'With her connivance? Pouf! I'll have a word with Master Brodie. But they will say she is a slave and a Moor, she has no rights: which is why I suggested to Raoul that we send for you. I hoped you would be able to stand up for her - stand between her and Masters Brodie and Skinner - while you hunted down the real culprit. I still hope so.'

'She's a Moor, Jaufre. "Just a Moor" - weren't those your words? If she were to die, the world would be well rid of her ...'

'She is not *just* a Moor. She is a woman. I was speaking of Abdelwahed ben Youssef, a man, and of *his* status here in Christendom. A man is defined by and *cannot escape from* his birth - his family, his religion. His nationality even, as Coucy has found.'

'And a woman?'

'A woman can change all that without a second thought, as she does when she is given in marriage and goes to join her husband. For her, these things are superficial, may be put on and taken off, like clothes.'

Very chivalrous - and of course there was some truth in it. She might remarry, and change her family allegiance, three, four, times in her life: many women did, for in general they lived much longer than men.

'You, for instance,' he went on. 'You are - what? Scottish? Spanish? A little bit Moorish, I suspect, from the way you walk? And yet you live in London and everyone thinks you are English. Is that not so? If *I* lived in London, no one would think *I* was English.'

That was for sure. But how much could I trust him? I looked into his eyes. He thought I might be partly Moorish not for any logical reason - such as my fluency in Arabic - but from the way I walked. I smiled. 'You are right. I am not simply Scottish and Spanish.' I smiled. 'My Spanish side *is* only half Spanish: the other half includes my Jewish great-grandmother; and her husband, my great-grandfather, who was indeed a Moor, was in fact half Arab, half Chleuh.'

'Chleuh?'

'Berbers, from the High Atlas region; though my great-great-grandmother was a dancer from somewhere among the oases in the Oued Drâa, the Drâa valley, whom my great-great-grandfather received as a gift when he was out in the desert on a political mission.' I laughed. 'Or so the story goes.'

'There you are then. Spanish, Jewish, Arab, Berber - and Scottish.'

'The Scottish side is not that simple either. My father's roots were part Gael, part Norse - my grandmother's maiden name was Gudmundsdottir. That's six. And I also, it seems, have Elpin blood in my veins.'

'Seven. And each no more than a veil that you cast aside as you dance. Beneath is the real woman.'

I had misjudged Jaufre. I was beginning to think that if Raoul were not around, I might easily end up doing the dance of the seven veils for him - and I had not done it since Granada - but then Jaufre's interpreter, Roger, joined us and the conversation became more general, and the noise in the bar gradually louder and more convivial as the evening wore on, until I realised suddenly that Kari was fast asleep with her head on Jaufre's lap.

He carried her upstairs for me while I held the two candles, and laid her on her bed; then he glanced at mine. I gave him a kiss and one of the candles and sent him to his own bed.

I put the other candle on the small table and took out my almagest, but it was too dark with only the one candle and my eyes were tired. I decided to leave it till morning.

ELEVEN

A Resurrection, and Two Deaths

In the morning, all I had time for between my exercises, in which Kari joined enthusiastically, and my breakfast, was a quick glance at the almagest. I consider the position of the Moon at the time of birth to be almost as important - perhaps as important - as the position of the Sun. I discovered that on Bella's birthday the Moon had been in Cancer, which indicated that her one ambition, her single dream, was likely to be a home and a stable marriage. Security, and love. In that order. What could that have to do with this murder? Nothing, so far as I could see. And besides, my mind was now on Souad.

Kari and I were still quietly enjoying breakfast, and I was thinking that Jaufre was right, it was my duty to intervene on Souad's behalf, when Raoul knocked at our door. I asked him to sit down and drink some tisane with us. 'Some bread? It's still warm from the oven.' I broke off a piece and gave it to him. 'Sit down.'

He took a bite, but remained standing where he was. 'I just thought you might like to know that Master Skinner has reappeared from the sea.'

'Really? When?'

'Late last night.'

'How do you know? Ah. You were there. Please, Raoul, sit down. Good. Now, tell me about it. What time did you ride out to the Skinner steading?'

'The sun was going down. But I hadn't eaten, so it was still quite early. She asked me if I had eaten.'

'Bella?'

He nodded. 'And she offered me some soup. Only it was *soupe de poisson*, fish soup, with shellfish, and shellfish always upset me. I didn't want to seem to criticise though, so I just said I wasn't hungry and asked if I could take it with me when I went.'

'Can we come to the point?'

'You told me once, in Paris, that everything was to the point in an enquiry such as this.'

'Yes, you are right, I am sorry.'

He gazed at me. He gazed like a man in love - wistful, desperate - only it wasn't me he was in love with, not any more. Coll had been right. If Raoul was "the other one". Right about him, at any rate. Was she right, too, about Bella?

'Is she as much in love with you, Raoul, as you are with her?'

He showed no reaction. Kari looked at him and grinned. How much of our conversation - which was in French, of course - was she managing, somehow, to follow? I decided to send her out for some fruit. 'There were cherries to be had in Dyngvale. See if you can find some here. Take this.' I gave her money and off she went, still grinning.

My mind flew to her mother again.

Then I turned back to Raoul. 'Does the skinner's resurrection from the ranks of the presumed dead make any difference?'

'It doesn't seem to. Not to your enquiry. Unless he is the murderer - or saw the murderer. It will make a great difference to Bella, though, *bien sûr*. And to poor Coll.'

'Yes. But not to Rachid, now. Or to Drostan.'

'Drostan?'

'The condemned heretic.'

'Ah, Master MacDalorg. Yes. I heard of him in Avignon.'

'They are past being tortured. Anything more would kill them. Raoul, I need someone - not a shoulder, but an ear. I need to think aloud.' He smiled, and I went on: 'My main suspects so far have been Hugh of Foulis -'

'*Le petit baron*?'

'You know him?'

'*Ah oui, bien sûr*. I met him in Dyngvale, visited him at home, in that tower of his. Our main dealings are with such as he. Who else do you suspect?'

'Thorfinn Skinner, and Bella.'

'Bella? But why? She of all people is - '

'She was there. And she lied to me about what happened that

evening. Why?'

'Yes, I know. I asked her what she had told you. She says she told you she didn't go out because she was frightened. She panicked, that's all.'

'Yes, but if she lied to me - which she did - she might also lie to you, Raoul.'

'No.'

'And Skinner himself. Why the disappearance? Was it set up? Or was it only in the minds of those expecting him back, while he himself was unconscious of being missed? Either way, we need to get the times right. Was Skinner still on shore when ben Youssef died? Was Jaufre still out and about? Was Bella? We know Coll was. We know Whin and her children were.'

'Whin?'

'The tinkler woman. Kari's mother.'

'And what did she see?'

I told him.

'Then there's the whole question of the mutilation,' I went on. 'That sounds like Coll rather than Bella, but might have been carried out afterwards. And with his own knife perhaps - which doesn't seem to have been used for the murder, but was missing from the body. Why?'

'That could have been Coll, as you say. She's capable of anything.'

'Why do you say that? Because she's not - human?'

'I think *you* have forgotten *me*, Mariana. I am probably the only person in this town - the only person in this whole country - apart from you - who would never entertain such a thought.'

My Raoul.

My Raoul?

'Or,' he went on, 'it could have been this Whin.'

'That's true. Except that I have had the story separately from her and her two children, one of whom is Kari, and they all agree: they left the area together soon after the rider - it may not have been the same rider - passed them by for the third time. Probably some time before the mutilation took place, though I suspect that by then ben Youssef was already dead.'

I refilled my cup with the tisane, and this time Raoul joined me.

'Then there is Jaufre. He was there too. I had a chat with him last night at the Spider, but my mind was on Souad, and on Whin. Anyway, I'd like to get Bella's story clear. Also, I need to talk to Baron Hugh as soon as possible. It seems he coveted Souad, wanted to buy her, but ben Youssef would not - '

'*Le petit baron* develops a terrible lust for the hunt whenever something eludes him.' He grinned. 'Have *you* been eluding him?'

'We haven't met.'

'Then you have that honour still to come.'

'I look forward to it - and shall be at my most elusive.'

He laughed. 'But as regards the murder, I imagine he could prove he was not in the area that night.'

'He wouldn't kill the man himself.'

There was a knock at the door.

It was Raoul's man, Arnaud. 'Milady, *vous m'excusez*?' He turned to Raoul. 'Monsieur, you remember that *soupe de poisson*? Well, it is your dog that - '

'My dog? What - ?

'*La Pauvre. Elle est morte, monsieur*. She is dead.'

'What? But how? Why?'

The fish soup. So, it had started.

'Arnaud, are you telling us that you gave the fish soup to the dog of Maître Raoul, and the dog died?'

'*Oui*, milady. Raoul gave me the soup, but I sniffed it and I didn't like it, so I gave it to the dog. *La Pauvre*.'

'You didn't like it so you gave it to *La Pauvre*?' wailed Raoul.

Arnaud nodded miserably, seemingly only too well aware that in his master's eyes he ranked considerably lower than a stray dog - or at least than this particular stray dog.

'And then?' I asked.

'After a few moments, she began to vomit, milady, then to have convulsions - '

A tear ran down Raoul's cheek. 'She was like me; she could not abide *les fruits de mer.'*

'Raoul, shellfish do not cause convulsions. Certain poisons, however, do.'

Arnaud did not agree. 'Milady, shellfish can cause

convulsions if they are contaminated, if they are poisonous.'

'I understood that these were stale. You think they may have been contaminated? But in that case, anyone who ate them, even when they were fresh, would have become ill, would probably have died.'

Raoul leapt to his feet. 'Bella! Excuse me, Mariana, I must - ' He went running out of the room.

I followed, shouting, 'Raoul! Be careful! Skinner is there now!'

There was no answer, only the sound of feet racing down the stairs.

I turned to Arnaud, who had followed me onto the landing. 'Go with him, Arnaud. Oh, and tell him I'll come back here, and hope to see him, as soon as I can.'

Thoughtfully, I finished my breakfast. When Kari returned, I shared with her the wrinkled apple which was all she had found, then sent her out along the coast to observe the comings and goings at the Skinner steading, while I went to see what more I could find out about Souad and Rachid and whether there was anything I could do for them.

Mona - Mistress Brodie - told me Souad had been crying all night because no one would help her brother, no one would even take her to see him. She also told me that she accepted my version of Souad's and Rachid's testimony; and so, she believed - or at any rate hoped - did her husband. However, others insisted that Souad too should be put to the question, for how else would they know whether or not she had been telling the truth? Those "others" included, she thought, Margaret, Countess of Sutherland, and Baron Hugh of Foulis, who had arrived in Tain together that morning after a night out hunting along the coast.

Lady Margaret? Maybe. Why should she care? But I found it hard to believe that Baron Hugh would let them spoil Souad's beauty. Would he, though, if he couldn't have her himself? I needed to find out much more about him.

Mona told me that Baron Hugh and Lady Margaret would be there later for dinner, and invited me to join them. I accepted, eagerly.

Then the Bailie himself came in. Mona left us together, and I was informed once again that the Countess of Sutherland and Baron Hugh of Foulis would be meeting there for dinner at midday. And that I was invited. This time, for "invited" read "commanded". Still, as I say, I was not displeased. I had questions for Sir Hugh that might be easier to ask - certainly easier to get an answer to - in the presence of the fabled Red Countess.

I was also informed that certain documents had been found at ben Youssef's lodgings.

The Bailie, very distant and bureaucratic this morning, was still not managing to get to the point any faster.

'What documents, Master Brodie?'

'I'm not sure that I should - '

'Master Brodie! I was brought up here to act as interpreter and to help you solve this riddle.'

'Yes, my lady, but you have no official - '

'What language were they in, these documents? The Gaelic?'

Sarcasm was wasted on him. He simply looked at me as though I was stupid.

And saw me, for the first time, as a woman.

You can have breasts or you can have brains, was clearly his view. And the way I was dressed that morning made it quite obvious where my talents lay.

'Gaelic? No, of course not.' Impatient. But kinder, too, and in a strange way, more patient. 'Some were in Arabic, they tell me, and others, the ones that concern us, in French. Those have been translated - quite competently, I am sure - by Master Finlay MacKay.'

'And the others? The papers in Arabic?'

'They will contain nothing of importance that has not already been ... However, I wouldn't like you getting upset, so perhaps it might be a good idea if - '

'Yes, it might be a very good idea. And the papers in French?'

Did he think he was interviewing for the post of wet-nurse? Somehow, I had to get his attention back onto what I was saying. 'The papers in French, Master Brodie. Shall I tell you what they are? What they say?'

It was going to be a guess, but not such a wild guess. After all,

Souad had said, "I don't *want* to be free!" and racking my brains now I suddenly realised what this implied: it implied that she was free. I also realised that Master Brodie might be right about my talents. All that time to make this one simple connection! And if he was, then he might also be right about my function in life.

However, I didn't let these humbling considerations affect my apparent confidence. 'Among them,' I announced, 'are certificates of manumission stating that she is free.'

That focussed his attention. 'How did you know that? How could you have known?'

And there was an answer to that question in his eyes, a sudden fear. I remembered thinking the previous night that I must be more careful here in Scotland, where what was different or not well understood was feared - like Tinkman and Rachid and Agnes the witch and Master MacDalorg - and what was feared was racked or hanged or burnt to ashes.

At least they didn't boil you here as they did to women in certain cases in England. I would hate to be boiled. It would be so embarrassing to be hoiked up out of the pot afterwards on a meat hook in front of everyone you least liked. So much nicer, so much more mysterious and dignified, to be blown away as ashes on the morning breeze. At dawn. The party over.

It was Raoul. He always did this to me. Or not to me, but to my mind. I think my mind was still a little in love with him. It has a will of its own sometimes, and strays off down paths through bluebell woods that I would never consider taking. Not alone, anyway. Perhaps with him.

I'm not very good at diplomacy, either, at choosing my words; but I did my best. I smiled - open, innocent, sweet. 'You forget, Master Brodie. I have spoken to them. They knew they were free. Souad told me herself. And, interestingly, she said she didn't like being free, didn't want to be free. Can you understand that?'

'Did she now? And did you believe her? Come, my lady. I think you and I had better go up and question the girl again. Together.'

'Tell us about the manumissions, Souad,' I said to her, after we had talked once more, but with her very much taking the lead this time, about where her brother had been and what he had done that night, and what they had done to him, and about how they would maim her, make her ugly and stupid and crooked and valueless - if they didn't kill her, too.

Kill her, too? Was he dead, then? Did she know? How could she know? I recognised the questions: I was beginning to think like Master Brodie - and Master Robert. But she was right to be frightened. Even the Bailie seemed to have made up his mind.

It was those manumissions.

'The manumissions? What about them? Sidi Abdelwahed insisted on them. We were in Paris, and he had been ill. He was worried. Everything that we had with us was to be mine, too. There's a paper that says that somewhere, as well. And I was to look after my brother. He worried about my brother.' She began to cry again.

'Is her brother dead?' I asked the Bailie.

He shrugged. He didn't know - or care. 'He was in a bad way last I heard, but still alive. Did she say anything new?'

I translated the bit about all ben Youssef had with him going to her.

He nodded. 'Ben Youssef carried various letters of credit, one of them on a Paris bank and another on a London merchant. He was also carrying quite a lot of gold in French *livres d'or* and English nobles. That will all be forfeit, of course, and fall to the State, if she is found to have been her brother's accomplice in the murder. As she will be. We know already that she gave false testimony when she spoke to us, through you, earlier.'

'How do you know that?'

'She portrayed the boy as innocent, my lady.'

'I see.' I turned back to Souad. I told her I was going to check up on her brother, and would speak to her again later, after dinner. Did she have any message for him?

'Message? Lalla Mariana, what message? Rachid is dying. Or he is dead. They have killed him. Kiss him for me. Kiss those lips that I knew when they were the sweet, firm lips of a little boy. His well, his oasis, our father called him then, the gift of Allah, a spring of joy and hope in the desert of life. "And me?" I used to say to him, "And me?" "Ah, you, my little dancer, you are a slender palm tree growing by that spring.'"

A guard was now posted outside the holding-room but he seemed to know who I was. He waved me on through without a word.

Inside, Master Thorfinn the skinner was back in charge. Another big man, though slimmer than Master Robert, and with a full brown beard now speckled with white.

'Where's Rachid?' I said, looking round. The rack and the bench were both empty.

'Ah. Lady MacElpin, I presume. I've been hearing a lot about you, my lady.'

'And I a little of you, Master Thorfinn.'

'So I understand. And I must ask you to refrain from bothering my girls out at the steading, my lady - at least in my absence.'

'I had no idea you were absent. Indeed, it was to you that I wished to speak. In a moment, perhaps, you will favour me with an account of your - er - prolonged absence. But first, I came here to check on, and to talk to, the boy Rachid. Where is he, Master Thorfinn?'

'Dead, my lady.'

He nodded towards the corner of the chamber that lay furthest from the door, and from daylight.

Kenneth piped up: 'We chucked him over there, out of the way. He may still not be quite dead though. I mean, if you want to speak to him.'

Ignoring, for the moment, young Kenneth's insolent manner, I went over and found Rachid face down on the stone floor. I knelt beside him, turned him over, and supported him on my lap and in my arms again, to help him breathe.

'*Salaam wa laikum*, Rachid. Rachid? It's me. Lalla Maryam. Can you speak? No? Can you nod? I know, squeeze my hand with yours ...'

His eyes were open, and seemed to see me now, and there came a little squeeze.

'Rachid, squeeze once for No, twice for Yes. You understand?'

Nothing.

'Squeeze twice for Yes. Like this.' I squeezed his hand twice.

'You understand?' Two slight squeezes. 'Good. That's fine, Rachid. Your name is Rachid, isn't it?' Two squeezes. 'Am I your sister, Souad?' One squeeze. Good. 'Am I Lalla Mariam?' Two squeezes. Right. 'Did you love your master, Sidi Abdelwahed?' Two squeezes. Yes. 'Did you kill your master, Sidi Abdelwahed?' No. 'Did your sister kill him?' No. 'Do you know who did kill him?' No. 'A few days ago, Souad received a visit from a French officer, Captain le Fou. Is that right?' Hesitation - then Yes. 'Did she get visits from other men?' Hesitation. 'From another French officer?' No. Right. Good. 'From a local man?' Hesitation. Then No. But he was weakening fast now, in my arms. Giving up. 'Rachid, listen. When you were a boy … When you were at home, with Souad, before ever you met Sidi Abdelwahed … what language did you speak? Did you speak Arabic?' Yes. 'Did you speak Spanish?' Hesitation. Then Yes. 'What language did you speak with your mother? Was it Spanish?' Yes. 'And what was your mother's name? Do you remember?' Oh, *merde*! He can't tell me. And I can't go through all the - yes, I can, the most common ones. 'Was it Maria?' No. No. Was that two No's? Or was it Yes? 'Maria?' No - but his hand continued to squeeze mine, and he whispered, 'Katerina. She was just like Souad. Only taller.' And he died.

After a moment, I opened the hand that lay, now so relaxed, in mine, and holding it up towards what little light there was, I studied it. His life - and his death - were written all over it. Now I had to see Souad's hands: they were going to be, to some extent at least, very similar, and the differences would be revealing.

I closed his eyes, laid him down, and got to my feet.

Only the skinner was there. I said, 'Master Thorfinn, the boy was a Christian. His mother was a Spanish woman named Katerina, and he was sold into slavery as a child.'

'Is that so? Then I will ask Father Gilbert to see to the disposal of the body. Is there anything else, my lady?'

'How is Master MacDalorg this morning? Can he - ?'

'Drostan? No, don't worry. He is not dead. Better for him if he were. But Brother Arsenius left strict instructions that during his absence no one - no one - was to be admitted to the cell of the condemned prisoner. I'm afraid that includes you, my lady.'

'Yes. Yes, of course. Thank you, Master Thorfinn.'

Before I returned to the Bailie's house I wanted to see ben Youssef's body, so I made my way to the church. I found Father Gilbert outside and introduced myself. He peered at me through eyes long clouded by cataract. I wondered how much he could see. How much he could hear. He had made no response, so I said, 'I'm looking for the body of the murdered Moor, Father.'

'It has been taken away, my daughter. It - he - was buried yesterday, in the Judas Field.'

The Judas Field: the unhallowed plot they kept for suicides, and for the unbaptised.

'I see. Father, the Moor had a servant, a young man called Rachid.'

'I know, I know. The one who killed him.'

'That is unproven. But they have killed him, in the holding-room. And he was a Christian, Father.'

'A Christian? How do you know?'

'Because he told me, Father, before he died. His mother's name was Katerina.'

'Then tell them to bring the body to me. We will find room for him in the cemetery.'

'Thank you, Father.'

'My daughter, tomorrow is St Arsenius' Day. Would the good brother like me to celebrate Mass for him, do you think?'

'The good brother?'

He could see almost nothing, I knew, yet he too looked at me as though I had clotted cream for a brain and milk flowing through my veins. A cross between a man and a cow.

'The Black Friar, Brother Arsenius,' he explained, patiently. 'Do you think you could ask him for me?'

'Yes, Father.' No more sarcasm.

I turned away. Turned back. 'On second thoughts, Father, the boy, Rachid, would probably rather lie beside his master, whom he loved, than among strangers.'

'Had he been baptised, my daughter?'

'No, Father, probably not.'

TWELVE

A Leo At Heart?

Back at the Bailie's house, I told Mona of Rachid's death and asked her to inform her husband.

Then I went upstairs to tell Souad.

She had been expecting it. There was no scream, no hysterical wailing. She simply raised her hands like claws to rake her eyes and cheeks.

I grabbed her and held her to me.

Her whole body began to shake, and went on shaking, as she cried out the pain and the loss; the loss of everything and everyone, the loss of home, the loss of family, the loss of comfort, the loss of hope: the loss that is so total it seems far worse than death. These last few days had only completed losses that had begun when she was still a child.

I remembered Job. Would this girl curse God? Would she curse man?

How strong was she?

Slowly, she calmed down. I told her, in Spanish this time, that before he died Rachid had spoken of their mother. 'He told me her name was Katerina, and that she was a Christian.'

Souad said nothing, merely went on sobbing.

'Claiming to be a Christian might help you here, in this country.'

For a moment or two, she still said nothing. Then she began to speak. Her face was all wet and her body was shaken by occasional sobs, but she had herself under control now. It was true, she said, yes, that their mother had been a Christian; however, their father had not and they had never been brought up as Christians, had not been baptised, did not want to be Christians, did not want to be free, did not want Sidi Abdelwahed's gold or anything else of his, they only wanted - '*I* just want - *me*! I'm all that's left! - I just want to go home now to Andalucía! There must be somebody there, or over the sea in Oran or Tangier - or Fès - that's where we were going to live with Sidi Abdelwahed - there must be somebody, somewhere, who would give me a home, a place in his harem. I am beautiful. I please - "For that, you were created", poor Sidi Abdelwahed used to say - poor Sidi Abdelwahed, who loved me and cherished me like a precious stone, and whom I loved so passionately in return. But what will happen to me if they break my poor body - look how defenceless it is! - if they break my poor body on the wheel, or whatever it is they do in this cold, hard country, whatever it was they did to poor Rachid? What will happen to me then?' she wailed. 'What will happen to me when I am no longer pleasing to look upon, pleasing to be with?'

I took her hands and held them out in mine, palms up. I had been expecting all this, but the next question, after a pause, and the start of another bout of sobbing, did take me by surprise.

'And where is Capitán le Fou? Is he still in Tain?'

The sobbing became uncontrollable again.

Le Fou?

I waited, studying her palms. As Jaufre - le Fou - had observed, there was no henna on them, though she had intricate patterns all over her toes and the tops of her feet and on her ankles, forming a background to the gold anklets. Patterns such as I used to have on my feet; anklets such as I too used to have to wear at all times and still did wear whenever I could, though not of course under the boots I wore most of the time up here.

She had a small but surprisingly Martial hand, with a long, strong, well-developed thumb, and a clear Line of Mars curling round within the line of Life. Quite different from Rachid's hand. Her Line of Life merged early with the line of Head. Her Line of Fate ran right up through the Mount of Saturn and onto the middle finger. Rachid's got lost somewhere between his Line of Head and his Line of Heart.

The sobs were becoming less frequent.

'When I was living in a harem in Grenada,' I said, 'I had henna drawings on my hands as well as my feet.'

'You lived in a harem, Lalla Mariana?'

'Yes. My last master was Ibn Khaldoun. He gave me my freedom when he left Andalucía for Fès.'

'Fès ... Sidi Abdelwahed was from Fès. Do you think your Ibn Khaldoun still lives in Fès? And that maybe he is still alone? No, that is not possible. I am a fool. And anyway, I am not like you, I am small and dark and - '

'Souad, you are beautiful!'

'But I am not you! If he liked you, then he will have bought himself other girls with green eyes and skins bathed in moonlight and laughing voices like your voice, and he will dream that he is once again with you.'

'Souad, I don't believe there exists a man whom you would not delight.'

'I know men.'

'Do you? Or do you only know Sidi Abdelwahed?'

She looked at me from beneath those long thick lashes, unsure to what extent she could confide in me.

'Can you tell me the date when you were born, you and Rachid?'

'Yes, our mother used to ... I'm sorry ... Our birthday is on the twenty-second of July. The day before hers - our mother's. She was born on the twenty-third of July. Which makes us different, doesn't it? I don't remember exactly. Since she - since we - since then, I haven't thought about it.'

'Yes, it makes you different. She was born under the sign of Leo, you under the sign of Cancer.'

But this Souad is almost a Leo, I was thinking, and that "almost" can mean so much. A Leo at heart, unlike her brother the Cancerian. Oh, you could see the moodiness and self-pity of the Cancerian in her. Her situation would bring that out anyway. But there was also something of the vanity of the Leo. Was she then influenced by the Sun? By the heart, and by fire, rather than by the breast and by milk and flowing water? It did seem that she might be.

'And do you know more exactly when you were born? The time? And whether you were born first, or Rachid?'

'I don't know the time, no, though we were born late in the day because I remember my father saying he had waited all day for his son to be born, and then at the end of the day got a daughter. He said he had refrained from questioning the will of Allah, even in his heart, and so Allah had looked kindly on him and sent him a son ten minutes later. And what did he do with that son?'

She burst into frenzied tears again and I held her to me till she stopped.

'Do you want to tell me all about it?'

'Another time,' she sobbed.

It had nothing to do with the murder, but there was something strange about their background and I was curious.

'How old are you now, Souad? Eighteen? Nineteen?'

'I am eighteen. Almost. I will be - and Rachid would have been - eighteen this year.'

'This month. On the day of Santa María Magdalena. Let me see. Next Tuesday.'

'Where shall I be next Tuesday?'

Where indeed?

'What am I going to do, Lalla Mariana?'

'I don't know yet. All you can do now is hope, and pray. And remember that I am your friend. I am on your side. I won't let you fall into the hands of the torturers, I promise.'

But how was I to keep that promise?

In the event, I didn't have to. She and Mona - Mistress Mona, the Bailie's wife - did more than hope and pray. They took action. And it was a good thing they did. But not for Jaufre le Fou.

THIRTEEN

Red Queen, White Queen

When I came downstairs again, Baron Hugh had arrived. Master Brodie himself introduced us and, when the Baron observed that a Bailie must have many pressing things to do, excused himself - with some relief, I thought - leaving the Baron and I seated at a table by the fire with a flask of whisky and another of water.

From what I had heard, I expected a hunter, a man supple and tough as a willow withe. I expected him to look like the predator he was, with the nose and eyes of a hawk and teeth like a young wolf's; but he was plump and pink and covered with ginger bristles like a piglet brought up by the fire on sweetmeats and trencher scraps, and he had a sweet, self-deprecating smile that stretched the corners of his mouth up almost to his ears, and made him look even more like a baby pig.

He had come early, he said, to have a long chat with me about this murder case on which I was rendering the authorities such valuable assistance and in which he, as one of the authorities - he gave me another sweet smile - took such interest.

In the vain hope of catching a glimpse of Souad, I suspected, but that may have been my natural modesty: he did seem quite content to sit and gaze at me instead while we awaited the arrival of the Countess, Lady Margaret. So I asked him one or two questions that I realised he might find easier to answer without the Red Countess sitting there listening to his every word.

'Sir Hugh, had you met the dead man, ben Youssef?'

'Me? Yes. He was with that French Captain, le Fou, at one of our less formal meetings.'

'Apart from that? Did you ever visit him at home?'

'Ben Youssef? No. Why on earth should I?'

'No reason. I simply thought you might be able to give me some background information on the girl Souad and her brother, and their master. However, if you never met her ... '

'Met her? Met her? No, of course I never met her.'

'So you wouldn't know her if you saw her.'

'Oh - well - yes, I think I did glimpse her somewhere, I don't remember where. But I would recognise her, yes. Not many around here like her. Not even you, Lady Marian, for though you have something sultry about you, something of her darkness, you have the eyes and eyelashes and soft cheeks - and soft white bosom, if I may say so - of the Gael.'

'You may say so, Sir Hugh.' I said sweetly, and fluttered my eyelashes at him. Then let my voice become a little less sweet. 'However, we are not discussing me.'

'Pity. Then let me tell you something of Master Brodie's other dinner guest: dear Lady Margaret, the Countess of Sutherland. You have not met, I believe?'

'No.'

And so he changed the subject and I had no choice but to follow him. It didn't matter. I would get the information from elsewhere. His lies didn't help me, anyway: they were just as likely to be motivated by shame or embarrassment as by guilt. More likely, in fact. Meanwhile, I learnt a little of the Red Countess.

She was, he told me, not only the wife of Robert, sixth Earl of Sutherland, but also the granddaughter of the king. And she was a passionate huntress, which was hardly surprising, for her father had been King Robert's black-hearted, black-souled, younger son, Alexander, known as "the Wolf of Badenoch".

'I arrived here at dawn,' said Phorca, beginning at the beginning. (I named him Phorca in my mind, from the old story of the four little pigs. Why Phorca, rather than Porca or Borca or Torca, the three other brothers in the story, I do not know. It simply seemed right for him.) 'I had been out all night, going up and down the beaches and dunes and creeks and marshes in pursuit of a woman - '

'A woman, Sir Hugh? But surely there are easier ways - '

'Not just any woman, Lady Marian. One of the wild women of

the woods.'

'Ah. I see. You favour such women.'

He gave me his smile again, though I was trying his patience. 'What I favour is ladies, ladies like you.' (Slave-girl/ladies, like me and Souad; serving-wench/ladies, like me and Bella. Wild-woman/ladies, like me and Whin.) 'These so-called "wild women",' he went on, 'are not women at all. They're brownies, I think, or shelts or elphs, or something like that, though some say they're not, they're simply mermaids with legs, I mean wearing legs when you see them on land: and that seems right, for she does take the form of a mermaid at times, this one. I almost had her down on the Cromarty Firth yesterday evening. She'd been running for hours, then at the last moment, just before she took to the sea, one of my men got a shot at her - '

Oh, Whin. You knew this was going to happen.

'You mean with an arrow, Sir Hugh? Where? About here?' I touched my thigh, at the point where I had seen the scar on Whin's leg, the mark of a wound made by another huntsman's arrow.

He gasped. 'How did you know?'

'I am one who knows, Sir Hugh.' No being careful today. 'I am descended from generations of spaewives. But tell me the whole story from the beginning.'

'You'd like me to? Really? I mean, I know ladies - I don't mean Lady Margaret, but - ladies - don't enjoy the hunt, and tales of the hunt, as we men do, though of course some do, and there are some great ladies who are hunters and great hunters who are ladies but not, you know, lady ladies, like you …'

He was getting lost in my eyes. I blinked to wake him up. 'I understand, Sir Hugh, of course I do, and I know what you mean. Still, I would love to hear the story.'

'You would? Well … It all started last Monday, when they let that tinkler brat escape from the Court House in Dyngvale, and then went after him without informing me! Oh, "it was not that kind of hunt," Master Robert says: they had already sold him, they had to bring him back alive. Why? And why had they already sold him? What was he worth? Ninepence? Why wasn't he offered to me? Oh, if he had been, if I'd been hunting him and he'd been already mine, I would not have let him live. Even if he hadn't!

Here - have your ninepence! For there are not many left of them. I would have had his head up on my wall. Next to his mother's. Yes, she's his mother, this one I was chasing yesterday. I've been close to her before, very close at least once - once for sure, because I sighted her clearly and she's quite unforgettable. Anyway, those curs in Dyngvale had their tails tucked right up between their legs when - '

What I could not understand was how this poor pink Phorca had ever come to be so pleased with himself. So superior. But on second thoughts, I had met aristocrats in England and France; some exactly like him. 'Curs, Sir Hugh? What - ?' What was he talking about?

'The Executioner, the Sheriff, and the others. Anyway, I soon found out that the mother and her mate were down by the Beaulieu Firth somewhere to the south of Dyngvale. That was on Friday night. By Saturday morning I had gillies out there combing the woods for them with lymers, but they'd disappeared. And they'd split up. The man was spotted that afternoon over on Black Isle, but he wasn't hunted - he didn't have to be - he was simply bound and carried across to Foulis, where he is now, caged and waiting. He's worthless. Not made of the same stuff at all as his mate.'

He picked up the iron poker and prodded at a half-burnt log, levering it over onto its side in a blaze of sparks.

'Then the next day, Sunday - yesterday - we hunted *her* with all we had: running-hounds, greyhounds, rachets - even a couple of elp-hounds - they're like alaunts, ugly, vicious things with big, heavy heads; they have to be kept muzzled - they go for men and horses - but they frighten the life out of elps. And women and children.' He laughed, and his little eyes gleamed.

'Well, as soon as she scented us - heard us rather, for the hounds were baying - she took off through the wood like a hind cut off from the herd. Going south, we reckoned, for all the veering this way and that. So when we lost her, we carried on south - till we found we really had lost her. Then the dogs picked up her trail again heading east to Loch Ussie. And there she took to the water, which didn't surprise us; but something she left there did, something none of us had ever met before: a cooked rabbit, in pieces, on the ground at the water's edge. Before we could stop them, the leading hounds had snapped the bits of rabbit up and swallowed the lot. She had gone on across the north-west corner of the loch, as I say, but we didn't know at that point whether in fact she had taken to the water. And if she had, where she might be coming out or might have come out already. So we were fortunate that a shepherd spotted her on Cnoc Farrel. From the top of Cnoc Farrel, she could see back down to Loch Ussie, where the hunt was now, see what was happening. Nothing was happening, not yet - but she decided, don't ask me why, to race off north-west now 'twixt Strathpeffer and Dyngvale. We skirted Cnoc Farrel, so as to catch up with her, then some of the dogs started staggering and, even as we stopped, one began to vomit and soon the others followed suit. Now I understood: what she had been looking for was happening. "Come on!" I shouted. "Leave them! She's getting away! Leave them, I say! They've been poisoned! It was that rabbit!" Six greyhounds died there, in convulsions, according to the boy we left with them, the Sheriff's boy, from Dyngvale. Oh, the bitch is clever.' Another prod at the big log which had caught his attention.

'That wasn't just clever,' I said. 'Her son had been badly mauled by those same dogs only days before.'

'You mean she was - avenging him? But how did she know? And how could she think of that?'

I sipped my whisky. 'Never underestimate your enemy, Sir Hugh.'

'She's not my enemy. She's my quarry.'

'That may be how you see her, but I think you can be reasonably sure that she regards you as her enemy.'

'She regards me? And the deer, whom I regard as venison - ?'

'She's running now, because she's outnumbered. I'd hate to be you if she caught you alone in the forest.' *Phorca.*

'Oh, Lady Marian,' he laughed, suddenly understanding that he didn't have to take me seriously. 'I'm sorry, but have you ever seen one of them? How small they are? It would be like a fight between me and some human girl-child of nine or ten years old!' The smile did reach his ears … 'Anyway, we chased backwards and forwards and up and down until, hours later, we had her trapped in Glen Glass. Or thought we had. We thought she'd go on up the glen then try to cut across to Loch Mouri, but no - suddenly the running-hounds could find no trace of her. "We missed her!" I cried. "She's off down to the sea!"

'It was what I'd been fearing.

'So we raced down the glen again, back to the steading where we had stopped and turned round before - where we had lost her. Now we went on.

'Again, not a whiff of her. Whiff! That was it! "The midden!" cried one of my men. "She's been in that midden back there, these are her tracks!" He shoved a few noses in it, and that was enough. We were away!

'By the Black Rock, we got confirmation: she had been sighted, "Running naked!" "Running like one of those that run with the Queen!" "Queen? What Queen?" "The Queen of Elphame!" "Running like a hunted animal!" "Running like one of the old gods, like Wul-herself!" Oh, I would have her! But she took to the water, washed off the shit, confused the spore, and we lost her! Again! "On! On!" I cried. "She's off down to the sea!"

'But she wasn't. Oh, she's cunning, she's sleekit, she's worse than an otter or fox, she's - she came out of that river five times, six, to the south, to the north, then finally, I imagine - I don't know - went up one of the burns that washes down off Cnoc Cislein: and then kept going, north, into the hills. "On! On!" I cried, in my simplicity. "To the sea, as fast as may be! And there's a gold *livre* for the first confirmed sighting!"

'By the time we realised the truth, that she had turned back, away from the sea, we too were exhausted. "She'll go on up. We've lost her," said one. "No, she'll turn again, to the sea," said another. "Why? Why should she?" "Yes, why should she? She knows she has won."

'"Won?" I cried. "Won? She has not won! She's just proving her worth, giving me more to brag about when I show off her head." "Only her head?" someone shouted. They all laughed, with what little breath they had left, but I said, "When we have her, we'll see what's worth keeping. We have to catch up with her first, and we won't catch her standing here bleating and yacking like a flock of old women. Now, I say she'll make for the sea. She thought she'd be too exposed up at Loch Mouri, and she was right. She'll reason the same now. She won't risk it, she's far too exhausted, and if we did go on after her, even she couldn't escape. No, she'll still make for the sea. But further up - at Alness, I imagine. Alness Point, somewhere like that. Three of you, take the dogs and go on, go after her. Find her and harry her. Don't give her a moment to breathe. And as you bring her down to the shore, sound the horn. Keep sounding it. We don't want to miss her. The rest of you come with me. We'll line Alness Bay all the way round from Balconie north. The tide will be right in soon, and she'd be able to swim off from anywhere along the shore."

'And what happened? She doubled back down to the Glass and across to the Sgitheach again and we heard the hunt coming out to the south of Balconie Point and my men all spread out to the north like fools! What a creature! I was at Balconie Point because I'd had a feeling … I saw her break cover and race for the sea. She was perfect! The dogs were at her heels now - just like the sign of the Whore & Hounds in Dyngvale - yes, she was naked, as she should be, and the sun was still above the hills and shining straight on her back. She had blood running down the backs of her legs. The front runners had had their teeth in her at some point but they had failed to bring her down and now they were at her again. Even as we watched, one leapt at her and bit, but slipped away. Another, a brachet, small but even more relentless, more unforgiving, got its jaws to her rump. It didn't have the weight by itself to pull her down, yet it dug in its teeth and hung on as she dragged it along behind her. She knew that if she could just get into the sea …

'Two men were with me, William and Fingall. We all raised our bows and let fly at her. Nothing. Again. Our last chance. One, we thought, went through her thigh. Another transfixed the brachet that had its teeth in her rump, and it fell away from her. With the arrow clear to be seen now in her leg, and the dying dog left thrashing about on the beach, she threw herself, she flew, across the shallows and into the sea - and as she turned, sitting in the water, to pull the arrow out, her legs up, before our eyes those legs became a silver tail and it was out of that tail that the arrow slid, not out of a leg at all.

'While they ran to fetch a boat, I shot my last arrow, but she was out of range. I ran for the arrow she had pulled out of her tail, but she had snapped it before she chucked it onto the beach. I held it to my nose. It smelt of fish. Then we rowed out after her.

'She seemed to be having trouble swimming because of the arrow wound or because of the goodly bites in her rump and the backs of her legs. What a tragedy about that dog! I didn't know whose it was, but it had been the pick of the pack that day.

'"On! On!" I hissed. "Hurry!" At last, he got the boat close enough for me to plunge a spear down into her, or so I thought, but the boat moved, or she moved. I tried again and again, desperate to kill her, for by now, although she was wounded, she was mocking me. Mocking me. Then William, who had been watching the sport with a grin while Fingall rowed, put his last shaft to his bow. She must have seen him. It was as if she had run out of patience with us - her with us! - for she suddenly upended like a porpoise, and was gone. The last we saw of her was her long tail golden in the setting sun. The arrow sailed harmlessly past it and lay floating on the sea like a marker; all that was left of my Great Hunt.'

And a loud, clear, voice from behind us said, 'Don't believe a word of it, Marian! All that stuff about mermaids and tails! And as for the smell of fish on that arrow - it had been in the sea! The water there in that part of the firth simply reeks of dead fish and seaweed. No, what Hugh really admires about the creature is not her fishiness, it's her sheer determination to survive. Which is what makes her such wonderful game, of course. You are Marian, aren't you?'

She was tall, as tall as me. Not particularly beautiful, unless you liked hair so flaming red it seemed it could only have been grown by a plant, and eyes greener than emeralds and full of power.

Sir Hugh, the womaniser, the bully, shrank like a spent penis in her presence.

'Ah, Margaret! Yes, this is indeed Marian. Come and sit down with us.'

So the introductions were made, with little formality, and I found that we were all on first-name terms. So different from

Spain; even from Paris and London.

'I heard that you were involved somehow in this "Great Hunt", Margaret.'

'Oh, I love it. Any kind of hunting.' She showed her teeth. 'Though I don't normally go after what few elphin and glaistig may still be around, and shelts and brownies and uriskin and so on, and nor would I normally permit Hugh to hunt them either, not north of the Firth, anyway. But this one is different.'

'She didn't drown,' breathed Phorca. 'She couldn't drown. And I will have her, one day. I don't care what or who she is: a fish, a hunted animal, the goddess Wul, the handmaid of the Queen of Elphame, I will have her.'

'The Queen of Elphame! Really, Hugh.' A good ten years his junior, she nevertheless always spoke to him as if to a foolish child ripe for a whipping.

But Phorca wasn't listening. 'To bend not one but five birch trees and leave them there with their heads hanging as a message to us - to me! - while she was being hunted for her life! What a creature! Perhaps she herself is the Queen of Elphame.'

Margaret snorted.

What was this about birches? I would ask Whin when I saw her. Tell her how impressed Hugh had been. If I saw her ... 'What happened then? Did she come ashore somewhere? Did anyone see her?'

Margaret answered: 'They think she came ashore in Sutherland, somewhere up on one of the great sand beaches around Dornoch or to the south of Loch Fleet. Word was brought to me from the ferry point, where Hugh and his men were waiting.'

Like good boys, she meant. She was purring. I had thought of her as a red wolf, but she was more a wildcat. A wulcat. Are there red wulcats? And do they purr? And are they safe when they are purring? Or at their most dangerous?

'I authorised Hugh to land and carry on the hunt, and rode down with a couple of my own dogs to join him.'

'On your own?'

'My friend Don Alfonso is staying at the castle but he didn't wish to come. He was after other prey, he said. So, yes, on my own.'

Don Alfonso? The man in black?

'You haven't seen her dogs,' smiled Phorca.

'My maid, and her maid, and my page, and a pair of men-at-arms, arrived this morning. They were late.' Those teeth again.

'And your fool?' Hugh asked. 'Is he here? I rather liked - '

'With a page-boy like this one, I don't need a fool. If you like *him*, you can have him.'

I wanted to know about Whin. 'Did you find any trace of her?'

'No. And now we await word from the look-outs I have posted all along the coast. They're to follow and harry her, but not to kill her. That's for me.'

'Me,' said Margaret. Her mouth was too big, and so were her teeth: she was a wolf, after all, like her father before her. 'If they don't lose her.'

I thought of Whin in the forest, and of Margaret in the forest. I feared the great forest, but they were at home there, each in her different way: one the prey, one the predator.

The Countess smiled at me. I smiled back.

She was lithe, she was supple and tough and graceful, yet somehow it was not her but Souad, I suddenly realised - Souad - with the small mouth and tiny teeth, it was Souad who had about her the aura of the cat - of the lynx we used to see sometimes at home when we rode out into the foothills of the high sierras.

Phorca, incensed, said, 'They won't lose her. I've told them: the men who lose her, lose their eyes. And the man who kills her, dies. Slowly.'

And I was sure that none of his men thought for one moment he might be bluffing. That nice fat smile was for the ladies.

Phorca was used to having his own way.

'Hugh,' I said, 'when were you born? What is your birthday?'

'My birthday?'

'She dabbles in astrology - do you not, my dear?'

'Somewhat more than "dabble", Margaret. I studied astronomy in Spain under Jewish and Moorish masters, and I studied astrology at the university in Paris. In London, I have cast horoscopes for, and read the palms of, some of the greatest in the land.'

'For instance?'

'For instance, Queen Anne and Joan of Kent.'

'Then you must read Margaret's palm and cast her horoscope,' laughed the fat Baron, 'for she is among the greatest in this land.'

'I am a Scorpio,' she said.

The same as me. Sometimes, still, I am taken by surprise. Not this time.

'The date?'

'I was born on St Margaret's Day.'

'Do you happen to know what time of day?'

'Yes, it was in the morning. My mother had been in labour all night.'

'Before or after sunrise? Do you know?'

'Does it make a difference?'

'Oh, yes.'

'Then guess. Surely it must be obvious, if it makes such a difference.'

Mars rules in the day house of Scorpio. 'Probably after sunrise,' I said.

She nodded, and smiled.

'Hugh?'

'I'm two weeks younger than Margaret - and seven years older - being born on St Andrew's Day, November 30th, 1355. What does that make me?'

'A Sagittarian.'

The same as Whin and Newt. Now that is interesting. And something else to look up later in my Almagest.

'What time of day, Hugh?'

'I've no idea. I suppose I could find out for you, if you're really interested. My nurse is no longer with us -' he crossed himself - 'but my mother is, and if she does not remember, there are one or two other old women doddering around still who might.'

'Now do, please, read my palm, Marian!' cried the Red Countess. 'I'm fascinated.'

I took her hands in mine. They were cool and slender. I laid them, palms up, on top of my own palms. Another Martial hand, like Souad's - in this case, what I expected. I concentrated … Then gazed into her eyes. The eyes of the Red Queen. She had ordered deaths while still a child. Had killed with her own hands. Should the opportunity present itself, she would kill Whin: Whin meant nothing, but a chance to best Hugh was not to be missed.

She had not, however, killed ben Youssef. Or anyone else, in the last month or so. That was quite clear.

As soon as we had eaten, I made my excuses and left. (She didn't eat like a wolf; on the contrary, she was very much the great lady, the Red Queen. He did, of course, eat like a pig.)

I hurried back to the inn, hoping to meet Raoul. I wanted him with me when I went out to the Skinner steading.

Instead, I found Jaufre waiting outside.

He gave me a passionate peck on each cheek and stood back from me, still holding my shoulders, gazing down into my eyes. *Down* into my eyes? Had he grown taller since Paris? Or had I grown shorter?

'I'm leaving for the north again this afternoon. I need to see Raoul. You're meeting him here?'

I nodded.

The way he was holding me pressed my breasts together. He squeezed a little tighter, playing, liking the effect.

I pushed his hands gently away.

'And how is the investigation going?' he asked, eyes wistful but voice under control.

'I am finding out all I can about ben Youssef, and those who knew him. This was no casual killing. He was either killed by someone who lives here -'

'Such as, for instance, Master Thorfinn Skinner.'

'Or by a visitor to the area, someone staying here openly - '

'Such as me.'

I gazed at him. 'Exactly.'

'Or by a secret visitor,' he carried on for me. 'A stranger no one knew was here.'

'Mm. Who came here for that purpose, to kill the Moor and leave, with no one the wiser. Not even the Moor, if he was shot - as I suspect - with an arrow from a distance.'

'But you don't really think it was that.'

'Someone unknown? No. Why? Do you?'

'He might have been mixed up in some secret activity - on behalf of, say, Coucy ...'

'But you have no evidence.'

'Only a suspicion. No concrete evidence.'

'And there is no evidence of any stranger being in the vicinity at the time. Apart from a certain rather Spanish or Italian-looking gentleman dressed all in black who will probably turn out to be Lady Margaret's friend, Don Alfonso.'

'Don Alfonso?'

'He's staying at Dunrobin.'

'Is he now? Well, I'll be spending a night at Dunrobin so I'll see what I can find out for you.'

I seemed to have recruited an unlikely - but very welcome - assistant.

'Don't go riding into danger, Jaufre.'

He laughed. 'Any Don Alfonso I can handle. Lady Margaret, however, *is* titillatingly dangerous - '

'Jaufre, this is serious. One murder has already occurred.'

'All right. So. What else do you have?'

'We have witnesses - '

'Of what? Not of the killing?'

'Unfortunately, no. But of your ride. How many times did you pass along that road, Jaufre? And at what times, roughly?'

'I went out to the farm midway between vespers and compline, and rode back into Tain with Bella soon afterwards, still before compline.'

'And then? You took her back to the farm? At what time?'

'I would have taken her back, but ... she ran away.' He looked as though he could still hardly believe it.

'Incroyable,' I murmured, but it was his conceit that was unbelievable. No, perhaps not, from a Leo. Was he a Leo, in fact? He must be. 'Are you a Leo, Jaufre?'

'Un Lion? Oui, bien sûr.' He grinned at me.

'And so? What happened? You washed your hands of her? You didn't ride out after her, looking for her?'

'I am a stranger here. How could I have found her if she didn't wish to be found?'

'True … Apart from Raoul and that Finlay MacKay, who else did ben Youssef know and spend time with?'

'He talked to everyone. But *en passant*, you know. And - ah yes: he knew Bella's master, the skinner.'

'He did?' This was new.

'Oh, not well, how should he? But I did see them talking together one morning - just along there, where Raoul is now with your two horses.'

I looked and saw Raoul coming towards us, leading my horse. He waved.

'And?' I said.

'It seemed quite a serious conversation - they had both dismounted - and I remember wondering what they could have to talk about. Then forgot it. Is it important?'

'It could be.' I smiled at Raoul as he came up to us. Raoul, dressed always in grey: so different from Jaufre. 'Raoul, *ça va?'*

What language did Thorfinn use with Bella?

As we rode out of the town a few minutes later, Raoul told me he had gone out to the Skinner steading. There, he had seen Bella from a distance, working outside the house. She had seemed well enough, and Skinner had been there with her, so he had not approached lest he cause more trouble.

Instead, he had taken La Pauvre's body to the local apothecary.

The man had not been able to help. It could have been the mussels in the soup - though that seemed unlikely if no one else who ate it was ill - or it could have been a poison extracted from some toxic plant such as the yew. 'Do you know the yew? Apparently it's not widespread up here, but … common enough.'

Oh, I knew it. And I knew what had caused the deaths of those other six dogs, as well. But was there any connection? That was Whin. This was - Bella?

He read my mind. 'No,' he said. 'Not Bella.'

'That soup was a weapon as deadly as any spear, Raoul, and it was aimed at you. I want you to be very careful what you eat from now on, and where you go. Don't go anywhere alone, and especially, don't go near Bella.'

'That is ridiculous.'

'Who else could have introduced poison into that soup? All right, don't go anywhere near Bella or Coll.'

'What you're suggesting is that Bella murdered ben Youssef and tried to murder me - that she might try again to murder me. Or might murder someone else, for that is what she is, what she does. But you don't know her, Mariana. She is …'

'Beautiful,' I said, gently.

He was about to agree, but then he looked at me. 'Don't mock me,' he said.

'I'm not mocking you, Raoul. We are just talking, as we used to talk - '

'We are not "just talking". This is real, this is life - and she is too beautiful to be a murderess. Too good.'

'Why? The beautiful is the good? Go back to Paris. Study philosophy this time.'

He stopped his horse, and I stopped mine. He gazed at me, and I saw all the sadness of the intervening years, culminating in this. 'I wish I could. Would you come with me? You could be my Heloïse? You have no maniac uncles, have you? I mean I shouldn't like to be castrated.'

'No, I don't think so. Only Ferchard - Farquhar -'

'Farquhar! Yes -'

'I can't imagine him doing anything like that.'

'I can. We'd have to be very careful. Couldn't we leave him here?'

'Oh, Raoul. Do you remember how you used to sing:

I'll follow the wild geese, my love,
Till they bring me back to you ... ?

I always thought it sounded very Scottish.'

'I followed the wild geese, my love - flew north, north, north with them one sunny day. They brought me back to you.'

'Oh no, not to me. But it was good, wasn't it. And it was something we did, not simply something we once were and have now outgrown.'

'Accomplishments, too, pass away.' Oh, he was so sad.

'So beauty is not different in kind, it simply passes more quickly than deeds; but they too, like flowers, are ephemeral.'

'It is simply a matter of emphasis. Like the difference between you and Bella.'

'What difference?'

'The difference between you and Bella, between Bella and all others. Between you and all others. Mariana, you are beautiful, even more so now than when you were in Paris; yet when I describe you I don't think of, don't mention, your beauty first. When I describe Bella I do mention her beauty first. Only in post-script, as an after-thought, would I mention her sweetness and innocence; her sheer harmlessness. The first thing, the key thing, about her is her beauty. Beauty is what Bella is - and that is what makes, what has always made, her life so difficult.'

The sun had gone in. There was a cold wind from the east blowing in our faces. It didn't look as if it was going to rain: it looked, and felt, quite suddenly, as if it was going to snow! In July?

I was cold. And not only cold but jealous. Hurt. And biased against tall blondes with the bodies of Nordic goddesses and faces men would die for. Kill for. I said, 'And when you describe me, what is it you mention first?'

He didn't hesitate, didn't need to think. 'It is your interest in the arcane, your passion for truth, your care for the wronged. Bella is an angel; you are a fighter, a leader, one of the great shining lights on the side of the angels.'

'That's ridiculous.'

'It is not ridiculous. Look how your presence lightens the darkness up here.'

'I think I would rather be … not just beautiful, no, but - just an angel, an ordinary angel. Like Bella.'

'No, you wouldn't. For if you were, who would help Bella? Who would help you?'

Who would help Souad? That dark beauty too looked like an angel. I was far from sure that she was one, but I was sure that she had no knowledge of her master's murder.

Phorca, though? He had the motive, he had the means - he had a private army - and he had no scruples: in fact I was quite sure he enjoyed killing. Yet there was not one shred of evidence against him.

Skinner himself could easily have turned back, committed the murder, and put to sea again. And he may well have had a motive too, or thought he had.

On Souad and Baron Hugh I would suspend judgement until I had looked up their birth dates in the Almagest; in neither case had reading their palms helped me much, though Souad did seem to have more potential for passion and violence within her than I had suspected.

'I must tell you, Raoul, *mon amour*, that at this moment all - well, almost all - the evidence points towards Bella: one, she murdered ben Youssef because she was having an affair with him or because - and this is more likely - he knew about an affair she was having with somebody else, and was planning to inform her master; was perhaps on his very way to inform him. After all, he was a master himself, a slave-owner, a good Muslim and a believer in the absolute sanctity of the harem. And Skinner would have killed her, or as good as killed her.

'Two, she attempted to murder my good friend Raoul. Why? Because he knows something? I would say now that Jaufre is in danger, as well as you. And it is also fairly obvious that Master Thorfinn Skinner can only hope to survive the next few days if Bella doesn't. And if Coll doesn't. And I must say that on this count at least I agree with them - so let us add me to that list.'

'And me: if he has laid a finger on Bella, I will kill him myself. Which will save you and Bella and Coll - and Souad - the trouble.'

We were approaching the Skinner steading, and I was expecting Kari to appear at any moment.

Raoul heard her before I did, or rather a voice which he took to be hers, calling softly from among the bushes at the side of the road. But when we got down off our horses to investigate, I saw that it was not Kari at all.

'Whin?'

'Call me Kari, my lady.'

'Kari? Ah. Kari.'

'Does this one understand us?'

'No.'

'Kari's gone. Pretending to be me. She let herself be glimpsed swimming north. But she's gone south. She's not to come ashore till she is south of the Cromarty Firth. On Black Isle, in the heart of the Millbuie Forest, we know some people and she can get some clothes. Then she'll go through the forest to the head of the firth, and on to Dyngvale. I told her to tell your man, Sir Farquhar, at Master Robert's house, that you sent her. I hope you don't mind, my lady.'

Mind?

She looked up at me. She was so small. She was tired and the suffering was beginning to show, but her eyes were still the same beautiful blue-green. 'And I would like to stay with you now, for a while at least, my lady.'

'Of course, yes. We'll talk later. Listen, is the skinner there, do you know?'

She nodded.

'You're sure?'

'Oh yes. He's been skinning a walrus he brought back with him. Kari and I were watching him earlier, before the hunters came by and she had to leave. She was undressed and ready. We knew they were coming and what we would do.'

'You can tell me about it afterwards, Whin, and I'll explain what I'm up to here. For now, though, I want you to stay with Raoul, and wait for me. Keep an eye on the gate. I may come back up here and fetch you, or I may have to set off in the other direction, towards Balintore, on my own. If I do, bring Raoul and follow me there.'

I repeated all this in French to Raoul, who, of course, had no Gaelic. 'Let yourself be led by Whin. She knows the way and can make sure you're not seen by anyone.'

'Whin? Ah.' He smiled down at her. 'Whin. *Je suis enchanté, demoiselle.*' He gently took - and kissed - her hand. She gazed up at him in awe. It was the only time I ever saw Whin at a complete loss for words. It was probably also the only time in her life when she was treated as she should at all times have been treated, for she truly was a pearl among her people; as even Phorca, the porcine Baron Hugh, was beginning to realise. The difference was that whereas for Hugh that meant she had to be hunted and killed and collected, for Raoul it meant that she was to be worshipped.

The gate was open. At my approach, Wolf-bane came charging out, barking and yammering. He had on a spiked collar today, like the ones the wolfhounds wear in France, and seemed very pleased with himself, but as neither the mare nor I showed any fear - I thought of him as Butterfly-bane and smiled to myself - he soon stopped his noise and merely pranced around us, sniffing at my booted foot and the gloved hand I held down to him.

The skinner appeared next. 'Ah, it's you, Lady Marian.'

I dismounted, and he eyed the three of us - me, the mare, and his supposedly vicious dog - sourly. 'You seem to have some - ah - influence over animals.'

'As you are well aware, Master Skinner, I have been here before. No doubt he recognises me.'

'And I asked you not to come here again.'

'No, you told me not to come here again - in your absence. I should like to put some more questions to Bella, and to Coll. I also have some questions for you, if you wouldn't mind.'

'On whose authority?'

'On the Bailie's authority. Baron Hugh of Foulis is also supporting my enquiries, as are Countess Euphemia of Ross and Countess Margaret of Sutherland.'

As I had hoped, the last two names did intimidate him. As they would intimidate anyone who knew - or knew of - the good ladies, the one so young still and the other so old.

'Well, you had better come in.'

I tied the mare up by the gate and he ushered me in, closing the gate behind me.

'I can tell you right now that Coll is not available. Bella may be, though she still feels sorry for herself. I had to chastise her, you see.'

I saw.

One of her eyes was black and her lips and face were swollen. She had trouble walking, though she tried not to show it.

Thorfinn and I sat down. Bella remained standing there awkwardly in front of us.

'My lady? I didn't think you would come back.'

'I said I would. You've been in trouble, Bella.'

'Yes, my lady.'

I wasn't sure how much of this, if anything, Thorfinn understood. I spoke to him now in English, to see, including him in the conversation. 'What had she done, Master Thorfinn, to warrant this?'

'Are you questioning my judgement, or my right to chastise her?'

'I wasn't, no, I was simply asking; but what is your right, exactly? I understood that she was your son's wife - his widow, now.'

Bella was gazing longingly at me: she knew I understood nothing of the sort.

'And if she were? In certain circumstances - these, for example - I would have a right, a duty, to chastise my daughter-in-law.' He paused, and looked at me; then looked at her.

I did not speak. Nor did Bella. She would not have dared.

'In fact, she *belonged* to my son, who had her from her previous owner, all properly documented. And now she belongs to me.'

We both looked at her.

I loosened my cloak, letting some air to my throat. It was hot with the fire burning in the hearth. 'What circumstances were you referring to, Master Thorfinn?'

'I said if she were my daughter-in-law. As it is, I don't need special circumstances.'

'Of course, I understand that. I am not stupid, Master Thorfinn. I have girls - and a woman - and men - who belong to me. I need no excuse to have one of them chastised. Nevertheless, I believe you were referring to the special circumstances that apply in this case - this murder case - and I should like to know what you had in mind.'

'She has been playing the whore, my lady, for whore she is, whore she was when my son bought her - literally - and whore she always will be. Playing the whore with some Frenchman.'

Raoul? 'You know the identity of this Frenchman?'

'Oh yes, I know. He is their captain. One le Fou. And fool he is, for I will kill him.'

Bella's face was white beneath the bruises. Her eyes were cast down. She would not meet my gaze.

'Master Thorfinn, let us solve the first murder before you commit another.'

'And what do you mean by that? Are you suggesting that I committed the first?'

Yes, of course. 'No, of course not. But where were you when the first murder occurred?'

'When did the first murder occur?'

Good question.

'It seems that you put to sea early in the evening. You did not return?'

He shook his head.

Interesting. Is he shy of outright lies?

I persisted: 'There was a brief storm. It did not drive you back?'

Again he shook his head. 'That was no storm. That was Coll playing games. She has paid for it.'

'Is Coll also yours, to do with as you will?'

He nodded.

'And you have.'

He nodded.

'And did this include branding her? Rebranding her?'

'You know much about us, my lady. Some would say too much.'

'Yes or no?'

'Not yet. But it will.'

'So you did not come ashore again that evening. Nor did you come home the next day. Or the next. Where were you all that time, Master Thorfinn?'

'It has nothing to do with the matter in hand, but I was hunting a walrus. I had seen it several times, always on different beaches and always headed south. This time I was determined to hunt it down.'

'And did you catch it? Kill it?'

'Finally, yes, my lady. You want to see it? I've been skinning it.'

'No.'

'Squeamish? But I wouldn't like to think you doubted me. Bella? Lead the way.'

We went round to the back of the house, and there it was: a mound of raw flesh. To one side, spread out, lay the skin, bloody side up, and next to that, two huge tusks, which had been hacked out, roots and all, not sawn off at the base as I should have expected.

'Beautiful, eh?'

Beautiful? I looked round for weapons.

'I'd give you one of the tusks, my lady - both - to commemorate your visit, but ... I am a poor man. I cannot afford such noble gestures.'

There were the various knives that he had used, presumably, during the flensing process, and there was a large spear with a cord attached. A harpoon. That could hardly have been the weapon used to kill ben Youssef.

'Was it in the water or on the beach when you killed it, Master Thorfinn?'

'On the beach, my lady.'

'And how - I mean how did you get it back? How did you get it into your boat? It's enormous.'

He laughed at my simplicity. 'I waited for the tide to come in and half float the beast, then towed it back. Not easy, but - I had no choice. It was dead. It's easier if it is only wounded.'

And so much more fun, I thought.

'All right, I've seen enough. I believe you, Master Thorfinn.'

I led the way back into the house.

'You stay out here,' he ordered Bella. 'Make a start on scraping that skin.'

Back inside the house, we both sat down again in the same places.

I said, 'So you know nothing of the riders who went back and forth between your steading and the town of Tain that night?'

'I won't say I know nothing. I usually know something at least of what is going on. But ask Bella. She knows.'

'She says she doesn't.'

'She is a liar as well as a whore. And ask the Frenchman, if you can get to him before I do.'

'Will you call her?'

He nodded, then changed his mind and said, 'She'll be all bloody. We'll go out to her.'

She was indeed all bloody, right up above her elbows. And her legs too, for her feet were bare and her skirt was caught up out of the way between her thighs. Beneath the blood, her legs bore the bruises left by Thorfinn's belt.

'Bella?'

'Yes, my lady?' She sat back on her haunches. I noticed the gold anklet she was still wearing, now smeared with blood. She can't have had that on her when Thorfinn's son bought her. Slaves are always sold bare of all adornment.

'Who gave you that anklet? Master - what was your son's name, Master Thorfinn?'

'Harald.'

'Master Harald?'

'No, my lady.'

'Then - Master Thorfinn?'

Thorfinn laughed

'No, my lady. I had it on when I came to Master Harald.'

'But - '

'My son was a fool. He bet his boat - my boat - against her as she stood. And won her as she stood, gold and all! And when he was dying, his last thoughts were for her: would I swear to care for her - by Hel I swore - and never to remove the gold anklet from her while she lived. I swore again, swore that too by Hel.'

Then *he* had a very good motive for killing *her*. That gold anklet was worth more than she was. No, on second thoughts, perhaps it wasn't. I sighed.

The skinner misunderstood my sigh. 'He was always a fool, but not that great a fool. She must have put a spell on him.' He looked at her, distaste etched round the corners of his mouth and nose, lust on his lips and in his eyes. And she, who had been gazing up at us, wondering what we were saying - we were speaking Gaelic - dropped her eyes in confusion.

I said, in English, 'I see. Well now, listen, Bella.' She looked up at me. 'Last time I was here, I asked you about the night of the murder.' She dropped her gaze again. 'I will ask you once more, but this time I want the truth.'

'Yes, my lady. You asked me last time if I had gone out and I said I hadn't. That wasn't true. I did go out. My master knows, so I may as well tell you. Jaufre - '

'Jaufre!' Skinner spat. 'Call him le Fou! Captain le Fou!'

'Captain le Fou came after my master had left - '

'Left? You mean in his boat?'

'Yes, my lady.'

'You saw him go?'

'Yes, my lady. I carried his things down to the boat and helped him load them. I threw the rope to him as he left.'

'I see. Well, go on.'

'I came back to the house, and soon afterwards, Jaufre - the Captain - arrived.'

'Was Coll here? Did she see him?'

'No, Master Thorfinn keeps her in the byre, here, at the back, these days, since he - since I - '

'That's enough of that, Bella. Stick to the story, as I told you.'

'Yes, master. Captain le Fou didn't want to stay here, my lady. He wanted to take me into the town, to - to - '

'A tavern?'

'"To-to-to" lie with her, she means, my lady.'

'No, my lady. People would see us, would tell Master Thorfinn, so we went to his lodgings -

'Like a bitch on heat.'

'Then we came back here and ...'

'And?'

'And that was all, my lady. He went again, on his own, back to Tain.'

'I don't believe you, Bella. Everything sounded true up to where you said he brought you back here and that was all. If he brought you back here, then that was not all. But I don't think he did bring you back here.'

She was a Taurus. She was cautious, could be a liar; but a killer? Such a killer, such a crime?

I needed to talk to her alone, not like this; alone, and with her hands clean, so that I could hold them and study them and look into her eyes and find out all about her.

I did not say goodbye to her. I wanted her to feel my disappointment and my anger. I walked away with the skinner and left her there squatting barefoot on the skin with the scraper in her hands, gazing after us.

He took me to the gate, and lifted me onto my horse. I smiled down at him. 'Master Thorfinn, where did you learn your English?'

'In my youth, I was a roamer. I spent many years in the south, the far south, on the Channel coast mostly, doing this and that for - what harm will it do, you knowing now all these years later? - for Coucy, when Coucy was the Earl of Bedford and an Englishman, and son-in-law to King Edward.'

Well, well, well. I rode off along the track that led to Fearn and so to Balintore and Kattar-bol. And Mouraig, my grandmother.

As I rode I wondered what Raoul and Whin would do. Would he ride openly, while she scampered through the woods alongside him, keeping out of sight? Or would he take her up on his horse with him - behind him - or even in front of him, on the saddle, in his lap? I liked that picture very much.

And that was what I saw when I looked round for them after I had passed Loch Eye and the Skinner steading was out of sight. I stopped and waited, and we rode together down to the other coast, the open coast, the open sea.

FOURTEEN

The Open Sea Awaiting

The skinner's threat did not impress Raoul: Jaufre would not be back, he said, till Sunday evening. He would tell him then. And knowing Jaufre, he would immediately go looking for Master Thorfinn.

'Perhaps we had better not tell him,' I said.

We were squeezed into Mouraig's little house, Raoul and I, and Mouraig. Whin, having told us, very briefly, her story, had gone out to sleep in the herb garden at the back. We were cosy and warm, but we were not happy.

Raoul was worried about Bella.

I was worried about Kari.

Mouraig agreed with Whin that Kari would be fine. She was young, she was fast, she was clever; and she had had the best teacher in all Alba. Whatever happened, she would land on her feet. She had at least some of the nine lives of the cat and she had the seven lives of the mermaid. She had the blessing of Wul. And Colum had said of her, St Columba himself (for had she not been born on Colum's Day?):

A blessing on you, my child:
The blessing of the open sea awaiting you,
When the din of people, the hunting and shouting,
The fighting and the blood become too much.

I remembered her hands, and how they related to her star sign, Gemini. The same sign as Raoul. She did seem to have been born lucky. I couldn't see anything bad happening to her at this juncture other than, or worse than, the break-up of her family: and even that had been lucky for her in some ways.

But what about poor Sasunn Bella? I had hardly been able to prevent Raoul from galloping straight back to the rescue when he learned what had happened to her. Finally, though, he had agreed to wait until morning and then go with me: but this time he was coming in, he said. And I said yes. Better with me in the morning than on his own at night.

Now he broke the silence. 'You still suspect her, I know you do.'

'She's bound to,' said Mouraig. Her French was still quite good, even after all these years. 'The girl was there, and the girl has been lying to her. *Soit raisonable, mon cher.'*

'I am being reasonable, madame! You say she has been lying. But if so, why? To protect someone? Who? Who would she protect?'

'She would protect you, unless I am much mistaken,' said Mouraig.

I said: 'The best thing we can do for everyone is to discover the truth. If she thinks she is protecting you, then she must imagine you were involved in the crime. What possible motive might you have had - as she sees it?'

'I don't see that I - '

'Listen. I'm not asking about some motive you might have had for wishing ben Youssef dead. I'm asking about the motive Bella might have *imagined* you had. Did you ever speak of ben Youssef to her?'

'*Non!* I have hardly ever spoken to her at all! I simply saw her and loved her, and started writing poems once more. I hadn't written any for a long time …'

I did blush this time. He was not looking at me, his head was down, but Mouraig saw everything.

'It was Jaufre who chased her. You know what he is. Just for sport. After he found that the Moorish girl was unattainable.'

'But he preferred her - the Moorish girl.' Mouraig wanted to be quite clear about this.

'*Oui, madame*.'

'Then we have a motive of a kind for Jaufre le Fou. Perhaps she thinks she is protecting him.'

I was unconvinced. 'Her story doesn't protect him. *Au contraire*. It is not true, and it brings him back out to the steading, then has him leaving the steading on his own at almost exactly the time of the murder, so far as we can judge.'

We all sat in silence for a moment, digesting this. Outside, I could hear the waves pounding on the beach. The weather was getting worse, the sea getting rougher. Would Kari really be all right out there in a storm? But the mind is a strange thing: I heard myself say, 'Coll. She might protect Coll.'

'It wasn't Coll,' said Mouraig. 'Though the mutilation could have been.'

'Yes, but what if Bella knows about the mutilation and assumes that Coll committed the murder as well?'

'That's true,' said Raoul. 'Or of course she could be protecting the skinner.'

'Why?'

'Why not? Look how he has beaten her. And did you not tell us you formed the impression they had agreed on the story beforehand?'

I nodded. 'So we have Bella and the skinner as suspects, either one possibly protecting the other for whatever reason. And Jaufre. Because he was there. But was he?'

'Whin was there, too.'

'That's ridiculous.'

'It's a great deal less ridiculous than including Bella's name on your list of suspects. Whin could kill a man; Bella could not.'

I looked at him and thought about it, then turned to Mouraig and spoke to her in Gaelic. 'Mouraig, talking of Whin - and Tinkman - you may be able to explain one or two things I need to know. First, the name "Yewel".'

'It's an old Elpin name, and it's his real name. He's been called Tinkman now for so long even Whin forgets and snaps her fingers at him, but she knows, and I know, that really he is Yewel the sheltiman. The nearest thing they have to a sheltiman these days. Oh, there are teachers and healers and masters of the ancient lore like the old sheltimen - like the old druids - left still in the Faroes and Iceland and Greenland, and maybe in Sheltland itself, though I doubt it, but Tinkman - Yewel - is the nearest thing to a sheltiman they have here. At least he knows how to swerve off into the shelti-world when he is healing, or when he wants to find the answer to a hard question.'

'And does he use some kind of mushroom?'

'You did find out a lot in a short time! Yes, a mushroom we call flysvamp. Amanita, you would call it, I expect.'

'Ah. I've heard of that … And they dry it?'

'Aye, they hang them up by their stalks to dry in the sun, and then they store them. Tinkman must store them in some special place he has. Or special places. I'm sure he doesn't carry them around with him.'

'Would Whin have access to them? She would? Yes, of course, why not … And used wrongly, or if too much is taken, what would happen? They're toxic, aren't they?'

'Oh, yes. There are various different types and - I don't know, I'm no expert, you'd have to ask Tinkman himself - they would produce different results. I think it would have to be taken in quite large quantities to be fatal.'

'Tinkman, though, would know how to control it?'

'Of course. He is, as I said, a sheltiman, and that means an expert on herbs not only for healing but to induce dreams and visions and - and other alternative states.'

Raoul was getting impatient. 'Why is the *tinklair* not on the list of suspects? As I say, she was there and she could kill, unlike poor Bella.'

'Why don't we include the Queen of Elphame?' said Mouraig, smiling. 'She was there too, by all accounts. And she could kill a man.'

I looked at her in amazement. Was she serious?

'Sweign Pigsticker saw her, for one.'

'What is this *reine*?' asked Raoul.

'La Reine de Faërie, who is said to -'

'Ah, like Morgan - Morgana - in the stories, Morgan le Fay!' His eyes lit up for the first time that day.

'Exactly. They say she rides out at night - '

'Not only at night,' put in Mouraig. 'I've seen her, or one I took to be her, in bright sunshine. She wears a white cloak with a hood and rides on a horse and is always followed by one or more hounds. Some say the horse is a white one and the hounds are white too, and huge, with red ears. But that was not the case when I saw her.'

'If it was her,' I said.

'Who else could it have been?'

True. She knew everyone around here.

Raoul said, 'Those white hounds, the ones with the red ears, I have read of them. They are the hounds of Hel. Not Hell the place, Hel the goddess. In Normandie, and up here I am sure, the men of the north, the old men at least, and the old women, still remember her. Men with names like Thorfinn.'

Mouraig snorted. 'Remember her? Thorfinn still believes in her. Still worships her, in so far as he is capable of worshipping anything. And he's not the only one.'

I stared at her. 'You don't think - '

'I don't think it has anything to do with the murder and mutilation of the Moor. I still believe that was the work of Sir Hugh of Foulis Castle. Like le Fou, he was enamoured of this girl Souad; unlike le Fou, he is a Scottish baron, and unaccustomed to being told No. Whatever a man like him wants, he takes. Killing even one of his peers would mean little to him; killing a peasant, nothing; and killing a foreigner, a Muslim, less than nothing. It would be his pleasure. If the foreigner stood between him and the object of his lust ...'

'Yes, you're right, Mouraig. But if it was him, how could we ever prove it?'

'Publicly hand the girl over to him, then wait for him to start bragging about how he had arranged it, done it all, himself.'

'It's too easy.'

'You mean she would agree to it?'

'I mean, as a theory it is too easy. It leaves too many things unexplained. No, I'm quite sure Skinner and Bella are hiding something, and I'm going back there in the morning to find out what. I also intend to see Coll.'

The fire was dying down. We were full of good salmon; and I had drunk my share too of *uisge beatha*, "the water of life". I could talk no longer. I fell asleep on Raoul's shoulder, listening to Mouraig telling him something about a Frenchman she had known when she was young ... But in the night it was not of Frenchmen that I dreamed. It was the story Whin had told us earlier, before she slept, the story of the Great Hunt, that came back to me. At first I thought that in my dream [I knew I was dreaming] I was Whin ...

I had guddled a trout for Yewel. [Tinkman. But "guddled"? I didn't even know that word. Nor did I know how Whin/I had managed to immobilise it just by tickling it, but that's what we did, then scooped it up suddenly and threw it out onto the bank. I had seen bears scoop them out like that in Spain; she/I smiled - we had seen bears do it right here, by the Falls of Riga. "Riga"?] I had cooked the trout over a tiny fire - I still had the makings, though for how long this time? I had fed him.

I ate the rest myself, with some watercress. I saw some wild roses and got up and plucked and ate them, disturbing a grey-muzzled fox that had been lying watching me curiously. Tinkman couldn't eat roses or cress. The hornies had broken all his front teeth. ["hornies"?] - they'd probably done that first, punched him a bit - Tinkman with his hands bound, of course - before they gave him the whipping. They? That Hel's-spawn Master Kenneth, the curse of Mour on him. And when I saw his mouth bleeding later, I assumed he had bitten his tongue. He has, I see now, he's bitten it badly, his teeth have gone right though part of it. They can't have noticed or they would have cut at least that part out, if not the whole tongue.

I strip down to my cutty semmit, the short green smock that all my kind [her kind: but *it is my body*] make and dye and wear under the kirtles or skirts we get from women in the towns and villages. I listen. No one. Only the old tod. ["tod"?] What does he want? I pull my cutty semmit off my shoulders, let it slide down, then step out of it. I slip into the water, swim along beneath the surface. Wondering. Trying not to panic. After all, I have studied dreams. I have even taken part in shared dreams. I should not be panicking. I should be observing myself in the dream, I should be calm, detached. I should, but ... I come up out of the water, cool and refreshed. A roe buck is browsing just out of Tinkman's reach. He couldn't catch it anyway.

I hear hounds baying in the distance.

Is it for me?

The roe buck looks up and listens then carries on munching, unconcerned.

I glance at the tod. He gives me a look of disgust and trots away among the trees, apparently intent on putting the greatest possible distance between us.

I don't blame him. The hunt is for me.

'Gho! Gho!' Tinkman glubs, his half-severed tongue unable to focus on the broken teeth and swollen gums.

I pull my cutty semmit back on, determined not to lose that if I can avoid it, they're so hard to replace. An old kirtle I can always beg: the women find it shameful that I should show my legs.

'Gho! Gho!' [But what is he doing here? He should be on the Black Isle, not here at the Falls of Riga with me. This is different. Then I am not dreaming, I am being hunted - hunted in earnest.]

'Gho! You are the becht of women - the only woman! May Wul gho with you - an' may you be lughier in your necht man!'

My next man? I make the sign of AN-herself over him, and run.

I run lightly, easily, I find. I run along the path between the bushes till I am well clear of him before I slip back into the water - a wide, deep pool, here - and swim to the other side. Then I head north, settling into the long, steady lope of the hunted everywhere.

The sun moves higher above the trees.

I decide to confuse the hounds a little. I can't hear them yet, but they are coming. When I do hear them, I will have no time to do anything but run. I shin up a young birch, one of many all growing close to each other. As I near the top, it begins to bend under my weight. It comes close to another birch and I spring onto that one, climb up till it too bends then spring to another and climb up that. And so on. Seven times. On the eighth tree, the tallest, I ride the crest of it all the way down to the ground, then leap off and run to the edge of a lochan. Still no sound. I slide quietly in, careful not to disturb the two coots feeding peacefully out on the water. I relax. Cool down. Then come out again at the same spot and run back to the last tree, the one I swung right to the ground on. I intend to go back up it and repeat the process in reverse, but - I frigged it too well. The poor thing is hanging there, limp, quite unclimbable; and its seven brothers are also bowing to me, pointing droopily: MARIANA, they whisper in the breeze, MARIANA PASSED THIS WAY, MARIANA DID THIS TO US … A mistake, but so what? I smile to myself. Let them read it as an omen, a warning. In what other way can they interpret it? Childish, time-wasting folly? Not while I am being hunted for my life. Yet that's what it was.

Dancing lightly, I make my way back along my track till I come to a ditch full of nettles, then jump straight down into it without touching the edges. The stinging I hardly notice at the time, but I suppose it acts as a goad, keeps me moving, twitching, squirming, as I snake along on my belly under the nettles.

The ditch becomes a narrow burn and I find myself out in the open suddenly, slithering over pebbles and mud and through shallow water down to the Sgitheach, which is wider, and a little deeper, so I stand now and run up it, but still keep to the water.

A dog barks at me.

I sit down on the bank and it comes to me. I quiet it. A shepherd's dog. But has the shepherd seen me? He's down there to the south, so I come out of the stream now and head north to Glen Glass, where the stream is bigger, a river, with willows and alders along both sides leaning out over the water. Should I go up it to Loch Glass? Or carry on north, over the hill, to Loch Mouri? Or go down now, to the firth? I can see the firth, with Black Isle opposite me and Nigg in the distance. The tide is coming back in again now, a fast one, sweeping up over the empty mud-flats even as I watch.

So. Which? The afternoon is wearing on and I am tiring. There'll be people if I go downstream, none probably upstream. But if the chase goes on upstream as far as Loch Mouri, I'll have little or no cover, no hope of escaping. Down below, though, I can take to the sea.

But I must first survive until nightfall.

Nightfall?

I cross the Glass and run parallel to it, some way above and to the north of it.

I run and I run.

And run.

I trip and fall, pick myself up again.

And run. Mind blank now, exhausted.

Run and run, hour after hour.

Run …

Run …

I fall again - and lie there - just for a moment I tell myself - hear the hounds on my track, faint, but excited, up in the distance behind me. A good thing I do, or I might have slept. I get up and stretch, and trot on, heading on up to a bothie I notice rather than down to the river. And this time I am lucky. There is no man here, only a cuddy, an old donkey with a nice smile. I swing up onto him and urge him down into the trees, hoping I haven't been sighted by the hunters. Is the Red Countess among them? But why is she - why are they - hunting *me*?

I come to a steading. The hounds are louder now, but they sound confused. I remember the birches I left so sorry-looking when I was young and fit and full of life and I smile. Now, a whole day later, a whole life-time later, the sun is going down, my sun, and I am an old woman and can go no further.

There - a midden. That will do. Even if I never come up again, how much better than the hounds, than Phorca's fat, smug, foolish face. I put one leg up in front of me, then the other, my feet flat on the cuddy's soft warm back, then stand up. I balance, and as he ambles by the midden, I drop straight down into the water and refuse and ordure of all kinds which fill the pit and form a great heap over it, slide down through the smooth cool slime and sharp scratching bits that must be twigs or feathers - and there are thorns - fragments of bone perhaps - and rotting flesh? - slide down into it with gratitude and disgust, and stay still.

Nothing moves.

Nothing.

Till I move. The donkey, if he is still there, still waiting and wondering, if he is watching, sees the tip of a nose, two nostrils, covered in brown slime. Nothing else.

I hope he is not one to stand and stare; for there they stay, that nose, those bubbling nostrils - I can't help that - until the silence is broken by the shouts and barking of the hunt, when they are pulled, imperceptibly (I hope), back down under again.

When I can stay down no longer, I let my whole head up and out - silently - and listen.

The birdsong is normal. The hunt has gone.

Now what?

At least I have rested a little.

I stand up, covered with grits and bits and slime. Now the cutty semmit will have to go. I pull the shoulders down, then ease it off my body, pushing it down my legs with my feet and trampling it into the bottom of the midden. I look down at myself. I look more like a pig than Phorca ever did.

All I need is some piglets to feed.

Master Brodie would enjoy this scene, too.

I climb out, run down to the river to wash. Stop myself on the edge of the water. No. It's the perfect camouflage. They won't see me. They won't even be able to smell me.

It's filthy, it stinks, but it's marvellous.

I set off, running faster, down through the forest towards the firth. The firth!

But there are the hounds. They are on to me. They know. I take to the water again, come out the other side, run for a while, dive in and swim under water a while, come up the same side, clean now, I notice, and naked, and wet. And run, and run, and run ...

But I am sleeping as I run, and suddenly - there are people, people pointing, people chasing, people laughing, calling, shouting, LOOK! THE QUEEN OF ELPHAME! LOOK-AT-HER LOOK! THE QUEEN! LOOK-AT-THE-HOUNDS! THE HOUNDS! THE QUEEN! LOOK-AT-HER LOOK-AT-HER! LOOK! THE QUEEN! THE QUEEN! THE QUEEN!

I woke. It was night still. Mouraig was holding my head on her lap.

I was soaked

'That's not river water,' she said. 'You're sweating.'

I looked up at her. 'Were you with me?'

'Some of the time. I left you when you jumped into the midden.'

I laughed.

'I woke up. A few minutes later you seemed to be getting very upset, so I woke you too. What was happening?'

'I was running naked like a hind or a whore or - and everyone was shouting and pointing and chasing after me, and …'

'What were they shouting?'

'Look at the Queen - the Queen of - '

'Elphame?'

'Yes.'

She smiled. 'Let me find you some dry things to change into.'

I looked round in the light of the small lamp she had lit. Raoul was sleeping on the floor wrapped in a blanket and some kind of fur - it looked like a bearskin. He was snoring. Perhaps he was a bear in his dream.

When she came close again, I said, 'Who undressed me last night? Put these things on me?'

'Oh - we did. I understood that he was - or had been - your husband - more or less. And when I saw how gentle he was with you - you were no help at all, you were like a dead thing - and how charming he was to me - I could understand your terrible jealousy of the Sasunn slave-girl, what's-her-name. I would be broken-hearted too, in your place.'

What could I say?

FIFTEEN

A Hole For A Hole

I woke again.

I looked around.

Raoul was still asleep.

The dream. Only a dream?

Mouraig was down on the beach - I could see her through the open door, sitting on the enormous cat-skin she used to keep the chill out of her bones. She was meditating. Or maybe just gazing out to sea. The weather was better. I wanted to meditate on the beach for a while too.

But first I had to make sure about that dream. About Whin.

I went out and round to the back to talk to her, and met her coming to the front, still half-asleep. She wanted to lie in the sun, just as Kari had that first day.

I walked back with her, sat down beside her. She was so quiet, so peaceful; so able to sleep anywhere, any time.

'Whin?' I said.

She opened her eyes, looked up at me.

'Whin, are you - you - this morning? Are you Whin?'

She looked at me.

'There is nothing of - of me - in you?'

'You have lost part of yourself, my lady?'

'No … it's not that. I had a dream last night in which I was you, and - '

'Was it the hunt, my lady? Were you being hunted?'

I nodded dumbly. Helplessly.

'It was? For a while, when I was about to give up for the first time - when I nearly slept - I was not alone. There were two of us. And only so, only because you were there with me, was I able to go on and on, even when that Hel's-spawn dog, that brachet - had its teeth in me. We were lucky there, though, at the end, weren't we? To reach the sea, I mean.'

'Not "we": I wasn't there then.'

'You were. Perhaps you just haven't remembered that part yet - dreamt it yet. You left me when I left them. I swam away fast and when we were alone out on the waves, suddenly I noticed that I was alone: you'd gone. You remember the seal that came up and took an interest in us? In me? No? No, you'd gone by then. She came with me across the firth and kept watch while I slept somewhere off Embo. I was never alone.'

'You slept on the sea?'

'There were men on the beaches, keeping watch.'

'For you?'

She nodded.

'I was there when you bent the trees - '

'And when I was nearly caught, and doubled back - '

'And rode on the donkey - '

'The old cuddy, aye. And when I jumped into the midden.'

'Oh yes! And I put out my nose, like this - to breathe - just my nose, and when they came I had to go back under and stay under, thinking I'd need to breathe, but I didn't, I didn't, not till they'd gone, and then I stood up and it was so disgusting, I ...'

'You keep saying "I", my lady, now, not "we". And you showed me with your nose what I did. You really were there.'

'I know. The poor birch trees - you remember them? - they said, "Look at us, look at us, Mariana did this, Mariana was here, Mariana, Mariana ...".'

'To me they said "Whin did this, Whin was here." ... We were both there, but I *was* there. Look.' She hardly needed to pull up Kari's skirt, it was up anyway, but she twisted and adjusted it so that I could see the arrow wound that had all but obliterated the old scar; and the raw flesh where the dog's fangs had sunk so deeply into her buttock then been torn away, and other tooth marks on the backs of her legs and her ankles, all bruised still, yes, and yet not gashed and torn as I should have expected, but healing - healed already, for the most part - fast and clean.

'It's the sea,' she said, reading my thoughts, and smiled. 'I've been in the sea almost continuously since then.'

She pulled the skirt down over her legs, tucking them up under her so that they were covered. She waited. She wanted to see if I too bore the marks of our sufferings, but didn't dare ask. I smiled and pulled aside the chemise, which was all I was wearing. There was no mark to be seen.

'I was with you in spirit,' I said.

'If I were your spirit and had such a home, I should not wander.'

I laughed.

And behind me, Raoul said, in French, 'I'm sure she said you have a beautiful body. And if she didn't, let me say it.'

'Raoul!' Still laughing, I adjusted my chemise, which covered very little. 'Raoul, go away! Go back into the cottage. Get yourself some breakfast. I'm going down to the beach to do my exercises and to meditate a while - and I intend to do so with the minimum of clothes on.'

'I have seen you with less than a minimum of clothes on, my lady - many times.'

'Not in the company of my grandmother, you haven't.'

And as I said it, I remembered, and knew what he was going to say even as he said it:

'Who do you think undressed you last night? Took you outside and helped you piss while you were half - more than half - asleep? And your grandmother laughing in the background.'

'That is not the kind of thing you mention to a lady afterwards.'

'It is not the kind of thing a lady needs help with from some passing Frenchman.'

'If the lady needs help, then a young and handsome Frenchman who happens to be passing might be just the thing. *Bien*! You may come and watch me exercise - and join me in my meditations, if you care to.'

We leave Whin to her well-earned slumbers in the sunshine and walk down onto the beach, Raoul fully dressed and booted, me barefoot and free.

I feel like an elp still. Like prey. Tempting, of course, and exposed, out there in the open.

Like an Elp.

But Raoul is no hunter. He has that adoring look on his face again. His courtly look. The young chevalier. Such a look in a woman's eyes, on a woman's cheeks, might indicate pregnancy. He is about to give birth to a poem.

Men have such short memories, even the best of them.

Which may not be such a bad thing.

'So she is your grandmother. I knew there was something ... *Elle aussi, elle est merveilluese, de sa façon.'*

She too is wonderful, in her way.

Oh, Raoul.

We left Whin with Mouraig.

She wanted to come with me; she said her best cover was as my maid. I did not agree. She needed to rest. Mouraig could look after her. And if anyone approached the cottage she could disappear up into the cliffs, among the wulcats - or out to sea again, whichever was easier. With me, in the town, there would always be the risk of someone recognising her for who, or what, she really was. To Mouraig's mind, Lady Margaret was no fool; and even Baron Hugh was not such a fool as to let his prize walk past under his nose. I thought he might be, but I agreed with her about the Red Countess. The thought of either of them now, since that dream, made me want to run for cover, but she was the clever one, the laughing one, the implacable one: Whin/I would not have got away if she had been there. Perhaps it was meeting her that had made me identify with Whin.

But I had met them after the hunt. I did not understand. (I noticed, for instance, that in my dream I - we - did not poison the dogs. Why?) I would understand, though, when it was all over and I applied my mind to it, and Yacoub ben Amar's systems for thinking and working things out.

Passing by under their noses was, of course, exactly what Whin had in mind. Circling round, and approaching the hunter. And laughing.

I knew Whin now.

I also wanted to discuss this whole question of dreams, and the Sight, with Mouraig. How had she come to share my dream?

And done so without Whin knowing that she was there. And how had she known who I was in the first place, even known why I was going to Tain?

They always said I inherited my *taibhsearachd,* my ability to See, from her.

When we got to the Skinner steading, Raoul came in with me. I thought for a moment he too was going to learn what it felt like to have a wolf-hound's teeth clamped in his buttock, but in the end Butterfly-bane allowed him to pass through the gate for my sake.

'I thought you'd been here before, Raoul,' I said, as we went on into the house.

'I have, once. The beast wasn't impressed by me then, either. He adores Bella, of course. And he seems to have taken to you. I think he's one for the girls. Where is Bella?'

'Not here. Let's try round the back.'

The door at the back of the building opened into a quite separate byre. It wasn't locked, but Coll, cowering away from the door, was clearly a prisoner. Perhaps she had simply been ordered to stay there.

'Coll? You remember me?'

That barely perceptible nod. But she kept glancing nervously at Raoul. The hound, seeing this, also started giving him meaningful looks.

I said, 'This is one of the two foreign gentlemen who visited Bella. Which one is it, Coll?'

To Raoul, who of course understood nothing, I said, 'She doesn't know you by sight, but she may recognise your voice.'

'She has never seen me or heard me. All I know of her is what Bella and Jaufre have told me.'

'She would have heard you from in here. I don't think she sees very well, not in bright sunlight at any rate, but her hearing may be as good as a dog's - or a cat's, even. Say something else.'

But Coll interrupted. 'Coll hears.'

'Aye, Coll hears. And which one is it?'

'What did she say?' asked Raoul.

'Whisht. Which one is it, Coll? Is it the one Bella wants, and who wants her? Or is it the other one?'

She studied him - covertly, but she was less frightened now. Butterfly-brain settled down, lay at her feet. She put her left foot on him. He seemed content.

While she studied Raoul, I studied her. She was wearing less today, just a brief cutty semmit, a smock like the one Bella had worn, not much different from the silk chemise I myself wore under my bodice and skirt. I saw that her legs, which were in full view, and her arms too, were covered all over with fine silver down. And unlike poor Bella's, her legs were unmarked.

At last she spoke. 'This is the one.'

I waited. I said, 'The one Bella wants?'

The nod.

She was accustomed now to the presence of Raoul, and apparently indifferent to it. She - even more so than Whin - had none of our Christian modesty.

'Coll … The last time we spoke, your master was still away in his boat. Now Bella told me that when he came back he was going to brand you again. Renew his claim on you. Did he do that?'

This time she shook her head slightly.

'No?'

She shook her head again. 'Master Thorfinn nailed Coll to the wall. Over there.' She got up and walked over to the wooden wall, where she lifted her hair off her ear - the left ear - and held the ear out from her head and pressed it flat against the thick wooden plank.

I went over to her, and looked. In the wood was a deep blood-stained hole, made by a steel nail.

I examined her ear. It was bigger than our ears, and higher and more pointed. And a great deal more useful, as I knew. Now there was a big hole in it, held open by a wooden peg the size of my little finger. It was still raw and her whole ear was swollen.

'Raoul, in my saddlebag there are two jars of unguent. *Soît gentil*, and bring me the larger of the two.'

The pin needed to come out. The skinner might force it back in later and make matters worse than if I had never interfered. It would swell more though, if I did not. It was dangerous. I would have to take it out and hope for the best.

I said, 'Come outside.'

'Coll can't.'

'Coll can. Your master is not here, he is in Tain. And even if he were here, he would not argue with me.'

'Coll - '

'Come on! I need to wash that ear under the pump.'

I pulled her up and out through the door. She didn't struggle. Raoul pumped while I held her head under the gushing water, and worked on her ear, cooling it, massaging it, then popping the plug out of it without her even noticing till later when she felt my finger go through the hole, cleaning it, soothing it.

She said nothing.

I took her back in and dried her with a cloth that was lying there handy and seemed quite clean. Then I worked the salve into her ear.

When I had finished, I squatted in front of her and held her hands. She let me do that, but she wouldn't meet my gaze, would only glance at me, fleetingly, whenever she thought I might have looked away.

No one had spoken since before we went outside.

I was waiting. I wanted to know what was at the front of her mind.

She glanced at me, glanced away again, looked down at her legs, her long, thin feet, a little muddy from the pump, her brown pointed nails. And with her eyes still down, she said, 'Now Coll is his for ever.'

'For ever?'

The nod. 'For ever until she dies. Or he dies.'

Suddenly she flashed me that wicked grin of hers. 'Coll almost had him on the sea, in that storm. This time, with "blood of the unbeliever" mixed into the poppet …'

Blood of the unbeliever? Oh, no … But we'd been expecting that, hadn't we. The mutilation, not the murder.

I held onto her hands. The fingernails, too, were pointed and sharp.

Wasn't what she was planning now, though, murder? No different from the murder of the Moor? You can't say "It's all right to kill him, yes, he's unbearable; but you mustn't murder him, he's a nice man." Where do you draw the line? There is no line.

Countenance the killing of Thorfinn Skinner, and you become - like him - one of them.

But I nodded and smiled. 'Tell me about it, Coll.'

'First, you have everything ready, she said - '

Who said? Mouraig - the Witch of Balintore? Or the famous Witch of Golspie, whom I never met - successor to the old wise woman who aided Mouraig on her return from her travels? Had Coll perhaps known this Agnes of Strathpeffer that Big Robbie had hanged in Dyngvale? Or her beautiful daughter?

I never did find out.

Coll was still talking. ' … the Moor's blood, and his ballock, the blood on the ballock, and fresh blood of Taran the bull, and food - food he has fingered and left, food he has lickit and lippit and left, food he has chewed and spat out and left …'

She began to chant:

'I tuik the ballock, I tuik some food,
I tuik a spoonfu' of Taran's bluid,

Was that voice, I wondered, as I listened, the voice of the one who had taught her? Was Coll imitating? And imitating, too, the motions - the taking and grinding and so on?

I groun' them all, I formit the head,
I moulit the body, I meid it red,

I tuik a sliver of Taran's horn,
I gored the body and brak the bone.

I put my eyeball to the hole,
I lookit right thro him, deil tak his soul!

I lookit thro at the moon and the sea:
May the deil tak him and set me free!

Yes. Well. If he didn't, what sort of devil was he?

Master Thorfinn was not intending to bestow the benefits of his professional skills upon any bulls that day, was he?

Was he? I asked her.

Yes, she said. And smiled. I think she already knew that Taran had won.

Taran would: Taran was an ancient god. He hardly needed the help of Auld Cloutie. Auld Nick.

But better far than that Thorfinn should have been employing those same skills on the defenceless body of poor Souad. Or Coll here.

I no longer knew what I believed.

I knew only that I was on Souad's side; and Coll's, whatever she might have attempted to do, might somehow have managed to do; and Bella's, yes, whatever she might have done.

And I knew that Souad was my next priority, and the Bailie's house in Tain my next port of call.

SIXTEEN

If We Three Survive

In bright sunshine, Raoul and I rode on to Tain. And met a small procession coming out towards us: the Bailie and his men escorting home the wounded Thorfinn Skinner.

We all stopped.

I looked at Thorfinn, at Master Brodie. 'What happened?'

'He was gored by a bull.'

They had him in the back of a cart. His right side was soaked with blood, his face deathly pale and beaded with sweat.

'But - so many men?'

Niáll of Lairg was there, as well as half a dozen other official-looking men.

The Bailie looked at Niáll.

Niáll said, 'We have reason to suspect that this was no accident, my lady.'

'You mean - the bull did it deliberately?'

'I mean, madame, that it may have been witchcraft. Now if you will excuse us ...'

When they had gone, I explained to Raoul. He whistled. 'I hope they mean Coll, and not poor Bella.'

'Oh they mean Coll - for the moment. But whose name will Coll scream out when she is put to the question?'

'Not Bella's,' he said.

We would see.

We came into Tain, and learnt at the Bailie's house that Souad was no longer there.

'But they said - '

'No, not that,' Mona explained, 'though they wanted to - and they would have, too! No, she just … left.'

'You mean she ran away? Escaped?'

Mona nodded, frightened and pleased and shocked at herself all at the same time.

'But where? I must see her. I must help her. I promised to.'

'I don't know, my lady, of course, but … If you were to inquire of old Mouraig out at Kattar-bol, I've a mind she would be able to help you. You know Mouraig?'

Oh yes, I knew Mouraig. 'The witch?'

'Don't say that! Not now with that Brother Arsenius here, there and everywhere like a cross between a great black fly. He'll have them thinking the lass was spirited away.' She crossed herself.

'But she wasn't.'

'Oh no, she wasn't, my lady.'

I thanked her and turned away.

I was tired suddenly. I left my horse with Raoul, and walked to the inn, where I found the Black Friar in my room. Mona was right.

'Can I help you, Brother?'

'Ah - Lady MacElpin. Or is it plain Mistress MacElpin?'

He paused. I held his gaze but made no reply.

'Yes, you can help me - by telling me what you are doing here in Ross; and when you have told me that, you can tell me what you meant by certain of the statements you made to the condemned prisoner, Drostan.'

'I do not have to answer you, Brother.'

'Not today, no. But you will. Tomorrow.'

Tomorrow? So he intended to get Coll to point the yarrow at me, did he?

'Do not imagine that your "noble blood" will save you. Have you never heard of William de Soulis, Laird of Liddesdale? He was a disciple of the wizard Michael Scott. Ah - Michael Scott you have heard of. William de Soulis was boiled to death in a cauldron of molten lead. For witchcraft, my lady'

'And what has all this to do with me? Or indeed with Drostan?'

'Drostan is to be transferred to Edinburgh and executed there.

The King, God save him, is taking a personal interest in the case. He may wonder what you are doing here, talking to Drostan and mixing with the witches that he knows infest the area, especially down by the sea in Sand-vik and Balintore.' He crossed himself. 'Ah, well is it named the Black Isle, the half-isle to the south of here; but this, the land of Tain and Nigg, is blacker still, and the Devil himself has taken possession of it.'

He came even closer, face to mine. 'But *I* am here now, and - '

I held the door wide. 'Out.'

He went, and as he passed I thought he was going to take my chin in his hand, stare into my eyes. And what could I have done about it? He was so tall, so hard. But as it was, he simply muttered, 'God bless you, my daughter.'

'And God bless you, too, Brother,' I murmured back sweetly.

I slept.

And was woken in the middle of the afternoon by Raoul. He lay down beside me and stroked my face and forehead and hair. Lovely.

'Why am I so tired?' I murmured, languorously

'It's the weather. It's warm.'

'Not by my standards.'

'London's so warm?'

'As warm as Normandy.'

'I've been living in Avignon, remember,' he said.

'And I grew up in the south of Spain, remember.'

I had things to do. I pulled myself up, slipped off my chemise and sluiced myself with cold water from the basin. His eyes on me were soft, admiring, but - he hadn't tried to hold me, hadn't slipped me out of the chemise himself, hadn't -

'Let's go and see what is happening with Thorfinn Skinner,' he said.

He meant: Let's go and see Bella.

I dried myself while he watched me, then as I dressed I said, '*D'accord*. But you stay in the background. Don't let him see you with me.'

Did I really need to see Thorfinn? Or did I simply want to be with Raoul?

As we set out, I told him about my visit from Brother Arsenius.

'But Mariana, you must leave! Now!'

'I can't, Raoul. Anyway, the Church has a long arm. I'm as safe here as I would be anywhere in Scotland. It would take me how long - weeks - to travel south to the border and into England.'

'You would be safer there?'

'Yes. Arsenius represents Pope Clement.'

'Take a ship - a ship to anywhere for now - then later make your way to England.'

I smiled at him. 'What makes you think there's a ship leaving today? And what about Ferchard and Kari? And Souad? I promised to help her. She will be caught and she will be tortured and there will be no one to speak for her.'

'What use will you be to her, hanging from the next set of manacles?'

"What use will I be?" I had heard that same question before, but where? And who had been speaking? Ah. Yes. Tinkman. And where was Tinkman now?

'I'm not that easy to catch and hang up, Raoul. If Brother Arsenius thinks I'm about to play little grey mouse to his great black skeletal cross between a fly and -' (I smiled at the memory of Mona Brodie's desciption of him) 'and a tomcat at midnight - he's in for a shock.'

'*Mariana! Je t'implore!*'

'*Je ne peux pas quitter mon poste.*'

'*Bien*. Then le Fou and I, with our men, will be obliged to come to the rescue. Masked, of course, and without a word spoken. It would not do at all for the French *Armeé Royale* to be seen to be acting against the Church and the Scottish Judiciary.'

'In defence of a maiden in distress? It would do wonders for their reputation! And Jaufre would certainly wear his uniform of *capitaine* along with the mask … But I am touched, Raoul.'

'You can depend on me - on us.'

It was comforting, but somehow I couldn't see it happening. I could never have guessed that le Fou would be dead though; murdered in his saddle, just like ben Youssef, before ever I was arrested.

'For in a sense, you are one of us, Mariana.'

'I know, *mon cher*, I know.'

Butterfly-bane knew my scent now even from a distance. He did not bark at all. And nor was the gate bolted, so we arrived completely unannounced.

I peered into the house, Raoul close behind me in the doorway. Sensing our presence, Bella turned from where she was kneeling at her master's bedside and looked straight at me. I had been almost sure she was ben Youssef's murderer. And that she had also attempted to murder Raoul with the fish soup, and had quite possibly murdered her previous master, Harald Skinner, as well. But when she looked at me, I wavered. I could not believe it. As I had been unable to believe it when I had been face to face with her before, even though she had lied to me.

She got up and came towards us.

I backed out of the doorway, pushing Raoul out behind me as I went.

'How is he?' I whispered.

'Bad, my lady.' She had tears in her eyes, had been crying.

'He's still bleeding?'

She nodded, looking past me at Raoul, questioningly. 'Yes, and he's coughing up blood.'

'Is he conscious?'

'Some of the time. But I don't think he makes any sense when he speaks - especially when he goes on about my anklet. It's mostly Gaelic, so I'm not really sure.'

'What language does he normally use with you?'

'French, my lady.'

'Ah. *Tu parles bien*?'

'*Quelques môts* - I understand him, but I often answer in English.'

'*Elle parle merveilleusement*.'

I gave Raoul a pained look, and he closed his mouth. The pain was real. *I* speak French *merveilleusement*.

'Let me go and see him. I may be able to help. No, you stay out here, Raoul.'

I knelt with Bella beside the bed and studied his face and

eyes. I felt his forehead, read his pulse. He had lost a lot of blood. His breathing was shallow, his pulse rapid and fluttery.

I studied his palm. A violent and solitary man - and now his time was up. 'He's dying.'

'I know. They sent a message to the Abbey and Father Basil came out here. And Brother Martin. And - and they cut away his tunic and tried to staunch the bleeding. Brother Jacob was helping Father Basil, but they couldn't do anything so they bound up the wound as you can see and - and Father Cyril had to go outside, he couldn't stand the sight of all the blood - '

'Father Cyril? The Abbot? He was here?'

'Oh yes. And Brother Eusebius suggested some kind of leaves - I don't remember what - but they wouldn't listen to him - '

'Brother Eusebius? Was the whole monastery here?'

'No, Father Kenneth is old now, he couldn't come, but he sent me his - his blessings.'

'His blessings. I see. And did Father Basil leave you anything to give Thorfinn when he woke up? Any pills? Any powders?'

'Only this.' She held out a little glass bottle. 'They told me to give him three or four drops of this in a little water every hour or so. And I have, when he would take it.'

I smelt it. It was a decoction of mandrake root plus something else. Sea holly?

He started coughing and she held him up, supported him, as she should, while she wiped away the bloody froth on a rag.

His liver had been pierced and the blood vessels leading to it broken, or so I guessed. In addition, his whole right side was bruised, some ribs were cracked, and the lung was filling with blood.

'I have something else he might be able to swallow. If he can, it will help him sleep.'

I went out and fetched from my saddle bag the opium I never travel without.

'What's happening? Can I come in?' Raoul hissed.

'No! I'm going to give him something to make him sleep, then we'll come out to you.'

I mixed the opium in with the other filtre. We waited till he coughed again, then, as soon as he had done coughing, we got him to drink it. We waited. It stayed down. And after a while his breathing grew slower and he slept.

Bella looked at me. She was extraordinarily beautiful, even when her face was swollen with tears: or was it still swollen from the beating? The black eye had faded to blue and yellow, but the white of her eye was still discoloured, and the swollen cheek was not from crying. Upset? In her place, I would be celebrating.

I nodded towards the door.

Raoul was now sitting on the ground, with Butterfly-bane beside him. Their four eyes gazed at us. I laughed, I couldn't help it, and Bella, relaxing, smiled too. Then she said, 'I'm sorry, my lady, monsieur - would you like a drink? You prefer water, my lady?'

'Usually, yes, I prefer water, or wine, but this evening I'll try some of that beer you recommended the other day.'

Raoul nodded. 'Sounds good. Shall I help you get it?'

'No, you shan't help her get it, you'll sit where you are and wait. She's quite capable - '

'I was simply being polite. You are quite *capable* of opening a door for yourself.'

'Yes. Right. You are right. I apologise. But she will manage. Now, listen. It must be very late.'

'No, you listen. I'm going to stay here with her.'

'Stay here? You? But it would be better if I - '

'I'll stay outside. I'll guard the place - and her. And I'll be here if she needs help.'

'And me?'

'You've given him a sleeping draft. He'll be all right. He may die, but he'll be all right.'

Bella returned with the beer and we sipped in silence, tired and thirsty. It was good.

'Some time, I want to have a long chat with you, Bella.'

'Oh, yes, my lady.'

'But not now, I'm afraid. Now it is late, and I at least must go.'

She glanced at Raoul.

He said, 'I will stay here with you, keep you company, make sure you are all right.'

She smiled. Such a smile. Coll had been right.

'Bella, if anything happens to your master - '

'If he dies, you mean.'

'Yes - when he dies - you come to Mouraig's house in Kattarbol. That's just to the north of Balintore - Port-an-Ab. You know it?'

'Yes, but I don't know Mouraig, my lady.'

'It doesn't matter. I will be there. It's where I stay most nights now. And if I'm not, wait there with Mouraig till I return.'

'Is she the one they call the witch?'

I nodded. I would have to tell her my secret. 'She is my grandmother, Bella. You can rely on her.'

'Your grandmother? Oh, my lady, I didn't - '

'It's all right. Just trust her. If Raoul is still here when - '

'I'll be here till morning. Then I must leave. But I will return in the evening.'

We sat together in silence for a while. There was no moonlight and the sky was darker than I had seen it since coming so far north.

'You see those two bright stars there, Raoul? No, there. Yes, those.' They both gazed up. 'Those are the Twins. Castor and Pollux.'

'The twins?'

'Gemini. Your star sign. The Twins.'

'Oh, I see! Sorry. And that's them? That's fantastic. No one has ever shown me them before ... And what's that other one - there - nearby? The very bright one?'

Why did he have to ask about that one?

I'll fight most things. Like the Red Countess, I am a fighter. I too was born under the rule of Mars in the day house of Scorpio. But fight fate? Fight the stars in their courses? I, of all people, should know that fate will hit you in the face, again and again and again. And go on hitting you till you bow to it.

I bowed.

'That is Aldebaran,' I said. 'Aldebaran in Taurus.'

'Taurus? That is Taurus? That is your star, Bella! Oh, look how bright it is! And that cluster there, just beyond Taurus?'

'The Pleiades.'

Bella looked at Raoul shyly. 'How did you know I was

Taurus?'

'Mariana told me.'

'Mariana? Oh - my lady. Yes. And ...?'

'Tell us about Taurus, Mariana.'

'Taurus? Taurus is ruled by the planet Venus, the planet of love and harmony. And of firmness of purpose. Determination. And in people born under Taurus this determination can turn into stubbornness.'

'And?' Raoul wanted to hear more of his beloved.

'And what? Bella and I will talk alone together one day - one day very soon - and then we shall see what we shall see.'

'But - but her colour? Her lucky number? You know.'

'Your number is seven, Bella. Your colour is green. Your stone is the emerald - or no, maybe the turquoise in your case. Your metal is copper, your flowers the clover and the rose, your trees the alder and the birch, your birds the sparrow, the dove and the swan.'

'My lady, that's - '

'And your symbol is the girdle.' I laughed, and so did she, and we both knew I had much more to say to her later.

'And Gemini?' asked Raoul.

'Gemini? I am more interested in Thorfinn Skinner. Do you happen to know his star sign, Bella?'

'Yes, I do. Master Harald told me. He's a - '

'Don't tell her. Let her guess! She's fantastic at this!'

'Raoul,' I protested, 'it's not a game!'

'She guessed that Jaufre was a Leo. He *is* a Leo, Mariana - did I tell you? Did he tell you?'

'Jaufre was an easy one. Leos usually are. But Thorfinn ... From everything I've seen and heard, and from having met and spoken to him, from having just now held his hand and read his palm, I would say that overriding all else is arrogance: pride and ambition chained down by a fear and self-doubt that he does not understand and will not admit to. He despises the herd but his self-doubt keeps him down among them. And among them he feels, he is, isolated and cold, mean, and fundamentally pessimistic. Yes? His ruling planet is Saturn and his star sign is - Capricorn.'

Raoul looked at Bella, and grinned as he saw that I was right.

'Yes!' she cried. 'That's wonderful, my lady!'

'But,' I said, 'take note that both Capricorn and Taurus are Earth signs, which means that you are likely to share certain characteristics with your master.'

'Bella? She couldn't be more different from Thorfinn Skinner!'

I ignored him, spoke to her. 'You are shrewd and practical, and cautious. You will not take risks. You will aim to be rich.'

'You've got that completely wrong,' objected Raoul. 'Bella is not practical - or not very - and she is certainly not interested in money.'

'Oh yes she is.'

We both looked at Bella.

She looked back at us.

When she was born, the Moon was in Cancer. I knew what she would say.

'I would like to buy my freedom, Raoul. And for that I need money. I would like to have my own home, a home like this perhaps, but my own - or a home in a town - in Colchester - with beautiful things, things that are mine, and a man I love and who loves me. And I would like to wear beautiful clothes … like my lady wears.'

I smiled at Raoul.

'*Oui, mais alors, pourquoi pas*?' he blustered. Why not?

'*Pourquoi pas*, indeed. And perhaps you could persuade her to substitute Chartres for Colchester? Then, if we survive the next few days, I will come to your wedding.' I will even play bride's mother, in the great Cathedral of Chartres. If we three survive …

I stood up, glanced in at the dying man, and took my leave.

SEVENTEEN

The Queen Of Elphame?

I was sleeping when the Bailie and his men arrived, but Mouraig had seen them coming along the sea path. Whin and Souad had fled up the cliff into the bushes.

I joined Mouraig at the door.

She smiled. 'That Souad would make a good wulcat.'

We watched the half-dozen men approach.

'How does she get on with Whin?' I asked.

I hadn't had a chance to speak to them or observe them together. When I arrived, they were asleep.

'Oh, and that too. She took to Whin like a tinkler bairn, and Whin responded. She's had a gap in her heart since they stole her two bairns away from her. No word of either of them, I suppose?'

'No. How could there be?'

'Of Kari? Who knows? Otter may surprise you though.'

The Bailie stopped his horse in front of us. He opened his mouth to speak, without bothering to dismount. Mouraig, offended - on my behalf? - got in first: 'She's not here.'

'Who's not here?'

'The one you're looking for.'

'Oh yes she is.'

As I had feared: Brother Arsenius ... But Mouraig had been so sure it was Souad they were after - and possibly Whin.

'Mouraig of Balintore, you are wanted for questioning in connection with the deaths of the Moor Abdelwhatsit ben Youssef and of Thorfinn the Skinner - '

'Thorfinn's not even dead yet!' I cried. 'At least, he wasn't a few hours ago.'

'As you say, my lady. Now he may well be. Fetch your things, Mouraig.'

'Was it Coll put the yarrow on me?'

'It was. And that's all I'm saying. Now, will you comc of your own free will or do we have to - ?'

'I'll bring her,' I said. 'She'll come with me on my horse.' I fetched the horse and saddled it. I mounted. No one helped me, but two of the men lifted Mouraig up behind me, side-saddle.

'You'll regret this, Master Brodie,' I said, breaking the silence.

'My lady, I - '

'You don't know who she is.'

'Leave it, Marian,' muttered Mouraig.

'She's the Witch of Balintore,' he replied, refusing to raise his voice. 'And more than that, she has been named the Queen of Elphame and enemy of the Church and of mankind.'

'The Queen of Elphame?' I laughed. 'Look at her. She's over eighty! She can hardly stay up on a horse!'

Some of his men were beginning to fidget and look doubtful.

'Who knows what she can do when the magic is on her?' he responded.

'You have no idea, have you, who she is - who she was, long before you were born.'

'Marian!'

'It's all right, Mouraig. I shan't tell him. But be advised, Master Bailie. Send word to Euphemia, Countess of Ross; ask her this: Is the Witch of Balintore a body I should arrest and put to the question? Or is she someone I should, if I value my position and your patronage, leave in peace? Simply ask her that, Master Bailie. You have nothing to lose, and everything to gain.'

He thought about it. He was a cautious man. Yes, he had nothing to lose. He nodded to one of his men. 'Donald, you go. She's in Inverness, or was the last I heard.'

'But - '

'Take the Nigg ferry and pass down through the Black Isle. I want you back in Tain tonight.'

Donald rode off at a gallop. We followed, but at a slow walk, the Bailie and Niáll of Lairg up in front of us, and three more men behind.

'They say I have the fath-fith,' Mouraig said, suddenly.

I looked at her, looked at them: they were talking quietly together but I couldn't hear what they were saying.

'The fath-fith?'

'The power to change form. That I'm a shape-shifter.' She "listened" a bit more, then whispered: 'They thought *you* were me,' and laughed.

Well, they were not so far wrong. I thought I was Whin.

'Now they think that we are both the Witch of Balintore.'

'You mean both the same one witch - or two witches?'

She "listened" some more. Then: 'Now they've seen us together, two witches. I think.'

Brother Arsenius' influence. But who was this Queen - the one they all called the Queen of Elphame? In Kabbalistic terms, the Queen was *Malkah*, the Sephiroth *Malkuth*, a girl crowned and enthroned and surrounded by a rainbow. Who could that be, among us, here, and now?

In those same terms, ben Youssef had been *Hesed*, protective love, the Father, husband of *Din*. But *Din* was so slippery. *Din* the destructive goddess? The Mother in her destructive aspect, symbol of anarchic violence, the sword, the spear, the scourge, the chain? Was this, could this be, Souad? Was she the one whose colours were red and black and the orange of flame?

But *Din* was also Justice.

'Those are interesting thoughts,' Mouraig murmured. 'But where do Raoul and Jaufre le Fou fit in? And where do you? And I?'

Where indeed?

Coll had been scourged and was hanging by her wrists from a ring set high up in the wall. They had turned her round to face us. She had taken one frightened look at Mouraig and sobbed, 'No, not her. Coll didn't mean her.'

The Bailie was unsurprised. Coll's fear of Mouraig was greater than her fear of the whip. But he had no choice. He ordered Mouraig's release and when I pointed out that she was exhausted thanks to his folly, said she might rest on the bed there in the holding-room.

The men dispersed.

Of Brother Arsenius, there was no sign; only skinny Master Kenneth, smirking at the poor tormented glaistig hanging there muttering and sobbing and crooning to herself.

'You did that.'

'Who else? My father's not coming now there'll be no executions. He'll come up and join the Brother and me, of course, if we catch a whole nest of witches. Coven, I should say: coven of witches. Do you think we will … my lady?'

'Not if poor Coll is the only witness you have.'

'Ah, but she's not. We're looking for the Moorish slave-girl - and for that tinkler woman. You remember? The one we had down in the chamber at Dyngvale and let go again. There's a conspiracy here, the Brother says, but we'll get to the bottom of it.'

'We?'

'We, my lady.'

'Poor Coll,' said Coll. They had turned her face to the wall again, but she was conscious, it seemed, and listening.

'I wanted to cut her above the breath, but the Brother said she was harmless enough, none of the magic she used was her own. I spat at her, though, between crossed fingers, the way we do around here, before I whipped her. And I keep her turned to the wall, just in case.'

The little Hel's-son. 'Have you ever seen someone cut above the breath?'

He was going to say yes, but he knew I would catch him out. 'No. I learnt about it. They can't put the Eye on you then.'

'I've seen it. They do it in France.'

'The Brother says there's no reason we can't do it here. He says we will, if we catch a real witch. The old one's a real witch - ' he nodded towards Mouraig, who had her eyes closed, though I doubted very much whether she was asleep. 'But she's no good. She'd die before we finished cutting her. Was the one you saw young?'

'Quite young. She was cut across her face - here - above her nose - '

'Not "cut", *scored*, my lady.' It was the Black Friar. He had crept in behind me, and his slimy voice was right beside my ear as he went on: 'It's not a cut, it's a deep scratch, and I mean deep, made with - ' he picked up and brandished a nine-inch awl with a viciously sharp-looking point - 'made with something like this. A wavy line, scored - ploughed - across her forehead from temple to temple.'

I looked back into his pale, staring eyes. Gazing, not staring - gazing like a lover, into my eyes and backwards and forwards over my forehead. His mouth was closed, but I knew that if he opened it a dark forked tongue would come darting out.

He opened it. 'Like this,' he murmured, putting the tip of the awl to my forehead.

There was a moment of absolute silence. Then Drostan coughed in his cell. Another brief pause. Arsenius grinned. 'I'm just showing you, my lady.'

Kenneth smirked. He would have loved to be able to grin like "the Brother".

Arsenius, face straight again as though the grin had never been, as though I had imagined it, ran the point gently in a wavy line across my brow. 'Like that. But hard. As hard as the goodman can do it. After that, her breath and her glance are powerless. Then she is left for eight days, by which time the scoreline on her brow will have opened - the scalp is very tight, you know, and tends to pull away from any cut, making it wider and preventing healing.'

He was right. That was what I had seen - the result, after eight days.

'The ordinary folk -' he went on, his face still far too close to mine, but I refused to back off, 'the ordinary folk, when they see that line, believe that the head has been opened and closed by the Devil - opened and closed, perhaps many times - and something awful, something the witch agreed to, done to her. And for that alone, they argue, she deserves to die at the stake.'

'I see.'

'I have spent the last few years working in Carcassonne. Hundreds of witches have been sent to the stake there, and in Toulouse and Avignon.'

We held each other's eye for a moment. Then he said, 'The old one there, your grandmother, will never reach the stake, not now. She should have been burned, or at the very least hanged, years ago. Now it is too late. You will not be so lucky.'

Again, we held each other's eyes, and then by some mutual understanding, turned away simultaneously, I to my right, he to his. Before me lay the items they must have found and considered incriminating when they took Thorfinn Skinner home to die and arrested glaistig Coll.

Of course, not being "one of us", she had no rights. And not being "one of us", she could not, presumably, be a witch; the reason she had not been scored above the breath, I realised. But she had been scourged, and would be further tortured by our young "master" - with the pilliwinks? on the rack? - until they had the names of the witches, and the identity of the Queen of Elphame.

Did Coll know? I suspected that she did.

Looking through the pathetic bits and pieces of wax and bone and blood-stained cloth, I realised too that ben Youssef's dagger - the knife that Coll had used to slit his scrotum and sever one of his testicles - was not there. The knife was missing. Important? Probably not. But curious. They must have searched the place.

The more I thought about that dagger, the more interesting I found it. It had been in the wound when Coll first saw the body. Yet I didn't believe it was the murder weapon. It was too small. It couldn't have made the large hole in ben Youssef's back. In fact, now I thought about it, our original idea must have been right: he had been killed with an arrow - or a spear, or a harpoon - from behind and from some distance. Where had I seen a bow and arrows? Callum Vass, wee Magnus Vass's father, had taken a bow with him. What for? And if he had one, would not Thorfinn Skinner have had one as well?

'May I speak to Master MacDalorg before we leave?'

'Who?'

'The prisoner known as Drostan, Brother.'

'No. He is being held incommunicado until he is transferred to Edinburgh. We do not wish him to bring poor simple souls into jeopardy with his devilish rantings.'

"Poor simple souls"? Like me? Ah well. But "devilish"? Drostan?

'Thank you, Brother.'

I had no wish to bring up the question of when we might meet again. Arsenius's "tomorrow" was today, and I was still free. However, from now on, I would have to take not just every day, but every hour, every minute, as it came.

EIGHTEEN

The Baron Makes His Bid

By midday, I was on my way back to Kattar-bol, with Mouraig up behind me again clutching a flask of whisky that Brodie had given her on his return by way of compensation. Or sweetener. Or please-don't-mention-this-to-Countess-Euphemia.

She seemed quite happy with her end of the bargain. But she also seemed very tired still. What the Black Friar had said worried me. Not his threats, but the implication that for Mouraig time was running out. Would he know? He might have some feeling for it - the hunter deprived of his prey.

As we approached Loch Eye, Mouraig asked me to stop beside a burn that fed into the loch. Was I hungry? I helped her down off the horse then squatted beside her on the river bank while she did something that I had done "myself" in my dream: she guddled a trout - caught it, just like that, with her bare hands. Then she showed me how: one hand in, right in, smoothly, gently, quietly … under the trout … now tickle it - but it jerked away from my finger as if from the scratch of a sharp stick, and was gone.

She looked at me. 'I'd have thought you'd be good at this.'

Practice? Apparently not. I'd already frightened all the fish away from this spot, so we would move along the bank a little, then she would do it.

She caught two more, one large, and another small one, then built a fire of dry sticks and set out a grill of straight green sticks across it. When all was ready, she laid the fish on the sticks and sat back.

I watched her, fascinated. I was relieved that she seemed all right, yet my mind was elsewhere. I was remembering again the little campfire by the stream where Whin had caught and cooked fish for Tinkman in that brief hour of peace between the torture chamber and the hunt. I remembered it as Kari and I had found it that night, in reality, and I remembered it as it had been in my dream, when it had been me that had guddled the fish. Me, there with Tinkman. Yewel.

It would be Thursday again tomorrow, I realised. Almost a week had gone by since we left Whin and Tinkman and made our way up through Black Isle to Callum Vass and Shusie and then via the Nigg Ferry to Sand-vik and Balintore and Kattar-boll - and Mouraig, my grandmother. And what had I achieved since then? Very little. Rachid had died. Souad had fled. Thorfinn was dying. Coll had been arrested and tortured. And a witchcraft case was blowing up, thanks no doubt to my presence as much as that of the Black Friar; and to the manifestations of the Queen of Elphame - or at least the perambulations of someone masquerading as the Queen of Elphame.

Mouraig turned the fish over. She was very skillful with sticks.

Being born under the sign of Scorpio is not so bad. When we believe, we believe passionately. We hold nothing back. And that applies, too, when we are in love - or so they say. We are easily hurt. Likewise, we do not conform, are not conventional, but have a keen instinctive sense of right and wrong, and we wish to know, to understand, whatever is hidden, is mysterious. Not so bad, as I say, but it can get you into trouble, especially if you see yourself as a Child of Light - for Scorpios can be either, Children of Light or - like the Red Countess, Lady Margaret? - Children of Darkness. I try to be a Child of Light, but find myself entertaining the dark thoughts of the scorpion rather than flying up to the sun with the eagle, the other, the better, symbol of Scorpio.

As now.

And thinking about who might be *Malkah*, the Queen, in the Kabbalah correspondences, reminded me that I was without doubt *Hod*, imagination and intelligence combined with logic and reasoning, combined like a ship dragging its anchor. *Hod* is the sphere of the mental faculties. Why did I have to be *Hod*? Why did my sphere have to be that of the mind? I could wish that I were *Malkah*. Or even *Din*, the destructive goddess - but this was merely the eagle and the scorpion coming out in me. I was what I was: *Hod.*

The fish was ready, cooling down on some big leaves she had found. We ate it with our fingers. We drank a little whisky from the flask and handfulls of water from thc burn. It was delicious, the fish, everything. I was thinking that I might very well come to live up here - I could learn to guddle trout - when I saw an old man standing at the water's edge downstream where the burn flowed into the loch.

He was watching us.

'Who's that?'

'Where? Oh - that's the pigsticker, Sweign. He's shy to join us while we're eating.' She laughed. 'Talking of Coll, he reckons that she belongs to him - that he saw her first - saw her many times. He never managed to catch her though. Poor Coll. Better for her if he had.'

'You never know when a worse fate may be in store for you.'

'Sweign!' she greeted him.

'Mistress Mouraig. Good day to you.'

'This is a young friend of mine. Lady MacElpin.'

'MacElpin? MacElpin?'

'That rings a bell, eh?' She passed him the flask.

'It does indeed. My lady?' He poured a little of the golden liquid into the palm of his hand, drank that, said 'Ah ... ' and passed the flask back to her. These two were old friends. I suspected that the performance with the palm of the hand was for my benefit.

'Master Sweign, I am the lady who is concerning herself - at the request of Sir Hugh and the Bailie and the French Officers posted here - with the murder of the Moor Abdelwahed ben Youssef.'

'Ay, I've heard of you, my lady. Though not that you were a MacElpin lass ...'

He looked at Mouraig and at me, and at Mouraig, and back at me again. It rang more than a bell, in my opinion. Mouraig, I realised, was probably wrong about the number of older people who knew who she really was.

'Over there it happened.' He nodded towards the north.

'Aye, about halfway between Tain and the Skinner Steading.

Or at least that's where the body was found. You live out here?'

'Aye.'

'Did you see or hear anyone - anything - that night?'

'Nothing out of the way.'

'Anything at all. Even if it happens every night. Was it windy? Was the moon shining? Did it rain at all? Did anyone pass by? On foot? On horseback?'

'My lady, it was not windy. As to the moon, it will have risen, but later. When I took my last look at the loch, it was still light in the sky over there beyond the forest, and the evening star was shining bright. There was no rain that night. There was a heavy fall of dew at dawn, though.'

'If I had only seen that body then! There would have been such clear tracks in the grass.'

'Aye, there would, my lady. But there was just the boy came looking for him and took him home slung across his own horse. It had been waiting beside him.'

'You saw all this?'

'No, my lady. I heard it afterwards.'

'So no one passed by.'

'Only the Queen, my lady.'

'Ah, yes. The Queen.'

'The Queen of Elphame. She passes once or twice a week - '

'At night, always?'

'No, I've seen her in the early evening, in broad daylight, and when the sun is setting - often when the sun is setting - and at night, especially in winter she rides at night, by moonlight. I've seen her in the snow, with that great hound of hers behind her - like Thorfinn Skinner's hound, but bigger, younger; and somehow quieter yet more alive.'

'And did you know her?'

'Aye, she was the Queen.'

'I mean, did you see her face - her hair, her eyes?'

'No, she always wears the same white cloak, my lady, made of silk and satin by the look of it, and trimmed with white fur, and she always has the hood up and her face in shadow. Though she smiled at me once, and from that moment the hound stopped snarling at me as he passed - warning me, you know, to keep my distance from the - from his mistress.'

He had been going to say "the goddess", I'm sure.

'And no one else?'

'No, my lady. Sometimes a fishwife from Balintore goes in early to Tain with her man's catch on a yoke across her shoulders or on a cuddy, and sometimes a monk from the abbey passes by this way or that on some errand, maybe of mercy, maybe not.'

'But you saw no one.'

He shook his head.

'I'll ask at the abbey and among the fishwives,' I said, but my mind was on "the Queen". Could it be Lady Margaret? The Red Countess - the Red Queen? It seemed too far away from Dun Robin. But who else was there?

'The Queen of Elphame ...' I said. 'Does she carry anything? A spear? A bow? Does she seem to be hunting?'

'Oh no, my lady.'

'Her hound does sometimes seem to be,' murmured Mouraig, and I knew that behind me she was smiling at the memory.

'Thank you, Sweign Pigsticker,' I said. 'I hope we shall meet again.'

'I hope so too, my lady. Good day to you. And good luck with your quest.'

'Thank you.'

'My lady? Don't waste your time thinking that the Queen may have killed the Moor. The Queen is good, my lady. If she had been there, the man would not have died.'

'You mean she would have intervened, have saved his life? The life of an unbeliever?'

'An unbeliever in what, my lady? He had seen the Queen of Elphame. He had spoken to her. He was the only man I ever saw her stop and speak to.'

So he would have known who she was.

'When was that, Sweign? Soon before his death?'

'Three or four days before. One evening when he was coming from the ferry and I behind him, she rode out of the forest, and they spoke and then she rode away at a gallop leaving him - and me - behind.'

'How long did they speak?'

'Just a few words.'

'Did they already know each other?'

He regarded me thoughtfully.

'Aye, they did, now I come to think of it. Now *you* come to think of it, my lady. For she rode out of Tarlogie Wood straight at him. As if she had a word to say to him. And he was not surprised.'

He took his leave of us and we raked out our fire and rode on towards Kattar-bol.

Mouraig said, suddenly, 'Sharing your dream was nothing, child. I had woken up, was sitting by the hearth, letting my mind wander - old folk are early risers - when I became aware of your thoughts ... much as I am now: that you have this and other questions to put to me. But I was not with Whin during the hunt, as you were.'

'I wasn't.'

'You were. One is unaware of these things - unless, like little Otter, one is able to control them.'

'Otter? You mean Whin's son?'

'Aye, I do. The one you foolishly left behind to his fate. But how were you to know?'

Otter ...?

'Nor were you aware of it when you appeared to me that night at Sand-vik. You were sitting on the beach - just as you were a few days later, when you rode up from Dyngvale with Kari. We had that same conversation, more or less; for some strange reason, things never turn out exactly the same. It was from you I learnt about the death of the Moor - before it happened. Though not before he arrived in Tain. I made enquiries immediately: yes, there was such a man. I sent a message to him. I don't know if he ever received it.'

Presumably not. The Moors, the people of the Maghreb, though Muslims, never ignore dreams and signs and portents.

'And you have no control over these things?'

'No. The one they call the Witch of Golspie has, however - a lass my old friend found one day on the beach after a storm. She took her in and taught her all she knew. *She* uses a magic mirror - '

A magic mirror?

'An art I never mastered. It is just a bowl half filled with syrupy water in which certain herbs have been boiled (mustard seeds, red poppy flowers, nettle leaves, stonecrop) then charged with fire.'

'Fire?'

'Mental fire, which you accumulate in a ball between your two hands, moulding and forming it … then feeding it slowly and smoothly into the mirror. I have watched them do it, both of them; I have seen the image appear on the surface of the mirror, but for me - it does not happen.'

'Do they add drops of solution of gold? Do they add drops of human blood?'

'Ah. You know about these things. Yes, they do. And they would not have held anything back from me.'

'Were the drops of human blood that of a virgin?'

'A virgin?'

'Yes, it's important. My teacher in Spain used drops of *my* blood.'

'He *what*?'

'I was the only virgin available.'

'And your father *let* him?'

'My father never knew. It was nothing.'

She shook her head. 'Nothing, the lass says … So you *know* how to make a magic mirror.'

'No. He said not till I grew up. It was dangerous knowledge. But I haven't seen him since I grew up, haven't spoken to him …' Except in a dream in Paris, when he came to my aid at one of the worst times of my life; but there was no need to go into that now.

We lapsed into silence. I had much to think about.

Mouraig, sensing this, held her peace till we reached home.

Where Whin was waiting. 'They've taken Souad!' she cried, as soon as she saw us.

'Who's taken her?'

'The Pig.'

Mouraig laughed. 'Sir Hugh, she means.'

'I know. Phorca, I call him.'

Whin liked that. She knew the tale of the Four Pigs.

'He's taking her to Foulis, to his tower, and - '

'Let's all sit down,' Mouraig suggested, 'and you can tell us everything, starting from when you left here this morning.'

Mouraig and I went in. Whin, who was used to living out and didn't like being in houses, sat by the door.

'We were on the banks of the Balnagown, not far from Balichraggan, when there came a sudden silence. Even Souad noticed and listened. Then in the distance, we heard the baying of hounds, coming from the south. I took her up the river, then north and west into the forest, and when I was sure I had them heading west I doubled back east towards the sea. But he knows me now, the Pig - Phorca. And he knew I had Souad with me. At least, I think he knew. We must have been sighted. If I'd been alone, I would have gone up across the marshes and onto the Whiteness Sands and tried to strand and drown some dogs out there before I took to the sea; but Souad was tiring, and she can't swim.

'When we heard them close behind us, I headed this way. I thought *you* could protect at least her from the hounds. But long before we got here, she collapsed and they caught her. They almost caught *me*, for I was watching, and when he had them hold the hounds off her, they came straight for me! I saved myself, I had to - then hid underwater in a black-water lochan I found suddenly at my feet. When I came out, all was quiet, so I circled round to see what they were doing with Souad.'

She liked doing that.

'I heard them say they were taking her to Nigg, Phorca and one other, and that's where they'll be now, waiting for the tide to turn.'

Mouraig nodded. 'Aye, they'll have a little boat. They wouldn't want to be seen with her. Not if he's taking her for his own.'

'How much time do we have?' I asked.

'Time enough, maybe, on your horse,' Whin said. 'But then?'

'Then? We'll see. Let's get there first.'

'But will you be able to ride direct?' wondered Mouraig. 'What about the other hunters?'

'I don't know. They're probably still north of here.'

'Put this cloak on.' She gave Whin a white woollen cloak, and helped her on with it. She pulled the hood up over Whin's head and face. 'They won't recognise you like that. Especially not on a horse, and with Lady Marian.'

'They'll probably think she's the Queen of Elphame.' I meant it as a joke, but Whin was shocked and frightened. She made the sign with her hands, warding off evil, and tried to take the cloak off, but Mouraig insisted: 'Marian's just being silly again.'

Again?

Whin gave in.

She was much more frightened though, I noticed, of insulting the Queen than she was of Phorca and his gang of cutthroats.

'Won't he use the ferry?' I asked as we rode.

'No, he won't want to be seen, as Mouraig says. And he'll want to go direct to the jetty at Foulis.'

That was true.

'So what will he do, do you think?'

'I don't know, my lady. He's your kind, not mine.'

True again. We rode on in silence for a moment, then she relented.

'He'll take a boat the same as he took Souad.'

'He thinks he can take whatever he wants,' I said.

'He can.'

That too was true.

Outside the Ferry Inn, people were waiting to cross over to Cromarty. I asked them.

'Baron Hugh?' a woman answered. 'Aye, he took a boat belonged to the old man there.'

'Did he have anyone with him?'

'No, he was alone.'

I thanked her and led the horse over to the old man, with Whin still up on it, swathed in her cloak.

'He told me I should collect it from Foulis tomorrow, my lady. He said the rest of his party were waiting away along there under the cliff, and he could manage. So I helped him launch her, and that was that.'

'Then he's gone.'

'No, that's them pushing off now - down there, do you see? They haven't waited for the tide, so they'll have heavy going for a while.'

'When will it begin to flow?'

He surveyed the beach, the choppy grey water. 'A quarter of an hour maybe, my lady, or a wee bit more.'

I rode west along the beach, away from Sir Hugh, but in the direction in which he was now heading.

Whin said, 'How's your swimming, my lady?'

'Good. Not so good as yours, but - '

'Can you row a boat?'

'Not a boat as big as that. It wouldn't help anyway, would it?'

'No.'

I stopped the horse and we watched the boat coming slowly towards us. It was heading further out into the main channel where the current was stronger; no doubt to lessen the risk of being noticed. But where was Souad? All I could see was the two men. They must have tied her up and thrown her in the bottom of the boat.

'Listen,' Whin said. 'What I suggest is …'

I listened, and I liked it. It reminded me of the time I escaped from a ship that was carrying me away from Andalucía, my home, and over to Oran, to the slave market.

We rode till we were out of sight of the little port, then tethered the horse, took off our clothes, and slipped into the sea. It was cold, but wonderful. I should have swum with Kari that first evening instead of sitting grumping on the beach like some old grandmother. But if I had, perhaps I would never have met my grandmother.

I would have met her.

'There they are!'

They were coming towards us quite fast, and would pass us by some fifteen yards further out. I stayed where I was, while Whin swam out till she was directly in the path of the boat. As it came up to her, she gave a cry and I saw Hugh leap to his feet.

'It's her! And look - she's injured. I got her! I did get her!'

So Whin, playing at being injured, tempted him to lean over, catch her, pull her out, up into the boat.

'I'll have the two of them!' he crowed. 'I'll have them both!' He leant right out and caught her by the arm and by the hair - and when he was completely off balance she gave a tug and in he went.

Meanwhile, I had swum up to the other side of the boat and was waiting.

Hugh shouted, 'Here! Help! Give me a hand in, dammit!'

And as his man leant over to pull him in, as he took the weight of him and the boat tipped, I lifted my side up with all the strength I had and - yes! - the boat jerked and I heard another great yell and splash and more yells.

Then, mysteriously, the boat began to move again, fast, on into the loch, and left me face to face with the two struggling men. They were not looking at me. Hugh could swim, but his companion could not and was hanging onto Hugh, dragging him down, drowning him. Then Hugh, too, panicked, and did what he would do: he pulled out his dirk and thrust it into the man, who jerked up half out of the water almost as though Hugh were lifting him, then sank.

Now Hugh turned his attention to me. 'Marian,' he hissed. And I, who had been watching aghast, suddenly realised that it might be my turn. I duck-dived. For a brief second, he had only my legs to look at - to lunge towards, knife still in hand - then they too were gone.

Would he claim later that they had changed into a tail?

I swam on underwater till I could go no further, then surfaced. Whin, towing the boat, was far ahead of me. I glanced round and saw Hugh making for the beach.

Our perfect plan had one enormous drawback.

He would come out just where we had left the horse and our clothes!

What to do? Whin and Souad would get away. She would beach the boat somewhere near the mouth of the Balnagown and take Souad on from there. They would be as they had been before Hugh caught up with them - except that Whin, once again, had no clothes.

But nor did I. And this was no dream.

I had Hugh, in a rage, between me and my horse and clothes, and other hunters, the rest of his gang, on their way down here to join up with him.

I could not swim back to Kattar-bol. If I tried, I would be

caught long before I got there. I could perhaps swim across to Cromarty, but might drown on the way. And if I got there, what could I do? Go to Callum Vass and Shusie? Go to the hermit Farquhar, at Red Nose? Naked? Swim ashore here, to the north, somewhere out of Hugh's sight, and go up the hill, take to the forest? Try to get back to Mouraig's that way? Around Balintore the land was mostly clear of woods. Perhaps at night, in the dark …

No, there was only one thing to do. I had to get to those clothes, that horse, before Hugh did. He had seen the horse, was trying to make his way to it, swimming against the current. I raced after him. Too much thinking, not enough action. *Hod.* Now if I were more like Whin …

I stopped for breath and to see where he was. He had changed direction again, exhausted, desperate now simply to get to the beach without swimming any further than he had to. Easier to walk back along the sand.

I was tired but not exhausted. I swam straight for the horse, as fast as I could.

When I looked up again, I was nearly there - but so was he! He was coming up out of the water onto the beach. Staggering.

I swam on, felt the waves breaking, felt sand under my hands, ran up out of the water - and found myself in a race with him. But he was nearer. Then he suddenly fell flat on his face. I was there!

I undid the bridle, seized the clothes, and sprang up onto the horse. But he was up again, and he too leapt. He missed me, but grabbed at the clothes in my hand as the horse started moving. I wrenched most of them out of his hand, as I thought, and cantered away into the evening. But I was wrong. All I had left in my hand was the old cloak Mouraig had given to Whin.

If I put that on, *I* would be mistaken for the Queen of Elphame.

I slowed down.

Stopped.

I was going about this all wrong. What was I hoping to achieve by running away? As though *I* were the criminal.

It was that dream. He was the hunter, I was the prey.

I turned back.

He was still there, staring after me in disbelief.

'Hugh?' I said, sweetly. 'I suddenly realised it was you. I thought I was dealing with a *common* criminal.'

His mouth fell open. It only needed an apple in it.

'Can I give you a ride somewhere? You are wet.'

'So are you.' His eyes could not stop running up and down my body. 'Get down then, let me up in the saddle. You can ride in my lap.'

'Oh, no. I stay right where I am. You can come up behind me.'

'Behind you?' His fat face opened in that unforgettable smile, while his eyes continued to flick up and down from my face to my feet and back up from my legs to my lips. And my eyes. He looked *at* my eyes, I noticed. He didn't look into them.

'But first you put those clothes down there - just there - yes - and turn your back while I dress.'

He sighed, and did as I had ordered.

I jumped rather than slid down off the horse. Saddles are most unpleasant when you are wet and naked, especially that saddle. Couldn't Ferchard have found something a little more suitable for me? I pulled on my clothes - and realised I had Whin's clothes there too. Had he noticed?

'How do you come to be in the company of that tinkler bitch, Marian?' he asked, his back to me.

'Tinkler?'

'The one you were with. The shape-shifter. Don't tell me you didn't see her change into a mermaid again out there? Just as she did the last time I saw her, after I hunted her into the sea.'

'Was that her? The poor creature you were hunting that day? But this was a woman, Hugh. You can't go around hunting women. Or kidnapping them, come to that.'

'She's not a woman, she's a tinkler - and a selchi, or something, you know, that changes. And the other one isn't one of us either. She's that slave-girl - a Muslim. Nothing.'

'Not nothing, Hugh. All right, you can turn round now.'

I swung up into the saddle and he clambered up behind me.

'I'm going to Tain,' I said.

'Aye, that'll do me.'

We started off along the road at a slow trot, his thumbs on my hips, his index fingers pressed into my groin, both sides, and the rest of his fingers over the sides of my buttocks. Well, it could be worse. Would be much worse if he had got to the horse first and had the whip hand - literally - as he so nearly did.

'You haven't answered me, madam,' he grunted.

'You haven't asked me, sir.'

He made a piggy noise that may have been a chuckle.

'I'm not sure you're not a better catch than all the others put together, Marian.'

'Ah, but I'm not a catch, am I? I'm another one that got away. A good thing Margaret didn't witness that performance.' I laughed.

'You won't tell her?'

'Listen, Hugh. I was riding along, enjoying the view up on the hill with the open sea on one side of me and Nigg Bay on the other, and in the distance, snow-capped, beyond the hills, what I took to be Ben Wyvis, when I heard "Lady! Lady!" and the tinkler woman - whose name incidentally is Whin - burst out of the bushes crying, "Lady! They're after me - and they've taken Souad!" "Souad? The Moorish girl? How do you know her?" I demanded. "She was lost! She'd run away from them! I've been looking after her!" "I see."

'Well, Hugh, as you know, I have appointed myself in some sense Souad's protector, so I said, "Where is she? Where are they taking her?" And she showed me two men - two criminals - and the poor girl in a boat heading into the Cromarty Firth. "Will you help me rescue her?" I said.

'She said she would. And we did.'

'Hm. I'm not at all sure you have told me the whole story. But then you are not the sort of woman who would tell a man the whole story.'

'Who would tell anyone the whole story.'

'There's something wild in you, Marian.'

He was quite romantic for a Phorca.

'You are the woman I always dreamt of but never believed in: something between Margaret, the wild huntress, who prefers leather to silk, and the ordinary, silly women we are surrounded by all our days. Something better than either ... Perfect.'

I wondered about his mother; but all I said was, to provoke

him, and to keep the conversation going, 'Sounds more like Whin than me.'

'Whin? You mean the tinkler?'

'Yes. She's the one who roams thc hills and forests, the one you cannot catch for all your men and all your dogs, and she a poor naked defenceless woman.'

'Defenceless? She killed half my dogs the other day. Drowned a trusted servant of mine today.'

'She did not drown him. I tipped him in. You knifed him. She was busy saving life, not taking it.'

He was silent for a moment, thinking. Then he said, 'Aye, but you're a lady.'

'A lady-lady,' I laughed.

'Aye, my Marian, you're a lady-lady, unlike Margaret. But you're more, much more, than that. Will I tell you a strange thing?'

I didn't answer. I knew he would.

'I would have got to the horse first, but something tripped me. Yet there was nothing there.'

I snorted.

'And will I tell you another strange thing? ... I have just realised who it is, is riding round the country posing as the Queen of Elphame. Posing it may be. Perhaps she really is the Queen of Elphame. After all, with her name and ancestry ...'

Nigg Bay on our left was filling rapidly now. We rode north into the evening in silence, leaving the Bay behind and I thought about what he had said and wondered what name he could mean, what Margaret's ancestry was, apart from being a Bruce and of the family of "the Steward". I was still sneering in my mind at the pretensions of the Bruces when he said, 'How will I ever catch the tinkler woman or the runaway slavegirl if you are protecting them? I mean if they are your friends - if they are Whin to you, and Souad, then ...'

So that was it.

So be it.

We rode on towards Tain in silence. Even his hands on the sides of my buttocks seemed reverent now.

CHAPTER NINETEEN

The Sweet Influences Of Pleiades

I woke with a start, and for a moment did not know where I was. Then I remembered bringing Sir Hugh to the Spider, declining to eat with him, coming up to my room. And remembered too that it was Thursday.

I got up, washed, did my exercises, meditated.

I would ride out to Kattar-bol. I needed to know what was happening. Perhaps Whin and Souad were there. Perhaps Thorfinn Skinner had died and Bella was there. And Raoul.

As I rode along, I thought about Raoul, his infatuation with Bella. It was understandable, predictable even. But what was *her* situation now, in fact? And what could he do? She was not free, any more than Souad would have been free without the certificate of manumission Ben Youssef had prepared for her. She would go with the house, as the livestock would go with the farm, to whoever was Thorfinn Skinner's heir. She and the boat, and the great wolfhound, Butterfly.

And who was his heir?

In fact, only Bella was there. She was sitting with my grandmother. Raoul had gone back into Tain the previous evening, had not been seen since.

'But didn't he say he would ride back out to you for the night?' I demanded, not realising how upset she was. I was tired and worried. My temper was short.

'Perhaps he did, and Bella had already left,' said Mouraig. 'She arrived here yesterday evening quite early.'

'Then why didn't he follow her here?'

They didn't shrug. They merely looked at me.

'All right,' I said. 'I'm sorry. You'd better tell me the story, Bella. In your own way. From the beginning.'

'Have you had anything to eat or drink today, child?' asked

Mouraig.

I shook my head.

'Then wait till you have.'

I went outside. It was a clear, calm day. The beach was deserted apart from some birds - a pair of jackdaws, the usual wagtails, a few gulls soaring and swooping where the sunshine bounced and sparkled over the sea straight at me. It reminded me of home - home in Spain, I mean, the coast where I grew up, which also faces east into the morning sun: warmer, much warmer, than this, but no brighter.

I sat on my usual rock. It had a smooth, flat, slightly concave surface that I liked.

Hugh had thought I was the Queen of Elphame.

Whin thought the Queen was the goddess Mour, riding out still as she had always ridden out since the beginning of time.

What had Abdelwahed ben Youssef thought? Or rather, what had he known? And had there been any connection between that knowledge and his death?

Was Raoul right when he suggested that ben Youssef might have been some kind of secret agent and his death politically motivated? Jaufre also seemed to consider that possible.

Was Drostan right that it had probably been the murder of an outsider, a foreigner, an unbeliever - of someone who is not "one of us" - and not personally motivated at all? Or hardly at all.

Was Mouraig right when she observed that there were beautiful women close to the heart of the story, that they were sure to be involved somehow, at least in the motivation?

It had crossed my mind more than once over the past few years that when a second death occurred, the leads which had seemed so baffling came together and began to make sense.Thorfinn Skinner was dying. Was presumably dead, as Bella had turned up here on her own and stayed the night. Did that help?

Then Bella came out with my breakfast: some oatcake, some honey and some herb tea.

'Shall I stay, my lady?'

'Yes. Oh, this is nice. Thank you. Sit down - there will do.'

She sat on another rock, facing me, close to me, but not too close, and slightly lower than me.

'You told me - you told me to stay with him until he died, but - oh, my lady! I couldn't! I just couldn't. You see, he … He was worse, my lady, he didn't know what he was saying, what he was doing, and all he could think about was the …'

'What did he say? Anything about the death of the Moor?'

'The Moor? Oh no, my lady, my master doesn't know anything about that. He was out in his boat and he never came back that evening, nor any of the following days. I'll swear to that.'

'What makes you so sure?'

'His bow, my lady. He forgot his bow. By the time he realised, it was too late. He had to creep up on the walrus and use his harpoon on it, like a spear - for it was not in the water, it was out on land, on the beach somewhere.'

'He told you that?'

'Oh yes, it was the first thing he said when he arrived back and saw his bow standing there where he had left it, in the yard. And I already knew. I noticed it there soon after he left. I'd have expected him to come back for it, but he didn't.'

A good alibi. Too good? And economical, too, if the alibi was also the murder weapon.

'So you were there most of the evening, you and Coll? One of you would have seen him if he'd come back.'

'Oh yes.'

'Yes what?'

'Yes, my lady.'

I laughed. I was feeling better now. 'I don't mean that, silly. I mean yes one of you would have seen him or yes you Bella were at home most of the evening?'

'Both, my lady.'

'Bella, it's time for the truth. If you knew it wasn't Skinner who murdered ben Youssef, and if you knew you hadn't murdered him yourself, then why did you lie to me? Who were you protecting? Captain le Fou? He doesn't need your protection. No one suspects him.'

At least I thought not. Perhaps on second thoughts Jaufre was still a suspect. Especially if it had been a political killing. However, there was no need for Bella to know that.

'It wasn't for him,' she said, 'it was for me.'

'Of course it was for you. By claiming that he took you back to the steading you made him the one who was wandering around out there alone at the critical time. In fact it was you who was alone out there. Captain le Fou stayed in Tain.'

'My lady, you said I was to tell you the story my way, from the beginning - but which story do you want? The story of that night? Or the story of yesterday afternoon?'

'Both. But let's start with that night, shall we? And I want the truth. The whole truth.'

'Yes, my lady.'

'So. Master Skinner left on his boat. Did you see him go?'

'Yes. I helped him put his things on the boat.'

'And you didn't notice the bow?'

'No, that's something he always sees to himself.'

'And then? Where was Coll?'

'I don't know. With the pigs. She came in later. Into the house, I mean. She wasn't allowed in there any more, not since ...'

'Bella, was your master sleeping with you? Making love to you?'

'Sleeping with me? No, not sleeping. And not love. But yes, he was fucking me.'

'Did you mind? Did you try to stop him?'

'What did he care if I minded? He preferred it that I minded. He liked to rape a girl, not love her. Some men do ... Before Harald - long before - when I was still a little girl, I was sold to a brothel-owner by my mother. I remember her saying goodbye to me. She must have had a good reason. And I was there in that brothel till I was fourteen. That was in St Edmundsbury. Then I was sold to another brothel, a bigger, better one, in Colchester. Now my owner was a woman and life was easier - in some ways, though you can't do what you like with a woman the way you can with a man. I was there till I was twenty. Then I was bought out by Master William of Wivenhoe.'

'Why? What for?'

'Because he loved me.'

'And he was good to you?'

'Oh yes. We were happy. Really happy. He was going to free

me, marry me, but - he was a gambler. When he bought me it was with money he'd won. I found that out later. Anyway, he lost me, in a bet with Master Harald Skinnerson. Against Harald's boat ... So you see, when you've worked in a brothel - grown up in a brothel - you don't mind being fucked. You hardly notice. It isn't something ...'

'I was kidnapped, Bella, and bought and sold, and beaten, and ... yes, I understand. It mattered more to Coll than it did to you.'

'He made her live out in the byre at the back, like an animal, but - no, I don't think she minded. I think she preferred it.'

'I see. She was indoors though, in the house, when Captain le Fou arrived.'

'She slipped away when the dog started barking. She didn't want to be seen in the house.'

'You wouldn't tell Master Thorfinn?'

'Me? No, of course not.'

'But she knew it was Captain le Fou?'

'Oh yes, she hears everything, even from the byre. Anyway, Captain le Fou had seen my master's boat leaving and had come out to talk to me.'

'Was this the first time?'

'No. He'd been - twice - before.'

'And had you encouraged him?'

'No. He was sweet, but he was like a customer - you know, in the brothel - a nice customer - even a favourite customer - but ... not like Master Raoul.'

'Raoul - loved you?'

She nodded. 'He'd seen me in Tain, and came out to bring me a poem he'd written - a poem about me.'

'Did he make love to you?'

'No!' She blushed bright red.

'And le Fou? The Captain?'

'Oh, well - yes - of course - but that wasn't "love".'

'That night? The night ben Youssef died?'

'No, I - I wasn't in the mood. I thought Master Thorfinn might come back for his bow. I thought Master Abdelwahed might come.'

'Why? Had you been letting him fuck you too?'

'No!' This time she was not only embarrassed, she was angry. 'Do you think I let anyone fuck me? Do you think I charge them for it? I've never charged anyone for it. I let Jaufre do it because he needed to do it. I've been dealing with men like him all my life. It's my trade, what I was trained for. But Master Abdelwahed ... you must understand, my lady: Master Abdelwahed was a friend. My first real friend since I was brought here to Scotland, apart from the monks. Master Raoul, though … he loves me. That's different.'

There must be many who are whores by trade who are not whores at heart. And many who are whores at heart who are not whores by trade. A disquieting thought.

'Bella, your friend Abdelwahed is dead. I'm trying to find out who killed him, to stop another innocent person being tortured to death and bring the real killer to justice. Now, tell me what happened next.'

She looked lost. I smiled. 'Between you and Jaufre le Fou.'

'He took me with him into Tain, said he would show me his room, take me downstairs for a drink. I wanted to go. I never go anywhere now except with Master Thorfinn. But in his room I still wasn't in the mood, and when he said "Then let's go for a drink, *ma belle*," I suddenly realised that of course I couldn't go into the tap-room with him. Everyone knows me, and that I belong to Master Thorfinn. So I left him and went back to the steading alone.'

'But what did he say? He wouldn't like that. I know him. He would at least want to take you home. Perhaps he followed you. Did he follow you, meaning to take you home on his horse? Was he out there when Abdelwahed was killed?'

'No. No, I'm sure he wasn't. He didn't follow me because he didn't know I'd gone. You see he left me in his room while he went for a drink and a meal. I told him I would feel better if he left me alone, let me sleep for a couple of hours in his bed - then I would be ready for him.'

That rang true. Jaufre would love sitting in a bar knowing that he had this waiting for him at home, warming his bed. The anticipation.

'You didn't mean it, though,' I said.

'No. Oh, I don't know. He went, and - and after a while, I crept out of the house and ran through the town and ran and ran till I had crossed the river and felt safe. Now he would never know I'd been there. Then I started walking. I walked slowly. I was happy. I was enjoying the evening. And I kept off the road so if Jaufre did follow me he wouldn't see me.'

'And then what happened? Remember you're telling me the truth this time.'

'What do you think happened, my lady?'

She could be cheeky, this one.

I wondered where Kari was, and what was happening to her. Another cheeky one.

I wondered if Sir Hugh saw me as I saw them. No, he did not. Though he might if he got to know me better and the glamour wore off.

The glamour. If he went to the Bailie, it wouldn't be cheek he charged me with.

Ferchard used to say I was cheeky. Now he boxed the ears of anyone who was cheeky to me.

I couldn't see him boxing Bella's ears. If he was nothing else, my Farquhar, he was a gentle knight. Unlike Sir Hugh.

'I think Abdelwahed ben Youssef came riding along, and you, realising it was not Jaufre le Fou, let yourself be seen. And he stopped. And you talked. And he took you up on the horse - where? Behind him, or in front on his lap?'

'Behind him, my lady.'

'And then what happened? He took you home and dropped you off and rode away again? Or he took you home and went in with you? Or he never reached the steading because you didn't like what he said - he intended to report you to your master? - and you - or somebody else - killed him on the way?'

'My lady, you see now why I lied to you. It is too easy even for you to imagine awful things like that once you know I was out there at the time.'

'So what did happen?'

'He took me home and came in with me. We talked for a while, then he left.'

'You spoke French?'

She smiled and nodded.

A breeze was blowing up. I looked along the beach. I could see herring gulls now, wheeling over the sea, but they were wild and shy, not like the black-headed gulls.

'And what did you talk about?'

'Nothing to do with the murder.'

'What did you talk about? You promised to tell me everything.'

'Yes, my lady. Well, you see, we had met on - on other occasions, and Abdelwahed liked me ...'

Her life would be a great deal less complicated if she were plain - or even ordinarily beautiful. Like me.

'And?'

'And he wanted to buy me.'

I looked at her.

She smiled. 'That surprised you, my lady.'

'No, it didn't, actually. Remember I've had Souad's story. Had he spoken to your master about this plan you dreamed up between you?'

'Yes, and Master Thorfinn said no. Then Abdelwahed said money was no object - and Master Thorfinn said yes. But Abdelwahed was a good man. His main concern was me, what I wanted, and Souad, whether she liked the idea. He came that evening to inform us that Souad raised no objections: she said if we didn't get on, he could sell me again later. And after all, whoever he sold me to, it couldn't be worse than my present situation.' She hesitated, looked at me, obviously wondering whether to tell me. 'He had the purse of gold with him. The gold to buy me with.'

'And he took it away with him again when he left?'

She nodded.

What happened to that?

'How had all this come about? These earlier meetings you mentioned?'

'He stopped me one day, told me he knew a slave when he saw one, knew an unhappy slave when he saw one. Would I like a change of master? I would.'

'How had he stopped you? I thought you weren't allowed out

on your own.'

'I go out sometimes when my master is not around.'

'I see. So you would have expected to be sold to Abdelwahed when your master came back from this fishing trip. And you liked the idea.'

'Oh yes, my lady. And if he did sell me again it would be to another good man, and it would be in a warm country, he said, with beautiful trees and flowers and horses and fountains and women - but none so beautiful as me. No women, anyway. The horses were more beautiful. He made me laugh. He could see I was sad and he wanted to make me laugh.'

'So for you his death was in fact a catastrophe.'

'Yes, my lady. And for poor Souad.'

'You've met Souad?'

'No, but he talked about her. And Jaufre, too. Jaufre told me she was small and dark - exotic - quite the opposite of me.'

'That's true. And more to Jaufre's taste,' I said, cattily.

'Oh, I know. He told me. I wasn't his thing at all, he said, but he didn't mind, for a change. As no one else was available, he meant.' She laughed.

Mouraig had emerged, and was looking up and down the beach. She came over to join us. Bella stood up.

'No, no, you bide there, child. I'll just sit here.' She sat down carefully on a sea-bleached log that must have been washed up some time when the tide was exceptionally high. It had now dried out, and was probably more comfortable and certainly far warmer than the rocks we foolish virgins had plumped for.

A Biblical allusion: the term "virgin" is used loosely in that - and other - Biblical contexts. And in this. However, "foolish" did apply, literally, to both of us. Only Sir Hugh, I think, looking back on it, and perhaps le Fou himself, could compete with Bella and me on that score.

'So what should we do, do you think, Marian?'

'About what?'

She looked at me. 'About the situation at the Skinner steading.' She peered at Bella, dazzled by the sunshine. 'You haven't told her the situation?'

'No, my lady, I - I didn't - '

'It's my fault. I was asking her about ben Youssef. So tell me, Bella. You had been entrusted with the care of your master. What happened? Why did you leave him?'

'He got worse, my lady. All day he slept, on and off, but each time he woke he was worse.'

'He would be. He was dying.'

'Let her speak, Marian. Go on, child.'

'Worse in the things he was saying. He wanted to take me with him.'

'You mean - ?'

'He wanted to kill me, and take me with him. He said he had been born alone; he wasn't going to die alone. Why should he? I was his thrall. He could do anything he liked with me. He could kill me if he wanted to. He could have killed me any time he liked.' She turned to Mouraig. 'Is that true, my lady?'

'Something like that, yes. It's the old law of the North Folk - of whom, in part at least, I am one. But the old laws do not run, not here, not now. Thorfinn would say, of course, that in his own home a man's will is the law, no matter where, no matter when. And he is right, to some extent. Sir Magnus would have said the same.'

Sir Magnus. My grandfather. Yes, but there has to be some control over evil men like Thorfinn Skinner, doesn't there?

'So what did you do?' I asked Bella, anxious now to hear the story.

'I kept away from his hands. It was difficult because I had to give him the filtre you left, I had to hold him up when he coughed. The last time I held him, he seized hold of me and pulled a knife out from under the mattress. I wriggled and struggled and as he raised the knife I slipped out of his grip - he was all wet and sweaty - and he missed me and slashed his own arm. Then slept again, I think. Or at least lay there quietly, his eyes now open, now closed, now open again. His arm was to his lips, so there was blood on his face, round his mouth. The next time he coughed, I refused to go near him. I know I should have, he was coughing blood, but I'd put him in a rage, I didn't mean to. It was my eyes, I think, my eyes always made the blood go to his head – I tried not to look at him - and the anklet, if he couldn't take me, he wanted the anklet, to take the anklet - the Magdalene Anklet, he was calling it now, though he never had before - but he'd promised Master Harald and Harald had promised Master William ... I don't know. There are things about me that sometimes make men mad. Anyway he pulled himself up, swung his legs off the bed and came for me, arms wide. I ran out through the door. He staggered after me. He had his knife raised. Butterfly started barking at him, dancing around behind him. I jumped up on the horse and turned and faced him. He swung his knife at the horse, the dog, me, I don't know. The horse shied up, the dog flew at him, the horse came down on him, then he was lying on the ground all bloody and he was dead - or not, still - I didn't look, I couldn't look.'

'You just left him where he was?'

She nodded.

'What about the horse? And Butterfly? Did you leave them there?'

'They were his.'

As you were his, I thought.

'They'll be all right,' she said, brightly. 'Everything will be all right - except the the goats. They need milking.'

'You rode to the gate?'

She nodded.

'And the hound followed you?'

'No. I don't know. He wasn't with me outside the gate. I slipped down off the horse and shut it inside, and ran. I ran till I could run no further, then walked, and in Balintore a woman told me how to come along here to Mouraig's house.'

'In what language?'

'My lady, I'm telling you the truth. I've learnt a few words of Gaelic but we didn't need them, not really. She knew the name Mouraig, and showed me the path. I'd been crying, and she wanted to help. She described Mouraig's house. She used her hands to help me understand, and I did, I understood everything.'

I am surprised all the men of Balintore didn't turn out to escort her.

Mouraig, reading my mind, gives me a baleful look.

I ignore her.

'So, Bella, come here, closer, and give me your hands. And let me look into your eyes. That's it … Now tell me about yourself. How do you feel about your mother, now that you are a woman and you know how difficult - how impossible - life can be?'

She has the ability to open right up. No doubt something else that makes her irresistible. Her eyes are like invitations - or rather declarations: I am all yours. And the soft, sweet voice so characteristic of the Taurus is lulling me, lulling me … Just like Big Ferchard, another Taurus. Another victim. What is she saying?

' … so I think on the whole, if she couldn't keep me, and if there was no one who wanted to give me a home, then she probably did the right thing. I mean a home is a family, isn't it? A home is filled with love. She wouldn't have wanted me to be a little skivvy, a slave to the real children. And if she'd taken me to a convent, they wouldn't have paid her for me - and from what I've heard of nuns and convents - and priests - I wouldn't have been very happy. So …'

She's right about that.

She has the tapering fingertips of the comfort-loving.

'My hands are not the same as they were before I came up here.'

'You mean they used to be beautiful, but now with the cold and the hard work …'

She nods.

The skin was once fine, yes. Will be again if she gets the chance to indulge her natural laziness - as I'm sure she will. And the nails, though rough and in one case broken now, are clearly the perfect oblongs indicative of a sweet and gentle nature.

The little finger on both hands bends inwards slightly: diplomacy, a tendency to deceive when she deems it necessary.The largest mount is the mount of the Sun, so the third finger is important too. It is perfectly formed on both hands. This, with the pronounced mount, indicates physical beauty - well, we know that - and a tendency to shine, be charismatic, but also to be the object of envy. She will be versatile and adaptable - but she will be vain. Interesting …

The mount of Venus is also pronounced. A love of home and family. She will be sweet and kind, and hate to cause harm to anyone or anything. She will love peace and harmony. She could though, if bad, become morally corrupt - in fact completely depraved.

The Line of Life and Line of Head are long and unflawed. However, the Heart Line starts between the index and middle fingers - sign of a potential for happy love but also the likelihood of suffering before that happiness is finally achieved.

I feared that the Line of Fate might terminate at the Heart Line - as Raoul's does, I now remember - but it does not, which is a relief. In fact it does not seem at all that the situation she is now in is anything more than a passing difficulty: there is every indication of a rewarding union and lasting happiness.

'Bella,' I say, 'I believe you. In my opinion, you will come out of all this without suffering any real harm and will enter a new and happy phase in your life.'

'Will I get married?'

'You will. And have children.'

And you will get married again in later life, when you are still beautiful and your first husband is for some reason no longer with you. But there is no need to tell her that.

I am also relieved to find that the mark in the mount of Venus which indicates following love as a profession, profiting from it, is absent. Nor is there any indication anywhere of any murderous or criminal tendency.

'And a home? I'll have a home of my own?'

'You will have the home of your own that you have dreamt of for so long. But ...'

She smiles nervously.

'But people have a way of putting you on a pedestal, treating you like a goddess, worshipping you. It is not your fault. It is written in your hand and in your star-sign. But they do, and that can give rise to danger. Two dangers. First, that of vanity. Vanity is not only sinful, it is foolish. Beauty passes like the flowers in the field. Don't take your beauty - or your admirers - too seriously.'

She knows what I mean. With those eyes, who would - who could - wear jewels?

'That's not really a danger, my lady.'

No? 'No, but jealousy is. People will envy you. Or will envy those who have you, which can be equally dangerous.'

'I know … And the other danger?'

'I have mentioned two.'

'No, my lady, you've mentioned one.'

Mouraig smiles. At her, not me.

I laugh. 'Then, "my lady, you tell me" what the other danger is.' I quote back at her.

'There's a danger of being caught out. Of people discovering that you are not what they take you for, not what you seem.'

Mouraig sighs. 'That happens to all of us in the end. All but the most simple, the most innocent, of us. I must go in, I am getting stiff. Which of you will give me a hand?'

Bella goes in with her, and I walk north along the beach, then stop and sit down again and look back past a series of jutting green headlands, one behind the other, down towards Nigg - and the Black Isle - is that the Black Isle? - in the far distance.

I take my clothes off and walk into the sea.

An hour later, completely refreshed, I swim up onto the beach and look round. No one. I stand up and walk quickly to my clothes. I dress without drying - I have no towel with me - and hurry back to the house. I want to ride out to the steading, now, straightaway, to see what the situation is, and I want Bella with me.

She is not there.

Niáll of Lairg is there, come looking for news of Souad - and to check up on me, I am sure.

When he has gone, Mouraig tells me that Bella saw him approaching and fled up the hill at the back, following in the footsteps of Whin and Souad. But where she has gone, we do not know.

She will certainly not have taken to the woods.

Am I wrong about her again?

While I change my clothes, my grandmother watches and listens.

'Mouraig, there are aspects of the Thorfinn story that I do not understand. For instance, how does he come to have a son the age of Harald, Bella's late master, when he himself can be no more than forty and he spent years away in England - possibly even elsewhere - in the service of Coucy? Did he go away after Harald was born, leaving the boy alone here with his mother? I find that difficult to believe.'

'Thorfinn was not Harald's father. Thorfinn had an elder brother, Dub. The steading belonged to Dub, and Harald was Harald Dubson. When Thorfinn came back from his travels, he found Harald and his mother alone, Dub having disappeared on a journey somewhere in the west. He took over. Harald's mother was Mary, the "wife" I told you about.'

'The one Thorfinn worked -'

'And beat - '

'To death. Yes, I remember.'

'Another thing that might interest you: Thorfinn's mother died in childbirth, having him. I know. I was there. It was soon after I got back from my travels.'

'That would explain his saying that he was born alone.'

'Exactly.'

'Hmm. So who is Thorfinn's heir?'

She shook her head. 'Is it important?'

'His heir will be Bella's new owner.'

'Aye, that's right, poor lass.'

But why has she fled? I want her to go with me to the steading. I want to know if everything is as she left it. I want to see her reaction to the scene, now, the next day.

I go alone.

Everything is more or less as she described it. The horse is grazing on the far side of the enclosure. The pigs are snuffling around in the same area as the horse. The goats come running up to me, bleating. Sorry, girls.

The great wolfhound that Bella calls Butterfly and refers to as a dog is lying on the ground near his dead master. He has his head between his paws. He does not raise it, but he watches me. He growls a little. A warning. Nothing serious. I say 'Oh come on, Butterfly, it's me - your next best favourite lady.' His tail moves. I am in.

Now for Thorfinn.

He is lying on his front. His back had been to the house when he fell, but he fell forward, away from the house. Why, if he fell back, as Bella said, away from the horse's hooves?

And why is the back of his head broken and sticky and covered with flies?

Someone did this to him - did it from behind while he was still standing. Or at least kneeling. If the horse's hooves had hit him, they would have caught his forehead, the front of his head, or his shoulders. Unless Thorfinn had turned away from the horse. But he hadn't. And the marks of a horse's hoof would be different. This was done with something heavy and rounded and blunt.

Yes, there it was: where it had been thrown down only a few yards away after it had done its work.

I picked it up.

Butterfly growled again and backed away from me.

I talked to him, calming him down, while I examined it.

The club - a heavy piece of wood, rounded, part of a branch - still had blood and hair on it. But that was all, of course. No indication who might have wielded it. But I knew who had wielded it. And I knew why. I just didn't know why she had lied to me - again - when she told me the story.

If it had been anyone else, the hound would have defended Thorfinn.

I turned him over - and swerved away, retching.

I have a strong stomach, but this ... His nose, half his face, had been torn away. Butterfly? No. That was done by the horse. Well, Thorfinn. When even your horse turns against you, even your dog will no longer defend you ...

But there were no hoofmarks anywhere on the front of his head, either.

I went back to Mouraig, leading Thorfinn's horse, his hound following us.

I told her I suspected Bella again. We talked. We did not agree. She was right. And yet I was right. This must have been Bella. And why was she lying to me?

Yet her hand, her horoscope, was all against it.

I needed to establish how and where she fitted into the scheme of things as laid out in Kabbalah. My old teacher Yacoub's system.

She didn't fit in. She didn't fit in at all.

I went for another walk. Not by the sea this time but up over the hill of Kattar-bol and down the other side. And there I met a child, a little girl.

She looked at me. I looked back at her. I smiled.

She said, 'Are you the Queen?'

I was going to laugh and say Of course not, but instead I said, 'Do I look like the Queen, flower?'

She looked me over. 'Aye, you look like her. But you are not her.'

'You've seen her then?'

She nodded. 'My da thinks we saw her today, but we didn't. We saw you. He thinks you are the Queen.'

'Where did you see me?'

'Down there.' She pointed, vaguely. 'You were leading the Queen's horse, and her hound was with you, as he always is with her. But she wasn't there.'

'That was Thorfinn Skinner's horse and hound.'

'It was her horse. I know it. And I know her hound, too. The way it holds its head and tail, and looks around, watching out for any danger to her. It's the best dog in the whole world ... Why was he with you? Where were you taking them?'

'To the Witch. She's looking after them ... My name's Marian. What's yours?'

'Mona. Sweign's my grandda - Sweign Pigsticker. He agrees with me. "Lady Marian MacElpin she is," he says. "The Queen of Elphame she isn't."'

'And what makes him - and you - so sure, Mona?'

'The Queen has yellow hair, yellower than mine. I've seen it. So has Grandda.'

Yellow hair. Her horse. Her dog.

'Mona, are you sure? Quite, quite sure?'

'Oh yes, she threw her hood back once, right off her head, and smiled at me. She has blue eyes, too, but blue, blue, blue. You're the same as her - tall and pretty, like a queen - but you can't change the colour of your hair, can you? Or of your eyes.'

I laughed. 'My hair, maybe. But not my eyes.'

I gave her a kiss. 'Mona, you've been a great help to me. Here …' I took out a gold noble, the pair of the one I'd given to Shusie for Wee Magnus Vass. 'Take this home and hide it. Don't lose it - it's gold.'

'Gold!'

'Yes. Put it away and keep it for one day when you're older, when you might need it. And remember it was given to you by Lady Marian, who is definitely not - and you can tell your da this from me - definitely not the Queen of Elphame.'

I ran back over the hill, almost falling down the cliff through the bushes to the house, and thinking how could Whin, how could anyone, run - get away - in a skirt? She had no choice but to strip, it was that or be caught and be killed. Me, I was merely in a hurry to get my horse and ride back to the Skinner steading, but still ever since that "dream" I had the urge to run free through the trees and down the hills.

It was late, but I had to go. I had to find that white cloak, the cloak of silk and satin trimmed with white fur.

Was it possible? Had Hugh Skinner's son loved her so much? No. More likely it was this William of Wivenhoe, or some earlier admirer.

Of course: the gold anklet. William of Wivenhoe had staked her as she stood against the boat as it stood. And she had been wearing a white cloak. *The* white cloak.

But Mouraig wouldn't hear of my going. Go in the morning. All right. All right … I was very tired. I began to undress, ready for bed.

'No, child, I want a walk on the beach with you first.'

'But you're tired, too.'

She took the pouch she always carried - always, except that time she was arrested. Had she known it was her they were coming for?

I wanted to ask what was in it.

She looked up at me. 'There's a blade we'll be needing. And my shell. And the talismans of the World Tree: I shouldn't like to be without them this evening or during the coming days. Will I show you?'

I nodded, and she emptied it out on the table. From among the bits and pieces - not so different from Coll's bits and pieces, after all - she picked out a patch of reddish bark and said: 'The World Tree has its roots in the Underworld, it grows up through this world, and on up, up, into the Heavens. The Tree is said to be a yew. This is a scrap from the bark of a great and ancient yew that grows not so far from here. A squirrel runs up and down, up and down, between the worlds. This - ' she picked up a small furry pelt with a bushy tail - 'is the skin of a squirrel. Around the roots of the World Tree, a great snake is coiled. This is the skin of a snake. And finally, on its topmost branches an eagle sits. This is an eagle feather.'

She put it all back onto the pouch, tied it to her waist, and patted it. 'While we have this with us, we're in touch with everything, with all that is.'

We walked past Balintore and onto the beach at Sand-vik.

'Someone is out to do you harm,' she said.

'"Someone"?' I laughed. 'We *know* who - '

'Whisht, child. We never name the one we curse.'

'Curse?' Oh, no.

'Aye. No one is named, thus it is safe. Whoever sets out to harm you, brings it on himself.'

By this time we were far from any dwellings. The wind had died down, the sea was calm and quiet, the sun was low over the hills behind us.

'Look through here.' She held her hand to my eye, fingers and thumb curled to form a tube.

I peered, saw nothing, only windswept sand.

'Do you see the body? Do you?'

With the one eye she allowed me, and in the gathering darkness, I searched the beach. 'Yes! There!'

We walked towards it.

It wasn't a body, though it had looked like one. It was part of a tree, stripped white, sea-bleached, a trunk, branches like cropped limbs.

She squatted beside it, opened her pouch, took out a knife and proceeded to carve various runes in the smooth white surface.

When she was satisfied, she murmured, 'Give me your hand.'

I held it out to her. She took it, and with the same blade she nicked the ball of my thumb. 'Your blood,' she said.

I had a ridiculous urge to point out that my blood was no longer the blood of a virgin.

She understood, of course. Looked up into my eyes. 'This is not a joke, child.'

Marian being silly again.

I smeared my thumb over the wood, reddening the runes with my blood.

'What does it say?' A question I rarely have to ask.

'This is Death. And this is Pain, and Shame. Your blood protects you.

Deid body I see, but no heid.
So maun it be to him who would
bring deith to thee.

Body nakit, hurt and shamed.
So maun it be to him who would
bring hurt or shame to thee.'

No head?

We walked home in silence, and in silence drank some water and prepared for bed.

Lying there, I puzzled over what I had witnessed on the beach. That it was spell of power, I did not doubt. But how could it possibly be made to apply to the Friar?

My thoughts went back to Thorfinn Skinner, and the curse Coll had put on him. She hadn't minded the risk of naming him. Perhaps she hadn't known the danger. Or perhaps she'd thought things couldn't get worse.

She'd been wrong about that, I thought, ruefully.

And what was this about the anklet? Had it been nonsense, just something preying on Thorfinn's mind? But *Magdalene* anklet. What memories that brought back … If there was some legend attached to it, perhaps Drostan would know.

I slept. And I dreamt again.

TWENTY

Follow Your Heart

For a moment I thought I was Whin. I wasn't, I was me. But the boy staring at me was Whin's son, Otter.

Was I achieving with this tinkler family - this Elpin family - what I'd been trying in vain to achieve for so long? Ever since I'd arrived in Paris and begun to remember and try to recapture the skills I'd developed with Yacoub when I was a child?

Otter, sitting on some straw in a corner.

'Is that your bed?'

He nodded.

'But you're not sleeping?'

He shook his head. Then he said, 'I was sleeping. And in my dream I saw you, my lady.'

'You saw me?'

He nodded, green eyes huge-seeming in that little pinched face.

'You were in a place like the place where they did that to my da, and you were hanging from the wall by your wrists. And the one who paggered me - '

'"Paggered" you?'

'Skelped me.'

'Ah. Master Kenneth.'

'Aye, him. And a monk, tall and thin, with icy eyes.'

'What colour robe was he wearing, this monk?'

'Black, my lady.'

Brother Arsenius.

'You saw the holding-room in Tain, Otter. You saw it as it will be.'

'My lady, there were two others with you on the wall, hanging. They were not shown to me, not clearly, but I think one of them was the woman who was not a woman on the beach that night.'

'Coll. Yes. She is already there. And the other one?'

'The other one had been whipped.'

'Been whipped? But I had not?'

'Not yet, my lady.'

Not yet. "No" would have done quite nicely.

'They had her facing the wall, with her back to me. But I think it was my ma. It felt like her.'

There were tears now, running down his face.

'And you woke up? And you called me - in my sleep?'

He nodded.

Well. 'Fetch Sir Farquhar - and Kari, if she is there with Sir Farquhar. Run away from your master - don't worry, I will protect you. Find them, tell them the story, and come to Tain with them. Sir Farquhar will know what to do.'

'Yes, my lady.'

His eyes were full of trust. Could I protect him - I, who would be unable even to protect myself? Who would have to depend on them to rescue me?

But there was something else, something more immediate. I had gone to sleep puzzling over the mystery of the Queen of Elphame, the white cloak, and the anklet. Did Otter know the answer? Had I been searching for him, too, in my dreams? Had we met because we were both trying to - as had happened with Yacoub and me?

'Otter, that night on the Tarbat coast, the night you saw Coll weaving her spell ...'

He nodded.

'Did you also see the Queen of Elphame? Did you see her ride out on her horse, with her great hound following her?'

He shook his head. 'I saw only the prisoner, the lady with the Viking hair who is being held captive there in the steading. She rode out early with one man then rode back later in the evening with another. But neither of them was the man in black.'

'The man in black?'

'Aye, him. He is here to rescue her.'

I sighed. As Whin had said, he was a wonder at making up stories. 'So you must have noticed her before, have known her, if you recognised her, knew who she was in the distance that evening?'

He nodded.

'Had you spoken to her? Ever?'

'No.'

I got the impression, though - why didn't it surprise me? - that he wished he had.

'So it was just from the colour of her hair that you knew her?'

The nod. 'That and the way she holds her head.'

Ah yes.

Ah yes ...

I woke up, knowing that I had dreamed. What was it? Then it all came back to me. And there was someone knocking on the door - a messenger? - talking to Mouraig, riding off again fast.

The messenger had been speaking French. French? I leapt out of bed.

'What was it?' I asked. 'Is it Raoul? Has something happened?'

'Yes. Yes, something has happened. Your friend Jaufre le Fou has been murdered.'

Jaufre? Jaufre? It was Raoul who was in danger ... wasn't it? 'Where? When? How?'

She smiled at me. 'Who? Why? On the road from the Mickle Ferry, by Tarlogie Wood. He was found at dawn by the Earl himself, whose party had ridden through the night from Inverness on their way north to Dunrobin. He had been stabbed with a Moorish knife. It sounds like the murder of Sidi ben Youssef all over again.'

I nodded. It did. 'Listen. Bella is the Queen of Elphame.'

'So you said last night.'

'And the Queen haunts Tarlogie Wood. I know that. It was from Tarlogie Wood that she rode out and accosted ben Youssef as he came from the ferry.'

'Yes, I remember you telling me that.'

'Could Jaufre have known something? Have seen something? If he rode back out of Tain after her that evening, he might even have witnessed the murder.'

'And she might have just realised this. There are a lot of "ifs" here, a lot of "mights", but not one fact.'

'She is the Queen of Elphame.'

'She is not the Queen of Elphame. She is a girl riding out on a horse with a big dog behind her. A beautiful girl, in a beautiful cloak, riding out when her master's away. If people are foolish enough to take her for the Queen of Elphame, is that her fault? I doubt she is even aware of it.'

'Maybe she wasn't, at first. But she is now. Ben Youssef's first interest in her was as the Queen of Elphame.'

'This is your *fact*? And what connection is there between this *fact* and any of the murders?'

'The Queen rode out the night that ben Youssef was murdered. If she did not kill him earlier when she rode home with him as herself, as Bella, perhaps she rode after him later and killed him as the Queen of Elphame. As herself she gave Raoul poisoned fish soup. As herself she battered her master to death with a wooden club. As the Queen she rode out of Tarlogie wood last night and accosted le Fou as she had once accosted ben Youssef in the same spot, and killed him.'

'How did she manage that, when her horse and her hound were here, and her cloak, as I'm sure you will find, was with her other things at the Skinner steading?'

'Mm.' I hadn't thought of that. 'But if she'd had her horse with her, she would not have been able to appeal to him for a ride into Tain - as she once did with ben Youssef. No, it was as herself that she rode behind him and stabbed him, with the dagger Coll took from ben Youssef's body and which was still at the steading. It was not among the objects the Bailie removed when he arrested Coll - presumably because Bella had already put it with her things.'

'So she murdered three people - and attempted to murder another. And does this fit in at all with what you know of her hand, her horoscope, her character, her - how does she fit into Kabbalah?'

'She is the Queen,' I said, as that at least came clear to me. 'She is *Malkah*, the beautiful girl on the throne, with the crown on her hair and the rainbow around her.'

'A killer?'

'Of course not.'

'Then?'

'Then I shall have to rewrite the sciences of cheiromancy and astrology. And rethink the Kabbalah.'

She laughed. 'Did you not tell me that *Hod*, your own correspondence in Kabbalah, tends to reason too much, to think too much?'

'I did. And I am. Am depending too much on my own unaided reason, I mean. I admit it.'

'And I admit that things do look black for Bella. So - I will present the evidence against her. You try to find fault with my reasoning.'

I smiled. She was so good, yet she didn't look well today. 'Are you sure?'

'Yes, yes, don't fuss. So. The idea that ben Youssef's murder was a disaster for Bella is based on a story she could have made up. That ben Youssef wanted to buy her may have been no more than a daydream of hers. In fact, he may well have been going to report her to Thorfinn - after all, he was a believer in the sanctity of the harem, and Bella was slipping out at night when her master was otherwise engaged.'

'So she could have killed him to save herself from being whipped by Thorfinn. Yes. Though there is some independent evidence that ben Youssef was intending to buy her. He had spoken to Souad of it. Still, he could have changed his mind - could well have done so. He caught her sneaking out at night - may even have seen her with le Fou: the greatest sin of all in the eyes of a man like him, and deserving not just of a whipping but of death. Go on.'

'Someone saw her kill him, or saw her bringing his body back on the horse, or saw her drop his body off. That someone must have been either Raoul or Jaufre. She doesn't know which. She thinks first it was Raoul and tries to get rid of him. Then, talking to him - the other night, when they spent the night alone together? - she realises that he knows nothing. So it must have been Jaufre.'

'Yes, but - first of all it was a man who rode back alone, heavily, on the horse, presumably with the body.'

'Perhaps Jaufre not only witnessed it, but - shocked by what he had seen - got involved in it. Told her to go in, and stay in, while he got rid of the body.'

'And she then followed him - as the Queen - and made sure he did get rid of the body. That he didn't ride on into the town with it and report her to the authorities.'

'Exactly. But you're supposed to be defending the poor lass.'

'Easy. Jaufre would never have done as you suggest. If he had witnessed the murder, he would have seized her and taken *her* into Tain slung over his saddle, not the body. It's not in character at all.'

'So. Then perhaps it was Raoul who followed her out there. He would have helped her cover up the crime.'

'He would help any beautiful girl cover up a crime - on the assumption that if she is beautiful she must be innocent; if she did commit a crime, she must have been driven to it - but she is innocent at heart still, and by nature. You only have to look at her to see that.'

'My dear, are you still quoting Raoul, or is this your defence of Bella?'

I laughed. 'I spent a lot of time with Raoul once. We influenced each other's ways of thinking.'

'He made a romantic of you.'

'More than that. We were a romance. I found myself on a pedestal.'

'And liked it there.'

'I got - restless. Bella was born to be there.'

'She wants a home, a family - you said so yourself. She too is restless.'

I thought about that.

'And you: what did you make of him?' she went on.

'He was already a poet. I made a mystic of him. Or tried to. Tried to make him less concerned with consequences.'

'Yet he is very much the diplomat.'

'And still dresses in grey, grey, grey. But I left an ember smouldering inside him that is still there - '

'And can be fanned into flame any time by a beautiful woman. So, there you are then. It was Raoul who, with total disregard for the law, dropped the body off. And she has her motive for wanting him out of the way. But then she realises he is no danger to her - he adores her - and might well be useful alive. She also learns that he told Jaufre - not the whole story, but enough to make him suspicious: he let slip, shall we say, his detailed knowledge of the crime. Le Fou would realise at once that Raoul knew more than he ought to know. Once again: Jaufre must die.'

'Yes, but ... how would she have known that Jaufre was going to be on the ferry?'

'Who knows what Raoul told her that night?'

'I doubt if they spent much time talking.'

She looked at me.

I blushed.

I said, for something to say, 'We have no evidence that Bella knows anything at all about poisons - or healing herbs. It is much more likely that Coll poisoned the soup ready to give to Thorfinn.'

'Good. Anything else?'

'No. But I'm clearer about things now, thanks to you. And although I think Bella committed all three murders, I don't believe it. My brain tells me she did. My heart tells me otherwise.'

'Follow your heart, my child. Follow your heart.'

I found Raoul, and Roger, le Fou's interpreter, with the Bailie and Niáll.

They could tell me no more than I already knew. The only difference between this killing and the killing of the Moor was that le Fou had definitely been killed with the Moorish dagger, whereas in ben Youssef's case the dagger seemed to have been thrust into the wound afterwards.

'If the second killing is a deliberate copy of the first, then the murderer seems to be unaware of our suspicion that ben Youssef was in fact killed from a distance, probably with an arrow.' Master Brodie, the Bailie, looked at us, looked at my breasts, beamed with delight. It was his brain that delighted him, as much as my lack of one.

Niáll was cleverer though. 'In that case, the two murders cannot have been committed by the same person.'

I wish I had said that. I wish I had thought of it. I glanced down at my breasts. Men were right. You can't have everything. I didn't mention my suspicions concerning Bella to them. I didn't even say that the Skinner was dead. I supposed that they knew. They were men.

'Raoul, come with me.' He hadn't understood much of what was going on, despite Roger's mumbling, so I explained. And I explained why I now suspected Bella.

He stared at me in disbelief. He too was beginning to think I might be just for decoration.

We left Roger in Tain, Raoul promising to meet him and Armand and the two other French soldiers later at the crossroads, ready to ride down to Inverness. For now, I wanted him with me. I wanted to go back to the steading, search again. And as we rode I wanted to hear him defend Bella. I wanted him to convince me.

He started with Thorfinn.

'Mariana, I was there.'

'You were there? But she said - '

'She didn't tell you the truth.'

I sighed. Then laughed.

'Why are you laughing? I do not understand you any more. You jump to conclusions. You are not at all *sympathique,* even with someone caught up in such terrible circumstances as poor Bella, and so good and so brave about it.'

'Would you notice all that if she didn't have a pretty face?'

'It's not just her face. She - '

'Raoul! Tell me what happened.'

He glared at me. Then smiled.

It wasn't simply my face, either.

'Then understand that it was not *amusant, pas du tout*. When I arrived, no one heard me or noticed me, not even the dog. Then I saw Bella up on the horse, the horse rearing back from - the dog, I thought at first. Then I saw Skinner standing and walking and brandishing a dagger at the horse, at Bella - I didn't know. The horse came down again, catching the dog with its hoof - by accident, I am sure: the dog was barking at Skinner, trying to drive him off, drive him back, away from Bella, and was under the horse's hooves. The dog yelped and ran out of the way, and the horse did something I have never seen or heard of before: it bit Skinner's face, bit at his nose, pulled it right off his face. I've heard of an ear being bitten off, but a nose …'

'And then?'

'Then? Bella screamed. I mean, she saw his face, what was left of it, just in that second as he collapsed onto his knees and covered it with his hands. Me, I was paralysed. The dog flew at him - yes - it had only been barking before, but now it flew at his hands and face. With a roar he punched it away and stood up. Bella was screaming. Skinner was roaring and howling, one hand on his face, the other still clutching the dagger. The horse backed away a few feet, then would go no further. It stood there, trembling. The dog was about to attack him again. I didn't know what to do. Everybody, everything, was hysterical. I wanted Skinner to lie down, be quiet …'

'Be dead.'

'Be dead. Yes. I don't know. I picked up a piece of wood - I needed a weapon, it was the nearest thing - and hit him with it. But not hard enough. He stopped. He turned and faced me. Looked at me with what was left of his eyes through the fingers of the bloody hand that was holding what was left of his face together.

'I backed away.

'The dog sprang at him and they fell over.

'And now Bella screamed: "Stop him! Stop him!" Who did she mean? Then I knew who she meant. I hit Skinner hard again on the back of the skull, and again and again. Till he was dead and still on the grass.

'I looked round. The dog was watching me. The horse was watching me. Bella was watching me. Had I done right? If not, I was a dead man, too. Then Bella smiled. The horse shook its head and stopped trembling. And the dog came up to me and licked my hand. I had done right.'

We rode on in silence for a minute. Then he said, 'Now don't you tell me I did wrong.'

'Raoul … *Au contraire*. You have restored my faith in you. A queen needs poets around her sometimes, yes, but quite as important as that is a man of action to be there and to defend her in time of need.'

We had reached the steading.

We stood well away from the body.

'I'll tell them he was delirious,' I said. 'Violent. He attacked the girl and she fled and told me and Mouraig her story. We gave her shelter. Then he must have attacked the horse. We won't bring you into it.

'Now come into the house with me. There's something I'm looking for.'

'Something?'

'You'll see. If we find it. As I am sure we will.'

And we did, very fast. It's easy when you know what you are searching for, know what to expect.

I held it up. Pure white. Silk and satin. Fur trimmed.

'But - but what is that?'

'It's the cloak your queen wears when she rides out on her horse with the great wolfhound behind her.'

'My queen? My Queen? You mean that Bella is the Queen of - *comment dit-on*? - Elphame?'

'The one they call the Queen of Elphame. I'm not even sure that she knows. I am sure she wasn't conscious of it at first, but I think she does know now. I think she must.'

'But that … that is *incroyable*!'

'Pas du tout. It is obvious. Has been since the beginning. Even I - but what's this?' I gasped.

This second find was not expected.

'It's his dagger,' said Raoul, 'ben Youssef's dagger. I've seen it many times. It's the one that was found in his body. But how did it get here?'

'Coll brought it here, after using it to mutilate the poor man.'

'Then - that is all right. You know about that.'

'Yes, but Raoul - don't you see? I thought Bella had used this knife to murder Jaufre. I mean, I knew she had this knife, so she was the obvious suspect when he was stabbed with a Moorish dagger, on a night when Bella was missing, and in a spot the Queen of Elphame is known to haunt.'

'But if the knife is still here …'

'Then another knife must have been used. Another Moorish knife. And who would have access to another Moorish knife?'

'Souad,' he breathed.

The weather was changing. When we came back out and mounted our horses, the sky was dark grey, and the grass all around us more silvery even than usual. A pair of huge hooded crows flew by, so large I thought they must be ravens. Then I saw little Mona, Sweign's granddaughter, standing staring at us.

'Hello, Mona. What are you doing here? It's going to rain.'

She looked at Raoul. Back at me.

'Do you know about birds?' I asked.

'Birds? You mean the two hoodies?'

'They were so big I thought they might be ravens.'

She shook her head.

They weren't ravens? Or she didn't know about birds?

'Listen, Mona. How old are you?'

'Eight.'

'Eight. Yet you seem clever, and very grown up. Will you deliver a message for me if you happen to see Bella - Master Thorfinn's slave-girl? Do you know her?'

She shook her head. 'Not really. I've seen her in the distance, with Master Thorfinn, or with glaistig Coll. She looks a bit like the Queen too, doesn't she?'

'She does indeed. If you see her anywhere - or if you see Mouraig, the Witch - say I said Bella's to go to the lochan and hide there among the wild roses and brambles and cover herself with clover and wait there, just wait, for me or for one who says she comes on my behalf. And tell her to weave herself a crown of roses and carry a birch wand with her when she goes there and hold it in her hand. All this and only this will protect her when they hunt for her - and when the real Queen of Elphame rides out. Can you remember all that?'

'Oh yes.' She repeated it for me, then ran off, while we turned west into the ever-darkening sky. But suddenly I didn't want to go into Tain with Raoul. I had to get back to my grandmother - fast!

I explained to Raoul.

He had no choice. He and le Fou's soldiers were going to Inverness to report the murder of the *capitaine* and await further orders. But he promised he would come straight back, on his own if necessary, whatever the orders were.

TWENTY-ONE

The Mantle And The Ring

Mouraig was lying on the floor.

I tried to pick her up.

She opened her eyes. 'No, no, don't move me. Lie here beside me.'

'But - are you all right?'

'It depends what you mean by all right, child. I'm dying - '

'*What*?'

'I'm all right, though - I'm fine. Lie down here. Quick now.'

'But Mouraig! Grandmother! I - '

'Will you please just do as I say.'

I lay down beside her, on my back, as she was.

'Close up, lass. Press against me.'

I shuffled sideways, pressing the side of my leg and my hip, and my arm and shoulder, against hers.

'Like that?'

'Aye. We haven't much time. You've been on a shelti-trip, you say? You know something of the shelti-world?'

'Yes, but - '

'We must go together. It'll be easier if I follow you. I can. You may not be able to follow me. Use the same way in you used the last time you went.'

She waited.

But I couldn't. I'd only ever been once. And I was shocked. To find my grandmother and then lose her again, just like that!

'Lass, those are not the thoughts we need at this moment. We were lucky to meet at all. Now, picture that cave, or whatever it was.'

I pictured it. My mind was elsewhere, and I don't think I

expected anything to happen, but a second later she had me by the hand and was leading back into the depths of the cave.

All was as I remembered it, the concentric rings of stone that formed the walls, the gently sloping rock floor, the slight light coming from nowhere.

But we didn't come out through a cave-mouth halfway up a high cliff, this time. We came out behind a waterfall in the mountains somewhere. We were standing on a kind of beach with the water thundering down in front of us. The air was full of spray, everything was wet with spray, the pebbles we were standing on were green and slippery.

Mouraig looked at me. *Do you know this place?*

Me: *I'm not sure. No.*

I took her hand, pulled her across the narrow beach towards the edge of the fall.

Mouraig: *We can go through it, you know. Things like this are not a problem here.*

I realised suddenly that I was understanding her without words - something she could do in the real world, but I could not. I knew also that she was quite right. We were not here in body.

Holding hands, we walked into the torrent. It was hammering down on us, but we felt nothing. Then we were through - and walking on water - yes! - walking on the surface of the lake.

She smiled at me. She liked my shelti-world. But we had things to do ...

We headed for the point where the lake began to be fringed by forest. The shore beneath the forest was a muddy bank, riddled with holes - the homes of water-voles, she informed me - and just as she said that one appeared from the water then disappeared into its hole. It was like a rat but 'cuddlier'. Mouraig looked at it, looked at me, but said nothing. Then we stepped - almost floated - up over the bank and onto a path that led between the trees.

Then my own fears hit me. First there came a screaming and a hammering and a bull appeared on our path, coming straight at us - a bull that had been flayed, that had no skin, was all bare bloody flesh, yet was still alive and screeching, screeching, screeching. It was almost upon us.

I screamed. Mouraig held onto me. I tugged at her but she was stronger than me here, we were *both* going to die - then it passed through us, screeching as it went. And dragging along behind it, caught up in the rope of a harpoon which stuck out of the bull's back like a banderilla, was the skinner, also screaming. He too passed through us and was gone.

I was shaking. The screeching had all been in my head. This world was totally silent.

Mouraig led me on.

Then we came into a glade and saw two black things fighting a silent battle to the death. Almost silent, for one of the contestants was a gigantic black beetle which was mortally wounded but chattered and rattled still as it were under its breath. The other was an enormous black slug, slow but clingy and suffocating. Now the beetle had had enough. It tried to limp away, its cracked shell oozing its own dark ichor over the slime of the slug, and only two of its legs, both on the left side, functioning at all; but the slug came after it, inexorable as time, and slowly, quite carefully, slithered up over it.

Mouraig: *Don't interfere. Don't do or say anything.*

We waited.

Eventually, the slug moved on, leaving the slimy remnants of the beetle in the grass behind it. And as I watched, an owl - my little heart-faced white-breasted owl - came flapping down and picked up the slug - *the little slug* - and ate it.

Mouraig: *Your shelti-creature is the barn owl?*

Me: *I - I don't know. Perhaps.*

Mouraig: *I've never seen a barn owl eat a slug before. But come. I have to take you somewhere, show you something.* (*Say farewell.*)

She hadn't said it - hadn't thought it *at* me - indeed, as the thought crossed her mind she tried to conceal it - but I had caught it.

She knew at once.

Sadly, she took my hand, led me on.

Sadly, I went with her. On and up, to the end of the path, the end of the forest.

As we came out onto the sunlit hillside, I glanced back and saw the owl again.

Me: *You know where we are now, where we are going?*

Mouraig: *I shall know when we get there.*

We walked across the flowery meadow, and I bent to pick a buttercup. As I did so, I wondered if she would stop me.

Instead, she smiled. *That's the first flower you've ever picked in this world? The buttercup is your flower then.*

The buttercup? What does it signify?

You tell me.

It comes under the Sun. It probably signifies reflected glory.

No. You are right about the Sun - which is something new for you, I think, and must reflect changes in your personality. But that is all it reflects: in itself, it signifies pure radiance - radiant beauty, it may be, or some other faculty or power radiating out from you.

My mind flew back to Raoul and Bella. It sounded like what he had said of her. But what had he said of me?

Mouraig was with me, of course. *He was right. You do radiate beauty, but more than that you radiate goodness and intelligence and concern. In your company, people - good people, at any rate - feel blessed; those in need of understanding feel understood, those in need of protection and sustenance feel protected and provided for. No bad thing.*

I looked round. Down there was the lake and the waterfall. Beyond was the sea.

She too looked, then turned her back on all that. *Come.*

We found the river that led down to the waterfall. As we followed it further up towards its source, it grew narrower, more turbulent.

Here? It's too high.

Here.

We turned a corner and saw a cave.

She went in.

I waited.

A great bear emerged. It was her, I knew - our minds were linked.

She resumed her human form. *Here I shall stay for now, Marian. Here you may come and visit me. No, don't speak, lass, there is nothing to say. And don't weep. Not here. You may weep a little over my body when you return.*

I knew she had more to say. I waited.

After a while, her thoughts cleared. *So you only visited this world that once, so long ago? You almost lost your shelti-creature, your owl. Watch out for it. I think it's showing itself to you again. You've seen it twice. Twice more, and it's still yours. Whatever appears to you four times is making itself known. But you must entertain it, dance it,* be *it, from day to day - or rather from night to night, hunting in the dark - or it* will *leave you. And you must visit it here, often, not only when you have a question to put to it.*

Me: *And the bear? This bear that is you?*

Mouraig: *Ah, that. The bear became my fylgia, my totem-animal while in the land of the Algonquin. Which is where, in a sense, we are now.*

Me: *And the wulcat?*

Mouraig: *That's different, that's shape-shifting. Like when you dreamed you were in Whin's body. A little like that, only more so. When I shape-shift I am in my cat-body, not my human body, which is lying empty at home. You will experience it one day, my dear - though not as a cat. You're not one of them, any more than little Kari is. They know you, though, and they'll support you in your hour of need ...Burn my body on the beach. Give my ashes to the wind and the sea. But first, remove the ring - the ruby ring - it is yours. My mantle is yours. My pouch is yours. Everything is yours ... Now go.*

She kissed me, and I went.

When I looked back, I saw the bear watching me. *Ask Euphemia! Trust Euphemia! Trust only her, and Whin. But not together!* There was a laugh with that last "not together". *Don't ever mix your friends, especially ones as different - and yet as similar - as that.*

I wanted to go back to her, join in that laugh, gossip about Whin and Countess Euphemia of Ross, discuss the incompatibility of friends in general, but she wouldn't, couldn't, let me. So, I left her on that laugh.

And realised, as I went back down across the flower-strewn meadow, that she was already dead.

I intended to find a way out through the lake - I was still happiest in water - but before I got there, in a glade in the forest (the same glade? - there was no sign of the beetle) - the owl came flapping down again and perched on a branch growing out of a log and looked at me.

I stopped.

He turned his head to the left, and from the left I heard the screaming in my head again, coming my way, the screaming of the bull, the screams of the man. I wanted to run, to hide, but the eyes of the owl, the way it cocked its head, said: *Does the Witch of Balintore run?*

The Witch of Balintore?

And they were on me. But this time I held out my arms and said: *Stop.* Quite quietly. If I had screamed, my scream would have been lost in their screams. As it was, the bull fell silent to hear what I had to say, the skinner fell silent to see why the bull had stopped.

I walked past the bull. Poor thing, it was meat not flesh. Its place was the butcher's shop or the kitchen of a great house or tavern, not the field or the farm, and certainly not the forest. Why had the skinner left it alive? I took hold of the *pica*/the harpoon, and tugged. It slid out easily. Like King Arthur's sword, I thought. Does it prove something?

I dropped it in the grass. Then, still ignoring the skinner, I went back round and took the bull by one horn. I led it down to the edge of the lake, dragged it in, felt its relief as the cool water washed over it. *Wait*, I told it.

I had to go back to the skinner. But what to do with him?

The owl was there close by him. That was four times. It caught my eye, knew that I knew.

I knelt down beside the skinner, held his head. Was he going to die again, this time with his head in *my* lap? Then I remembered how he *had* died. It was strange that this time his face was quite unmarked. He must have managed to hold it up while the rest of he was being dragged over the rough ground and all the skin grazed off his body, dirtily, roughly, quite unlike the neat job he had done on the bull.

I looked back at the owl.

It cocked its head as though listening.

I listened.

The anklet.

The what?

Marian?

Yes.

The Magdalene Anklet. That's what they all want, lass. You'll understand.

But -

You'll do what has to be done.

Of course, but -

Aye. That's all right then. I knew you'd understand.

He sighed a great sigh of relief - and vanished.

All *who*?

I went back down to the lake, waded in, took the poor bull by the horn once more and swam forward slowly, letting him find his feet on the bottom, for as I had suspected, he did not float. The water covered us. He walked and I swam on, deeper and deeper. At last, while there was still murky light enough left to see by, I told him: *You stay here. I must leave you now.*

You will return?

Oh, yes.

I swam on down into the dark depths and entered a water-filled tunnel.

As I came out into the light in Mouraig's cottage, on Mouraig's floor, beside Mouraig's body, I wondered if I had acquired another, very weird, shelti-creature in addition to thc wonderful owl that would now, I knew, be mine for life.

I lay there for a moment, readjusting, then leant over and kissed her forehead. It was ice cold. She had been dead for a long time.

The light came from the open door. Had I left it open? I stood up and went outside. No one. I walked down onto the beach and sat - not on my stone, no, not this time - on Mouraig's log. And waited.

Nothing happened. Nobody came.

Tell Euphemia, she had said. Trust Euphemia.

Despite the name, despite the grandmother, despite inheriting her mantle - for that must have been what she meant - I was a stranger here.

I went back in and took the ring from her finger. It slid off easily. I put it on, murmuring 'Thank you, grandmother,' and made for the back where the horses were. I had to go to Tain. There I could report Mouraig's death - and Thorfinn's, if they didn't already know. And get a message delivered to Euphemia, Countess of Ross.

I started at the Bailie's house.

As I arrived, the rain began again.

They told me they knew about the skinner, that a party of men had gone to the Abbey to pick Bella up. The Abbey? Yes, she always goes there, they adore her there.

And they proceeded to take my horse away from me. Simply took it, without explanation, but with that horse-faced and patronising firmness dutiful men display in dealing with a bad woman.

I decided not to mention the death of my poor grandmother.

I remembered my rendez-vous with Brother Arsenius. But why *now*? As they hustled me ungently towards him through the downpour and puddles and mud, all I could understand of what that man of few words, Niáll of Lairg, was shouting at me, was that a few hours earlier, Coll had finally told them the truth: she had meant *me*. *I* was the witch, *I* was the Queen of Elphame. And the tinkler woman Whin, who had also been arrested, was another witch and a shape-shifter.

Thoughts flashed through my mind as they dragged and prodded me through the torrential rain.

I'd had at least three warnings and had ignored them all.

They wouldn't handle Bella so roughly. With the exception of Skinner, she brought out the gentleman in everyone. Unlike me. I brought out the gentleman in Skinner.

Coll hadn't named Bella - Raoul had been right - but it was strange, for Coll must know that Bella was the Queen of Elphame, or at any rate that she was riding out dressed up as the Queen.

Was Raoul right then about everything? In that case, who did *he* think had killed Abdelwahed ben Youssef?

I had never bothered to ask him.

Let's hope they left me a little of my beauty. It was all I had.

And one last thought, as we came to the door: Otter must have contacted Ferchard and Kari by now. They would be on their way. I hoped. Perhaps that, too, had been only a dream, like my dream of solving this crime. Jaufre had died while I was cleverly persecuting the innocent Bella. And cleverly leaving her alone in the hands of Skinner, the man who - as Raoul obviously realised - had murdered the Moor and would have murdered her, too, if Raoul had not saved her.

Be calm, I told myself. Panic and hysteria won't help you.

Whatever happens to you now, you deserve.

They removed my cloak, my boots and hose, my skirt. I was not wearing a tunic, as it was summer. They removed my armlets and earrings, and Mouraig's ring. They left me only my chemise. Then, as Otter had predicted, they took me over to where Whin and Coll were hanging by their chained wrists from rings set into the wall and chained my wrists and hung me between them.

After I had got over my shock at the sight of Whin's back, I realised they had also left me my hair. Both Whin and Coll's heads had been shaved. Or rather, scraped. More of Kenneth's work: their scalps were as raw as poor little Otter's had been in Dyngvale.

I think one of the reasons I had taken so few precautions, had walked straight into all this, was that I wanted to see whether Otter was right, whether the dream had been accurate: it was. Whin had been scourged, then hung up on the wall, not long before I arrived, by the look of it. The blood was running down her back. And Coll's back was raw still from the scourging she had received two or three days earlier.

Master Kenneth was smiling. Working on that grin.

Whin could not speak. I would have to wait at least another hour before she could tell me what had happened. And in another hour, I might not be able to speak myself.

Outside, there was a great crack of thunder - right overhead, it seemed.

Otter had been right in every detail, so it hadn't all been merely a dream. We had some hope of being rescued.

I decided to go on the offensive. 'What are we waiting for? The rain to stop?'

No response.

'If we wait for you to become a *real* master, to grow some hair and muscle, be a *man*, we'll still be waiting next century.'

'*You* won't.'

'Naughty. Wait till I tell your da you've been implying that I'm a witch again.'

'Wait till my da comes up here and finds you *are* a witch.'

'Mm. You'd have a point, if I were a witch. But I'm not - and he knows I'm not.'

'You'll confess all right when you're stretched.'

'Stretched? By *you*?' Despite my best efforts, my voice had sounded a little squeaky then.

'No such luck. He'll keep *you* for himself. He wants Sir Hugh here, too, to see and to listen - to be a witness - only Sir Hugh wants you cut first, you know, scored above the breath. I think he's frightened of you.'

'And you're not?'

That must be the reason I still had my hair. Kenneth hadn't dared cut it.

Hurry, Ferchard!

Now he crossed his fingers, on both hands. He came up close to me and spat in my face between the crossed fingers, which he held out like a curse.

I stopped laughing.

Whin, beside me with her face to the wall, must have been listening. 'You mean … you do … stretching?' she gasped.

The gob of spit was running down my cheek but some of it was in my eye and I couldn't get it out.

'Yes, I do stretching. And you call me "Master" when you speak to me.'

He winked at me.

Little runt.

Winked *back* at me, I realised. And pulled the grin he'd been working on for so long - managing something like a changeling baby with indigestion. He probably was a changeling.

'But - but how does it work?' She sobbed. 'How will you know that I'm not a witch from doing that?'

'Say "Master".'

'M-Master.'

'That's better.'

"Better"? It wouldn't be, not for him, if she ever went free.

I said: 'The pain makes you say whatever they want to hear, Win - in this case, that you're a witch. If you manage to withstand the pain, that of course *proves* you're a witch.'

Whin said nothing. I thought she nodded, though I couldn't see. She probably thought she'd be the first - and with Master Kenneth. And she must be suffering wave after wave of agony from the whipping, quite unable to concentrate on anything else for more than a moment.

Kenneth turned away from us, bored now. He peeped in on Drostan, then went up the stairs and out, leaving the door open.

Gone to watch the storm, probably.

I could hear the rain torrenting down and see lightning flashing through the open doorway.

I turned back to Whin. 'This isn't the first time you've been scourged, is it?'

'No. They scourged me once, years ago, before Kari was born, up in Helmsdale. Outside in the square, at the whipping-post, with everyone watching.'

'What had you done?'

I didn't see the expression on her face, of course, but I heard the snort of derision.

I said, 'I'm sorry, Whin.'

What had she done? She'd been born an Elp, a tinkler, one of the little people, and a beautiful woman what's more, in a world ruled by big men, that's what she'd done. And she hadn't lived a Yes-sir life.

I looked down at myself. The way I was hanging made my breasts stand up and out. I thought of Master Brodie and Niáll. And thought of Sir Hugh - Phorca. And of Kenneth who, though hardly a big man - hardly a man - could treat Whin like that - treat me like that, if my luck ran out - simply because he had a big man for a father and a wee pair of ballocks for himself. And I thought again of that father, Robert Ross, and wondered what he would say - and do - when he arrived. I had a very bad feeling about Big Robbie down in the pit of my stomach. He represented severity and justice, the sword, the spear, the scourge, the chain, the positive aspect of *Din/Geburah*, which in Souad was seen in its negative aspect as the destructive goddess of anarchic violence. And ben Youssef, I saw now, had been *Hesed*, protective love, the Father, and husband of Din. Souad.

The thunder crashed again.

And I thought of Big Ferchard, and forgave big men everything as I wondered was he on his way to me through the storm. And he was, indeed he was, as I discovered later …

TWENTY-TWO

Whom The Lord Loveth

The sun rose red in the sky on the morning Jaufre le Fou was found dead between the forest and the water, his horse grazing placidly nearby; the morning after Otter had come to me in the night, in my dreams, to tell me of his dream. Jaufre did not see that sun. Neither did I, for I slept late, was woken only by the news of his death.

Otter watched it from the spit he was chained to in the yard of the Whore & Hounds - the Queen, as his people called it - watched it rise as he turned and turned, both arms aching, both hands blistered. It coloured him red, redder than he was already from the heat of the fire, coloured even the dead goat as it went round and round and round.

It was nearly noon when his chance came. Fergus took him from the spit, where two hens were now cooked to a turn, cuffed his head for him to keep him on his toes, and told him to clear all the tables that were no longer in use. 'And clear those that are, too!' he shouted, aiming a kick at Otter's behind and missing and losing his balance, nearly falling over, to the delight of the drinkers at the nearby tables - though they soon lost their smiles when he turned to glare at them. A small, but violent, man.

Otter slipped out.

A few minutes later he arrived at the big house where Kari and Ferchard were staying. The executioner's house.

He dared not knock. Dared not clang the great bell, or indeed draw attention to himself in any way.

Eventually, the door opened. A woman came out and surveyed the sky - a big woman with long, chestnut-coloured, wavy, curly hair. And, yes, a kind face.

He showed himself.

'Are you the lady of the house?'

Her face hardened, then relaxed into its former smile as she saw that he was alone and small. And tame. His shaven head and welted legs attested to that.

'I am. And what is that to you?'

'I'm wanting someone, Mistress.'

'If it's the executioner you're wanting, you've come to the right place.' She examined him, not unsympathetically - for there was a deep-down kindness in Effie. 'Who sent you here? Were you sent for a whipping? Master Robert has no time for that sort of thing today. Was it him whipped you last time?'

'No - no, the young master.'

'Master Kenneth. Aye, he'd give any lad was in trouble a skelping free of charge. But he's away up in Tain with the witch they have there, and a heretic monk, and some black-skinned and black-hearted murderers hanging won't do for, they'll have to be burnt or boiled. Tain's a terrible place by all accounts, and the poor boy on his own up there like a journeying knight.'

'No, Mistress, it's not Master Robert or Master Kenneth I'm wanting, it's Kari - my lady's girl -'

'Kari? Why didn't you say so?' She fetched him a totally unexpected clip on the ear that sent him reeling into the mud, and, with a snort and a 'Wasting my time!' went swishing back into the house and slammed the door.

He grinned. She was big, and powerful, but her hand was soft and her eyes were soft. If he had to be bonded, why could he not be bonded to her, instead of that skinny Fergus at the Queen, whose hand was like wood and who had the eyes of a stoat?

He got up and waited, rubbing the mud off himself with his hands as best he could.

A few minutes later, Kari came out. He stared at her.

She had a chunk of oatcake and a cup of milk for him. 'She says she knows who you are, now, and you shouldn't be here. You're to eat this and go.'

He drank the milk, gazing at her over the rim of the beaker.

'What are you staring at? Have you never seen anyone dressed like this before?'

'You're b-bonny like that, Kari.'

She too softened, and smiled. 'And you? Why are you so red? You look half cooked.'

'I am half cooked.'

She waited while he ate some of the oatcake.

'Did you have a message for me? From my lady?'

'Aye. She's in trouble, in Tain.'

'In trouble? How can she be in trouble?'

'She is, in a place like where they broke our da's fingers - '

'But she can't be - '

'She is! Or she will be. And she needs Sir Farquhar - fast.'

She believed him. 'Don't go!'

Half an hour later they were on the road.

They had two horses. One a great grey gelding ridden by Ferchard, and, following him as best she might, Kari on a gentle - but temperamental - brown mare, with Otter clinging on behind her, a grin of excitement on his hungry little face. Kari had never ridden a horse before, never been on a horse except that once when she had sat up behind her lady, but she wasn't going to admit that when Ferchard said 'You can ride, lass?' and lifted her up bodily into the saddle. She simply smiled and said, 'Thank you, sir!' Then cried out to Otter, 'Get up behind me! Quick!' Quick, before the horse ran away with her, the poor child meant.

In the afternoon they rode into the storm and had to stop. They led the horses off the road a little way, among the trees but keeping clear of two tall pines that looked as though they might attract a lightning bolt, and crawled in beneath a white willow - a sally - beside a burn. An aspen growing over it lent them more shelter, and Ferchard and Kari sat and watched the water rushing and swirling by just below their boots, while Otter dangled his bare, sore, dirty feet in the water and groaned happily.

Kari glanced at him, torn between pulling her too-tight boots off and joining him, and maintaining her new dignity. She glanced at Ferchard. Anyone seeing them now would never guess what she really was, they would take her and Ferchard for equals; they would think only Otter was different ... She saw Otter suddenly freeze, ears pricked.

'What is it?'

Otter ignored her.

'What is it?' asked Ferchard.

'Shh. He's listening.'

'He must have very good ears to hear something in this.'

'He's got more than good ears. He knows things. He - he senses them.'

'Someone is coming,' Otter whispered. 'And she's in trouble, from the way she's running.'

'Anyone would be in trouble out there on foot,' grumbled Ferchard. 'Unless they were at home in it like you two are. Well, go and see, lad. And if you're right and it's a lass on her own and in distress, bring her here to us. Otherwise keep out of sight.'

Otter slipped silently away.

'You can see why he's called Otter, can't you,' laughed Ferchard, cheering up and quite enjoying the situation suddenly.

'It's not just that. Oh, he's good in lochs and rivers - and in wet undergrowth like this. He's not so good in the open sea, though. I'm better there. He's definitely an inland otter. But, the thing is ... You know how otters look after the old?'

'No. Tell me.'

'Otters have special tables - flat rocks, usually - where they leave food for the old ones, and not just the old ones, any too toothless or blind or maimed to hunt for themselves. These tables - we call them "altars" - are often in sea-caves, and we like to know where they are.'

'We?'

'Us. The Elpin. Then we help ourselves to the freshly-caught fish,' she laughed.

'"Elpin", you call yourselves?'

'Mm. And Otter's called Otter because he's like an otter: he brings back his catch and offers it, shares it, I mean. Presents it, like on an altar. He always has.'

Then Otter came back, leading a half-drowned Souad by the hand.

'She's drookit,' said Otter.

'Drookit?' asked Ferchard.

'Wet. Soaked,' explained Kari.

'I can see that. I thought he might be saying something helpful, something about who she is, what she's doing here.'

He looked at the girl. Was she a local lass? Those black eyes did not look local.

Now they fastened on him. Did they see something not local in him? In that skin dessicated by ten thousand suns such as they never saw once in a lifetime up here? In those eyes, so blue, yes, but that had swept the desert at dawn and at dusk and followed the showers of falling stars as they swept over the oases?

They saw something in each other's eyes.

And they were right, for their paths had crossed once many years before.

'Usted habla castellano. señor?' Her teeth were chattering with the cold and wet.

He took his cloak off and put it round her.

Kari watched in wonder.

'*Sí*,' he said. Then realising suddenly who she must be, added, 'I speak Arabic, too - better than I speak Spanish.'

Souad gazed at him. Was this man the answer to her prayers?

They began to talk. They talked and talked, while Otter and Kari watched and listened and tried to understand. And as they talked, he fell in love, though she was not a third his age. He had always had a soft spot for the almond-eyed girls of the Kasbah, but had never come across one before so like a fish out of - no, like a warm golden houri *in* ice-cold water; and so in need of his help.

And as she watched him fall in love, Souad knew that if she had not done that thing she could be his. But she had done that thing. And should she tell him? While he did not know, it seemed that there might still be some small hope.

But what was this?

'Did your master ever mention the Nazrani - ?'

'My master was Sidi Abdelwahed ben Youssef of Fès.'

'I know. You have said that.'

'And he bought my brother Rachid and me at the slave-market in Tangiers almost exactly ten years ago.'

'I know that, too. But you were not from Fès or Tangiers; you were from Granada, in Andalucía, you and your brother, the poor little eunuch, Rachid.'

'Yes, lord.'

'I ask you again, did your master ever mention the big white-haired and white-bearded Nazrani who helped him to buy you - to pay for you?'

She gazed at him for a long moment. 'He did, lord. But he did not need to, for I remember that big Nazrani with the white hair and white beard and piercing blue eyes. I am yours.'

'You are not mine, Souad. That money was your grandfather's money. He could do nothing else to help you when your mother - died - but that: to try to ensure that you went to a good, kind master. To buy you myself, if I wanted you and would be good to you -'

'You did not want me?'

'You believe that? You were the most beautiful child there that day - that week - that year for all I knew - and even before the sale began I knew that not all my money and your grandfather's together could buy - one toe of you.'

She laughed. She was getting warmer.

Kari was still awed. Never before had she seen or heard of a man giving his cloak to a woman. 'She must be very special,' she whispered to her brother.

'She's a princess,' he whispered back.

'But at the tavern, the night before the sale,' Ferchard went on, 'I had got talking to a man - a scholar, a traveller - and he was, in so far as you can find one such in such a city, a good man. And when I saw him bidding for you, and saw his smile fade as the bidding went up and up and up, I went close to him and said, "Abdelwahed, my friend, if you bought them, the two of them, would you be kind to the boy?" He said he would, that Allah would smile on one who was good to that boy. I gave him your grandfather's money.'

'And he bought us, lord. And he was always good to my brother.'

'And now your brother is dead, you say, and you fleeing for your life. Did you not see Lady MacElpin? Lalla Maryam? Did she not speak to you? Try to help you?'

'Oh yes! And she spoke to Rachid before he died. She was

very kind, but she could not save him.'

'So you did not trust her to save you. Well, you were right, it seems, for now she herself is held prisoner in Tain.'

'No!'

'Yes, and I ride to her rescue. Kari,' he turned to the child, and spoke now in Gaelic, 'is there anywhere you can take this lady where she will be safe - and warm?'

'I can take her to Mouraig, sir.'

'Mouraig? Who's she?'

'The Witch of Balintore. Lady Marian's grandmother.'

He had the feeling, suddenly, that he had stepped out of the real world.

He shook his head. Looked round.

The rain was easing, the thunder had passed over, and time was pressing.

They did not know *how* time was pressing.

Slowly, they got themselves organised. Kari took Souad up with her on her horse, then at the next crossroads turned east for Balintore.

And Ferchard and Otter, my two heroes, came galloping north to Tain.

* * * * *

'But why?' sobbed Whin. 'Now they should let me go. Or hang me, if that's what it says. Or give me to Phorca.'

'Phorca?'

'So he can maim me.'

'Maim you?'

'Aye, so they can catch me.'

'I don't think even Phorca would stoop to that, Whin.'

'I'm prey. And he has my scent. He has my scent and he will never give up.'

I tried to look at her. Was she serious?

'But to treat me as if I were a - a *person*, and a witch ...'

'Whin, there've been three murders, at least. And they believe witchcraft is involved. After all, the Moor was mutilated. And they think the Queen of Elphame may be involved too in some way.'

'But what has that to do with me?'

'Don't you see? They know you're a shape-shifter. They *suppose* you're a witch.'

'Why?'

'Witches are shape-shifters. All right, they don't think you're the Queen of Elphame, but they do believe you may have some knowledge of her, some connection with her.'

She brooded a moment, then muttered: 'That's not why.'

'Then why?'

Outside, through the open door I could hear the yowling of what sounded like huge cats. Mouraig's wulcats?

'Because *she* put the yarrow on me. And she put the yarrow on *you*, too.'

'She did that to stop the pain, you know she did; and we were the names they were feeding her at the time. Why your name? Because Sir Hugh gave it to them. He's the one has accused you of being a shape-shifter. Because he has seen you change into a mermaid. And because he wants to get hold of you, wants you in his power. Because he "has your scent", as you put it. And that has nothing to do with poor Coll.'

She let her head hang forward against the wall, and gave up.

My wrists were going numb. Pain was shooting down my arms into my shoulder-blades and spine. I was so much bigger, so much heavier than Whin or Coll.

But they had been scourged.

Would I be scourged? Would I be stretched? Would I really? Would they dare? I was a lady. The others were not even women. They had no rights. But what rights that I might have would a Black Friar recognise and respect?

I remembered what had happened to me when I had been the *abbé*'s prisoner in Paris. I had been a "lady" then, too.

Kenneth hadn't shaved my head.

Perhaps that was merely an oversight.

Or perhaps Hugh had decided I was not "one of us" at all, that I was an Elp - if a distinguished one - and had no more rights than Whin.

Perhaps that was what my dream of running from the hounds,

running with Whin, like Whin, like the Queen of Elphame, had meant.

Perhaps they were afraid to shave my head until Arsenius had scored me above the breath, rendered me harmless.

Perhaps I was in much, much bigger trouble than I had thought.

If I had realised only twenty-four hours earlier, I would have fled the country, jumped the nearest boat.

No, I wouldn't. Yacoub ben Amar, my mentor, had said, 'Finish the task in hand. Put the terrors aside along with the daydreams, and finish the task in hand, the task you have been set.'

The task you have taken on.

I turned to Coll, hanging on my left. A glance, which was all I could manage, showed me that she was awake and had been listening to me and Whin. And the cats, which were getting louder, more insistent.

'Coll hears,' I said.

'Coll hears,' she agreed.

'Did Coll hear Whin that night? The night the Moor was murdered. Or Whin's two children?'

Silence.

I strained my head round towards her as far as I could.

'Did Coll hear them?'

It was the strange little raising of the eyes and eyebrows that, I remembered, meant No.

'Did Coll hear horses - a horse - going by?'

The little nod. Yes.

'Did Coll hear, or see, the Queen of Elphame?'

Just a smile, a little smile, through the pain. She knew. At least she knew about Bella, and supposed that was what I meant. She probably knew much more.

'Did Coll hear words, any words, spoken out on the marshes that night?'

'Only …' She paused. 'Coll heard only Mona …'

Mona? 'Mona? You mean the wee lass that - ?'

The slight toss of the head. No. Then silence. I should not have interrupted! But Mona? Wait a moment. Mona was also the name of the Bailie's wife. Mistress Mona. Was it possible? Was there some great scandal here? Had the Moor been having an affair with the Bailie's wife? Had he been murdered for that?

Then Whin spoke: 'You shouldn't believe her, my lady. She's a liar. She lied about me. She lied about you. And she *is* a witch.'

'She is *not* a witch.'

'She cast a spell that very evening, called up that storm. And it was her cut off the Moor's cones, wasn't it. Or one of them. *One*?' She laughed, bitterly.

'It was, yes, yet she is not really a witch any more than you are. She was just making use of an old spell someone had taught her because she needed to kill Thorfinn Skinner. And she knew no other way. She tried poison. She tried magic.'

'She tried the knife once,' said Coll.

'Who? You mean you did? Coll did? Or Bella did?'

'Coll did. And Coll nearly died for it. Bella couldn't kill a chicken. Bella set a fat hog free once - let it run off into the woods - when it was all tied up ready and waiting for Master Thorfinn to come with his knife.' She paused.

So they didn't use Sweign Pigsticker. But Thorfinn wouldn't. A very private place, the Skinner steading.

I peered round at her.

Her eyes were wide. 'What happened to her then, *she* should have run off into the woods. Run with the little fat hog.' She giggled. 'The hog came home all by itself before the sun went down. But Bella is tamer even than that. When Master's around.'

'Was around. She's free now, Coll.'

I turned towards Whin. 'Which are you more like, Whin? You who claim to be prey? Not Bella. I remember Kari describing to me how you swim up behind a shag on a rock, the shag all unwary and with its wings out to dry, and you grab its ankles and yank it down and - drown it? Wring its neck? *You* are a killer, Whin, a hunter and a killer. It's easy to catch a foolish, hunted thing, a partridge, a trout, a hare, a deer. It is not easy to catch a hunter, a fox, a wulcat … you. Don't blame Coll for trying to kill Thorfinn - for killing him - yes, she was one of several who had a hand in his death, including his horse and his dog. Don't blame her for anything. She's not like you; she's like a partridge or a trout. A glaistig - '

'She's got claws.'

'A glaistig, a foolish, hunted thing - like that fat hog. No, not quite. Bella's more like the fat hog. Coll turned on her tormentor. Would you not turn on your tormentors if you could? By any means at your disposal? Did you not turn on those dogs? What would you do to Phorca, who hunted you and wanted you up on his wall? To Kenneth, who scourged you, and wanted your tongue?'

'I would cut off their nuts and scuts with their own daggers. Then I would stretch Master Kenneth out over a bramble bush and tie him there and leave him there for the hoodies to do the job, for they enjoy the job - as he does - more than I. But Phorca I would hunt through the forest, his dagger only in my hand, and every time I caught him I would slice off one more part of him in memory of my man's ears and of poor Badger, whose thumbs Phorca gave to his hounds before driving him to his death in the open sea - for he could not catch him.'

Nice.

'I'm sure Coll would have been more than happy to do the same to Thorfinn were she able. But she is not. So she did what she could. All she could. And Thorfinn is dead. Phorca and Kenneth are still alive. Unfortunately for us.'

Whin had the grace to strain her head round and smile at me, and then - past me - at Coll.

I, too, turned back to Coll. What had she been saying? 'Coll heard "Mona"? Coll heard no other word?'

'Coll heard the body drop off the horse onto the ground. Coll heard "blur-blur-blur-blur-Mona-mí-blur-blur-blur-blur". And then Coll heard the man walk away - heard the footfalls, the swishing of the grass, the night-birds falling silent, one giving an alarm. Then nothing.'

'Which way did he go? To Tain?'

The nod.

Who might say that? My Mona ... The Bailie? Little Mona's father? Grandfather? But why? What could that mean? Surely the Moor hadn't been planning to buy - or to abduct? - the child? But then why not? She was the same age, more or less, as Souad had been when he bought her … It didn't sound right, though. Bella, yes, he might well have been going to buy her, take her with him: but little Mona? Then again, how old had Bella been when she'd been sold? And by her mother. Seven? Perhaps the arrangement had been between the mother and ben Youssef, and the child had known nothing of it - yet. But the father had, and had intervened.

I would have to speak to Mona's mother and father. But how? And when?

Mona. My Mona.

'Coll took the dagger,' she said, suddenly. 'But that wasn't what …'

'Wasn't what killed him?'

'What wasn't what killed who? Pheeuw!' Kenneth back again, in the doorway. 'It reeks in here!'

It did rather smell. Whin had been unable to contain herself.

He called a man in with him from outside, and together they came down the steps to us.

He stopped below Whin. 'Filthy bitch.'

She had shit running down her legs, I saw now, shit on the floor below her, half washed away by piss.

'Help me get her down.'

They carried her through to the cell beyond Drostan's. Then they carried Coll through.

Now I was alone on the wall.

They both came back. The man stared at me. Kenneth said, 'And you? Are you going to shit yourself, my lady?'

The man laughed.

'Yes,' I said. 'Same as you would if you were left hanging here for hours on end.'

They took me through to the cell, too. I could walk, but my arms and shoulders were agony, and they left me manacled, of course, which didn't help. There was a torch burning outside the cell that lit it up when the door was opened. Whin and Coll were lying on their faces on the filthy floor. In the corner was a bucket.

I used it, gratefully, ignoring the two staring men in the doorway.

Then I went to sit down on the floor against the far wall.

'No, you come back out. The Brother will be here soon and it's you he'll want.'

They made me clean the floor, which was difficult with the manacle on, but I didn't mind, it gave me a chance to move, to stretch a bit. Then they hung me back up on the wall. Despite myself, I sobbed with the pain as they let me drop after putting my manacle back through the ring.

'Will I wait?' the man asked. 'It's cold outside now. And I don't like the sound of those cats.'

'No, don't wait. This one's not going anywhere, cats or no cats.'

'Good night, then, Master Kenneth.

'Good night.' Kenneth turned his gaze back to me. 'So. What were we saying? Ah, yes. What was not what killed who?'

'The whip was not what killed Rachid. Incompetent use of the rack by a mere apprentice working on his own was what killed him.'

He grinned. Ominously well.

But I ploughed on. 'I shall make sure the authorities know that when I return to Edinburgh. Rachid's sister already knows. You heard what happened to the man she thought killed her master? Imagine what will happen to the boy who killed her brother.'

'She will be caught. Probably already has been. And you, my lady, will never see Edinburgh again.'

'So sure?'

He hesitated. 'No - not so sure. Sure that you will be scored tonight. Sure that you will be stretched, tonight - tomorrow. Sure that you will be found guilty of witchcraft, of murder, of being in league with the Devil. And that if you ever do see Edinburgh again, it'll only be that you've been taken there - like Drostan - to see the King before you wear the scarlet cloak.'

'Like Drostan? Then I shall be in good company: such company as I would choose to live or die in. But who am I supposed to have murdered?'

'It seems that the powders found by Master Thorfinn Skinner's bed were not the ones the Brother Apothecary left for him. And it seems that you could as easily have murdered the Frenchman as the Moorish slave-girl could. More easily, in fact. And you knew him, she didn't. What motive could she have had?'

'She believes he murdered her master.'

'That was done by her brother, by Rachid. He confessed as much. And she had planned it, arranged it. So you see she is not one to commit a murder herself. And who else apart from her might have had a Moorish knife? You, my lady.'

'But I was - oh, never mind. I assume someone with the authority to question me will be here soon.'

'The Brother will. And Sir Hugh will be here, looking for some fun. The Brother won't want Sir Hugh disappointed …'

I opened my mouth. Closed it again. Even I could envisage little alternative in the way of an evening's entertainment for everyone, given the circumstances. Little runt. He was skinny and white, his body was hairless all over as far as I could see, and I had noticed, as they lifted me down and put me back up, almost completely odourless - apart from the pervasive odour of leather and death. He was like something from under a stone or rotting tree trunk that someone had foolishly lifted. Like a tough white worm. Or a white slug. Not like the slugboys of Newgate Prison in London, though: the one or two of them I had met I had liked.

'I'm for a wee sleep, my lady. It promises to be quite a night.'

He went and lay down on what had obviously become his bed, in the corner by the glowing coal fire and the gleaming instruments, most of which he must have brought with him from Dyngvale. A whip - whips, hanging there. They looked very long, very hard, but whipping I could face, I'd been whipped before. Though not as hard as he would do it, not like Whin had been whipped, and poor Coll. But being scored above the breath? Just the thought horrified me - not so much the pain and the humiliation but the effect, the great red witch-line across my forehead from ear to ear that would be there for ever - if, by some chance, I escaped the fire: which nobody with a witch-line and the witch-marks "the Brother" was sure to find somewhere on my body ever did … And as for the rack …

Ferchard would get here first.

I listened to the wulcats. They seemed to be all around us. Was it something natural? Or was it Mouraig …? How could it be?

Long minutes went by. The yowling grew louder and louder,

closer and closer. It sounded like *hundreds* of cats.

Suddenly they all stopped.

The door opened. Brother Arsenius came swiftly down the stone steps.

Anyone else wearing flip-flop sandals like he was wearing would make a flip-flop sound on those stone steps. Not him. He entered like a draught, silently.

He gave me barely a glance.

He went to Drostan's cell and unbolted the door, went in and stayed there a moment, no doubt to check how the old man was.

When he came out, he put his hand in the wide breast pocket of his soutane and took out a pointed tool not unlike the awl he had shown me - was it only yesterday? - but newer, shinier, sharper. He came up to me. Straight face. No grin now.

This was serious.

For once I agreed with him. This was serious. And whatever Uncle Yacoub might say to the contrary, I again had a serious problem that I was helpless to do anything about.

Where was Ferchard?

Ferchard was nearing Tain, but on foot, and slowly, limping through the mud, one hand on little Otter's shoulder, the other pressing down on a stout stick Otter had found for him.

'Old fool!' he kept muttering. 'Useless old fool. She should have brought Tom with her!' (Tom, whom he hated with a passion, and whom I had left behind in London.) 'Her life in danger, and what do I do? Sit in a forest talking to some other lass. Then when I finally tear myself away I let my horse collapse under me and end up walking - shuffling - Sir Farquhar - knight to the rescue … You be Sir Otter, lad, from now on. I'll be Ferchard the Fool.'

They limped and staggered on a few more steps, a few more yards, a furlong, step by step, another furlong, another. What little light the clouds had left was fading too now. At least the rain had stopped. An evening bird of some kind tried out its song. And liked it. Did it again.

'What's that?' he gasped. 'I can't even remember the names of the birds.'

'It's just a thrush. A missel thrush. Will we stop a while?'

A missel thrush. Ah yes. A mavis …

'No, no, let's go on. A woman is a dangerous animal, lad. And by now she must be ready to kill.'

Otter said nothing. Simply trudged on, and nodded sagely. He remembered a time he and his da had hidden in a lochan for hours breathing through reed stems while his ma had been on the rampage, a big blackthorn stick in her hand. He grinned. But no one could escape his ma. She must have known where they were and decided to leave them there for the afternoon, out of the way …

In truth, it wasn't Ferchard's fault that the horse had slipped and fallen in the mud, and that while Otter, of course, had sprung clear, he himself had got caught and had sprained his knee and ankle. Though he could have spent a little less time with Souad. They were coming, that was the main thing, my two heroes. No, I'd better amend that: my one young hero, bearing the weight of Ferchard the Fool on his shoulder as well as the whole responsibility for rescuing his mother and poor Coll. And me.

But it was his foresight, Ferchard's foresight, that saved us. Years ago, he had taught me how to use my feet and legs as a weapon. I had nearly killed Tom once, practising, and he had had to wear wooden splints to hold up his head. Then another time I had dislocated Ferchard's knee, and he had been laid up for weeks. That same knee that was now giving him so much pain. Poor Ferchard. But I didn't know that …

I knew only that the devil was coming closer, coming to me, and that I would have one chance. My foot flexed and hardened. I took a deep breath. I saw the beginning of a smile on his face. My leg, my whole body, shot out from the wall and his neck snapped, his head flew back and his body flew away from me as I hung there for a second up in the air then fell back, thud, against the wall.

The runt was stirring. 'Stay still, you. Or you'll wish you had.'

I stayed still. Very still. For once he too was right.

But what now?

The body lay on the floor, half naked. Legs like any other

dead felon. Gallows meat. Skinny and tough.

Oh Ferchard, Ferchard! Come! For the love of God - for the love of Christ and his Holy Mother - and the Magdalene! - come! Come now!

Ferchard was not doing well that day - even God had given up on him - but my prayers were answered and another old man - not quite such a fool as Ferchard - though fool enough in his own way - whispered: 'Shh.'

Drostan.

The friar had left the cell door open.

Drostan shuffled across to us, making as little noise as he could. Made the Sign of the Cross over the body, then bent and tried to pull it away.

Why? I mouthed at him.

But he wasn't looking at me.

He dragged the body slowly, slowly, over towards his cell, and every instant I expected Kenneth to wake, sit up …

He got it to the doorway, into the cell. Gone. I breathed a great sigh - then gasped as I realised how loud the sigh had sounded.

Drostan appeared again. 'Kenneth!' he called, in his quavering voice. 'Master Kenneth!'

Was he mad?

'Master Kenneth! Please! Help me! Help me …'

Kenneth roused himself from his bed, muttering, 'Old fool … What does he want?'

'Help me!'

'Shut up, old fool!'

And I realised that Drostan was behind the open cell door. Oh no … Oh yes! If he could do it. If he was quick enough.

I watched Kenneth go round to the cell, go in. I saw - and heard - the cell door slam shut, saw Drostan's raw finger-ends fumble at the bolt, heard Kenneth's shout from inside the cell … Saw the bolt slide home.

I cheered.

Then the street door opened and Sir Hugh walked in.

TWENTY-THREE

Where Angels Cannot Go

Drostan faded back into the shadows.

Kenneth fell silent, realising perhaps that, with no window in the cell, no one could hear.

Hugh stared at me. I gazed back at him, as wide-eyed and desirable as my breaking wrists and shoulders would allow.

Sir Hugh. Baron Foulis. Phorca. Not the answer to a maiden's prayer.

But perhaps to the prey-turned-hunter's. Which was why I must be me, not Bella. Yes, Raoul.

'Marian. What a pleasure. Or should I address you as the Queen? For though your realm has shrunk, your lineage is awesomely ancient.'

'Hugh. A pleasure indeed. "Marian" will do, as always.'

'And the mermaid?' he said, looking round. 'The tinkler bitch? The elph?' Eyeing my breasts appreciatively, he tutted. 'You are becoming like her, Marian. You have no shame. You run through the hills like that, you take to the sea like that … You can hang here like that, too.'

He was going to tear off what was left of my chemise.

The door was opening.

Say something!

'Hugh, I took you for a pig and called you Phorca in my mind but you're not a pig. You're a ferret.'

Oh, let it not creak this time! Let there be no sudden draughts!

'Marian. Your majesty. In what have I offended you?'

I dared not glance at the door.

And Drostan was creeping up behind him, a heavy wooden club raised high over his head. A club such as they used for beating people senseless.

I didn't believe it.

I couldn't look at him, couldn't look at the door. There was a cat at the door!

I said, 'Hugh, when we met I was rather taken with you. If only because I could see you were taken with me - with my eyes and breasts at least, if not my brain - which was flattering, for you see so many beautiful women. No, don't tear my poor cutty semmit any more than it has been already - I'm not some tinkler bitch, though to you, with your pure blood, I suppose I must seem - must be - some kind of half-breed, a half-elp. Well, go on then, if you must. You've seen me before.'

I made it sound almost an invitation. His eyes gleaming, his mouth watering, he put his hand up to my breast, to what was left of my chemise.

Get out of the way, Drostan!

It was too late. I had no chance to kick him as I had kicked Arsenius. Instead, as he seized the front of my chemise and pulled, I swung my legs up each side of him. He thought it was a game - a more overt invitation. Foolishly, he laughed as my legs rode down the sides of his head and onto his shoulders. Oh, what a treat he thought was in store for him.

Now at last I was able to glance round. The door had closed. There was no one. The wind? Or had someone peered in, then gone? Gone for a drink perhaps, seeing I had everything under control?

Or had I been right? That wulcat …

I closed my thighs on his neck, locked my ankles.

Still he laughed.

No ferret would have laughed in that position.

He was a pig after all. Shoving its snout in after the honey, regardless of all risk.

Well, come on, Drostan, someone! Or do I have to do it all myself?

I tightened my grip.

Now he began to struggle.

Really struggle!

And he bit me. And again. His teeth in me, cutting deep into me - *no*! Ferchard never told me this could happen!

'Drostan!!' I screamed. 'Quick!!'

The club rose up before my face. I looked into Drostan's eyes as it descended - then realised neither of us was watching what he was doing. I looked down. I thought it was going to break my legs. I nearly let go. But it came down on Hugh's back with a back-breaking thud, well below my legs. It jolted us both upwards so that as he dropped away from me I fell back down again, nearly tearing my hands off. The club came down on his head once more with a wonderfully final crack, and that was that.

I knew how Raoul had felt.

How Bella had felt.

Drostan dropped to his knees.

It was suddenly very silent.

I was suddenly very silent. I realised I had been screaming. Well, I had been bitten by a rat. Not what I had been expecting, but - now that it was over - bearable. Things could have been much, much worse.

'He was a man,' Drostan mumbled.

'He was a rat!' I sobbed. 'And he died in a corner as a rat should die!'

Some corner.

And did he have to die with his teeth in me?

I had another point to add to the list of points I wished to discuss with Sir Farquhar. Before I sent him back to his buxom niece and told her she could keep him.

I let out another great shuddering sob.

Blood was running down my leg.

Life with Effie's too good for you, Ferchard. Perhaps I'll leave you to the gentle ministrations of Father Cyril at the Abbey.

I looked down at Drostan. He was sobbing too, now, over the man he had killed.

'Drostan,' I said, 'don't waste your tears.'

'In every man there is something of God.'

I hesitated, avoided the glib answer, said simply: 'That's Kabbalah.'

'That's St Paul. According to Meister Eckhart, when St Paul wrote that we carry the Spirit of God within us, he meant it literally: he meant there is something of God in every man. Which, as you say, is Kaballah. I came to the Kaballah through Meister Eckhart.'

He gazed up at me. Me on the wall in the flickering torchlight like a crucifix.

Blasphemy.

I blushed.

Then retracted the blush. I had not hung myself up here.

'We have done so much.' he was saying. 'You have done so much. But now you can do no more. No one could. For this is the hour of the *Counterfeit Din*, and in that hour who can re-establish the balance of justice?'

'The *Counterfeit Din*? Then you do know Kaballah.'

'Oh yes. Kaballah teaches that there is *Din*, justice, true justice, on the one hand, and *Hesed*, loving-kindness, mercy, on the other hand. Justice must be tempered by mercy, but mercy must acknowledge the legitimate demands of justice. True justice. But not the false and lying judgments of the *Counterfeit Din*. Which is what we had here - '

'Still have - '

'Yes, what we still have …'

He considered me. What was left of my chemise was hanging from one shoulder. I was almost naked. I hoped the blood was not still running too obviously down my leg. I was more than a little ashamed of that manoevre, now I looked back on it.

He said: 'When, as a Kaballista, you meditate on the Tree of Life, what aspect of the personality of God do you see yourself as embodying? Have you thought about that?'

Kaballista. I liked that. I didn't deserve it, but I liked it.

'I am *Hod*,' I said.

He smiled. 'Because you champion truth and justice and thereby support and maintain the power of the *Divine Din*. Yes, you are right. But when the law lets you down, when justice becomes unjust and the power of the Other Side, the *Counterfeit Din*, intensifies - as now - and you are left in a limbo - why, then you find yourself forced into the role of *Netshah*, renewal, supporting *Hesed*, love and mercy, which is not at all the role you were predestined for.'

'Predestined?'

'Yet one must adapt. How do you read me?'

'You are *Hesed*.'

'Now, yes. And yet I was not, always ... And in my veins flows the blood of ancient kings.'

There was a rattling of chains, and Whin came wandering through like a hairless ghost of herself.

'Whin? How are you?'

'Bad. And you, my lady?' She examined me with her eyes, glanced at the old man, then looked at the body on the floor. 'Is it him?'

I nodded.

'And the other?'

'The runt? He's in there.'

'In his cell?' She nodded at Drostan. 'And the monk?'

'He's in there too. He's dead.'

'Dead, too? Oh, my lady. And you said *I* was a killer?'

I was going to point out how helpless I was, give the credit to Drostan. I changed my mind. He was in a state of shock. He did not need to be classed as, and admired as, a killer, by two killers like me and Whin, though under normal circumstances I was sure he could handle it. With his name, it must be the ancient kings of the Picts from whom he claimed descent. Warriors indeed! But for now it would be better to carry on with the theological discussion, give him time to recover.

Whin knelt down by the body, opposite Drostan, and turned it over. She stared down at the mortal remains of her tormentor. She had one regret, I knew. But there was still Kenneth.

Drostan looked back up at me. 'I undid the bolt on their door while I was hiding there. They were both asleep.'

'*Hesed*.'

He smiled up at me. '*Netshah*.'

'My teacher, Yacoub ben Amar, taught that false judgment is judgment based on what a man is rather than what he has done.'

'All of society is based on that, my daughter. What did you call yourself when you were speaking to - him? "Half-breed", you said. And you referred to his "pure blood".'

I smiled. 'I was mocking him ... My poor father came from

the same kind of background as Sir Hugh. And in discussion once with Yacoub he observed that Muslims may own Muslim slaves but they do not enslave another Muslim as they would a Christian - after a battle, for instance. Yacoub argued that the same is true of Christians - and Jews - though it is less obvious. The slaves have to be somehow different. No landowner, he said, will marry a serf; he - or she - will marry an aristocratic outsider, so that although serf and master are of the same stock originally they soon become very different. My father wouldn't accept that at first, but - '

'That's true all over Europe. And in cities full of real slaves - Avignon, for instance - where every cardinal and bishop has slaves attending on him - most of the slaves are foreign, often black - '

'Yes, yes, they are. I noticed that, too. And yet - how does it go? - in the eyes of God, there is neither black nor white, man nor woman, slave nor free -'

'That sounds a little like St Paul again,' Drostan smiled. 'Not many men, though, take that God-like view. Most men judge other men by their - '

'Yes, but why? To a bird, a bird is a bird.'

Whin sighed and said, 'Have you ever seen what black crows do to a white crow?'

There was a moment of silence.

Sometimes I talk complete nonsense.

But Drostan should know better.

He winked. Drostan winked at me!

I winked back.

Well, some of his ideas were stupid, let's face it, as he must realise, but he was good and kind. And I was a slave-owner myself. Khadija I had inherited. Yahia I had been given. And both these were Muslims - by birth, at any rate: Khadija crossed herself these days a great deal more often than I did. And Tom Fletcher I had "claimed" when he was in trouble in France after drinking too much - I had saved him and he had never disputed my claim. Of course, he was different, too: he was English. Like Bella. And when the English go abroad they do seem to get into trouble. The unimportant ones. The great ones are always busy trying to conquer the place. Not in the least concerned with justice, only with increasing their own personal power and glory.

Coll came tottering through from the cell, another hairless wraith.

Whin sighed again. 'My lady, don't you think we might try to get out of these chains?'

'How, Whin? Drostan can't help us any further. Look at his poor fingers. We are waiting for Ferchard - Sir Farquhar - you remember him? The white-haired man in the chamber in Dyngvale with me? And for Otter. And -'

'Otter? But what makes you think -?'

'I spoke to Otter in a dream, Whin.'

Had I been building my hopes on a dream? Deep down, I had feared so all along. And yet it had been so real.

'You should have told me.'

'I wasn't sure. I might have been dreaming -'

'You were dreaming, my lady. But Otter wasn't. He will be here, and Sir Farquhar with him, if that was what he said.'

'Yes. And Kari.'

'Kari? They'd probably be better without her, but ...'

Drostan spoke again. 'This - this one. Sir Hugh, you called him. Baron Foulis, I believe.'

'Yes.'

'Why did he call you Queen, and Majesty?'

I laughed, and thought my ribs would crack. I couldn't hang here like this much longer. 'He was a foolish man. Part of his foolishness was to take me for the Queen of Elphame.'

'For any good reason?'

'No. Save that I ride a horse sometimes, and wear a cloak - and have on occasion been seen with Thorfinn Skinner's great wolfhound behind me.'

'So has Bella - on many occasions.'

'You know Bella?'

'Oh yes. I was one who could speak to her properly, not just smile and gaze and exchange the odd word like most of the monks.'

Of course. 'And did you ever hear tell that *she* was the Queen of Elphame? Or at least the one taken for the Queen?'

'No, but it doesn't surprise me. That anklet she wears - and that beautiful cloak. And that way she has.'

I knew someone else with a way. I peered round at Whin. 'Whin, have you ever ridden on a horse?'

'No, only on a cuddy - a donkey.'

Drostan coughed. 'There are precedents for that.'

I smiled at him. True. Very true.

'But when I was a boy,' he went on, 'and that was long before Bella or you, my lady, were born - the Queen rode on a great stag, or elk. And she was being pursued by the hound, not accompanied by it. Or so they used to say.'

His poor old eyes were twinkling again. But yes, that was what Whin had hinted at so long ago. A week?

'Drostan, have you ever heard of the Magdalene Anklet?'

'No. No, I haven't. Though it does sound …'

'Familiar?'

'Suggestive.'

I could see that, yes. Change the subject again.

'Have you ever ridden on a stag, Whin?'

'Yes, there was one who used to let me ride him. He gave his life for me. I rode him that day like the wind, rode him till we were clear of the hunters, as I thought, then slipped off and away. But they caught up with him again while he was still exhausted …'

A long silence ensued while I tried to fit this into the picture - and tried not to think how much worse the pain was getting. It would pass. Everyone was suffering. Everyone was thinking. Except the rat on the floor. Rat he had turned out to be. He, not Coll, had been responsible for my arrest, and he bore - or would have born - responsibility for giving the Inquisition, the Black Friars of the Holy Office in the person of Brother Arsenius, the opportunity to extend the auto-da-fé to witches in this part of Scotland.

I caught Drostan's eye.

He smiled. 'Meister Eckhart also said: By will a man could pierce a wall of steel.'

'We shouldn't have much trouble with these little chains then, should we?'

'No, my lady. But God works in mysterious ways, and many

and unexpected are his instruments.'

Not many, and not entirely unexpected, if my prayers were answered.

I glanced at the door. At Coll.

'Coll hears,' she muttered, only half conscious.

The door opened. A pinched little face peered in. Quite different from the broad-faced cat I had seen, or had imagined I had seen.

And on the floor, Sir Hugh groaned.

I nodded to Otter, beckoning him in with my head.

He came running down the steps and hesitated at the sight of Coll, then saw the other woman kneeling on the floor, also with her head shaved, and with her back and sides whipped raw: 'Ma?' He flung himself at her, stopped, fearful of hurting her, knelt before her, face to face. He touched her face, wiping away some of the blood and dirt and tears.

After a moment, he looked up at me.

'Otter,' I said. '*M'eudail*.'

Whin smiled now, at him, at me.

'Where is Sir Farquhar?'

'Outside, my lady.'

'Tell him to come inside.'

'He can hardly walk. We'd an accident with the horse - '

'And Kari?'

'He sent Kari to Mistress Mouraig - '

To Mouraig? 'But why?'

'We met another foreign lady. Her name was Souad. Sir Farquhar sent her to Lady Mouraig on Kari's horse.'

Things were happening out in the big world.

'Tell him to come in, bad leg or no bad leg. We need his help.'

Hugh groaned and moved his arm.

'Drostan! Hit him again! Quick!'

'I can't. I really can't.'

'Otter?'

But Whin had picked up the club herself. She held it in both hands, manacled as she was, held it over Hugh's head - or rather his face, for she had turned him over, on his back. Was she going to smash it down onto his face, club him to death? I looked away.

I wouldn't have blamed her, but …

I heard nothing. I looked back. She still had not hit him. She looked at me. She had been waiting for me. Now, as he raised his head slightly, she hit him on the forehead. With that great club it seemed no more than a tap - it was no more than a tap - but his head went back with a thud and he was out cold again.

'I mean to hunt him. Sometime. Just me. Just him,' she hissed.

'Who is it?' Otter asked.

'It's the pig - the rat - who hunted me. Who holds your da in a cage.'

The boy grinned at her, put his ear to Sir Hugh's cheek. 'He'll do,' he said.

The door opened again. Ferchard?

It was Kari. In the white cloak her ma had worn that day. She looked up at me, wide-eyed, then saw Whin and Otter and ran down to them. 'Ma? What have they done to you?'

'Only what they did before to my poor boy here. Still, you have enough hair for all three of us, squirrel.'

'Ma! Your back!' She was crying.

'No, don't start being silly. Go and ask your lady what you can do to help.'

She came over to me, wiping her eyes, trying to be brave. 'My lady?'

'Kari, my sweet. Where is Sir Farquhar? Did you see him?'

'He's outside, my lady.' She laughed through her tears. 'He says to forget him, he's no use. To leave him out there in the rain where he can do no more harm.'

I looked at her, at the boy. They could manage between them.

'Is my horse outside?'

She hadn't noticed.

'Aye, it's there,' said Otter, who was standing over poor Hugh with the club now, ready to hit him if he stirred again.

'Oh yes! Next to mine,' Kari remembered. 'I mean Bella's!'

'Bella's?'

'Mine was finished by the time we arrived, with me and Souad up on her, and all that way. So Mouraig told me to bring you Bella's horse. And I brought you Butterfly, too. He's outside.'

Butterfly? A few days ago she had been nervous even of my

mare, and terrified of the great wolfhound.

'Kari, Mouraig's dead.'

She stared at me. 'Oh no, my lady. Who - who told you that? She said you might need the real cloak, too.'

At least she hadn't worn that.

But Mouraig?

'And the cats?' I demanded. 'The wulcats?'

'Wulcats?'

Somehow the world outside had changed …

'Go and tell Sir Farquhar I agree, but he's to guard the door. And if he can't manage that, to set the dog to guard it.'

Kari smiled, irrepressible. 'At the moment, Butterfly's guarding him - I mean growling at him. He won't let him move.'

'Will you go and do as I say? And inform Butterfly that Sir Farquhar is a friend. Not a very good or reliable friend, but - '

'I don't think Butterfly likes men, my lady.'

'Kari! I'm in agony here! Say Ferchard's really a woman in disguise! Say anything! Just do it!'

'Yes, my lady.'

We heard the hound start barking, then fall silent again.

She came back. 'Butterfly didn't believe it, but Sir Farquhar said he was glad you understood.'

'Understood? Oh, I see.' I laughed, despite myself.

'And, my lady, Mouraig sent this unguent. She said you might need it.'

'You'll need it on your bottom if you don't get me down from here!'

'And when you've finished with her bottom, pass her to me,' muttered Whin.

Kari grinned.

'Coll hears. Then pass her to me.'

That did make Kari move. The dog and Ferchard she obviously had at her fingertips. Me she had in the palm of her hand - she thought. But Coll still terrified her.

'Coll,' I said, very seriously, 'if they haven't got us all out of our chains in two minutes flat, turn the girl into a spider, will you? And the boy into - '

'Coll will keep the boy. Coll's never had a boy before.'

The two children gaped at her. I thought for a second we'd overdone it, and they were going to flee out into the night and never come back. But then Kari came and stood up against me, while Otter swarmed up onto her shoulders. From there he could just reach the ring and the chain. And Coll, watching them, chanted,

'What kind o' spider will ye be?
What kind will ye be?
A big fat white one, waxy, bloatit?
A whitey-green one, lady long-legs?
A dear little brownie, velvet-coatit?
What kind will ye be?
Or a chancy wee black one spinning its threid
frae one who'll be lucky to one who'll be deid?'

Otter had the manacle open. He jumped clear and as I slid down the wall Kari caught me and laid me gently on the floor.

'Not like that, on the stone floor. Put something under her!' ordered Drostan.

They looked round.

'Over there. My - '

'No, not your clothes, my lady,' said Drostan. 'I have something in my cell - '

'Don't open that door!' I screamed, as his hand went out to the door. Took hold of the bolt. His old brain was slow now, after all that had happened.

'Please God,' I prayed.

His hand came away again. He looked round foolishly.

'*Don't touch that door*,' I begged. '*Please*.'

'No. No, I - '

It didn't matter. I was already sitting up, trying to get my poor hands and wrists working, rubbing unguent into them, then when they felt a bit better dabbing some onto the vicious bite between my legs.

Meanwhile, the children released Whin and Coll from their manacles.

I leant over to Whin. I didn't know what was in the ointment but it felt right on me and I trusted Mouraig. (Mouraig! How could that be?) I soothed it over her back and her wrists, and when she seemed better, I turned to Coll: 'Are you all right, Coll? Can you walk?'

The nod.

'Then wait for me ... Drostan?' The old man seemed finished now, physically, mentally, emotionally.

I wanted to get them all outside.

'Whin, what shall we do with the boy?'

'The runt? Leave him where he is. I can do nothing today. But I will.'

'Will you do - as you said?' I asked.

'I will see what I will do when the time comes. When he falls into my hands.'

Drostan, waking up, was listening, understanding.

'Will you hunt him?' I wanted to know.

'Aye, if I get the chance. If he ever wanders into a wood alone.'

I shuddered. Declined to catch Drostan's eye.

'And the rat?' Whin asked, gazing down at him contemptuously. 'The hunter?'

'Leave *him* to me, Whin. As you say, you can do nothing today with that back of yours. I was luckier.'

I had to get them all to a place of safety, fast. Kari could go to Mouraig's and wait for me there if Mouraig was all right. But Coll? And Whin? I couldn't think how to organise it. I needed Kari to escort Drostan.

'Whin, will you be able to walk?'

She nodded, put her hand out for me to help her up. When she was standing, I fetched her my skirt from where they had thrown our things. 'Put on this skirt of mine. I won't need it.'

I held her while Kari helped her step into it.

I looked at Otter. He would do.

'Otter, take your ma and Coll out of the town. Take them west. Travel slowly, but avoid all contact with people. When Coll is ready, one night, she will disappear. Don't worry. Don't wait or search for her. Go on, and spend a year, two years, away on the west coast, or out on one of the islands - though you may feel trapped on an island. No, Whin won't, of course. But will you, Otter?'

Whin smiled. 'He won't, either. He's almost as good in the water as Kari.'

I helped her fold the top of the skirt over and tuck it in.

'Anyway, stay right away from here. Stay right away from towns. Whin, don't kill cats. Don't beg. Live out - right out. I know you can - both of you. Otter, you'll catch fish for your ma, won't you, till she's well again. And even then. And hunt for her, and be a man for her.'

'And my da?'

'Your da. Oh yes.' And now the plan came together suddenly in my mind. It would take a while but I liked it. 'Wait for me by Loch Mouri, and I'll bring him to you. In three days, four. Five, maybe. If I don't come in a week, then wait no longer. I will not be coming, for he is dead.'

'He's not dead.' It was Otter, who knew.

'Then I will bring him.'

'As you come to the loch, on the north shore, my lady, below the oak wood, there … We'll be there.'

'Well. We'll talk again then.'

'Can she take the other cloak?' Kari asked me. I nodded. 'Ma, take this cloak with you and wear it when you can. I shan't need it.'

'Goodbye then, *m'eudail,* my star.' I bent and kissed him. 'Goodbye, Whin. Will I ever run with you again, before the hounds?'

'Not before this one's hounds, my lady - not if you do your job tonight.'

'I wish we could do this together, Whin.'

'Oh, so do I.'

We embraced as well as we could, and Kari accompanied them out to the street. Coll followed, a strange look in her pale eyes. Was it tears? Then, when I thought there would be no sign, she turned and gave a little wave from the door - and was gone. Now Drostan and I were alone - apart from Hugh, on the floor.

'What will you do with him, my lady?'

'You've started calling me "my lady". Before, it was "my

daughter".'

'Foolish presumption, my lady. I am in your hands. But please, don't kill him. For your sake. It's you I care about. And true justice, not revenge.'

'Justice will be done, justice tempered by mercy. And it will be seen to be done, believe me. But about you. Kari will take you to a young man I know, and he will take you to a place of safety. A good place, a suitable place for one such as you to spend his final days.'

'My lady. My daughter. My dear. How can I ever thank you?'

'Don't. Thank Heaven. Thank God in his *Din* aspect that for once true justice has prevailed.'

'And - and if they come now? Before we leave? That is what I have been fearing all this time.'

'Sir Farquhar is there - Big Ferchard - my father's friend and my protector. I have absolute faith in him. And should he be sleeping, then I have absolute faith in Butterfly - a great wolfhound you will see as you leave. Probably sleeping too.'

'Rather simply say you have absolute faith. And always had. You never gave up.'

Kari came back in, crying. And carrying Bella's white cloak.

'Kari, you remember Callum Vass? The man we sold our whale to? You remember where he lives? Take this poor ill-used old man, ride with him on my horse, and deliver him to Callum Vass. Say he is the Lady Marian MacElpin's friend, Drostan, a holy man, and he needs help. Callum should take Drostan in his boat to the hermit who lives in the cave on the coast out past Red Nose, and leave him there. The hermit - one Fursey MacFarquhar, if I remember rightly - will know what to do with him. Then wait there for me. Do not go to Mouraig's again by yourself. Here, you will need money.'

I found some coins for her and took her and Drostan out into the night. Ferchard lifted her up onto the horse - with some pleasure, I noted - then the two of us managed to get Drostan up behind her.

'Hang on,' I told him. 'Hang onto her. Don't fall off.'

'Farewell, my lady. God be with you.'

'Farewell, Master.'

'Goodbye, my lady! Goodbye, Sir Farquhar!'

'Shh! Goodbye, Kari. Go now.'

At last.

I turned to Ferchard.

'I need you,' I said.

'You needed me. I was not here. I have the soul of a woman.'

'That is high praise if Whin and Coll and Mouraig - and little Kari - are anything to go by.'

'And you, my lady. Oh, and you.'

'Come inside. I do need you. Leave the hound on guard. Butterfly! No, stop that. Stand there. Right.'

We went in.

'Who is that?'

'That is Sir Hugh - Baron Foulis. And within the cell lies the Dominican Brother Arsenius of the Holy Office. Dead. And the foul young "Master" Kenneth, Big Robbie's son. Still very much alive, to my intense regret.'

'You have been busy, my lady. And indeed you did not need me, it seems.'

'No, as it turned out. But when you were teaching me, you omitted to mention that when a rat is cornered, it bites. I cornered a rat and it bit - most painfully.'

'My lady -'

'Marian.'

'Marian. I do not understand. What corner?'

'The only corner a lady has.'

He looked me up and down. I realised I was still wearing only my torn chemise. He suddenly understood, and blushed.

'Marian, that is not a corner a real lady ever lets a rat get into.'

'Then as we suspected, I am no real lady. But I am alive.'

'Is that the rat?'

'It is.'

'Let me deal with him.'

'No! All I want you to do is strip him and hobble him. I'll find some rope.'

'There'll be fetters here.'

'I prefer rope. The Queen of Elphame would not use steel. Hobble him, tie his wrists, too, behind his back, and put a long tether on him.'

'Round his neck? A slip knot?'

'No, a fixed knot, the noose too tight for him to get it off in any circumstances.'

'And him naked. Right.'

'Leave him his breech-clout.'

'I hope you know what you're doing.'

'Don't I always?'

'Do you ever?'

He tore off Hugh's garments, and had tied his wrists and was busy tying his ankles, when I said: 'There's an abbey at Fearn with a particularly obnoxious little abbot where I could leave you - '

'They don't take women in disguise.'

'Oh, they probably would. They'd pretend they didn't know. Shall I enquire?'

'I think I'd prefer Effie. Pass me that knife, lass.'

I was his lass again.

He peered up from his work. 'She's mature, for a start.'

'Ouch.'

'She doesn't end up on the wall of the local torture chamber, and blame it on everyone except herself.'

'Mm.'

'And she doesn't, and wouldn't, pick out for especial blame her oldest and most loyal and most devoted retainer.'

'Mm-hm.'

'And friend.'

'Ah.' I waited. 'That's it? I was only joking, but if that's how you really feel about me, Farquhar, then - '

'Shh - he's coming round.'

'Don't *shh* me! If the voluptuous Effie has you in thrall, then you can - '

'The voluptuous Effie does not have me in thrall! Now do you want the rat conscious, woman, or shall I whang him one?'

'Whang him one.'

He did so. With the side of his hand.

'Now put the rope round his neck and carry him out - drag him if you can't carry him - and sling him over my horse.'

While he did that, I found some water and washed my face

over the slop bucket - I used to be very particular where I washed my face before I came to Scotland! - then tried on Bella's cloak. It fit perfectly. My boots were there too, so I pulled them on.

Ferchard came back in.

'How do I look?'

'That cloak is beautiful.'

'You're supposed to say I am beautiful in this cloak.'

'You are beautiful in anything you wear, but not everything you wear is beautiful.'

Hm. 'I think I just may have to deprive poor Effie of you for another year or two. This is the cloak of the Queen of Elphame.'

'Really?'

'No, not really. But it is the cloak worn by the beautiful lass whom everyone takes to be the Queen of Elphame. And the horse out there is her horse, the dog her dog.'

'Don't tell me. The country is about to witness the Queen do justice on the wicked baron.'

I smiled. 'Effie wouldn't do that, either, would she?'

'Not in her wildest dreams.'

'Too mature.'

'Too conventional. Too civilised. Marian, look - there is food. Eat something before you go. And take some with you.'

'Join me, then. You haven't eaten either.'

So we ate what must have been young Kenneth's supper, and went on talking.

'Where exactly is Foulis Tower, Ferchard?'

He laughed.

'On the firth, a few miles this side of Dyngvale. You'll need to make for Alness first.' He drew a little map in the dust for me. 'We're here. I should keep to the forest for a while if I were you. Go due south to Balichraggan, then onto the road to Alness. Or south-west through the forest all the way to Alness.'

'Any rivers? Any landmarks?'

'You'll cross Aldie Water after an hour or two, then come to the Balnagown River after another two or three hours. If you're heading directly for Alness, cross it and keep heading south-west. If not, go down the river to Balichraggan and from there take the coast road south. You can't get lost because you'll always have a view of the firth on your left every time there's a break in the trees.'

'And what are we going to do with you while I ride the fells and forests of Ross with my great hunter friend here in tow?' I remembered that Hugh was not here but outside, and likely to come round again at any moment. 'We'd better go and check up on him.'

'He'll be all right. Me? I think I'd better follow that Spanish lass as soon as I'm able. Make sure she's not molested.'

Spanish? Yes, that's right, she is half Spanish. Same as me.

'I knew her when she was a wee lass,' he went on. 'I was there when Abdelwahed be Youssef bought her - '

'You were? But how?'

'It was that summer I was searching for you, lass. I was in Granada - but it's a long story, and it'll keep. She needs help now though, so if - if you don't need me any more …'

We looked at each other - and laughed. We were both in pain, both exhausted.

'I'll get a message to you if I do, old friend.'

'And I will come to you, though snails overtake me on the way. I will come.'

'I know you will. Kari left Souad at Balintore with my grandmother. You know her?'

'I knew her when *she* was Lady MacElpin.'

'Yes, of course you did. I'd like you to go there for her sake as well as for Souad's. Make sure that *she* is all right, and - and if she *is* all right, stay there with her. With them.'

'Of course I will. How do I find her?'

'Ask for Mouraig, at Kattar-bol, near Balintore. Wait for me there.'

'Aye, my lady. Here, take this as well. For him, not for the horse.' He handed me a whip. 'And the hound could do with a taste of it from time to time.'

I took it. He was right. I might well need it - but not for Butterfly.

We were ready to go.

Out in the street, I realised I had forgotten Kenneth. But what could I say to him? Stop torturing people? Silly. It was his job, his trade. And if he made enemies in the course of it - as do I, as do I! - then he would have to face that, face them, when the time came.

But I was glad my enemies did not include Whin.

I shrugged, kissed Ferchard, clung to him for a moment, then led the horse away up the street.

Butterfly followed, yawning, at my heel. And turned and gave Ferchard one last look. I'll swear he was gloating.

TWENTY-FOUR

Justice Is Seen To Be Done

I took to the woods, as Ferchard had suggested, heading south toward Balichraggan. I didn't want to be seen too soon, or too close to Tain, but there at Balichraggan I would go to the people with him, lead him along the main highway down the coast and through the villages, till we came to his home. And his mother.

With the dawn, he became restless, so I pushed him off. He hit the ground with a thud.

And a cry of pain.

Something sharp underneath him? Or his neck, or back, from the two blows he had received? No, three.

Three.

'Lady Marian?'

I made no reply. My hood was up and I intended to keep it up. I left him where he was, with the horse tethered nearby and Butterfly on guard, and walked off alone into the trees for a while to refresh myself. A good thing, a very good thing, that Ferchard had made me eat and drink before leaving the chamber - and bring more food and water with me. Though water there was in plenty everywhere in this country.

He was where I had left him. I took his tether in hand and mounted the horse. I gave the rope a jerk. No response. So while the dog stood watching I rode a few yards dragging him along on his belly behind me. I looked round. Phorca to the slaughter. Not this time.

I waited.

Still no response. I dragged him further. A lot further. Till he cried out. The hound started barking.

I stopped. He got painfully to his feet.

I walked the horse slowly forward. He followed. Butterfly trotted beside us - disappeared among the trees - trotted beside us once more. And the morning wore on, grew warmer, the sun brighter through the leaves and branches. A summer's day.

I dreamed.

Dreamed that I was married to Hugh. Woke up with a start of shock and horror, knew that he would not say no, that this was another of the myriad possible futures Uncle Yacoub used to tell me about, used to try to get me to imagine, to visualise. I had once imagined that my grandmother in Scotland was still alive.

I had never imagined - *could* never have imagined - anything like this, though.

I turned and cracked my whip at him - the torturer's whip Ferchard had thrust into my hand. I indicated that he should go in front of the horse.

Butterfly, getting the idea quicker than Hugh, chased him round to the front, snapping at his ankles.

How nice if he were to take a bite or two - as Hugh's hounds had when they were trying to bring Whin down before she could get to the sea.

When he was out ahead, I cracked my whip at him again, catching him square on the left doup - buttock. His doups were fat, but not at all feminine. They were fat in a long sense - I mean they extended right down the backs of his thighs. Porcine - as one might expect.

I gave him another welt, this time on the right doup - I found I was surprisingly accurate - and he began to move forward at, for him, hobbled as he was, a spanking pace.

We crossed Aldie Water.

How long could he keep this up?

With the help of the whip, quite a long time, probably.

And so it turned out. The sun was well past its zenith and we had reached the Balnagown, when he collapsed, sobbing. I let the hound dance round him, barking and worrying him. I let the rope fall to the ground. I rode off a little way among the trees, out of sight of the river, slipped down off the horse and slept between the roots of a huge oak.

In the evening we rode on beside the river, and when I thought we must be close to Balichraggan we stopped for the night.

I gave Phorca some bread and let him drink from the river, then set the hound to guard him.

I made myself comfortable among the trees once again. I lay there looking up through the leaves and branches at the stars, and I thought: For one who has always been scared of the great forest, I am doing well. Feeling at home.

Perhaps it was the Queen of Elphame persona I had adopted. After all, the horse and the wolf - the wolf? - were my animals. Perhaps it was true, Phorca was right, I was the real Queen of Elphame. Perhaps that was why I had taken over, told Bella she should be down by the lochan with the wild roses and the clover and the swans.

Ridiculous.

I should have brought Ferchard with me to keep my feet on the ground.

I should have brought Raoul with me, to make love in the starlight.

Raoul ...

Where would Raoul be now? Still in Inverness? Back in Tain? In Kattar-bol with Mouraig - and Bella? Or was Bella still sitting at the edge of the loch, covered in flowers and with a birch wand in her hand?

Raoul, mon ancien amour. Mon ami.

Mon ami. "Mona-mí."

That was it.

So Souad was right. Le Fou did go back again after Bella, on foot. And kill ben Youssef. And Bella was wrong. Or had been protecting him. Probably. "A favourite customer."

Though it could have been any French speaker, of course. Anyone who knew even a few words might address the French-speaking ben Youssef as "*mon ami*". Especially if he had just killed him.

Did Phorca know French? Yes, of course he did.

So did the Skinner.

It didn't help. Or not much.

I slept.

And was woken in the morning by the hound growling. Phorca had found me, was sitting on the ground quite close to me. Butterfly would let him no closer.

He was still bound hand and foot, so harmless. Harmless? I would never forget his teeth. As harmless as a trapped rat. In future I would go further away from him before I slept. And tether him to a tree.

'Marian? Undo my hands.'

I made no response.

'Just my hands. I can't run away with my feet hobbled!'

No, but you can attack me the moment your hands are free. The hound would kill you instantly, but do you realise that?

The front of his torn breech-clout was stained where he had pissed himself through it, but now he must need to shit.

I drank some water from the bottle, went up to him, undid the breech-clout and let it fall to the ground. His caber stood out free now, tall and red and proud.

I poured cold water over it. It reassumed what I took to be its usual abject posture - and he scuttled off among the trees with a curse which I shall not record here.

I went to the riverbank and washed my face and neck. I was feeling more and more like an authentic tinkler woman - tinkler bitch, as Hugh would have it. Elp sounded better than tinkler, anyway.

Then I mounted the horse and waited for him. I rode over to what looked like a wild cherry tree, but it had no cherries on it. The birds must eat them. I saw a little dog peering up at me from under the edge of a bush. A fox cub? Butterfly had followed Hugh, I realised.

They came back and the cub darted out of sight.

Hugh stood by the ragged breech-clout and looked at me.

I got down and tied it on him, from behind, a liitle nervous of his knees, as the hobble was quite loose to allow him to walk.

Then I mounted again and we were off.

Should I have told Drostan that I knew nothing really bad was going to happen? That this had not been, for me - or Whin - or indeed Bella, a time of danger? Letting him compliment me on having absolute faith … Yet knowledge was faith in a sense … And it had been so close.

If only I had had the chance to see le Fou's hands, look him up in my almagest.

We were coming into Balichraggan now, but nobody was taking any notice of us. Some rich and aristocratic woman taking a criminal or a slave of some kind to the Court House or the Bailie or the stocks. So what? And we were some way now from where Bella had ridden out as the Queen of Elphame. I was not recognised.

Until suddenly, a little girl cried, 'It's the Queen! The Queen of Elphame!'

'Where?'

'There! I've seen her before, in Tarbat!'

Soon a crowd was following me. As yet, no one had noticed who my prisoner was.

I rode in total silence. Even the hound was silent unless someone approached too near the horse - or Hugh. And then he simply growled a warning.

We rode on through and out the other side, down towards the sea. And the silent crowds stopped dead when a woman cried, 'I know him! That's Sir Hugh! Of Foulis!'

'Sir Hugh?'

'It can't be!'

'It is! I thought it was before, but - '

'The Queen's got Baron Hugh!'

'She has Sir Hugh in thrall …'

And they dispersed in fear and awe.

After Kilmuir, we found ourselves riding down to the firth and then along by the sea, with only a few children running ahead of us now, shouting the news.

I let them. I could have set the hound to scatter them, drive them away, but I didn't mind them, and I knew Hugh did. My happiest moment came when one of them cried, 'He's like a pig! He's not like a man at all!'

I threw that child - a little freckled lass - a silver coin, and then they all took up the cry. 'He's a pig!'

Luik, luik!
At its wul piggy een,
Its flab and its fat
And its wee bit o' lean!

It's a pig, not a man -
Fetch a knife, fetch a pan -
Its fat and its lean
Baith 'lang to the Queen.

'And what's its name?' cried one.
'It's Porca!'
'Porca!'

It's a pig on a string
That thinks it's a king!
A pig! Mak it hop!
A fat pig! Mak it sing!

Well, Porca was close enough. And they pelted him with bits and pieces, making him hop. I took little notice. He was walking behind me, but I knew they were doing it, and did not care. The sea was on my left with the sun shining on it from over the Black Isle. That fanatical fool must have been blind, wherever he came from. Could he not see that the Black Isle, so dark at dawn, grew bluer and greener as the day wore on until at dusk it seemed the very heart of light and colour and warmth? Land of the Devil? Oh, no: this - from Tain to Nigg and down to Kessock and to Muir of Ord - was truly, as my father always said, God's own country.

The bairns kept Phorca going that day, hour after hour, and older folk came out to stare, mostly at me.

'It's the Queen.'
'The Queen of Elphame.'
'Has him in thrall.'
'The Baron. Hugh.'
'Went hunting lasses.'
'Caught one he couldna' handle.'
'One was too much for any man.'

'Hark what the bairns are calling him.'

'He'll ne'er live this doon.'

'Where's she takin' him, do you think?'

'Home. To his ma.'

A ripple of laughter passed through the crowd.

Not one sympathetic face or glance. Not one.

At Dalmore, where the road turned away from the sea and into Alness, there was a blind man.

'Is that Sir Hugh, then, she has there?'

For him, I stopped.

They said, 'She's stopped! For you!'

'I ken she's stopped. But I canna see what she is!'

'She's the Queen of Elphame, in a white satin cloak. She's on a horse, and a great hound with her. And at the end of a rope, stumbling along behind, all filthy naked, she has the Baron, Hugh.'

Naked? I looked round. His rag had fallen off. Oh, well.

'He put my eyes out. He put my eyes out with his own two hands - his own two thumbs. For I had seen what I shouldna ha seen. But it was not I who had sinned! And when he did that - to my eyes - and left them hanging on my cheeks for all to see till some kind soul took pity on me and snipped them off - when he did that he sinned again, piling sin on sin, Deil tak him!'

'Aye, and he whipped my man half to death - he's never done a day's work since!' cried a woman's voice.

'He hanged Angus! He hanged my brother!' shouted a man.

'Tak me to him! Tak me to him!' cried the blind man.

Time to move on.

I rode round Hugh and when I was behind him, cracked my whip to left and right of him, then twice across his back to get him moving.

The hound pranced around him, barking.

But the crowd followed us into Alness, and there it grew greater as people came out of their homes to see. They began to stone him. This was not like the children throwing mud and beating him with twigs. This could kill him - would kill him.

Well, you are the Queen. Do something.

I stood up in my stirrups and cried in a loud voice, 'Let him -

or her - who is without sin cast the next stone.'

There was total silence. All had sinned. All feared the wrath of the Queen of Elphame.

They began to drift away. The eldest first, I noticed. One for St John.

We rode out of Alness almost alone. Just one or two awed, silent children followed at a distance, and never the same children for more than a few minutes.

The afternoon was wearing on. A heron flew across in front of us, and over the firth. We were approaching Foulis Tower.

'Hugh,' I said, speaking to him for the first time.

'M-Marian?' he croaked, desperate for communication.

'Take me to your mother.'

'My m-mother?'

The whip cracked.

'Ouch! … My mother. Aye.'

Let him get used to the idea.

And soon we were there. The guard at the gate stood speechless as we passed through. But he followed behind us along the road to the door of the tower.

I told Butterfly. He approached the guard, snarling, and the guard fled back to the gate.

At the door I ordered Hugh to ring the bell, call for his mother. He did so. Heads looked down at us from windows and battlements, and drew back, amazed.

Eventually, a lady appeared: a regal lady, unused to being summoned.

I remembered that the Queen of Scotland was her aunt.

She regarded me for a moment. 'Are you aware, madam, that this man is, through me, of the Ross kindred, and cousin to the Earl of Ross? And that he is close kin to the Royal House of Stewart?'

I said nothing.

The hound glanced from her to me and back again. She was a woman, but he didn't like her tone.

She tried again. 'Who are you?'

'Some call me the Queen of Elphame.'

She didn't laugh. But not because she didn't think it was

funny.

Hugh said, 'She is the Lady Marian MacElpin. I think it's true that she is also the Queen of - '

'MacElpin? MacElpin? Weren't your father and grandfather supporters of the Balliol pretenders?'

I declined to answer.

She said, 'If I call out, you will be seized - or killed - immediately.'

I said, 'Your son made the mistake of underestimating me.'

'My son is a fool.'

Now we were getting somewhere.

'But what has he done to deserve - this?'

'This? Some kind of justice has been seen to be done. But true justice has not been done. He deserved death. Ensure that in future he hunts nothing larger than a hare.'

'The hare is *geisa*.'

That's right, yes. I'd forgotten. Only the Elpin - and my family - ate hare. For all others it was forbidden by ancient custom.

'For you, yes.'

She looked at me, remembering old tales she had heard in her childhood.

'For Hugh, now, all is *geisa*. I would recommend fishing as a safe sport. As long as he is very careful not to catch a mermaid.'

'A mermaid?'

'Hugh knows. The last mermaid he almost caught has sworn to have, as she put it, his scut and nuts - for a start. He should keep very well clear of her. And then there is a glaistig of my acquaintance who is in the habit of removing just one testicle.'

'"Glaistig"? What is this?'

'Tell her, Hugh.'

'It - aye, it's true, Ma. She is a g-glaistig, she does nick out just one ballock - and of course she hates me.'

'I think you have been keeping very bad company. And I am beginning to think Lady Marian may be right. Right to bring you to me, to draw this situation to my attention. And yes, I will see that he - ah - limits his hunting activities from now on to what is acceptable.'

'And his dismembering activities. There are folk around here blind, crop-eared, lacking one or both hands. They want vengeance. Next time, I will let them have it.'

She looked at Hugh.

'It's truc, Ma. She saved my life from them today.'

'And finally,' I said, 'there were some children on the road today calling him Porca, mocking him. If I or my companions ever hear that he has taken revenge for that on any one of those children, then next time we will deliver him back to you on a spit. As pork. Is that understood?'

She nodded.

'*À propos*, Hugh,' I said, going into French, 'when you spoke to Abdelwahed ben Youssef, the murdered Moor, you presumably spoke to him in French. What exactly did you speak to him about?'

No answer.

I gave him a crack of the whip on his doup. Saw his mother flinch - then smile slightly.

I gave him another crack. The hound growled.

'I asked him - ' he began, in Gaelic.

'*En français*!'

'I asked him,' he mumbled, in French, 'I asked him …'

'You asked him how much he wanted for the girl Souad.'

'*Non*!'

'*Oui*! Now tell me that - in French!'

He did so.

'And he said *Non*? Or he said *Peut-être*?'

'He said *Non*.'

'And where were you the night he was killed? I asked you this once before but you declined to answer. Where were you when someone killed the Moor and, as they dropped the body off in the selected spot, said, "So much for you, *mon ami*."? Someone who could very, very easily have been you - risking your snout for yet another taste of honey.'

'Does all this mean what I think it means?' she asked, in French.

'Some of it, yes. Some of it, perhaps. Well, Hugh?'

'I don't remember!'

I cracked the whip.

'What night was it, Lady Marian?' she asked.

'It was the Wednesday night, ten days ago.'

'Wednesday? Then he was here. Yes, he was in fact here. I am much relieved. I had heard of this murder, and I was beginning to wonder if what you were suggesting might be true.'

'Do not be relieved. He has killed - who knows how many? And attempted to murder others - including me.'

'Those killings and dismemberings,' cried Hugh, 'most of them were simple justice!'

I looked at him. Looked at his mother. She raised her eyebrows.

'Justice?' I said. 'Talking of justice, I want the mermaid's husband.'

'Now you have lost me again, Lady Marian. What is all this about "mermaids", and why should her husband be here?'

'She is not really a mermaid. At least I think not, though Hugh in his simplicity believes her so - '

'And lusts for her, not as a woman but as a trophy - yes; but - her husband?'

'He has her husband here somewhere, in a cage.'

'The one who had been tortured? The one with the raw back and broken fingers? His wounds had become infected and I gave orders that he was to be put out of his misery.'

'Put out of his misery,' I repeated, tonelessly, my brain suddenly numb.

'You understand. He was dying. I wished to show him kindness.'

I sighed. 'I'm sure you did. But your son did not. He showed him "justice". I knew that man, Hugh. He was a good man, not strong or fast, but one whose children loved him and admired him. A man. Such a man as a mermaid might choose. You and he have nothing in common. Yet some day, some day, you may receive the same "justice" he received. Who knows?'

I threw the tether to the ground. 'Farewell, my lady.'

'Marian. You did not let me finish. When my men went to the cage to carry out my bidding, they found him gone.'

'Gone?'

'And one of the serving girls said she knew him, he was a

sheltiman - something like a sorcerer, a magician. No cage could hold him, she said.'

'So he did not die?'

'Not here … Farewell now, Marian.'

I turned and rode back out through the gate, and on towards the south. I had no wish to return by the same route, and Kari was waiting for me with Callum and Shusie Vass. Best to ride up through Black Isle along the road she and I had taken together the night all this began.

And that meant going first to Dyngvale.

I was still wearing only my ripped chemise under the silk and satin cloak. I would have liked to call at Effie's house to wash and get some kind of skirt at least, and a tunic perhaps, but Effie's house was the executioner's house, and she was Kenneth's mother.

I thought on the whole I had better ride round Dyngvale, not take any more unnecessary risks. Big Robbie was a Virgo, of course, and I couldn't see him treating me unjustly. Unless he was ordered to.

Round Dyngvale. Onto Black Isle. And then north through the night to Udale Bay, and Kari.

TWENTY-FIVE

The Ear Of Jealousy

I had found, while riding along beside the Balnagown with Hugh, that certain scenes caused a tingle of remembered excitement: a stretch of sheltered bank with a moorhen darting out of sight among the roots; a slope so steep suddenly that it was difficult not to go teetering down into the water; a group of alders and hazels like clustering bairns under the broad branches of a great motherly wych elm. These memories were not mine, of course; they were Whin's.

I wanted to see more.

I had a clear picture in my mind of Loch Ussie as it had appeared in the dream, and of the views from the summit of Cnoc Farrel, so after circling round Dyngvale I made my way there and slept with Butterfly in the shelter of the trees and bushes lining all that side of the loch.

I woke to a grey autumnal world. Autumn in July? A light rain was falling. The loch was small. I had feared it might turn out bigger, grander, but this was the loch I - she - had swum the corner of - that corner there - then gone on up the hill through those trees.

Now, though, I was cold. I had no food left. My cloak was wet and clinging. The rain seemed to have set in for the rest of the year. Shivering, I turned my back on Loch Ussie and rode east, with Butterfly making forays to left and to right among the trees, but always aware of me, always reappearing, and giving me great comfort. On Black Isle, I turned again and headed north, the rainswept firth once more on my left.

When I finally reached the Vass steading, I was exhausted. All I wanted to do, all I had in my head, was pick up Kari and leave again for Loch Mouri as quickly as possible. They would not hear of it. Shusie insisted that I needed food and rest. They made me undress, wrapped me in a smock and a sheepskin blanket, then told me Drostan had left me a message; Kari had it by heart, and was very pleased with herself: Think of Bella as the Soul, for she is not and never was *Malkah*, the Queen: and think of the others, all the others, as simply good or bad influences upon the Soul.

Bella? The Soul? This was Bella's story, then? Bella finding herself embodied in a world of illusion governed by the Devil; Bella beginning to feel her way back towards the world of light and goodness she had known before she died into what we think of as birth, and life. As indeed do we all in our own separate stories.

'There's more,' Kari said, watching me.

Watching me *think*?

'Tell me.'

'You are *Malkhut*, not Hod. You are the presence of God on earth, putting right that which is wrong here among the children in exile.'

Me, *Malkah*, the Queen? Oh no, you got that wrong, Drostan, you got that very wrong.

'There's more.'

'Tell me.'

'Remember that in re-establishing righteousness you are doing God's work. As Meister Eckhart said, God can no more do with us than we can do with him.'

Very true. Huh? *What*?

Then I laughed. 'Oh, Kari! God can no more do *without* us than we can do *without* him.'

'Yes. Isn't that what I said?'

Out of the mouths of babes …

'And Don Alfonso left a message for you too.'

'Don Alfonso? How do you know Don Alfonso? And what was he doing here?'

'He was waiting across the road, watching, when you saw me and Drostan off in Tain that night. You know? When Sir Farquhar lifted me up onto the horse?'

'*I* didn't see him.'

'He was dressed all in black and on a big black horse.'

'Why didn't you tell me?'

'I forgot you don't see in the dark like we do. And Butterfly didn't mind him; but that was probably because he was already there when we arrived.'

'And he followed you?'

'Yes - well, not followed us; came with us. At first I was frightened of him, I didn't want him with us, I didn't know him, but Drostan knew him, so ... He took Drostan up on his horse, which was bigger and stronger than mine - than yours, my lady - and - '

'But didn't you think he might just ride off with him, you silly child?'

'Yes, my lady, but what could I have done? Anyway, Drostan chose to ride with him.'

'And then?'

'He wanted to take Drostan with him on a ship he knew about that would be leaving next day, but Drostan preferred to remain here, do as *you* said, my lady. He told me. I didn't understand what they were saying together, but he wanted me to know so I could tell you. Don Alfonso went with Drostan and Callum to Fursey's cave to make sure he was all right, then rode off to the north, to Tain and Golspie, he said.'

And this Don Alfonso had stood quietly watching, almost invisible, outside the torture chamber while I went through all that? If I ever ...

'Oh! Wait! There was another message from Drostan. He told me afterwards, here, before they took him to the hermit, when we were by ourselves for a while. He said tell your lady it was given to Sarah's mother by her master - '

'He said *what*?'

'That! That's what he - '

'Yes. Sorry. Go on.'

'It was given to Sarah's mother by her master. One man in black represents the man in Rome. But remember Peter has two sons now. Both claim the whole inheritance.'

'That's it? That's all?'

She nodded, wide-eyed.

"It" was the anklet. Sarah's mother must be Mary Magdalen. Her master …? No wonder Drostan didn't want to say it openly. And the man in black? "One man in black." Which one represented Rome? Don Alfonso, obviously. The Black Friar, Brother Arsenius, represented Pope Clement in Avignon. But Arsenius had shown no interest in, no knowledge of, the anklet. Did someone else represent the French Pope? The man in grey? Raoul? Did he represent *Avignon*?

Raoul?

Raoul … I had known. I had known all along.

'Don Alfonso's words were … '

'What? Oh. Yes, go on.' Before she forgot.

She took a deep breath, then smiled and said, 'Drostan told me the words in the Gaelic,' breathed out, wiped the smile off her face, breathed in again and announced: 'You have earned his most profound admiration: not only did you accomplish your own task in a quite exemplary manner but you accomplished his as well. He is at present in the service of *La Reina Costanza de Castilla* and stationed in England and desires to make your acquaintance in London in the not-too-distant future.'

Constance of Castille. The wife of John, Duke of Lancaster, King Richard's eldest surviving uncle. We had met once, Prince John of Gaunt and I. I had rather liked him. And I was sure he would remember me, so Don Alfonso would have no trouble in discovering who I was and where I could be found.

Or had he already known?

I found myself nodding off: the warm room, Shusie bustling about, Kari beside me, and Wee Magnus - she even let Kari hold the bairn now - but no Callum, though he was expected. He had returned after taking Drostan to the hermit, Fursey MacFarquhar, and set off again almost at once with the basket of bait Shusie had prepared for him. The fish were running. He could not wait.

But there had been no difficulty, Shusie assured me. Drostan had been in a very weak state, but he had seemed to recover during the boat journey, rather than get worse as Callum and Don Alfonso had feared; and Fursey had promised to care for him as best he could. The rest was in God's hands. She crossed herself, and I followed suit. Kari, watching us wide-eyed, suddenly decided to cross herself, too - and nearly dropped the baby. I laughed: and must have slept.

It was dawn when I woke again.

The rain had stopped, but the sky was still grey and everything was wet and dripping.

The best thing, I had decided while I slept, was to write to Raoul. I opened my leather document bag, took out a quill and ink, and some sheets of paper.

It was a long letter and took a long time to write, though I never hesitated, never had to stop and search for ideas or for words.

By the time I had finished, everyone was up and about. I sealed the letter, and gave it to Shusie, who promised to give it to the lad next door. He would run it into Tain for me, find Maître Raoul and deliver in person.

That was that, then.

Shusie gave Kari and me hot porridge, and we set out.

Now finally Kari felt free to talk. 'I couldn't tell you, you didn't give me a chance. And then you sent me off with Drostan, and you still don't know. Do you?'

I agreed that I probably did not.

'The Countess is there - '

'What Countess? Where?' The Red Countess? Margaret?

'The Countess of Ross, they said. Lady Euphemia.'

'Where? Tell me the story, girl!'

'I'm trying to.'

It was more difficult to talk, it was true, for we were on separate horses now. She had my horse. I was still riding as the Queen of Elphame, though beneath my white cloak I had a warm shift and skirt that I had begged from Shusie, and paid her well for.

'She's at Mouraig's house. But she doesn't call her Mouraig, she calls her Marian. Like you, my lady.' She paused.

I said, 'She would. That's her name. Her real name.'

'Ah. Well. And while I was telling Mouraig - Marian? -'

'Mouraig will do.'

'Mouraig what had happened, how we found Souad and Sir

Farquhar asked me to bring Souad to her, and we were talking outside, she didn't ask me in, I think because she didn't want the Countess to know what we were saying ... Anyway, while I was telling her, Bella appeared. It was Bella, but she was dressed in flowers like Mart from the old stories, and up on her horse - that horse - '

'What? But - '

'There was a young lass there, Mona, and I talked to her after Mouraig had taken Bella into the home. Mona said you had told her to find Bella and take her to the loch. Her father thought Bella would probably be at the Abbey, so she went there, but she found the Bailie's men at the gate. She slipped round to the back, and was just in time to see two of the monks let Bella out and Bella go running off into the woods. Mona ran after her and gave her your message, then took her to Loch Eye. She helped her undress and cover herself in flowers, just as you had said. Then she left her there, sitting by the water, and went home.'

'And then?'

'Then Mona's da sent her to Mouraig to tell her where Bella was. He thought she should know. And when Mouraig heard, she told Mona to take the horse - her horse - that horse - to Bella, and the hound - '

'Don't tell me little Mona rode the horse? And in this cloak - '

'Yes! With Butterfly following her.'

I sighed. There was no controlling history; especially, it seemed, this little segment of history in which I had become so involved, this little story in which Drostan saw Bella not as the Queen but as the Pilgrim Soul. Bella's story, then. Bella's little segment of history.

'Well? Go on.'

'You told Bella she must wear only flowers from now on if ... so she didn't put on the cloak. Mona wore that, sitting up behind her.'

'And now they'll say they saw the Queen ride past dressed all in flowers. The Flower Queen. That was not meant to happen.'

'I don't think many people saw her.'

'Who?'

'I don't know. She mentioned only old Sweign Pigsticker -

because he's her grand-da. He dropped to his knees as they passed and bowed his head, so he saw very little. Mona said she was sure he didn't see her.'

'Didn't recognise her, you mean. She would have had the hood up.' I saw the laughter in Kari's eyes. 'She must have thought that was very funny.'

'She couldn't stop giggling - till Mouraig sent her home, told her she'd get her da to give her a good whipping if ever she mentioned any of this to anyone. "And *then*, if you're not very careful, *I*'ll turn you into a little fat pig and send you to your grand-da, and you know what *he* will do to you!"' Kari laughed. 'Mona didn't believe her, I don't think, but she swore she'd never tell, and ran off home. It was like when Coll threatened to turn me into a spider. She wouldn't, would she?'

'Who? Mouraig? She might ask her da to give her a whipping if the lass needed it. But that's all.'

'And Coll?'

'Coll? We'll see. Because I hope she'll be there still with your ma and Otter; and if she is, you'd better be very polite to her.'

Once again, the thought of Coll made the world seem much less amusing in Kari's eyes.

'And then?'

'Then after a while, Mouraig came out and sent me to you in Tain, with the horse and the cloak, and Butterfly. And she told me to tell you - '

'At last! Really, Kari!'

'She told me to tell you that the Countess and she were arranging to sell Bella and Souad. That the Countess herself had a ship leaving for somewhere called Bord - Border - Bordel -'

Now I laughed. And forgave her everything. 'Bordeaux. In France. I'll take you there one day, Kari.'

'Yes? To France? Oh, and she said that from there they would be taken on south and that you could guess the rest.'

Yes, I could guess the rest.

She must believe still, against her own better instinct and judgment, that Bella had killed Abdelwahed. Must think this was a good way to get rid of two beautiful young murdresses without actually handing them over to the Bailie and his men, and Master

Robert. And Master Kenneth.

Well, it would take a few days to organise, I hoped. Before we returned to Kattar-bol, I had to talk once more to Whin and Otter. And to Coll.

We rode for a while in silence. I was thinking about Whin.

I realised suddenly that it was long time since I had seen Butterfly. 'Where's Butterfly?'

'Over that way.' She nodded off to the right.

She heard and saw things I never could. That ability must be part of what helped keep Whin alive.

'Where was your ma born?'

'On Orkney. She's part of a fire-group who consider Orkney home. Me too, though I wasn't born there; it comes down through the lasses. We can't stay on Orkney, because the people there, Viking people mostly, like Thorfinn Skinner and Sweign Pigsticker - and Mouraig a bit, too, isn't she -'

'And me, I suppose, if Mouraig is,' I smiled. 'And she grew up there? On Orkney?'

'No, they were always on the roam. They had to be. But it wasn't just that. They liked it.'

'You say "they": and you?'

'I'm talking about when Ma was a child. But yes, it's the same now. We have to. And we like it - at least in summer.'

'You don't want to leave it all, do you? Leave it and come with me.'

'No. Yes. Oh, half of me does, half of me doesn't!' She laughed, then turned thoughtful. 'I've already left, my lady. Look at me. The way I'm dressed. And riding a horse. And talking to you …'

It was true. 'And her ma and da?'

'I don't think she knows who her da was. Her ma is my grandma. She stays up on the north coast now, near Thurso, where she can see Orkney. She … She's … They lopped her hands - for lifting, they said - stealing - and she's been helpless since. Ma's brother, Nebo, looks after her, brings her food and that, when he can.'

'When was that? A long time ago?'

'After Otter was born. I remember her with her hands.

Playing, showing me things. She was the first one took me down under the sea, showed me where everything was. She was the best of us all in the sea, my ma says. She liked never to come out at all. Now she never goes in.'

'She can't swim at all?' I bunched my fists, tried to imagine swimming with no hands.

'She can, but only … not like she used to, and it makes her sad almost to death. Ma says one day it will, and Grandma'll go down to the sea once more, and into the sea, and when she does we'll never see her again: she will have said farewell to the land and the sight of the land and the smell of the land for ever.'

And the dryness, I thought, and the dust and the dirt. And people. Oh yes, I could understand that.

We had been riding along a track which Kari said would bring us out somewhere on the Alness River, and when we came to it, and turned west again, I began to recognise more scenes from my run with - my run as - Whin. I even saw again the pit full of muck into which we had plunged in desperation; but of the cuddy there was no sign. I hoped they hadn't taken it out on him.

'What does her name mean? Whin? Whin is gorse, I know, the gorse bush. Mouraig was saying it had some other significance, but we were interrupted and she never got round to explaining.'

'Ma doesn't talk about things like that, but my da told me it's the Shelta name for Mart.'

'Mart?' A name from tales my father had told me - tales of "home".

'One of the old goddesses. Mart of the Pinks, Da calls her. She's the summer goddess. She arrives in spring, at Beltain, and all through summer she's here: all the world is pink and gold and green. Then at Samhain she leaves, she has to leave. She turns into a mermaid and slips away into the sea, under the protection of AN-herself.' Kari made a sign with her fingers as she said that name, the sign of AN-herself, the Great Mother Goddess.

'They named her well,' I said.

'She was named by Culbo, the last sheltiman. That's what they call him, anyway, though my da's a sheltiman, sort of. Culbo was still on Orkney then. Now he's in the Hebrides somewhere, in the west, my da says. Ma says he's gone on though, further west, across the Great Sea.'

Where Mouraig had been?

'She's off to the west herself now,' I said. 'She may have a chance to find out.'

'Mm. And my da. Didn't you say you would bring him with you when you came to Loch Mouri?'

I had forgotten him. Forgotten even to tell her he was alive, and free.

I told her now, and she began to weep. She was fond of her da, and had feared he might be dead. I pulled my horse over to hers and held her to me.

Loch Mouri is beautiful. We glimpsed it first between the trees as we rode through the wood that runs along the north side of the river and the loch. Beyond the loch, to the south, the hills rise again, covered with what looks like pine forest, but we were among oaks, with willows and alders increasing as we approached the water. I was learning fast.

Otter, expecting us, stepped out so suddenly that Kari's mare shied up and she nearly came off. She was furious. More for her dignity than anything else, I think, but she started shouting at him in their language while he just stood there and looked at her. He seemed unable to answer. If I hadn't known better, I might have thought he was slow-witted. Perhaps he was just slow to quarrel …

I said quickly, 'Kari, you are so good on that horse now! Anyone else would have fallen off.'

'You see?' she said, to Otter.

'Is Coll still about, Otter? Is she with your ma?'

He shook his head. 'When we came out of Inchlumpie Wood, at the fork of the river, she disappeared.'

'Could you find her? I want to talk to her.'

'I could, but it would take a while.'

'How long is "a while"?'

He smiled. 'Maybe tomorrow. Maybe not till next summer, if she didn't want to be found.'

It didn't matter. It didn't matter at all. It was better really, for now it was out of my hands.

Evening was coming, and Whin had fish for us on a little fire beside the loch. We talked of where they would go and where they would stay, of Tinkman, who would find them, Whin assured me, and of Culbo the sheltiman, and of the land beyond the Great Sea.

'Don't come back,' I begged them, 'not for a long time. And when you do come back, stay right away from Master Robert Ross and his son. Oh, Whin ... I too will come back, one day. The sea and the hills and the forest - and you - will be forever in my heart. But Otter, if before that, if in a year, two years, five, you should wish to come to me and Kari, make your way down to London - that is south, south, south, always south - and there ask for Mariana, Lady Marian MacElpin. Ask in Southwark. Ask anywhere. But first, before you get there, speak to me in a dream. Speak to me anyway, Otter. Will you promise?'

He nodded solemnly.

This was the good-for-nothing I had left behind in Dyngvale without a thought. More hasty judgments. More mistakes. More skin off other people's backs. Lives lost. Lives ruined. Will I never learn?

Now I must get back and save poor Bella. Try to do something right.

And little Mona. What had Mona done that she deserved a whipping? It was me, not her, should be changed into a pig and sent to Sweign.

Or to poor Hugh.

No.

That I did not deserve.

And yet why did I now always think of him as "poor" Hugh? Because for the first time in my life I had been the dispenser of justice. Had done Master Robert's job.

I had done more than re-establish righteousness. I had taken vengeance.

I never would again.

When we got back to Kattar-bol, Mouraig was alone. And alive - which I had already known, but only half believed.

We embraced. I was closer to sobbing that I had been in all the years since I had sworn at the age of - fourteen, was it? - never to weep again.

'Mouraig, what happened?'

'I don't know. Really, lass! I don't know. It was not much different from that time in Vinland, except that this time I wasn't buried and I wasn't frightened. I was lying on the floor, and I was very, very cold. But this time, too, I wasn't alone. Mona, poor lass, was kneeling beside me, holding my hand, great tears coursing down her pretty little cheeks. "Marian?" I said. My first word - thinking of you. See how close you've come to me in these few short days? But now the child was even more frightened. I squeezed her hand. "Mona, child, I ken you're not Marian. I was just wondering was she here?" Now she smiled. "I thought - I thought - " I reassured her. She helped me up, lit me a fire, made me a warm drink - brought me back to life. Figuratively. As she already had literally, in my opinion.'

'You mean …? Mouraig, you seemed dead, but you can't have been. Not really. Not this time, nor the other time, in Vinland.'

She gazed at me, letting me think things out for myself.

'But what was all that about in the shelti-world?' I went on. 'Either part of you is there still, is that bear, or the time is different, we saw the future - or the timeless, some world outside time. Or it was simply a dream, and all nonsense.'

'Marian, you are analysing again. You *must* learn to accept things more.'

Now I gazed. She was right. She was, but still, there must be -

'No, Marian, really. Leave it. We will see.'

She gave me a hot drink with honey and broom in it, and I imagined her sitting here then with Mona, sipping her drink, newly back from the dead. For the second time.

'One thing I knew,' she smiled. 'Wee Mona had called me back. But I didn't know what for. "Tell me, lass," I said. So she told me about poor Bella sitting there on the bank of Loch Eye wearing nothing but flowers, and I thought: Well, at least Marian's not using her head this time. That definitely came from the heart - a pity she doesn't do that more often. But I felt sorry for the lass out there in the cold - I was still cold as death myself - so I sent Mona to bring her in.'

'But why on the horse with the mastiff following, and her all in flowers? You must have known - '

'Who dressed her in flowers?'

True. 'And was she still wearing her gold anklet?'

'She was.' She peered at me. 'Why?'

'Oh. Nothing.'

'Nothing's nothing where you're concerned.' But she was smiling.

I smiled back. 'What happened about Bella and Souad? But wait. First, here …' I took off the ruby ring.

'Oh no, no, lass, that's yours now. This third life of mine - if it doesn't turn out to be a very brief one - will not be as Mouraig Gudmundsdottir, Mouraig the Witch.'

I still held it out to her.

'No.' She slid it back onto my finger. 'There. You are the witch now. I have moved on, become a sheltiwoman.'

I stared at her. *That* was what had happened?

Yes, of course it was.

But what about me? I *did not want* to be a witch. All my life I had struggled against it -

'Leave it, lass. I told you before, you must learn to accept your destiny … Now, let's get back to our two *filles fatales*, Bella and Souad.'

I laughed, I couldn't help it. That was exactly what they were. Even Bella, who was twenty-four, seemed to have no more idea than a precocious fourteen-year-old why men clustered round to help her, walked into things as she passed by, wagered ships against her "as she stood". And as for Souad …

They were to have left on the Countess's ship the previous Sunday during the night, the night I spent, exhausted, in the house of my friend Shusie Vass on Black Isle, where I had gone to pick up Kari. Their destination? Algiers, via Bordeaux and Marseilles. The Captain knew a trader in Bordeaux who would take them across country to Marseilles where another trader dealing with Arab captains would arrange for them to be shipped over to Africa.

That brought back memories.

'And their papers?' I asked. 'They would need papers, at least in France.'

'Their papers were all in order,' my grandmother replied. 'I, Lady Marian MacElpin, had seen to that. With the aid of my old friend Countess Euphemia - the spiteful wulcat! She wanted to have them both branded with her mark on their flanks.'

'Oh no!'

'Said it would make it all more convincing, as well as more official. I refused, said they were too beautiful to be branded like that. "All the more reason," says she. All the more reason - I ask you! Whose were they anyway? She gave in and got me the papers I needed: a certificate stating that I was the owner of the tall, blonde, blue-eyed Inglis girl who answered to the name of Bella; and licences to export the said Bella and another slave, a Moorish girl answering to the name of Souad -'

'But Souad was free! She had been manumitted!'

'No, she wasn't. The manumission was invalid. She belonged to Sir Farquhar. And he claimed her.'

'He *claimed* her?'

'Aye. Which left Bella. Your Raoul would of course have dearly loved to claim her, but he couldn't. Anyway, by the time he arrived back in Tain, and called here, she'd gone.'

Oh, Bella, I thought. And you couldn't have been more innocent.

'Oh, she was, yes. Everyone knew that except you. And Euphemia. She didn't take to Bella at all.'

'But couldn't you have - ?'

'Shh. I haven't finished. A messenger arrived from Dunrobin, from the Countess of Sutherland, whom I do not know. The message was not for me, it was for Euphemia. It asked her to scour the County of Ross for a blonde slave-girl, now a runaway, who answered to the name of Bella. She, Margaret of Sutherland, had a guest, Don Alfonso de León, who laid claim to her on behalf of the King and Queen of Castille.'

John, Duke of Lancaster, and his wife, Costanza, again. It must have been for the anklet - unless everything she had told me was a lie. No, don't start that again. 'What did you do?'

'We shipped her off to Dunrobin, with a sigh of relief.'

'And Raoul?'

'He was very upset ...'

He would have been. And not only about Bella.

I asked Mouraig who had killed ben Youssef, finally, in her opinion.

'Well, it wasn't Jaufre le Fou, as Souad herself realised eventually; and realised too what a terrible mistake she had made. It wasn't Bella: she had nothing to gain - on the contrary - and she was far too busy insisting that Thorfinn had not put in to shore again that evening. I think he did turn back. I think he picked up his bow from where he had left it; used it; replaced it; and sailed away again into the darkness. It was dark that night, what with the druid-storm and the murder, everyone says so.' She sighed, and gazed into the fire for a moment, then looked up again and smiled. 'The only other possibility is that it was organised from a distance by the heroic Baron Hugh, in order to liberate the girl for his own purposes.' After a moment, she added: 'But that is not how I see it. And I mean *see* it.'

I stayed with her at Kattar-bol three days, four, waiting to hear of a ship going south. Then one morning, a messenger arrived - but not with news of a ship; with a letter from Raoul.

TWENTY-SIX

The Letter From Raoul

I took it out onto the beach to read.

When I had finished it, I sat there on my rock. *Foolish virgins.*

'What is it, lass?'

'Oh, nothing. An answer to the letter I sent him.' I held it out to her.

She took it, but didn't read it. 'What letter?'

'While I was at Callum Vass's house. A week ago. I wrote …'

She gazed at me. 'You accused him of the murder.'

I nodded, unable to speak.

'What did you say exactly? Do you remember?'

I nodded again. Oh yes, I remembered. Every word.

'Tell me, lass …'

'I said … "You told me once, Raoul, that Bella was an angel, while I was a fighter for right and for truth. And I told you I would rather, much rather, be simply an angel. Your angel. You did not believe me. And I remembered afterwards that Rabbi Yacoub, my uncle, had told me once of a rabbi who, when asked which was more important, singing psalms or doing good works, replied: The Angels can sing psalms; only Man can redress the balance of good and evil here on earth … You said Bella depended on me to find out the truth. Very well then. I have done so. And having done so, it is for her sake as much as for yours that I have decided not to pursue the matter any further.

'"And also because they had one victim in Tain, they had poor Rachid, Souad's brother. Can justice ever be done now? Can Rachid be restored to life and health?

'"I know you saw yourself to some extent as the Knight

rescuing the Fair Maid from the Black-hearted Villain. The Fair Maid was indeed fair, and in great distress; Thorfinn Skinner was a monster; and you did achieve all that any Red Cross Knight could hope to achieve.

'"Remember, though, that your Sign is Gemini, the Sign of the Knights Templar.

'"*To liberate the girl for his own purposes*, Raoul. You remember that phrase, Raoul, *mon ami.*

'"It was not the Skinner you killed; Coll had already accomplished that quite adequately at the third attempt. No, *the man you killed was your friend and drinking partner and fellow philosopher, Abdelwahed ben Youssef.*

'"And the question is why? Did you mistake him for Thorfinn? Think you were shooting Thorfinn? Did you too believe Thorfinn was there, that he had turned back? Did you perhaps know that he had turned back and come in to shore to wait till the storm blew itself out? Had you seen him when no one else had?

'"Or did you know the rider was ben Youssef? I think you did. For after all, you spoke to him in French, called him "*mon ami*", when you dropped his body off, pulled out the arrow - no, not arrow, the bolt from your crossbow - and replaced it with his own knife in the wound. "*Mon ami*," you said: and what was the rest of it? "*Adieu, mon ami*. The bolt too is real theology." Was that it?

'"You were heard, heard by Coll, who can hear anything, anywhere, out on those marshes and among those dunes, at night. And she came and she took the knife, as you know.

'"But why, Raoul? Was the killing political, as we once thought when we - no, not *we*, when *I* - suspected poor Jaufre? Was it done at the behest of your master, Coucy? And was Bella simply conveniently placed, enabling you to accomplish two objectives with one (lightning) bolt?

'"Or did you know perhaps - had ben Youssef told you? - that he was negotiating the purchase of Bella? Had Bella herself told you? It must have seemed that the sale would go through. After all, he was a very rich man. And you could see Bella disappearing into the fleshpots of North Africa, being sold again, passed on from owner to owner, worth so much more out there than he would ever have paid for her in Scotland. And you thought, "Ah, for all your fine words, my Moorish friend, you turn out to be but another trafficker in human flesh and human misery." Is that how it was?

'"But in that case, Raoul, *you* were guilty of bigotry, for if Jaufre had bought Bella, planning to take her to France with him, you would have bowed to the inevitable.

'"And you were guilty of theft, for ben Youssef had a purse of gold with him, intended for Thorfinn, and you took that. Why? To buy her for yourself?

'"Or was it all about the anklet, from the very beginning? Was that why you came to Scotland in the first place - because your master (Clement, not Coucy) had received information that the anklet was here?

'"Then you fell in love.

'"Not so bad, so far.

'"But then you killed.

'"Did I ever mention to you Master MacDalorg's rather Nestorian notion that Jesus the man could and would fight back against the way things happened, against what had been ordained, as for instance when he healed the man born blind or raised Lazarus from the dead, or when he raised the little girl to whom he said "*Talitha, cum*!" ("Little girl, wake up!")? You too wanted to change the way things were, change them for the better. But when Jesus changed something, he gave life, he did not take it ..."

'I signed myself "Mariana MacElpin de la Manga."'

My grandmother gazed at me for a while, then, still without a word, unfolded Raoul's letter to me and began to read:

Tain,
La fête du Saint Barthélemy, 1382.

Mariana. My lady.

Tomorrow, I leave Scotland. De Vienne and his friends are still playing at invading England, but the Scots are more interested in what profit - "compensation", they call it - they can make out of *us* (the French) and *our* "invasion" of Scotland (and de Vienne's invasion of the Scottish king's favourite niece), than in facing two

English armies, one led by young King Richard and the other by the great Duke of Lancaster himself. I do not blame them. My master, Coucy (yes), has already lost interest in the whole non-event, and has summoned me and a few other civilians home before the situation gets any worse.

To me, Scotland will always be you and Bella. And Abdelwahed. And poor Jaufre.

But let me tell you …

I had returned to Tain from Inverness, and was debating what to do next, when I was handed your letter. Thrilled (for you had never written to me before, not even during those long years of separation), and desperate for news, I hurried into the nearest tavern, ordered a drink and broke the seal.

Mariana, how could you? To me, who always had such faith in you. Who placed you, unlike man, a little *higher* than the angels.

I had an alibi, in a sense. I was with Bella. She rode into Tain with Jaufre, who left her in his room. A little later, I met her creeping down the stairs, intent on escaping, and I rode home with her, back to the Skinner steading. And there, after a while, I left her.

Yet it was not an alibi, for when I left her and was on my way back into Tain, who should I meet riding out towards the steading but Abdelwahed?

So my alibi turns out to be quite the reverse; which is why Bella never once mentioned it. If it became known that I had been out on the marshes with Abdelwahed that night, everyone would immediately seize on me as the obvious suspect. I would be arrested, put to the question and hanged - by a gleeful Thorfinn Skinner. Or so she believed and insisted.

As even you came at last to believe me guilty, and did so without ever learning that I had been with Abdelwahed a matter of moments before he was murdered, it seems she was right.

Later, she rode out again with her white cloak on, and was taken for the Queen of Elphame. But that was after Thorfinn had been and gone without her ever knowing.

Mariana, I did not kill Abdelwahed ben Youssef. Why didn't you tax me with it, why didn't you ask me? And why did you not believe in me …?

But you were still wandering the hills and forests of Scotland. Bella had been sent up to Dunrobin, to Don Alfonso, who represents Pope Urban, and I could do nothing.

But I could do something else. Goaded by your letter, I decided to continue my investigation of the riddle which you, my heroine, my archangel, had failed so signally to solve. I had to. Only by proving someone else guilty could I prove myself innocent. Prove it to you, Mariana. Bella knows I am innocent. And although I had left her at home and was on my own when I met Abdelwahed, it never occurred to her to doubt me.

I say "continue" my investigation, for I had already - thinking only to help you - followed up while in Inverness the discrepancy between Thorfinn's story as he told it and the account you heard elsewhere. For you told me when you arrived in Tain that you had met a fisherman who had seen Thorfinn heading up the Moray Firth. This fisherman had been on the east coast of Black Isle at the time, and he must have seen Thorfinn going down through the narrow strait between the two forts - or he would not, from there, have described Thorfinn as sailing *past* him and on into the firth: he would have described him as sailing *away* from him, over to the opposite coast, towards Nairn and Findhorn. Believe me. I have been there. I have checked. Thorfinn was heading for Inverness.

Which was fine by me because I was in Inverness. I enquired at what passes there for a bank. "Enquired about what?" I hear you ask. *Allez, Mariana!* If he had killed Abdelwahed, then dashed straight back onto his boat, he was carrying a purse full of gold with him. The purse you accused me of stealing. That hurts. I would have left the purse.

The bank would tell me nothing.

I asked in all the taverns. I was directed to a small establishment run by a *maquerelle*: you know, a brothel in a back street masquerading as a workshop where penniless girls can earn an honest living. But who am I to preach? The *maquerelle* was a large, pale woman who looked as though she could throw bigger men than me out two at a time; fortunately, however, she spoke a few words of French. And liked the gold mark I held out to her.

Thorfinn had passed an afternoon there recently. She called a girl, Maeve, a sweet little thing, a bit like your Kari. Maeve told me, through her mistress, that she remembered Thorfinn's visit. It had been on the Thursday, she thought - which would have been the day after the murder. Why did she remember it? Because he had been in a good mood. Usually he just beat her and fucked her without a word and left her crying on the bed, but that day he had been *happy*. He hadn't taken his belt to her at all, just spanked her a little with his hand, then lain back on the bed and while she played with him - 'You know?' she asked, shyly - oh yes, I knew - he had talked to her. She didn't remember what about. She wasn't listening, she was doing her job, desperate to please - she didn't want him to change his mind and beat her properly after all. But she did remember something about a big fish because it was funny, and because she had dared to ask him a question, and then another as he hadn't minded. He had spoken of a big fish that sniffs at the bait, comes back and bites it off, then sails away with a smile on its face. *La petite* Maeve had asked him if fish really took the bait sometimes without getting caught. Oh, yes. And did they really smile? He had smiled. And when he left, later, he gave her a tip for the first time ever. 'Here, this is for you, lass.' Of course, she remembered.

"Sails" away, Mariana, did you notice? "Sails", not "swims".

Thorfinn had wanted the gold, but he had wanted Bella too. The money and the girl. Both.

And then? Then (the woman informed me) he would have gone to the Boar. That was where he always stayed.

At the Boar, they would tell me nothing.

I gave up, and seized the first opportunity to go to Tain. Where I was handed your letter. I called on your grandmother. She told me it had always been obvious that the murderer was either Thorfinn or Sir Hugh. You would not listen. Jealous, she said. Consumed by jealousy. You loved me, she said.

You loved me.

Not enough to trust me.

When a woman sees a man with another woman, she said, she no longer trusts him; she no longer knows what he will do, what he is capable off. But she still loves him.

We talked. We both believed Thorfinn was the murderer. As apparently had you, at first.

I rode over to the Skinner steading. It was deserted. No goats, no pigs, no geese. No dog. No horse. Inside, everything that could be removed had been removed.

I stood by the door, looking out over the wind-bent grass. The sky was that clear, pale blue, a colour so different from any I have ever seen in France, even on the coast of Normandy. A few wisps of cloud, high up, to the north.

I walked across the grass to the dyke, and up onto it, gazing at the grey sea with its flecks of white. Behind me, a little voice said 'Bella'.

I whirled round.

It was the strange creature they call Coll.

'Bella?' I responded, stupidly.

'Bella,' she replied.

I think we could both have gone on saying 'Bella' for the rest of time.

'Bella,' I murmured.

'Bella?' She wanted to know if Bella was with me, if Bella had returned.

I shook my head sadly.

She suddenly took me by the hand and led me to the little room at the back of the house where we saw her once - where you, Mariana, treated the poor thing's ear.

Nothing much was left, it had been cleared along with the rest of the house, but she had obviously moved back in with her bits and pieces. I suppose it is hard to stay out in the cold once you are used to having a roof over your head. That must be why your little gypsy friend, Whin, is so careful not to set foot in a house.

She sat me down, gave me a handful of berries and a cup of water. I don't know what the berries were, but they were delicious.

What did she have in mind, I kept wondering, this strange creature with the silver hair and eyes, in some ways so feminine, in others like a wild thing, an animal, in her innocent nakedness.

She got up to fetch more berries and I saw her back for the first time, criss-crossed with the scars of a brutal whipping. Was that Thorfinn? Or had it been done when she was a prisoner in

Printed in the United Kingdom
by Lightning Source UK Ltd.
130738UK00001B/292/A